中文详注剑桥莎士比亚精选

各如所愿

原版创始主编：[英] 瑞克斯·吉布森（Rex Gibson）
原版主编：[英] 瑞查德·安褚斯（Richard Andrews）
　　　　　[英] 维姬·维南德（Vicki Wienand）
原版编注：[英] 琳孜·布雷迪（Linzy Brady）
总主编：陈国华
分册主编：吴边　陈国华

社图号 21095

Cambridge School Shakespeare: As You Like It [Third edition] [978-1-107-67512-4] was first published by Cambridge University Press in 2015. All rights reserved.
This Simplified Chinese edition for the People's Republic of China is published by arrangement with the Press Syndicate of the University of Cambridge, Cambridge, United Kingdom.
© Cambridge University Press & Beijing Language and Culture University Press 2021.
This book is in copyright. No reproduction of any part may take place without the written permission of Cambridge University Press or Beijing Language and Culture University Press.
本书版权由剑桥大学出版社和北京语言大学出版社共同所有。本书任何部分之文字及图片，如未获得出版者书面同意，不得用任何方式抄袭、节录或翻印。
This edition is for sale in the People's Republic of China (excluding Hong Kong SAR, Macao SAR and Taiwan Province) only.
此版本仅限在中华人民共和国境内销售。

北京市版权局著作权合同登记图字：01-2020-4093 号

图书在版编目（CIP）数据

中文详注剑桥莎士比亚精选. 各如所愿：英文／陈国华总主编；吴边，陈国华分册主编. -- 北京：北京语言大学出版社，2021.9
　书名原文：Cambridge School Shakespeare：As You Like It
　ISBN 978-7-5619-5921-3

Ⅰ. ①中… Ⅱ. ①陈… ②吴… Ⅲ. ①多幕剧－剧本－英国－中世纪－英文　Ⅳ. ① I561.33

中国版本图书馆 CIP 数据核字（2021）第 157936 号

中文详注剑桥莎士比亚精选：各如所愿
ZHONGWEN XIANG ZHU JIANQIAO SHASHIBIYA JINGXUAN: GE RU SUO YUAN

项目策划： 李　亮	**责任编辑：** 孙冠群　李　亮
封面设计： 乔　剑	**排版制作：** 北京创艺涵文化发展有限公司
责任印制： 周　燚	

出版发行　**北京语言大学出版社**
社　　址　北京市海淀区学院路 15 号，100083
网　　址　www.blcup.com
电子信箱　service@blcup.com
电　　话　编辑部　8610-82301019/0178
　　　　　发行部　8610-82303650/3591/3648
　　　　　北语书店　8610-82303653
　　　　　网购咨询　8610-82303908
印　　刷　北京博海升彩色印刷有限公司
版　　次　2021 年 9 月第 1 版　　印　次：2021 年 9 月第 1 次印刷
开　　本　787 毫米 × 1092 毫米　1/16　印　张：13.75
字　　数　358 千字
定　　价　85.00 元

PRINTED IN CHINA

序

由于观察角度不同，评判标准不同，关于哪个国家哪位诗人或小说家的成就最大，世人可能难以达成一致；可是说到剧作家，大家的共识是，莎士比亚不仅是英语国家有史以来最伟大的剧作家，也是全世界最伟大的剧作家，在知名度、影响力和传世作品的数量上，没有任何一位剧作家可以与之比肩。正是由于其公认的文学成就和人文精神，在过去400多年里，莎士比亚戏剧的演出在英语国家和许多非英语国家经久不衰，莎剧的阅读和鉴赏已成为这些国家英文教学的必选内容。

莎剧进入中国，已经有100多年历史，莎士比亚全集已经有了四个中文译本。不懂英文的人可以通过译本来欣赏莎士比亚剧作。然而文学作品的语言，尤其是诗歌的语言，具有相当程度的不可译性，而几乎所有莎剧的大部分台词都是素体诗（blank verse）。例如《哈慕雷》（Hamlet）里主人公的名言"To be, or not to be, that is the question"，不论怎样译，都难以完全再现原文的深刻内涵和形式特点。要想真正欣赏莎士比亚的语言和戏剧艺术，还得阅读其英文原作。最早由剑桥大学出版社出版的这套莎剧精选，收录了最受读者和观众喜爱的14部剧目，涵盖莎剧的各个类别，以其独具匠心的设计和编排，成为所有英文原版莎剧中最适合英语学习者阅读、最适合戏剧爱好者排演的莎剧选集。

本选集的创始主编瑞克斯·吉布森（Rex Gibson）在本书引言（Introduction）里指出："不论做什么，都要记住，莎士比亚写下他的剧本是为了演出、观看和享受的。"秉承这一宗旨，这一新版莎剧选集有四个鲜明的区别性特点：

一、书的开本和页面的宽高比例特别适合学校的老师和学生以及剧团的导演和演员在排练莎剧时把书打开，拿在手里，随时参阅，而且左边页面上有许多有关排演活动的建议。

二、书中配有大量世界各国莎剧演出的彩色剧照，为莎剧爱好者和剧团排演莎剧提供了灵感。

三、书的正文部分打开后，右页是未经删减、原汁原味的剧本原文，左页是多种不同栏目，包括导演技巧（Stagecraft）、剧中语言（Language in the play）、人物分析（Characters）、主题分析（Themes）、写作练习（Write about it）及词语注释等。每幕之间（本幕回顾）和最后一幕后（本剧回顾）有与剧情相关的各种思考题。

四、在剧本之后有各种针对全剧的专题论述，以《哈慕雷》为例，包括视角与主题（Perspectives and themes）、人物分析（Characters）、《哈慕雷》的语言（The language of Hamlet）、《哈慕雷》的演出（Hamlet in performance）、笔论莎士比亚（Writing about Shakespeare）、笔论《哈慕雷》（Writing about Hamlet），还有一份莎翁年表（William Shakespeare 1564–1616）。

左页上的栏目对于解读和排演莎剧特别有帮助，剧本后面的专题论述对于撰写有关莎士比亚的文章特别有帮助，而参加莎剧排演，背诵台词，撰写论文，又是提高英语水平的极好途径。

为了方便更多的中国读者阅读、欣赏、排演莎士比亚原作，北京语言大学出版社携手剑桥大学出版社，将这套莎剧精选引入中国。我有幸应邀担任这套书的中文版总主编，组织起一个团队，对原版进行一定程度的改编和汉化，以适应中国读者的需求。我们不仅将原版提供的关键注释基本译成了中文，而且针对中国英语学习者和莎剧爱好者阅读理解上的难点，主要做了以下四件事：

一、参考 The Oxford Dictionary of Original Shakespearean Pronunciation (David Crystal 2016)、Oxford Dictionary of Pronunciation for Current English (Clive Upton 2003) 和 Shakespeare's Names: A Pronouncing Dictionary (Helge Kökeritz 1950)，给每个剧本前面人物表里的人名加上了国际音标。为了便于读者识别，我们将第一本发音词典里一般中国读者不认识的个别音标替换成了大家熟悉的近似音标。

二、为左页顶端的剧情简介添加中文译文。

三、左页中以及剧本后面论文部分里有一些具有挑战性的词和术语（如tableau），我们为其中的大部分添加了相应的中文释义。

四、适当增加了原版里没有的词语注释。

给剧中人物的名字加了国际音标之后，我们发现，现有莎剧中文译本里一些人名的中文译名与原文的读音差别较大且互不相同。根据定名不咎、译音循本、音义兼顾、音系对应的原则，我们给出了新译名。根据前两个原则，我们将剧本 Julius Caesar /ˈdʒuːlɪəs ˈsiːzə(r)/ 译成《儒略·恺撒》，而没有采用《尤利/力乌斯·恺撒》《裘利/力斯·凯撒》《居里厄斯·恺撒》等现成译名中的任何一个，因为从公元前1世纪到公元16世纪西方使用的儒略历（Julian calendar）就是以这位 Julius Caesar（拉丁文读音是 /ˈjuːlɪ.ʊs ˈkae̯sar/）命名的。根据音义兼顾的原则，我们将剧本 Hamlet /ˈ(h)amlət/ 译成《哈慕雷》而不是《哈姆莱特》或《哈姆雷特》，因为"慕雷"比"姆莱"或"姆雷"更适合用来给男子起名，结尾的辅音 /t/ 在实际说话中往往不发音。根据音系对应的原则，我们借鉴了曹禺的译法，将剧本 Romeo and Juliet 译成《柔密欧与茱丽叶》，没有将 Romeo 译成更常见的"罗密欧"，因为"柔 /rou/"比"罗 /luo/"更接近原名 Romeo /ˈroːmɪoː/ 的读音；同时我们将 Juliet /ˈdʒuːlɪət/ 译成"茱丽叶"而不是"朱丽叶"，因为这样做不容易让人误以为这个女孩姓"朱"。

这套经过改编并且带中文注释的《中文详注剑桥莎士比亚精选》不仅可以用作中国高中和大学的英文教材，而且适合中国所有具有较高英语能力的莎剧爱好者阅读和欣赏，将戏剧从书中提升到自己心中，将剧本从课堂搬演到戏台。

相信《中文详注剑桥莎士比亚精选》会带给中国广大英语爱好者一个惊喜。

陈国华

2020年5月于英国剑桥家中

Contents 目录

Introduction 引言	iv
Photo gallery 剧照精选	v

As You Like It 《各如所愿》

List of characters 人物表	1
Act 1 第1幕	3
Act 2 第2幕	35
Act 3 第3幕	71
Act 4 第4幕	111
Act 5 第5幕	135
Perspectives and themes 视角与主题	160
Contexts and sources 背景与来源	165
Characters 人物分析	169
The language of As You Like It 《各如所愿》的语言	180
Critics' forum 评论家论坛	186
As You Like It in performance 《各如所愿》的演出	188
Writing about Shakespeare 笔论莎士比亚	198
Writing about As You Like It 笔论《各如所愿》	200
William Shakespeare 1564–1616 莎翁年表	202
Acknowledgements 鸣谢	203

Cambridge School Shakespeare

Introduction 引言

This *As You Like It* is part of the **Cambridge School Shakespeare** series. Like every other play in the series, it has been specially prepared to help all students in schools and colleges.

The **Cambridge School Shakespeare** *As You Like It* aims to be different. It invites you to lift the words from the page and to bring the play to life in your classroom, hall or drama studio. Through enjoyable and focused activities, you will increase your understanding of the play. Actors have created their different interpretations of the play over the centuries. Similarly, you are invited to make up your own mind about *As You Like It*, rather than having someone else's interpretation handed down to you.

Cambridge School Shakespeare does not offer you a cut-down or simplified version of the play. This is Shakespeare's language, filled with imaginative possibilities. You will find on every left-hand page: a summary of the action, an explanation of unfamiliar words, and a choice of activities on Shakespeare's stagecraft, characters, themes and language.

Between each act and in the pages at the end of the play, you will find notes, illustrations and activities. These will help to encourage reflection after every act and give you insights into the background and context of the play as a whole.

This edition will be of value to you whether you are studying for an examination, reading for pleasure or thinking of putting on the play to entertain others. You can work on the activities on your own or in groups. Many of the activities suggest a particular group size, but don't be afraid to make up larger or smaller groups to suit your own purposes. Please don't think you have to do every activity: choose those that will help you most.

Although you are invited to treat *As You Like It* as a play, you don't need special dramatic or theatrical skills to do the activities. By choosing your activities, and by exploring and experimenting, you can make your own interpretations of Shakespeare's language, characters and stories.

Whatever you do, remember that Shakespeare wrote his plays to be acted, watched and enjoyed.

Rex Gibson
Founding editor

This new edition contains more photographs, more diversity and more supporting material than previous editions, whilst remaining true to Rex's original vision. Specifically, it contains more activities and commentary on stagecraft and writing about Shakespeare, to reflect contemporary interest. The glossary has been enlarged too. Finally, this edition aims to reflect the best teaching and learning possible, and to represent not only Shakespeare through the ages, but also the relevance and excitement of Shakespeare today.

Richard Andrews and Vicki Wienand
Series editors

This edition of *As You Like It* uses the updated text of the play established by Michael Hattaway in **The New Cambridge Shakespeare**. Some minor editorial differences exist between this and the previous edition, although pagination and line numbering remain the same.

▼ Duke Frederick has recently overthrown his brother and the kingdom's rightful ruler, Duke Senior, who now lives in exile in the Forest of Arden. Despite this conflict, the daughters of these two men – Rosalind, whose father has been exiled, and Celia, whose father now rules at court – are like sisters to each other.

▼ The play opens with a clash between another pair of brothers, the sons of Sir Roland de Boys. Orlando is mistreated by his elder brother, Oliver, who plans to kill him.

◀ Hoping that Orlando will be killed, Oliver persuades his brother to enter a wrestling match against Duke Frederick's dangerous star wrestler, Charles. Rosalind tries to dissuade Orlando from fighting, and they fall in love. She gives him a necklace to wear in her honour.

▼ Orlando defies all expectations by defeating Charles, but is dismissed as an enemy by Duke Frederick. Rosalind is also banished from the kingdom by her uncle, on pain of death, and she and Celia decide to run away together rather than be separated.

▼ The two women escape to the Forest of Arden along with the court jester, Touchstone. Rosalind disguises herself as a boy called Ganymede and Celia pretends to be his sister, Aliena.

▼ The three travellers come across country people, such as Corin the shepherd, and Touchstone enjoys conversing with them in order to show off his own superior wit and learning.

▼ In the Forest of Arden, Duke Senior enjoys a simple life, free from all the political manoeuvres and social ambitions of life at court. He is amused by Jaques, a melancholy and satirical courtier who reminds everyone that human folly and weakness exist even in the Forest of Arden.

In the forest, many kinds of love are in the air. Touchstone falls for Audrey, a simple goatherd (牧羊人), and plans to marry her. A shepherd named Silvius loves a disdainful shepherdess called Phoebe, but she rejects him and falls in love with Ganymede (who is really Rosalind in disguise).

▲ Meanwhile, Orlando has also fled to the Forest of Arden to escape his brother's murderous intentions. He spends his time daydreaming about Rosalind and writing her second-rate love poems, which he hangs in the trees.

▼ Rosalind reads the poems and meets Orlando while disguised as Ganymede. She tries to cure Orlando's lovesick fantasies and teach him about real-life relationships, making him treat Ganymede as if he were Rosalind. In this way, Rosalind also tricks Orlando into 'marrying' her.

◀ Towards the end of the play, Orlando saves the life of his brother Oliver. This formerly evil character is converted to goodness and falls in love with Celia at first sight.

▼ Rosalind tires of all the complications that her disguise has caused. She promises Orlando, Silvius and Phoebe that they will all marry the right person if they do as she says.

▼ At the end of the play, all the complications seem resolved. Rosalind abandons her disguise and reveals her true identity, at which point Orlando keeps his promise to marry her and Phoebe keeps her promise to marry Silvius. As the weddings are about to take place, a messenger arrives with news that Duke Frederick has also converted to goodness and restored the kingdom to Duke Senior.

▼ The play ends as everyone except Jaques plans to return to the court. Rosalind takes centre stage to bid the audience goodbye in a witty epilogue (收场辞).

List of characters 人物表

The court （朝廷）

The usurping court
（篡位的朝廷）

DUKE FREDERICK /ˈfredəˌrɪk/ （弗莱德瑞） younger brother to Duke Senior
CELIA /ˈsiːlɪə/ （希丽叶） his daughter (who disguises herself as ALIENA /eɪlɪˈenə/ [爱丽艾娜])
ROSALIND /ˈrɒzəlɪnd/ （若泽兰） daughter of Duke Senior (who disguises herself as GANYMEDE /ˈɡanɪˌmeɪd/ [甘尼密])
TOUCHSTONE /ˈtʌtʃstoːn/ （试金石） a clown
CHARLES /tʃɑː(r)lz/ （查尔斯） the Duke's wrestler
LE BEAU /lə ˈboː/ （勒博）
FIRST LORD （贵族甲）
SECOND LORD （贵族乙） } courtiers

The de Boys /dəˈbɔɪz/ （德勃伊） household
（德勃伊家人）

OLIVER /ˈɒlɪvə(r)/ （奥利沃）
JACQUES /ʒɑːk/ （雅克）
ORLANDO /ɔː(r)ˈlandoː/ （奥岚铎） } sons of Sir Roland /ˈroːlənd/ （柔岚） de Boys
ADAM /ˈadəm/ （亚当） servant to Orlando
DENIS /ˈdenɪs/ （丹尼） servant to Oliver

The Forest of Arden （阿登森林）

The banished court
（被放逐的朝廷）

DUKE SENIOR （老公爵） the rightful duke
JAQUES /ˈdʒeɪkəɪz/ （杰奎）
AMIENS /ˈamɪenz/ （阿缅）
FIRST LORD （贵族甲）
SECOND LORD （贵族乙） } courtiers
FIRST PAGE （侍童甲）
SECOND PAGE （侍童乙） } attendants on the Duke

The people of Arden
（阿登森林里的人）

CORIN /ˈkɒrɪn/ （考林） a shepherd
SILVIUS /ˈsɪlvɪəs/ （悉尔维耶） a shepherd
PHOEBE /ˈfiːbiː/ （菲妣） a shepherdess
AUDREY /ˈɔːdrɪ/ （奥卓依） a goatherd
WILLIAM /ˈwɪljəm/ （威廉） a countryman
SIR OLIVER MARTEXT /ˈmɑː(r)tekst/ （马泰克斯） a priest
FORESTERS （林官）

HYMEN /ˈ(h)əɪmən/ （亥门） god of marriage

The action of the play takes place in Oliver's home, Duke Frederick's palace and the Forest of Arden.

Orlando recounts how he inherited only £250. His father's will instructed the oldest son, Oliver, to educate Orlando. But Oliver treats him worse than the horses, and denies him status or education.

 剧情简介：奥岚铎讲述自己继承的遗产如何仅有250镑。父亲在遗嘱中要求长子奥利沃好生教养弟弟奥岚铎，但奥利沃待弟弟牛马不如，既不承认他的地位，也不让他上学。

Stagecraft 导演技巧

Dramatic grammar (in pairs)

The play begins in the middle of a conversation between Orlando and his family's faithful servant, Adam, about the will left by Orlando's late father. Orlando is clearly agitated (愤愤不平) as he talks about the unfair treatment he has suffered at the hands of his own brother.

a Read Orlando's opening monologue (独白) aloud to yourself as you walk around the room. Pay particular attention to the grammar by changing direction as you walk:

- At each full stop, make a full 'about-turn' (180 degrees).
- At each comma, semi-colon and colon, make a half-turn (90 degrees to your right or left).
- Think of gestures to make at question marks, dashes and exclamation marks (such as stamping your foot or clicking your fingers).

b With your partner, discuss how the grammatical structure of the monologue reflects Orlando's feelings and experiences. How would you enact (表演) these lines to convey his motivations at this point?

c How does the grammar of Orlando's speech change at line 24 compared with the monologue above? Why do you think this might be? Take turns to explore different styles of speaking Orlando's response to his brother in this line. Decide which style of speaking you think best expresses Orlando's inner thoughts at this point.

d Imagine you are planning to direct a production of *As You Like It*. Make notes on the set, the costumes and the general impression you would wish to create of Orlando, Oliver and Adam. These notes could form the first part of a Director's Journal in which you can record your ideas about staging the play as you read on.

1 Invent a scene (in small groups)

a Stage your own scene in which Sir Roland de Boys, on his deathbed, tells his three sons, Oliver, Jacques and Orlando, what is in his will and what he wants each of them to do.

b Alternatively, you could write the will of Sir Roland and perform a scene in which it is read aloud to the sons. All three sons should react to the will using facial expressions and physical gestures.

---

1 upon this fashion 以这种方式
2 bequeathed me 遗留给我
3 by will 根据（我父亲的）遗嘱
4 poor a = a mere
5 crowns 克朗（一种上面印有王冠的金币；一克朗值四分之一英镑）
6 charged ... blessing 责令我哥哥，他要是想得到祝福
7 breed 教养
8 keeps at school 供养上学
9 report ... profit （学校的成绩）报告把他的进步说得天花乱坠
10 rustically 像乡下人那样
11 stays ... unkept 把我关在这家里不管不问
12 stalling 圈养
13 manège （马的）步法
14 riders dearly hired 重金聘请的骑师
15 bound to 感激
16 something that Nature gave me 生身父母给我的东西（即出身）
17 countenance 态度；举止
18 hinds 奴仆
19 bars me 拒不给我
20 mines my gentility 毁坏我的高贵身份（mines = undermines）
21 mutiny against this servitude 反抗这种奴役
22 avoid 摆脱
23 Yonder 那边
24 Go apart 一旁站着
25 shake me up 整我，修理我
26 what make you here? 您在这里做什么？（奥利沃问题的意思是 "what are you doing here?"，奥岚铎故意曲解为 "what are you making here?"）
27 mar 毁坏

As You Like It

Act 1 Scene 1
The orchard of Oliver's house

Enter ORLANDO *and* ADAM

ORLANDO As I remember, Adam, it was upon this fashion[1] bequeathed me[2] by will[3] but poor a[4] thousand crowns[5] and, as thou say'st, charged my brother, on his blessing[6], to breed[7] me well: and there begins my sadness. My brother Jacques he keeps at school[8], and report speaks goldenly of his profit[9]. For my part, he keeps me rustically[10] at home or, to speak more properly, stays me here at home unkept[11] – for call you that 'keeping' for a gentleman of my birth, that differs not from the stalling[12] of an ox? His horses are bred better for, besides that they are fair with their feeding, they are taught their manège[13], and to that end riders dearly hired[14]. But I, his brother, gain nothing under him but growth – for the which his animals on his dunghills are as much bound to[15] him as I. Besides this nothing that he so plentifully gives me, the something that Nature gave me[16] his countenance[17] seems to take from me: he lets me feed with his hinds[18], bars me[19] the place of a brother, and, as much as in him lies, mines my gentility[20] with my education. This is it, Adam, that grieves me, and the spirit of my father, which I think is within me, begins to mutiny against this servitude[21]. I will no longer endure it, though yet I know no wise remedy how to avoid[22] it.

Enter OLIVER

ADAM Yonder[23] comes my master, your brother.
ORLANDO Go apart[24], Adam, and thou shalt hear how he will shake me up[25].
[*Adam withdraws*]
OLIVER Now sir, what make you here?[26]
ORLANDO Nothing: I am not taught to make anything.
OLIVER What mar[27] you then, sir?

Oliver is angered by Orlando's protest at being kept in poverty. He threatens to strike Orlando, but Orlando seizes Oliver and demands his share of the will. Oliver seems to consent.

剧情简介：奥岚铎抱怨奥利沃使自己陷入贫困，这惹恼了奥利沃。奥利沃威胁要打奥岚铎，反被奥岚铎揪住。奥岚铎要求得到他应得的那份遗产。奥利沃表面上同意了。

1 Brother against brother (in threes)

a Take parts as Orlando, Oliver and Adam, and rehearse lines 20–67 to experiment with how you would portray these characters on stage. Explore the points below to refine (改进) your ideas about the performance, and make notes in your Director's Journal on the most successful elements.

- **Language** Discuss why you think Orlando often echoes (重复) his brother's words. For example, the brothers call each other 'sir', but in what tones of voice and with what gestures? Locate each instance of Orlando's repetitions and decide how he might say them, and what he might mean by them. Try out a few different ways of speaking the lines to see what works best.
- **Status** Orlando appeals to his brother as a gentleman to treat him also as a gentleman. How would you show the difference in their status at this point? Think about the positions and postures of the actors.
- **Violence** Orlando is the younger brother, but he proves he is better at fighting than Oliver. Work out how you would stage the fight in a way that reveals the personality of each brother. The stage directions at lines 41, 42 and 59 suggest that Oliver begins the physical violence – but does he? Read the script without considering the stage directions, then discuss this point. Remember that the stage directions were not written by Shakespeare, but were inserted by the editors of later editions of the play.

b Write an **aside** (旁白) for Adam at each question mark in lines 20–67, to allow him to voice his opinion on the conversation from his hiding place. Perform the scene again, with Adam speaking these asides aloud.

1 **Marry** = by the Virgin Mary （"向圣母马利亚发誓"；这是一种语气温和的誓言形式）
2 **be naught awhile**　滚开
3 **husks**　麸糠
4 **What ... should**　我究竟挥霍了多少家产，让我竟然
5 **come to such penury**　如此一贫如洗
6 **better ... knows** = better than the person whom I am (standing) before knows
7 **in ... blood**　按照（我们）高贵的血缘关系
8 **so know me**　这样认我
9 **The courtesy of nations**　国家的礼制
10 **allows you my better**　让您比我高贵
11 **blood**　血统
12 **were ... us** = even if there were twenty brothers between us
13 **albeit** = although
14 **his reverence**　他老人家
15 **boy**　小子（称呼成年人为boy是一种辱骂）
16 **Wilt ... me**　你想打我吗（thou用于称呼身份较低的人，这里带有侮辱意味）
17 **villain**　坏蛋；贱种
18 **villein**　奴才，贱种（与上一行的villain谐音）
19 **railed on**　骂
20 **be patient**　压压火
21 **accord**　和气
22 **qualities**　品性
23 **exercises**　才艺（指要成为gentleman所学的剑术、防御术、马术等各项技能）
24 **become**　与……相配
25 **the poor allottery**　那可怜的一份（财产）
26 **testament**　遗嘱

ORLANDO	Marry[1], sir, I am helping you to mar that which God made, a poor unworthy brother of yours, with idleness.
OLIVER	Marry, sir, be better employed, and be naught awhile[2].
ORLANDO	Shall I keep your hogs and eat husks[3] with them? What prodigal portion have I spent that I should[4] come to such penury[5]?
OLIVER	Know you where you are, sir?
ORLANDO	O, sir, very well: here in your orchard.
OLIVER	Know you before whom, sir?
ORLANDO	Aye, better than him I am before knows[6] me: I know you are my eldest brother, and in the gentle condition of blood[7] you should so know me[8]. The courtesy of nations[9] allows you my better[10] in that you are the first-born, but the same tradition takes not away my blood[11], were there twenty brothers betwixt us[12]. I have as much of my father in me as you, albeit[13] I confess your coming before me is nearer to his reverence[14].
OLIVER	[*Raising his hand*] What, boy[15]!
ORLANDO	[*Seizing his brother*] Come, come, elder brother, you are too young in this.
OLIVER	Wilt thou lay hands on me[16], villain[17]?
ORLANDO	I am no villein[18]: I am the youngest son of Sir Roland de Boys; he was my father, and he is thrice a villain that says such a father begot villeins. Wert thou not my brother, I would not take this hand from thy throat till this other had pulled out thy tongue for saying so: thou hast railed on[19] thyself.
ADAM	[*Coming forward*] Sweet masters, be patient[20], for your father's remembrance, be at accord[21].
OLIVER	Let me go, I say.
ORLANDO	I will not till I please. You shall hear me. My father charged you in his will to give me good education: you have trained me like a peasant, obscuring and hiding from me all gentleman-like qualities[22]. The spirit of my father grows strong in me – and I will no longer endure it. Therefore allow me such exercises[23] as may become[24] a gentleman or give me the poor allottery[25] my father left me by testament[26]: with that I will go buy my fortunes.
	[*He releases Oliver*]
OLIVER	And what wilt thou do? Beg when that is spent? Well, sir, get you in. I will not long be troubled with you: you shall have some part of your 'will'; I pray you leave me.

Oliver resolves to get rid of Orlando. Charles tells of Duke Senior's banishment, Rosalind and Celia's great friendship, and of many courtiers joining Duke Senior in the Forest of Arden.

剧情简介：奥利沃决心除掉奥岚铎。查尔斯讲述了老公爵遭流放和若泽兰与希丽叶的深情厚谊，还说到许多朝臣追随老公爵逃到了阿登森林。

Characters 人物分析

Oliver's soliloquies (in pairs)

Oliver shows the unpleasant side of his nature, calling the loyal servant Adam 'old dog'. He then has two short **soliloquies** (独白), at lines 68–9 and line 75. The stage convention (常规) is that in a soliloquy a character speaks the truth, showing their true personality and intentions.

- Experiment with different ways of speaking the soliloquies. Use tone, gesture and dramatic pauses to convey Oliver's character and motivations. Decide how to deliver each soliloquy and share your interpretations with the rest of the class.

1 Setting the scene for the play (in small groups)

Charles's news helps to establish the play's context, relationships and themes. But how does the news relayed by Charles link to the story so far, and to the history of Oliver and Orlando?

- Use the list of characters on page 1 to help you draw a character web. Devise symbols or a colour code to show the status of characters you have met so far and the relationships between them. You could also include sketches of the characters and additional notes about their apparent temperaments and motivations. As you become familiar with more of the play's characters, add to your character web so that it serves as a useful 'who's who' of *As You Like It*.

Write about it 写作练习

Who, what, where, when, why?

Write a newspaper article about the Duke's banishment, using the details of Charles's account in lines 79–95. Embellish (润色) the article with features such as eye-witness accounts, quotes from the characters involved and language that is suitable for either a tabloid (小报) or a broadsheet (大报) newspaper.

1 *Exeunt*（剧本中的说明，两个以上或所有演员）退场，下场
2 *grow upon me* 顶撞我
3 *physic your rankness* 治治你的狂妄
4 *Holla* 喂，哎
5 *importunes* 恳请，请求
6 *good way*（杀死奥岚铎的）妙计
7 *morrow* = morning
8 *old Duke* 老公爵（即Duke Senior）
9 *good leave* 欣然允准
10 *her cousin* 她的堂姐／妹（即希丽叶，她和若泽兰是堂姐妹）
11 *bred* 养大
12 *to stay* = by staying
13 *of* = by
14 *merry* 快活
15 *Robin Hood* 罗宾汉（英格兰民间传说中的绿林英雄）
16 *fleet the time carelessly* 无忧无虑地消磨时光
17 *golden world* 黄金世界（即古希腊和古罗马经典著作中描写的黄金时代）

ORLANDO	I will no further offend you than becomes me for my good.
OLIVER	[*To Adam*] Get you with him, you old dog.
ADAM	Is 'old dog' my reward? Most true, I have lost my teeth in your service. God be with my old master: he would not have spoke such a word.

Exeunt[1] *Orlando* [*and*] *Adam*

OLIVER	Is it even so, begin you to grow upon me[2]? I will physic your rankness[3], and yet give no thousand crowns neither. – Holla[4], Denis.

Enter DENIS

DENIS	Calls your worship?
OLIVER	Was not Charles, the Duke's wrestler, here to speak with me?
DENIS	So please you, he is here at the door, and importunes[5] access to you.
OLIVER	Call him in.

[*Exit Denis*]

'Twill be a good way[6], and tomorrow the wrestling is.

Enter CHARLES

CHARLES	Good morrow[7] to your worship.
OLIVER	Good Monsieur Charles, what's the new news at the new court?
CHARLES	There's no news at the court, sir, but the old news: that is, the old Duke[8] is banished by his younger brother, the new Duke, and three or four loving lords have put themselves into voluntary exile with him, whose lands and revenues enrich the new Duke; therefore he gives them good leave[9] to wander.
OLIVER	Can you tell if Rosalind, the Duke's daughter, be banished with her father?
CHARLES	O no; for the Duke's daughter, her cousin[10], so loves her, being ever from their cradles bred[11] together, that she would have followed her exile or have died to stay[12] behind her; she is at the court and no less beloved of[13] her uncle than his own daughter, and never two ladies loved as they do.
OLIVER	Where will the old Duke live?
CHARLES	They say he is already in the Forest of Arden, and a many merry[14] men with him; and there they live like the old Robin Hood[15] of England. They say many young gentlemen flock to him every day, and fleet the time carelessly[16] as they did in the golden world[17].

Charles says he is reluctant to injure Orlando. Oliver falsely describes Orlando's character and intentions, and urges Charles to kill him. Alone on stage, Oliver expresses envy of Orlando's character and reputation.

 剧情简介：查尔斯说他不愿意伤害奥岚铎。奥利沃谎称奥岚铎人品差、心眼坏，力劝查尔斯杀死他。奥利沃独自站在戏台上，表达他对奥岚铎人品和名声的嫉妒。

Characters 人物分析

Charles: a pompous wrestler? (in pairs)

Charles is Duke Frederick's wrestler. He is very proud of his reputation, and warns of what may happen if Orlando insists on fighting him. He speaks formally, often using long words and unnatural word order where a simpler style would do.

a Discuss what effect Charles's overblown (夸张) speaking style might have on a listener. Think about the audience's impression, as well as how the other characters might react.

b Take turns to read aloud lines 97–107, then construct a verbal or written version of the speech that uses clearer wording and sentence structure. What difference does this make to the message? Why do you think Charles employs such complicated language?

1 A false brother (in pairs)

Oliver's descriptions of Orlando are often descriptions of himself. Psychoanalysts call this 'projection' – that is, attributing your own feelings or characteristics to others. Keep this in mind as you complete the following activities.

a One person speaks lines 108–23 in character as Oliver, pausing after every short section. In the pause, the other person judges whether or not Oliver is lying by proclaiming aloud 'True' or 'False'. Switch roles and see if there are any points in the speech when you disagree about whether or not he is being truthful.

b Take turns to read through Olivier's soliloquy at lines 127–34. Together, compile notes on Oliver's character and his behaviour towards Orlando. Write a psychoanalyst's report on Oliver, giving possible reasons why he might hate Orlando so much and why he might project so many of his own feelings and motivations onto his brother.

1 disposition 意图
2 disguised 乔装（当时出身高贵的人跟平民摔跤手摔跤有失身份）
3 fall 回合
4 credit 名誉，名声
5 shall acquit him well 就算表现不错了
6 loath to foil 不情愿打败
7 hither = here
8 withal = with
9 stay him from his intendment 让他无法理解
10 brook 忍受
11 a thing of his own search 他自找的
12 requite 回报
13 by underhand means 脚下使绊子
14 envious emulator 心怀嫉妒的仿效者
15 parts 品质
16 villainous contriver 恶毒的密谋者
17 as lief 宁愿，巴不得
18 look to't 当心
19 dost him any slight disgrace 让他吃一丁点儿亏
20 mightily grace himself on thee 占你一个大便宜
21 practise against thee 对你使坏
22 treacherous device 阴险手段
23 ta'en = taken
24 anatomise him 剖析他
25 go alone 独自走路（指被摔倒后站起来）
26 stir this gamester 逗逗这个不知天高地厚的家伙
27 noble device 高尚品质
28 altogether misprized 完全被人小看
29 kindle the boy thither 挑动那小子去那儿（参赛）

OLIVER What, you wrestle tomorrow before the new Duke?

CHARLES Marry, do I, sir; and I came to acquaint you with a matter. I am given, sir, secretly to understand that your younger brother Orlando hath a disposition¹ to come in, disguised², against me to try a fall³. Tomorrow, sir, I wrestle for my credit⁴, and he that escapes me without some broken limb shall acquit him well⁵. Your brother is but young and tender and, for your love, I would be loath to foil⁶ him, as I must for my own honour, if he come in; therefore, out of my love to you, I came hither⁷ to acquaint you withal⁸, that either you might stay him from his intendment⁹, or brook¹⁰ such disgrace well as he shall run into, in that it is a thing of his own search¹¹ and altogether against my will.

OLIVER Charles, I thank thee for thy love to me, which thou shalt find I will most kindly requite¹². I had myself notice of my brother's purpose herein, and have by underhand means¹³ laboured to dissuade him from it – but he is resolute. I'll tell thee, Charles, it is the stubbornest young fellow of France, full of ambition, an envious emulator¹⁴ of every man's good parts¹⁵, a secret and villainous contriver¹⁶ against me, his natural brother. Therefore use thy discretion: I had as lief¹⁷ thou didst break his neck as his finger. And thou wert best look to't¹⁸ – for if thou dost him any slight disgrace¹⁹ or if he do not mightily grace himself on thee²⁰, he will practise against thee²¹ by poison, entrap thee by some treacherous device²², and never leave thee till he hath ta'en²³ thy life by some indirect means or other. For I assure thee – and almost with tears I speak it – there is not one so young and so villainous this day living. I speak but brotherly of him, but should I anatomise him²⁴ to thee as he is, I must blush and weep, and thou must look pale and wonder.

CHARLES I am heartily glad I came hither to you. If he come tomorrow, I'll give him his payment; if ever he go alone²⁵ again, I'll never wrestle for prize more – and so God keep your worship.   *Exit*

OLIVER Farewell, good Charles. – Now will I stir this gamester²⁶. I hope I shall see an end of him, for my soul – yet I know not why – hates nothing more than he. Yet he's gentle, never schooled and yet learned, full of noble device²⁷, of all sorts enchantingly beloved, and indeed so much in the heart of the world, and especially of my own people who best know him, that I am altogether misprized²⁸. But it shall not be so long this wrestler shall clear all: nothing remains but that I kindle the boy thither²⁹, which now I'll go about.

Exit

Celia tries to cheer Rosalind, who thinks with sadness of her banished father. Responding to Celia's affection, Rosalind joins in witty wordplay about love, fortune and nature.

剧情简介：若泽兰想到父亲被放逐，十分悲伤，希丽叶试图让她高兴起来。为了回应希丽叶的关爱，若泽兰和她一起玩起了关于爱情、命运和本性的词语游戏。

Themes 主题分析

Fortune and her wheel (in small groups)

Fortune was commonly depicted as a blindfolded (被蒙上眼) goddess who used her wheel to raise people into prosperity and happiness before plunging them down again into misery.

- Look at the wheel of Fortune illustrated below and have a go at drawing and colouring your own. Annotate where Rosalind and Celia are on this wheel of Fortune, and show the direction in which they might each – or both – be heading. Where on the wheel are the other characters?

1 Fortune, Nature and witty repartee (巧妙机智的应对)

In lines 30–1 Celia says that Fortune bestows either virtue or beauty upon women, and that beautiful women ('fair') are rarely chaste ('honest'). Rosalind challenges her, as she believes that Fortune only affects 'gifts of the world' such as money and power. According to Rosalind, a person's looks, intelligence and moral qualities are 'the lineaments (特征) of Nature' – features given by Nature rather than Fortune. The theme of nature's relationship to fortune is central to the play, so keep it in mind as you read on.

- Rewrite lines 25–45 in your own words, to make the wit and wordplay intelligible and amusing to a modern audience. Some of the wordplay involves exploiting certain words' multiple definitions, so check the glossaries on this page and on page 12 to make sure that you have understood all the possible meanings.

1 thee/you 你 / 您（希丽叶用 thou 来称呼若泽兰，表示亲切；若泽兰用 you 来称呼希丽叶，表示尊敬）
2 coz = cousin
3 mirth 欢笑
4 still = always
5 so wouldst thou 你也会这样做
6 so righteously tempered 那么公平地锻造出来
7 the condition of my estate 我的处境
8 like = likely
9 perforce 用暴力
10 render thee again 归还给你
11 devise sports 想法找乐子
12 make sport withal 用它（指乐子）来玩游戏
13 nor ... neither 而且不超出游戏的范围（这里双重否定 "nor ... neither" 起强调否定的作用）
14 with ... again 只限于你我不过脸双一下就可以大大方方体体面面地从中抽身（这里有性暗示）
15 sit and mock 坐下来笑话一下
16 bestowed equally 赏赐得公平
17 blind woman 蒙着眼的女人（希腊神话中，命运女神赏罚人类时会蒙上双眼）
18 doth most mistake 错得最厉害
19 makes fair ... honest 很少让生来漂亮的有贞操
20 office 职能
21 gifts of the world 世间的馈赠（指财物、权力等）
22 lineaments of Nature 天赋的特征（指造物主赋予人的相貌、才智等）

Act 1 Scene 2
Duke Frederick's palace

Enter ROSALIND *and* CELIA

CELIA   I pray thee[1], Rosalind, sweet my coz[2], be merry.

ROSALIND   Dear Celia, I show more mirth[3] than I am mistress of, and would you[1] yet were merrier: unless you could teach me to forget a banished father, you must not learn me how to remember any extraordinary pleasure.

CELIA   Herein, I see, thou lov'st me not with the full weight that I love thee; if my uncle, thy banished father, had banished thy uncle, the Duke my father, so thou hadst been still[4] with me, I could have taught my love to take thy father for mine; so wouldst thou[5], if the truth of thy love to me were so righteously tempered[6] as mine is to thee.

ROSALIND   Well, I will forget the condition of my estate[7] to rejoice in yours.

CELIA   You know my father hath no child but I, nor none is like[8] to have; and, truly, when he dies thou shalt be his heir: for what he hath taken away from thy father perforce[9] I will render thee again[10] in affection. By mine honour, I will, and when I break that oath, let me turn monster. Therefore, my sweet Rose, my dear Rose, be merry.

ROSALIND   From henceforth I will, coz, and devise sports[11]. Let me see, what think you of falling in love?

CELIA   Marry, I prithee do, to make sport withal[12]: but love no man in good earnest – nor no further in sport neither[13] – than with safety of a pure blush thou mayst in honour come off again[14].

ROSALIND   What shall be our sport then?

CELIA   Let us sit and mock[15] the good housewife Fortune from her wheel, that her gifts may henceforth be bestowed equally[16].

ROSALIND   I would we could do so: for her benefits are mightily misplaced, and the bountiful blind woman[17] doth most mistake[18] in her gifts to women.

CELIA   'Tis true, for those that she makes fair she scarce makes honest[19], and those that she makes honest she makes very ill-favoured.

ROSALIND   Nay, now thou goest from Fortune's office[20] to Nature's: Fortune reigns in gifts of the world[21], not in the lineaments of Nature[22].

Celia comments that fools are sent by nature to sharpen witty people's intelligence. Touchstone jokes about honour. He hints at corruption in Duke Frederick's court.

 剧情简介：希丽叶说愚人生来就是用来磨砺智者的智力的。试金石说起了关于荣誉的笑话，并暗示弗莱德瑞公爵的宫廷有腐败现象。

Language in the play 剧中语言

Language games (in small groups)

Like all Shakespeare's clowns, Touchstone loves playing with language in order to entertain his listeners and to criticise the follies (愚蠢) of high-status people.

a Touchstone jokes to make a serious point, and seems to imply that Duke Frederick's court lacks honour. Read through his riddle-like story of the knight and the 'pancakes' in lines 50–65. Try to understand the meaning of the joke and how it relates to Duke Frederick.

b In lines 56–7, Touchstone tricks Celia and Rosalind into stroking their chins and swearing by their non-existent beards, in order to help illustrate his point. How might this affect the relationship and balance of power between the entertainer and his onstage audience?

c Find examples of Touchstone's puns, slapstick comedy (滑稽剧，闹剧), mimicry (模仿) and other comic features in the script opposite. Do you think that humour can be an effective vehicle for communicating criticism or discussion on serious topics? Why? Think of some characters in television shows or of some comedians who do this, and compare them with Touchstone.

1 fall into the fire 掉进火坑（指失去贞操）
2 wit 智慧
3 flout at 嘲弄
4 argument 讨论
5 too hard 太难对付
6 Nature's natural 天生蠢材
7 Peradventure 也许
8 wits 才智
9 reason of 谈论
10 whetstone 磨刀石
11 always 一直
12 whither 到何处
13 naught 糟糕
14 stand to it 坚持说
15 forsworn 发假誓
16 unmuzzle 展开
17 Prithee = I pray you（请问）
18 taxation 吹毛求疵
19 By my troth = Upon my faith（说实话）
20 Monsieur 先生（法语词，相当于sir或Mr）

Enter TOUCHSTONE

CELIA   No? When Nature hath made a fair creature, may she not by Fortune fall into the fire[1]? Though Nature hath given us wit[2] to flout at[3] Fortune, hath not Fortune sent in this fool to cut off the argument[4]?

ROSALIND   Indeed there is Fortune too hard[5] for Nature, when Fortune makes Nature's natural[6] the cutter-off of Nature's wit.

CELIA   Peradventure[7] this is not Fortune's work neither but Nature's who, perceiving our natural wits[8] too dull to reason of[9] such goddesses, hath sent this natural for our whetstone[10]: for always[11] the dullness of the fool is the whetstone of the wits. – How now, Wit, whither[12] wander you?

TOUCHSTONE   Mistress, you must come away to your father.

CELIA   Were you made the messenger?

TOUCHSTONE   No, by mine honour, but I was bid to come for you.

ROSALIND   Where learned you that oath, fool?

TOUCHSTONE   Of a certain knight that swore, by his honour, they were good pancakes, and swore, by his honour, the mustard was naught[13]. Now, I'll stand to it[14], the pancakes were naught and the mustard was good – and yet was not the knight forsworn[15].

CELIA   How prove you that in the great heap of your knowledge?

ROSALIND   Aye, marry, now unmuzzle[16] your wisdom.

TOUCHSTONE   Stand you both forth now. Stroke your chins and swear, by your beards, that I am a knave.

CELIA   By our beards – if we had them – thou art.

TOUCHSTONE   By my knavery – if I had it – then I were. But if you swear by that that is not you are not forsworn: no more was this knight swearing by his honour, for he never had any; or if he had, he had sworn it away before ever he saw those pancakes or that mustard.

CELIA   Prithee[17], who is't that thou mean'st?

TOUCHSTONE   One that old Frederick, your father, loves.

CELIA   My father's love is enough to honour him. Enough! Speak no more of him; you'll be whipped for taxation[18] one of these days.

TOUCHSTONE   The more pity that fools may not speak wisely what wise men do foolishly.

CELIA   By my troth[19], thou say'st true: for, since the little wit that fools have was silenced, the little foolery that wise men have makes a great show. – Here comes 'Monsieur[20] the Beau'.

Celia, Rosalind and Touchstone all mock Le Beau for his affected speech. He brings news of how Charles has seriously injured an old man's three sons. The news dismays the women.

剧情简介：希丽叶、若泽兰和试金石都嘲笑勒博言辞做作。勒博带来了查尔斯如何重伤了一位老人的三个儿子的消息。这消息让两位小姐感到悲伤。

Stagecraft 导演技巧

Mocking Le Beau (in small groups)

Le Beau (French for 'the beautiful') is often played as an overdressed courtier who puts on airs and graces (装腔作势) and uses elaborate gestures. He speaks with an affected accent (pronouncing 'sport' as 'spot') and is unable to keep up with witty wordplay of the other characters. Le Beau usually fails to see that Celia, Rosalind and Touchstone are mocking him.

- As a director, how you would advise actors to perform the script opposite for greatest comic effect? Discuss this in your group and write detailed notes in your Director's Journal, describing what you would want to see and hear on stage from each of the characters. Consider the following points in your actors' notes, then use your findings to perform lines 73–116 for another group. Try to make them laugh as much as possible!

Mimicry Celia speaks in French (line 76) and repeats Le Beau's words (line 79), while Rosalind and Touchstone use pompously (浮华地) exaggerated language (lines 81–2).

Imagery (意象) Celia uses an image from bricklaying (line 83), suggesting that Touchstone is thickly laying on the irony like a bricklayer slapping on a trowelful of mortar (灰泥，砂浆). Does Le Beau overhear her, and what is his response? Does he understand the joke?

Interruptions Le Beau's sad story of Charles defeating three sons of an old man at wrestling is interrupted in line 94 and lines 96–7. How does Le Beau react to the interruptions?

1 put on us 塞给我们
2 marketable （鸽子喂饱后因体重加大而）好卖
3 lost 错失
4 of what colour? 什么颜色？（希丽叶故意把sport曲解为spot）
5 fortune 好运
6 as the destinies decree 像命运女神下令那样
7 that … trowel = the colour that was laid on with a trowel （用泥瓦匠的瓦刀抹上去的那种颜色）
8 Nay … rank 好了，我要是没了自己的地位
9 loosest thy old smell 释放你的老气味（rank可表示rankness [恶臭]）
10 amaze 弄糊涂
11 lost the sight of 错过观看
12 match 匹敌，抗衡
13 proper 相貌堂堂
14 growth 身材
15 presence 仪表，风度
16 bills 告示
17 by these presents 借助以下文字（若泽兰在做文字游戏，既回应前面的presence，又以公告语言说出这句话）
18 dole 痛哭

Enter LE BEAU

ROSALIND With his mouth full of news.

CELIA Which he will put on us[1] as pigeons feed their young.

ROSALIND Then shall we be news-crammed.

CELIA All the better: we shall be the more marketable[2]. – *Bonjour*, Monsieur Le Beau, what's the news?

LE BEAU Fair princess, you have lost[3] much good sport.

CELIA 'Sport': of what colour?[4]

LE BEAU 'What colour', madam? How shall I answer you?

ROSALIND As wit and fortune[5] will.

TOUCHSTONE [*Imitating Le Beau*] Or as the destinies decree[6].

CELIA Well said: that was laid on with a trowel[7].

TOUCHSTONE Nay, if I keep not my rank[8] –

ROSALIND Thou loosest thy old smell[9].

LE BEAU You amaze[10] me, ladies! I would have told you of good wrestling which you have lost the sight of[11].

ROSALIND Yet tell us the manner of the wrestling.

LE BEAU I will tell you the beginning and, if it please your ladyships, you may see the end, for the best is yet to do; and here where you are they are coming to perform it.

CELIA Well, the beginning that is dead and buried.

LE BEAU There comes an old man and his three sons –

CELIA I could match[12] this beginning with an old tale.

LE BEAU Three proper[13] young men, of excellent growth[14] and presence[15] –

ROSALIND With bills[16] on their necks: 'Be it known unto all men by these presents[17]'.

LE BEAU The eldest of the three wrestled with Charles, the Duke's wrestler, which Charles in a moment threw him and broke three of his ribs that there is little hope of life in him. So he served the second and so the third: yonder they lie, the poor old man, their father, making such pitiful dole[18] over them that all the beholders take his part with weeping.

ROSALIND Alas!

TOUCHSTONE But what is the sport, monsieur, that the ladies have lost?

LE BEAU Why, this that I speak of.

TOUCHSTONE Thus men may grow wiser every day. It is the first time that ever I heard breaking of ribs was sport for ladies.

CELIA Or I, I promise thee.

The court and the wrestlers enter. Duke Frederick says that Orlando insists on fighting, but Charles is certain to win the wrestling match. Celia and Rosalind try to persuade Orlando not to fight.

剧情简介：君臣和摔跤手们上场。弗莱德瑞公爵说奥岚铎坚持要参加比武，但是查尔斯肯定会赢。希丽叶和若泽兰试图劝说奥岚铎放弃比武。

1 Why, Orlando? (in pairs)

Do you think Orlando volunteered to fight Charles, or did Oliver or others in the court force him? Conduct an interview with Orlando just before the fight, and try to determine what motivations or pressures were involved in his decision.

2 Friendly or menacing or something else? (in threes)

Duke Frederick greets Celia ('daughter'), then Rosalind ('cousin'). Rosalind is actually his niece, but in Shakespeare's time 'cousin' was used much more loosely than it is today.

a   In what tone of voice does Frederick say '– and cousin'? Remember that he has banished Rosalind's father and seized his dukedom. Also consider why and how Frederick says 'crept' in line 122.

b   Discuss the possible postures and gestures of Duke Frederick, Rosalind and Celia during this meeting. How might they physically interact with one another as they speak their lines? Write stage directions at lines 122–3 and 127–8, and take parts to perform lines 122–30.

▼ What do you think Orlando is really thinking as he responds politely to Celia and Rosalind? Is he distracted by their concern, impressed by their kindness or offended that they think he will not win?

1   any else longs = anyone else who longs
2   this … sides   肋骨折断（如同一把琴摔坏）的声音
3   dotes upon   （愚蠢地）喜爱
4   *Flourish*   小号奏花腔（表示王公或贵人的到来）
5   not be entreated   不听劝
6   forwardness   鲁莽
7   successfully   有获胜把握
8   cousin   侄女（这个词还可以称呼各个辈分的堂亲或表亲）
9   liege   殿下
10 such odds in the man   此人（查尔斯）优势太大
11 fain   乐于
12 general challenger   挑战天下人者
13 come but in   来参加比赛只是
14 try   比试
15 cruel proof   残忍的证据（指打败老人的三个儿子）
16 misprized   被人低估
17 suit   请求

ROSALIND But is there any else longs¹ to see this broken music in his sides²? Is there yet another dotes upon³ rib-breaking? Shall we see this wrestling, cousin?

LE BEAU You must if you stay here, for here is the place appointed for the wrestling and they are ready to perform it.

CELIA Yonder, sure, they are coming. Let us now stay and see it.

Flourish⁴. Enter DUKE FREDERICK, LORDS, ORLANDO, CHARLES, *and* ATTENDANTS

DUKE FREDERICK Come on; since the youth will not be entreated⁵, his own peril on his forwardness⁶.

ROSALIND Is yonder the man?

LE BEAU Even he, madam.

CELIA Alas, he is too young; yet he looks successfully⁷.

DUKE FREDERICK How now, daughter — and cousin⁸: are you crept hither to see the wrestling?

ROSALIND Aye, my liege⁹, so please you give us leave.

DUKE FREDERICK You will take little delight in it, I can tell you: there is such odds in the man¹⁰. In pity of the challenger's youth, I would fain¹¹ dissuade him, but he will not be entreated. Speak to him, ladies: see if you can move him.

CELIA Call him hither, good Monsieur Le Beau.

DUKE FREDERICK Do so; I'll not be by.

[*The Duke stands aside*]

LE BEAU Monsieur the challenger, the princess calls for you.

ORLANDO I attend them with all respect and duty.

ROSALIND Young man, have you challenged Charles the wrestler?

ORLANDO No, fair princess, he is the general challenger¹². I come but in¹³ as others do to try¹⁴ with him the strength of my youth.

CELIA Young gentleman, your spirits are too bold for your years: you have seen cruel proof¹⁵ of this man's strength. If you saw yourself with your eyes or knew yourself with your judgement, the fear of your adventure would counsel you to a more equal enterprise. We pray you, for your own sake, to embrace your own safety and give over this attempt.

ROSALIND Do, young sir: your reputation shall not therefore be misprized¹⁶. We will make it our suit¹⁷ to the Duke that the wrestling might not go forward.

Orlando says that he will lose nothing if he is defeated, because he is naturally unlucky and of no importance. Charles mocks him, but Rosalind and Celia support him. He defeats Charles.

 剧情简介：奥岚铎说，他即使败了也毫无损失，因为他天生运气不好，无足轻重。查尔斯嘲笑他，但若泽兰和希丽叶支持他。他最终打败了查尔斯。

Write about it 写作练习

The Arden Mirror

In role as a sportswriter reporting on Charles and Orlando's wrestling match for *The Arden Mirror*, complete the following activities as you research and write your report:

- Describe in detail the highlights of the match. Include eye-witness accounts and comments from supporters on both sides.
- Add quotations from the script opposite for each character, styling these as quotes from Arden's celebrity set.
- Sketch an image of the wrestling match and write an appropriate caption (说明文字) to accompany it.

1 **hard thoughts** 严苛的看法
2 **fair** 美丽
3 **trial** 比武
4 **foiled** 打败
5 **gracious** 受命运眷顾
6 **the world no injury** = do the world no injury
7 **only** 只不过
8 **supplied** 填补
9 **eke out** 增强
10 **be deceived in you** 低估您的实力
11 **gallant** 翩翩男子
12 **lie with his mother earth** 与其大地母亲躺在一起（倒地死去）
13 **a more modest working** 谦逊一些的盘算
14 **come your ways** 放马过来
15 **Hercules be thy speed** 就让赫丘力（希腊神话中的大力神）做你的保护神吧
16 **If … eye** 我眼里要是有霹雳就好了（希丽叶巴不得向奥岚铎的对手发出霹雳）
17 **down** 倒下
18 **not yet well breathed** 还没好好热身

ORLANDO	I beseech you, punish me not with your hard thoughts[1], wherein I confess me much guilty to deny so fair[2] and excellent ladies anything. But let your fair eyes and gentle wishes go with me to my trial[3], wherein if I be foiled[4], there is but one shamed that was never gracious[5]; if killed, but one dead that is willing to be so. I shall do my friends no wrong, for I have none to lament me; the world no injury[6], for in it I have nothing; only[7] in the world I fill up a place, which may be better supplied[8] when I have made it empty.	145 150
ROSALIND	The little strength that I have, I would it were with you.	
CELIA	And mine to eke out[9] hers.	
ROSALIND	Fare you well: pray heaven I be deceived in you[10].	155
CELIA	Your heart's desires be with you.	
CHARLES	Come, where is this young gallant[11] that is so desirous to lie with his mother earth[12]?	
ORLANDO	Ready, sir, but his will hath in it a more modest working[13].	
DUKE FREDERICK	You shall try but one fall.	160
CHARLES	No, I warrant your grace you shall not entreat him to a second, that have so mightily persuaded him from a first.	
ORLANDO	You mean to mock me after: you should not have mocked me before. But come your ways[14].	
ROSALIND	Now Hercules be thy speed[15], young man.	165
CELIA	I would I were invisible, to catch the strong fellow by the leg.	

[They] wrestle

ROSALIND	O excellent young man.	
CELIA	If I had a thunderbolt in mine eye[16], I can tell who should down[17].	

[Charles is thrown to the ground.] Shout

DUKE FREDERICK	No more, no more!	
ORLANDO	Yes, I beseech your grace, I am not yet well breathed[18].	170
DUKE FREDERICK	How dost thou, Charles?	
LE BEAU	He cannot speak, my lord.	
DUKE FREDERICK	Bear him away.	

[Charles is carried out]

What is thy name, young man?

ORLANDO	Orlando, my liege, the youngest son of Sir Roland de Boys.	175

Duke Frederick is displeased to find that Orlando is the son of his old enemy. Rosalind and Celia offer comfort to Orlando, but he seems unable to reply.

 剧情简介：弗莱德瑞公爵得知奥岚铎是他宿敌的儿子后很不高兴。若泽兰和希丽叶设法安慰奥岚铎，但他似乎无法回应。

Language in the play 剧中语言

From prose (散文；散体) to verse (韵文；韵体) (in small groups)

At line 176, for the first time in the play, the characters speak in verse rather than prose (see 'Verse and prose' on p. 183 for more information on these forms).

a Read lines 176–82 aloud together, concentrating on the beat of the **iambic pentameter** (抑扬五音步) – the rhythm is 'da DUM da DUM da DUM da DUM da DUM'.

b Now read aloud Orlando's prose at lines 145–52. Can you hear the difference between the rhythms in the prose and the verse? Describe in your own words the difference between them.

c Discuss why you think the characters switch from prose to verse in this way. What effect does it have on how the characters' words come across?

Stagecraft 导演技巧

Exploring the script (in threes)

Lines 194–212 provide a wonderful chance to try out some of Shakespeare's lines as actors. Orlando has won the fight and, it seems, the heart of Rosalind (if not of Celia, too).

- Prepare a dramatic reading of the script opposite, paying particular attention to the following lines. In your Director's Journal, compose detailed stage directions based on your interpretations.

  Line 198 'Wear this for me'. How does Rosalind hand over her chain, and how does Orlando receive it?

  Line 200 In what ways could Celia's goodbye to Orlando show how much or how little she cares about him?

  Line 204 'He calls us back.' This line often evokes audience laughter because Orlando has not called them back. Rosalind longs to speak to him again and, overhearing his aside, thinks he is talking to her. How might she show her desire to return to him?

  Lines 206–7 'overthrown / More than your enemies.' How long do they 'gaze upon each other' before Celia calls Rosalind away?

  Line 208 'Have with you' means 'I'm coming' or 'Hold on a minute'. How does Rosalind break her eye contact with Orlando?

1 house 家族
2 change that calling 交换那个姓
3 given him tears unto entreaties 流着眼泪苦苦恳求
4 Ere = Before
5 ventured 冒险
6 Gentle 高贵
7 envious disposition 恶毒性情
8 Sticks me at heart 伤透了我的心
9 have well deserved 值得敬重
10 But justly 只要严格
11 Your mistress 您的女主人 （希丽叶这里指若泽兰。西方进行马上枪术比赛 [jousting] 或摔跤比赛之类的对抗性比赛时，地位高的女性观众可以表示愿意做参赛者的赞助人或女主人；如果该参赛者胜出，其女主人会给他某种奖励）
12 one out of suits with Fortune 不再受命运女神眷顾的人
13 her hand lacks means 没有财力（这句话的意思是"心有余而力不足"）
14 better parts 魂魄
15 quintain （旧时供骑士练习冲刺的）靶子人
16 mere 纯粹
17 Have with you 就来

DUKE FREDERICK	I would thou hadst been son to some man else;
	The world esteemed thy father honourable
	But I did find him still mine enemy.
	Thou shouldst have better pleased me with this deed
	Hadst thou descended from another house¹.
	But fare thee well. Thou art a gallant youth:
	I would thou hadst told me of another father.

[*Exeunt Duke Frederick, Le Beau, Touchstone, Lords, and Attendants*]

CELIA	Were I my father, coz, would I do this?
ORLANDO	I am more proud to be Sir Roland's son –
	His youngest son – and would not change that calling²
	To be adopted heir to Frederick.
ROSALIND	My father loved Sir Roland as his soul
	And all the world was of my father's mind;
	Had I before known this young man his son,
	I should have given him tears unto entreaties³
	Ere⁴ he should thus have ventured⁵.
CELIA	Gentle⁶ cousin,
	Let us go thank him and encourage him;
	My father's rough and envious disposition⁷
	Sticks me at heart⁸. – Sir, you have well deserved⁹:
	If you do keep your promises in love
	But justly¹⁰, as you have exceeded all promise,
	Your mistress¹¹ shall be happy.
ROSALIND	[*Giving him a chain from her neck*] Gentleman,
	Wear this for me: one out of suits with Fortune¹²,
	That could give more, but that her hand lacks means¹³. –
	Shall we go, coz?
CELIA	Aye. – Fare you well, fair gentleman.

[*They turn to go*]

ORLANDO	[*Aside*] Can I not say, 'I thank you'? My better parts¹⁴
	Are all thrown down, and that which here stands up
	Is but a quintain¹⁵, a mere¹⁶ lifeless block.
ROSALIND	[*To Celia*] He calls us back. My pride fell with my fortunes,
	I'll ask him what he would. – Did you call, sir?
	Sir, you have wrestled well and overthrown
	More than your enemies.

[*They gaze upon each other*]

CELIA	Will you go, coz?
ROSALIND	Have with you¹⁷. – Fare you well.

Exeunt [*Rosalind and Celia*]

Orlando suspects he has fallen in love with Rosalind. Le Beau urges him to leave the court and so avoid Duke Frederick's malice, which is also directed at Rosalind.

剧情简介：奥岚铎怀疑自己已经爱上了若泽兰。勒博敦促他赶紧离开宫廷，以避免受到弗莱德瑞公爵的恶意伤害，这种恶意也是针对若泽兰的。

1 'The Duke is humorous'

Today, to say that someone is 'humorous' means that they are amusing, with a lively sense of humour. But in Shakespeare's day it meant moody, unbalanced, unpredictable. That is because Elizabethans believed that a person's nature was governed by four 'humours' (体液 [旧时认为存在人体内，影响健康和性格]) (see p. 132). These humours corresponded to different moods – anger, melancholy, bravery and calmness. If the humours were not properly balanced, it resulted in mood swings and extreme behaviour.

- How would you describe the temperament and balance of emotions in each character in the play so far? Make notes on every character as if you are a medical practitioner in Shakespeare's day, describing their emotions and behaviour and then relating it to the four humours.

2 How to play Le Beau? (in pairs)

Compare Le Beau's message and delivery here to his appearance earlier in the scene. Does he represent, after all, the kinder and more benign (善良) side of the court, or is he lying in order to get Orlando out of the court?

a Read the dialogue in two ways: with Le Beau acting as a trusted friend to Orlando; then as if he is trying to deceive Orlando.

b Discuss which interpretation seems more believable in the context of the script and the characters as you understand them so far.

1 passion 激情
2 urged conference 想要交谈
3 Or = Either （要么）
4 something weaker 某个更孱弱的人（即若泽兰）
5 Albeit you have deserved 尽管您赢得了
6 misconsters 误解
7 humorous 喜怒无常
8 More suits you to conceive 更适合您自己想象
9 indeed 实际上
10 whose 她们对彼此的
11 Grounded ... that 原因不是别的，只是
12 knowledge 了解
13 much bounden 感激不尽
14 from ... smother 刚出油锅，又入火坑

Write about it 写作练习

Disliking Rosalind, disliking Orlando (in small groups)

a Compare Le Beau's lines 229–33 with how Oliver explains his hatred for Orlando in Scene 1, lines 128–32. What similarities can you find?

b What advice would you give to Orlando and Rosalind, both of whom find themselves discriminated against because of circumstances and attributes over which they have no control?

c Compose three or four proverbs to help these characters make sense of their situation and find the courage to face the difficulties that come their way.

ORLANDO	What passion[1] hangs these weights upon my tongue?	
	I cannot speak to her, yet she urged conference[2].	210

Enter LE BEAU

LE BEAU	O poor Orlando! thou art overthrown:	
	Or[3] Charles or something weaker[4] masters thee.	
	Good sir, I do in friendship counsel you	
	To leave this place. Albeit you have deserved[5]	
	High commendation, true applause, and love,	215
	Yet such is now the Duke's condition	
	That he misconsters[6] all that you have done.	
	The Duke is humorous[7]: what he is indeed	
	More suits you to conceive[8] than I to speak of.	
ORLANDO	I thank you, sir; and pray you tell me this:	220
	Which of the two was daughter of the Duke,	
	That here was at the wrestling?	
LE BEAU	Neither his daughter, if we judge by manners,	
	But yet indeed[9] the shorter is his daughter;	
	The other is daughter to the banished Duke	225
	And here detained by her usurping uncle	
	To keep his daughter company, whose[10] loves	
	Are dearer than the natural bond of sisters.	
	But I can tell you that of late this Duke	
	Hath ta'en displeasure 'gainst his gentle niece,	230
	Grounded upon no other argument	
	But that[11] the people praise her for her virtues	
	And pity her for her good father's sake;	
	And, on my life, his malice 'gainst the lady	
	Will suddenly break forth. Sir, fare you well,	235
	Hereafter, in a better world than this,	
	I shall desire more love and knowledge[12] of you.	
ORLANDO	I rest much bounden[13] to you: fare you well.	

[*Exit Le Beau*]

	Thus must I from the smoke into the smother[14],	
	From tyrant duke unto a tyrant brother.	240
	But heavenly Rosalind!	*Exit*

Celia tries to cheer Rosalind, who seems downcast and love-sick for Orlando. She asks if Rosalind really has fallen in love so quickly, and jokes at her evasive reply. Duke Frederick enters, angry.

 剧情简介：希丽叶试图让若泽兰高兴起来，因为她看起来情绪低落，而且因为奥岚铎害上了相思病。希丽叶问若泽兰是否真的这么快就坠入爱河，并嘲笑她闪烁其词的回答。弗莱德瑞公爵上场，怒气冲冲。

1 A melancholy lover (in pairs)

The opening of Scene 3, where Rosalind appears so unhappy, contrasts sharply with Orlando's elation (兴高采烈) at the end of Scene 2. Both moods spring from the same cause: falling in love.

a Discuss how serious Rosalind's dejection (沮丧) is. Consider the following questions when coming to your judgement:

- Are her replies to Celia spoken in genuine sadness, and is she melancholy (depressed, dejected) because of love-sickness?
- Are her responses playful and light hearted, amusing both Celia and the audience as a parody* of the stereotypical melancholy lover?
- Does she want to shock Celia by referring to Orlando as the future father of her children (see line 8)?

b Role-play a conversation between a director and a costume and props (道具) designer, suggesting how you might interpret and visually present the opening of the scene. Describe what the characters might wear or carry in order to indicate their moods and emotions, and how they could use costume and props to emphasise certain lines or illustrate particular images in the script. It may be useful for you to have a look at an early seventeenth-century study of love-sickness – Robert Burton's *Anatomy of Melancholy*.

Language in the play 剧中语言

Wrestling as a metaphor (隐喻)

a After the wrestling match, Celia urges Rosalind to 'wrestle with thy affections' (line 16). Identify other moments in the play so far where wrestling seems to be an underlying **metaphor** (see p. 182).

b How might you suggest the metaphor of wrestling in this scene? Are there any particular words that could be emphasised and accompanied by gestures in order to bring this to the fore? Are the characters simply wrestling with depressed feelings, or is there perhaps some tension between them, too?

1 Cupid　丘比特（罗马神话中的爱神）
2 curs　狗杂种
3 lame me with reasons　用道理让我残废
4 laid up　害了病
5 briars　荆棘
6 working-day world　日常劳作的世界
7 burs　蒺藜
8 holy-day foolery　假日嬉闹
9 walk … paths　不走别人走过的小道
10 petticoats　蓬松长裙
11 coat = petticoat
12 Hem　轻咳
13 cry 'hem' and have him　轻咳一声就抓住他
14 turning … service　不开玩笑了
15 therefore ensue　因此
16 By this kind of chase　照此推论
17 faith　说真的
18 that　他的品德

* parody　戏仿，指对一部作品进行借用，以达到调侃、嘲讽甚至致敬的目的，例如周星驰的《大话西游》。

Act 1 Scene 3
A room in Duke Frederick's palace

Enter CELIA *and* ROSALIND

CELIA	Why, cousin; why, Rosalind – Cupid[1] have mercy, not a word?
ROSALIND	Not one to throw at a dog.
CELIA	No, thy words are too precious to be cast away upon curs[2]: throw some of them at me. Come, lame me with reasons[3].
ROSALIND	Then there were two cousins laid up[4], when the one should be lamed with reasons, and the other mad without any.
CELIA	But is all this for your father?
ROSALIND	No, some of it is for my child's father – O how full of briars[5] is this working-day world[6]!
CELIA	They are but burs[7], cousin, thrown upon thee in holy-day foolery[8]: if we walk not in the trodden paths[9], our very petticoats[10] will catch them.
ROSALIND	I could shake them off my coat[11]: these burs are in my heart.
CELIA	Hem[12] them away.
ROSALIND	I would try, if I could cry 'hem' and have him[13].
CELIA	Come, come, wrestle with thy affections.
ROSALIND	O they take the part of a better wrestler than myself.
CELIA	O, a good wish upon you: you will try in time in despite of a fall. But turning these jests out of service[14], let us talk in good earnest. Is it possible, on such a sudden, you should fall into so strong a liking with old Sir Roland's youngest son?
ROSALIND	The Duke my father loved his father dearly.
CELIA	Doth it therefore ensue[15] that you should love his son dearly? By this kind of chase[16] I should hate him for my father hated his father dearly; yet I hate not Orlando.
ROSALIND	No, faith[17], hate him not, for my sake.
CELIA	Why should I not? Doth he not deserve well?

Enter DUKE FREDERICK *with* LORDS

ROSALIND	Let me love him for that[18], and do you love him because I do. Look, here comes the Duke.
CELIA	With his eyes full of anger.

Duke Frederick banishes Rosalind on pain of death. She protests that neither she nor her father is a traitor. Celia supports her, saying that she and Rosalind have been inseparable friends.

剧情简介：弗莱德瑞公爵宣布放逐若泽兰，如不从命就处以死刑。若泽兰抗议说自己和父亲都不是叛徒。希丽叶支持她，说她和若泽兰已经成为密不可分的朋友。

1 Banishment or death (in large groups)

Duke Frederick's reasons for banishing Rosalind from court are that he does not trust her (line 45) and that she is her father's daughter (line 48).

a Create a mind-map of all the possible emotions that Rosalind might be feeling at this tense moment, showing how her feelings might change throughout her exchange with Duke Frederick.

b Take turns to speak Rosalind's responses in the script opposite in a way that expresses one of the emotions featured in your mind-map. Which response tells you most about her state of mind and her reaction to her banishment? Which emotion seems most fitting for each response?

c From what you know of the play so far, improvise (即兴创作) an imagined monologue for Rosalind about her suffering and her dilemma. Every member of the group should say a sentence or two in turn, and you should keep going until you feel you have explored all the relevant aspects of Rosalind's difficult situation.

1 dispatch ... haste 为了您的安全赶紧离开
2 You/Thou 您 / 你（从用you转为用thou称呼对方显示出言者的鄙视）
3 our public court 本公爵的开放宫廷
4 fault 罪过
5 If ... intelligence 如果我了解自己
6 frantic 发疯
7 dear 尊贵
8 unborn 尚未成形
9 purgation 自证清白
10 grace 美德
11 whereon 在什么之上
12 likelihoods 可能性
13 stayed her 让她留下
14 ranged along 一起流浪
15 pleasure 意愿
16 remorse 恻隐之心
17 Juno's swans 茱娜的天鹅（Juno多译作"朱诺"，她是罗马神话中主神 Jupiter [朱庇特] 之妻，为她拉车的是一对天鹅；天鹅的习性是雌雄天鹅结成稳定的配偶关系，彼此从不分离）

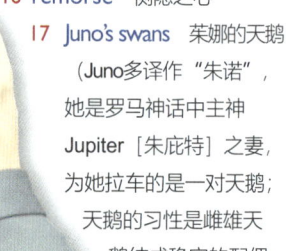

DUKE FREDERICK Mistress, dispatch you with your safest haste[1]
And get you from our court.

ROSALIND   Me, uncle?

FREDERICK   You[2], cousin.
Within these ten days if that thou be'st found
So near our public court[3] as twenty miles,
Thou[2] diest for it.

ROSALIND   I do beseech your grace   35
Let me the knowledge of my fault[4] bear with me:
If with myself I hold intelligence[5],
Or have acquaintance with mine own desires,
If that I do not dream or be not frantic[6]
(As I do trust I am not) then, dear[7] uncle,   40
Never so much as in a thought unborn[8],
Did I offend your highness.

DUKE FREDERICK   Thus do all traitors:
If their purgation[9] did consist in words,
They are as innocent as grace[10] itself.
Let it suffice thee that I trust thee not.   45

ROSALIND Yet your mistrust cannot make me a traitor;
Tell me whereon[11] the likelihoods[12] depends?

DUKE FREDERICK Thou art thy father's daughter, there's enough.

ROSALIND So was I when your highness took his dukedom,
So was I when your highness banished him;   50
Treason is not inherited, my lord,
Or if we did derive it from our friends,
What's that to me? My father was no traitor.
Then, good my liege, mistake me not so much
To think my poverty is treacherous.   55

CELIA Dear sovereign, hear me speak.

DUKE FREDERICK Aye, Celia, we stayed her[13] for your sake,
Else had she with her father ranged along[14].

CELIA I did not then entreat to have her stay,
It was your pleasure[15] – and your own remorse[16].   60
I was too young that time to value her,
But now I know her: if she be a traitor,
Why so am I. We still have slept together,
Rose at an instant, learned, played, eat together,
And wheresoe'er we went, like Juno's swans[17],   65
Still we went coupled and inseparable.

Duke Frederick rebukes Celia, saying that Rosalind steals her good reputation. He again banishes Rosalind with threats of death. Celia proposes that she and Rosalind go to the Forest of Arden.

剧情简介：弗莱德瑞公爵骂希丽叶傻，让若泽兰盗走了自己的好名声。他再次放逐若泽兰，并威胁说，如若不走，只有死路一条。希丽叶提议和若泽兰一同逃往阿登森林。

1 Standing up to tyranny (in groups of five or more)

a Read through lines 28–79 and discuss the following questions:
- Do you think this scene, where Duke Frederick banishes his niece and rebukes Celia, should be played intimately or in front of the court? What difference does it make?
- How might you best portray Duke Frederick's sentencing of Rosalind? Think about the actors' positioning and any props you might use.
- Suggest how the lords attending on Duke Frederick behave as they watch and hear his angry words to his daughter and his niece.
- How does Celia 'entreat' her father to let Rosalind stay with her? Is she on her knees? Does she hold Rosalind's hand or perhaps her father's hand?

b Prepare a tableau (定格；活人画) to represent one or two significant moments in the script opposite. Set your scenes in the court, and make sure that they capture the dramatic tension and the main character's emotions and relationships. Don't forget to include the lords of the court, as the positioning and expressions of these spectators are instrumental in creating the mood of the scene.

c When in position for the tableau, take it in turns to 'unfreeze' for a minute in order to describe your characters' thoughts and feelings at this moment.

Characters 人物分析

Celia's role (in pairs)

In deciding to hatch (制定) a plan for her and Rosalind, Celia begins to take on a more important role in the play.

a Look back at her speeches and interventions so far and discuss in pairs what characteristics she shows. Which of the following adjectives best describe her: loyal, impulsive, humorous, brave, rebellious, resentful, bossy, supportive?

b Make a list of character traits for Celia and put them in order of priority. Try to match these traits with moments in the play where she has demonstrated them.

c Take turns to sit in the hot-seat* as Celia and answer questions about her relationship with her father, with the court, with other characters and with Rosalind. The interviewer should make notes on Celia's character while listening to her answers.

1	subtle	狡黠
2	smoothness	油滑
3	name	名声
4	show	显得
5	doom	判决
6	provide yourself	做好准备
7	greatness of my word	君无戏言
8	sundered	拆散
9	devise … fly	商量我们怎样远走高飞
10	change	厄运
11	at our sorrows pale	= pale at our sorrows （因我们的悲伤而黯然）
12	Beauty … gold	美貌比金子更容易招贼

* hot-seat 热座位，一种课堂游戏，玩法是请一位同学坐到讲台上的一把椅子上，其他同学轮番给他/她出难题，哪个问题他/她回答不出就算输。

DUKE FREDERICK	She is too subtle[1] for thee, and her smoothness[2],	
	Her very silence, and her patience	
	Speak to the people and they pity her.	
	Thou art a fool: she robs thee of thy name[3]	70
	And thou wilt show[4] more bright and seem more virtuous	
	When she is gone.	

[*Celia starts to speak*]

                               Then open not thy lips!
                               Firm and irrevocable is my doom[5]
                               Which I have passed upon her: she is banished.

CELIA   Pronounce that sentence then on me, my liege,   75
             I cannot live out of her company.

DUKE FREDERICK   You are a fool. – You, niece, provide yourself[6]:
             If you outstay the time, upon mine honour
             And in the greatness of my word[7], you die.

Exeunt Duke and Lords

CELIA   O my poor Rosalind, whither wilt thou go?   80
             Wilt thou change fathers? I will give thee mine!
             I charge thee be not thou more grieved than I am.

ROSALIND   I have more cause.

CELIA   Thou hast not, cousin:
             Prithee be cheerful. Know'st thou not the Duke
             Hath banished me, his daughter?

ROSALIND   That he hath not.   85

CELIA   No? 'Hath not'? Rosalind lacks then the love
             Which teacheth thee that thou and I am one;
             Shall we be sundered[8], shall we part, sweet girl?
             No, let my father seek another heir!
             Therefore devise with me how we may fly[9],   90
             Whither to go, and what to bear with us;
             And do not seek to take your change[10] upon you,
             To bear your griefs yourself and leave me out:
             For, by this heaven, now at our sorrows pale[11],
             Say what thou canst, I'll go along with thee.   95

ROSALIND   Why, whither shall we go?

CELIA   To seek my uncle in the Forest of Arden.

ROSALIND   Alas, what danger will it be to us
             (Maids as we are) to travel forth so far?
             Beauty provoketh thieves sooner than gold[12].   100

To avoid harassment, Celia proposes to disguise herself as a country girl. Rosalind decides to dress as a young man. They plan to take Touchstone with them to the Forest of Arden.

 剧情简介：为了避免被骚扰，希丽叶提议自己装扮成一个村姑，若泽兰决定打扮成一名年轻男子。她们计划带着试金石一同逃往阿登森林。

1 Roman references (in pairs)

Rosalind's plan to disguise herself as a young man will result in all kinds of comic ambiguities. In Shakespeare's time, this effect was heightened by fact that the actor playing Rosalind would have been a boy acting as a girl (Rosalind) acting as a boy (Ganymede). More layers of comedy and confusion are added by the meanings of the names chosen by Rosalind and Celia in disguise.

In Roman mythology, Ganymede was a beautiful young man. Jupiter (Jove), king of the gods, fell in love with him and, disguised as an eagle, seized him and carried him off to Mount Olympus to become his cup-bearer ('page'). 'Ganymede' was also Elizabethan slang for a young gay man. 'Aliena' is Latin for 'the stranger'.

- Take turns to step into role as a young male actor in Shakespeare's theatre company. Describe your new role as Rosalind and how you feel about the disguises and 'sex-changes' in the play. Is it difficult to switch from acting like a woman to acting like a man? How do you expect the audience to respond to these disguises, and to the new names Rosalind and Celia have chosen?

2 Becoming a man (in pairs)

On the surface, Rosalind's image of a young man as having a 'gallant curtal-axe upon my thigh' and a 'boar-spear in my hand' refers to a romantic vision of hunting and nobility, rather than an everyday Elizabethan youth. It also has a second meaning that is a cheeky sexual joke – this kind of double meaning is known as a **double-entendre** (双关语). The description in lines 110–12 may also be Shakespeare's comment on the boastful frauds ('mannish cowards') who frequented London taverns. They had a swaggering, war-like appearance ('swashing and a martial outside'), and used it as a bluff ('outface') to sell false stories of their courage.

- Experiment with various ways of walking and talking 'like a man'. Advise each other on how to disguise 'feminine' traits and emulate (模仿) 'masculine' traits. What kind of man are you trying to be?

1. mean attire 破衣烂衫
2. umber 黄泥巴
3. smirch 涂抹
4. never stir assailants 避免招来骚扰者
5. suit me all points 把我自己从头到脚打扮成
6. gallant 漂亮
7. curtal-axe 短刀
8. boar-spear 晁（野猪）矛
9. a swashing … outside 大摇大摆、威风凛凛的外表
10. semblances 外表
11. state 境况
12. assayed 设法
13. The clownish fool 小丑似的傻子（指试金石）
14. travail 艰难旅途
15. woo 说服

CELIA   I'll put myself in poor and mean attire[1]
               And with a kind of umber[2] smirch[3] my face;
               The like do you. So shall we pass along
               And never stir assailants[4].
ROSALIND   Were it not better,
               Because that I am more than common tall,   105
               That I did suit me all points[5] like a man,
               A gallant[6] curtal-axe[7] upon my thigh,
               A boar-spear[8] in my hand, and in my heart
               Lie there what hidden woman's fear there will.
               We'll have a swashing and a martial outside[9]   110
               As many other mannish cowards have
               That do outface it with their semblances[10].
CELIA   What shall I call thee when thou art a man?
ROSALIND   I'll have no worse a name than Jove's own page,
               And therefore look you call me 'Ganymede'.   115
               But what will you be called?
CELIA   Something that hath a reference to my state[11]:
               No longer 'Celia' but 'Aliena'.
ROSALIND   But, cousin, what if we assayed[12] to steal
               The clownish fool[13] out of your father's court: 120
               Would he not be a comfort to our travail[14]?
CELIA   He'll go along o'er the wide world with me:
               Leave me alone to woo[15] him. Let's away
               And get our jewels and our wealth together,
               Devise the fittest time and safest way   125
               To hide us from pursuit that will be made
               After my flight. Now go we in content,
               To liberty, and not to banishment.
                                                                              Exeunt

As You Like It
各如所愿

Looking back at Act 1 第1幕回顾
Activities for groups or individuals

1 Mapping the characters so far

Visual maps and diagrams can help you place the characters in relation to one another.

- Continue to develop the character web you started on page 6 and add more characters to it, using additional symbols and extending the colour code to show status and relationships between the people you have met so far.

2 Summary tableaux

Act 1 is full of lively and exciting action: the clash of brothers, a murderous plot, the wrestling match, love at first sight, Duke Frederick's anger, the death threat against Rosalind and her banishment, and a planned secret escape. There are dramatic contrasts, too, as despair and tyranny alternate with laughter and friendship.

- In large groups, discuss what you think are the most important and dramatic events of Act 1. Prepare a series of tableaux that portray these moments as clearly and vividly as possible. Take photographs of the tableaux and use them to create a display that visually summarises Act 1. You could even use the photos of the tableaux to draw panels (展板，面板) that make up the first section of an *As You Like It* graphic novel.

3 Biblical references: the prodigal son (浪子)

In Scene 1, lines 29–30, Orlando refers to a story in the Bible about 'the prodigal son'. This parable (［尤指《圣经》中的］寓言故事) centres upon a kind father, a disdainful older brother and a younger brother who was so poor he lived with the pigs and ate their food. However, Orlando points out that he is not like this younger brother because he has not wasted his inheritance and dishonoured his family.

- Read the 'prodigal son' passage in the Bible (Luke 15:11–32) or look it up online. Make notes on the similarities and differences between the parable and Orlando's story so far in the play. What do you think Orlando is trying to say about himself and his brother by referring to this story? Predict how the feud (宿怨) between Oliver and his brother will end.

4 As you like it?

The title of this play might be interpreted as an invitation to the audience to make of the play what they will. It might also refer to the way that the characters seem to do as they like in spite of difficulties or conventional proprieties.

- List the ways in which the different characters you have met so far have done as they like, rather than what has been expected of them. Think about the villainous characters as well as Orlando, Rosalind and Celia.
- Predict what each of the characters would most 'like' to happen in the rest of the play. Write a social media update for each character, capturing their different perspectives at the end of Act 1.

5 Utopia

In Act 1 Scene 1, lines 92–5, Charles mentions the 'golden world' (from Classical literature) and the figure of Robin Hood (from English folklore).

- Research both of these concepts of what constitutes a utopia (乌托邦) (an ideal world), and make notes in a two-column table. What common ideas start to emerge? What differences are there? Do you think it is possible to have a utopia on Earth?

6 Banishment or liberty?

The first act ends, as the acts in Shakespeare's plays often do, with a **rhyming couplet** (押韵二行连句；对偶句) (see page 184):

> Now go we in content,
> To liberty, and not to banishment.

- Look at the images opposite and make notes in your Director's Journal about how you would stage the end of this act. Would you focus on the exciting prospect of liberty or show the characters' optimism in the face of exile and homelessness?

33

Duke Senior claims that life in the forest is far superior to life at court. Even its hardships are beneficial, and moral lessons are everywhere. He regrets that the deer are hunted and killed.

 剧情简介：老公爵声称森林里的生活远胜于宫廷生活，即便艰辛也使人受益，道德教训无处不在。他对鹿遭猎杀感到遗憾。

Stagecraft 导演技巧

First sight of Arden (in pairs)

The Forest of Arden has been depicted in a number of very different ways in productions of the play. It is contrasted with the corruption and tyranny of the court, and is clearly a rural retreat in opposition to the location of the court in the city.

- How do you imagine the forest? How would you stage it if you were an artistic director and set designer? Discuss the possibilities, then draw an initial sketch of your design in your Director's Journal. Use lines from the script, both here and in Act 1 Scene 1, lines 92–5, to guide your imagination. Compare your sketches with those of others in the class, and discuss the similarities and differences.

1 'Sweet are the uses of adversity' (in small groups)

Duke Senior claims that misfortunes ('adversity') are valuable, that good can come out of afflictions. He uses an image from an old myth: the ugly toad that has 'a precious jewel in his head'.

- Do you believe that troubles are good for you? Talk together about what you think of Duke Senior's claim, using practical examples from your own experience.
- What images or metaphors can you think of to express your beliefs about overcoming adversity? Compile a list of existing proverbs or meaningful sayings on the subject, or make up your own using some of Duke Senior's words in this speech (such as 'peril', 'chiding' or 'haunt').

2 Learning from nature (in pairs)

Lines 15–17 express the belief that humans can learn from nature, and that there are moral lessons in the landscape itself ('Sermons in stones'). Duke Senior even sees the bitter winter wind as a helpful 'counsellor' that does not flatter or lie to him.

- Take turns to speak Duke Senior's lines in different styles, and give feedback on your partner's readings. Then write detailed actors' notes to clearly instruct the actor playing Duke Senior how to perform these lines. Include an explanation for the actor detailing why you would like the lines spoken in that particular way.

1 co-mates 伙计
2 old custom 老风俗
3 painted pomp 宫廷的浮华
4 penalty of Adam 亚当受到的惩罚（即被上帝逐出伊甸园）
5 churlish chiding 厉声斥责
6 feelingly 深情
7 venomous 有毒
8 jewel 珠宝（这里指 toadstone，即传说中蟾蜍脑袋里长的蟾蜍石，据说是蟾蜍毒液的解药）
9 exempt from public haunt 免受公众叨扰
10 tongues in trees 树有言语
11 venison 鹿
12 irks me 我于心不忍
13 dappled 长着花斑
14 native burghers 原住市民
15 desert city 无人住的城市
16 confines 领地
17 forkèd heads 双叉箭头
18 haunches gored 屁股被射开大口子
19 melancholy 忧郁（当时的一种时髦心境，据说是体内黑胆汁过多造成的。参见第110页）
20 lay along 直挺挺躺着

Act 2 Scene 1
The Forest of Arden

Enter DUKE SENIOR, AMIENS, *and two or three* LORDS *dressed as foresters*

DUKE SENIOR Now, my co-mates[1] and brothers in exile,
Hath not old custom[2] made this life more sweet
Than that of painted pomp[3]? Are not these woods
More free from peril than the envious court?
Here feel we not the penalty of Adam[4], 5
The seasons' difference, as the icy fang
And churlish chiding[5] of the winter's wind –
Which when it bites and blows upon my body
Even till I shrink with cold, I smile and say,
'This is no flattery' – these are counsellors 10
That feelingly[6] persuade me what I am.
Sweet are the uses of adversity
Which like the toad, ugly and venomous[7],
Wears yet a precious jewel[8] in his head,
And this our life exempt from public haunt[9] 15
Finds tongues in trees[10], books in the running brooks,
Sermons in stones, and good in everything.

AMIENS I would not change it; happy is your grace
That can translate the stubbornness of Fortune
Into so quiet and so sweet a style. 20

DUKE SENIOR Come, shall we go and kill us venison[11]?
And yet it irks me[12] the poor dappled[13] fools,
Being native burghers[14] of this desert city[15],
Should, in their own confines[16], with forkèd heads[17]
Have their round haunches gored[18].

FIRST LORD   Indeed, my lord. 25
The melancholy[19] 'Jaques' grieves at that,
And in that kind swears you do more usurp
Than doth your brother that hath banished you.
Today my lord of Amiens and myself
Did steal behind him as he lay along[20] 30
Under an oak, whose antique root peeps out
Upon the brook that brawls along this wood,

The First Lord describes how Jaques, watching a wounded deer, draws moral lessons about society from the stricken animal's plight. Duke Senior looks forward to debating with Jaques.

 剧情简介：贵族甲描述杰奎如何一边看着一头受伤的鹿，一边从这头鹿的困境中总结出有关社会的道德说教。老公爵期待与杰奎辩论。

1 Learning more from nature (in pairs)

Duke Senior ends his first speech claiming that nature could teach all kinds of moral lessons about human life. Now he asks what lessons Jaques has drawn from the sight of a wounded stag (雄鹿), and the First Lord lists three of Jaques's conclusions that criticise society.

a Write out in your own words the three lessons, as described by the Lord in lines 46–57. They centre upon:

- the deer weeping into the stream
- the wounded deer abandoned by the herd
- the well-fed herd ignoring the wounded deer.

b Look back at what Duke Senior said about deer hunting in lines 21–5. Suggest how he now reacts to hearing himself so strongly criticised.

Themes 主题分析

Usurping at court and in the forest

Jaques criticises Duke Senior and his lords (lines 60–3). He sees them as usurpers and tyrants who have robbed the deer of their natural rights to the forest by hunting and killing them.

- Do you agree with Jaques? If so, why? How is this relevant to the action of the play so far?
- Write two paragraphs describing the different instances of usurpation that have shaped the plot and ideas of the play so far.

2 'the melancholy Jaques' (in pairs)

Jaques is tagged with an **epithet** (绰号) at line 41. An epithet is a term used to characterise a person or thing, such as in the title of 'Catherine the Great'.

a Create similar epithets for all the characters you have encountered in the play so far. Try to capture some aspect of their character in a single word.

b Write multiple epithets for each character, depending on how the other characters might see them. For example, Oliver might say 'dangerous Orlando', while Rosalind might see him as 'sweet Orlando'.

1 sequestered stag 落单的公鹿
2 languish 苟延残喘
3 leathern coat 毛皮
4 Coursed 流淌
5 Much markèd of 被……密切关注
6 Augmenting 加大
7 moralise this spectacle 就此情景讲大道理
8 similes 比喻
9 weeping in the needless stream 朝无须添水的溪流落泪
10 worldlings 世间凡人
11 sum of more 更多的量
12 velvet friend 身披天鹅绒的朋友（指长着柔滑皮毛的同伴）
13 part / The flux of company 使云游的同伴分离
14 Anon 马上
15 careless 无忧无虑
16 Wherefore = Why
17 invectively 尖酸刻薄
18 usurpers 篡位者
19 assigned and native 天赐而且天然
20 cope 见面，遇见
21 in these sullen fits 在这种忧郁发作时
22 matter = good sense（真知灼见）
23 straight = immediately

	To the which place a poor sequestered stag[1],	
	That from the hunter's aim had ta'en a hurt,	
	Did come to languish[2]; and indeed, my lord,	35
	The wretched animal heaved forth such groans	
	That their discharge did stretch his leathern coat[3]	
	Almost to bursting, and the big round tears	
	Coursed[4] one another down his innocent nose	
	In piteous chase; and thus the hairy fool,	40
	Much markèd of[5] the melancholy Jaques,	
	Stood on th'extremest verge of the swift brook,	
	Augmenting[6] it with tears.	
DUKE SENIOR	But what said Jaques?	
	Did he not moralise this spectacle[7]?	
FIRST LORD	O yes, into a thousand similes[8].	45
	First, for his weeping in the needless stream[9]:	
	'Poor deer', quoth he, 'thou mak'st a testament	
	As worldlings[10] do, giving thy sum of more[11]	
	To that which hath too much.' Then, being there alone,	
	Left and abandoned of his velvet friend[12]:	50
	''Tis right', quoth he, 'thus misery doth part	
	The flux of company[13].' Anon[14] a careless[15] herd,	
	Full of the pasture, jumps along by him	
	And never stays to greet him: 'Aye', quoth Jaques,	
	'Sweep on you fat and greasy citizens,	55
	'Tis just the fashion. Wherefore[16] do you look	
	Upon that poor and broken bankrupt there?'	
	Thus most invectively[17] he pierceth through	
	The body of the country, city, court,	
	Yea, and of this our life, swearing that we	60
	Are mere usurpers[18], tyrants, and what's worse,	
	To fright the animals and to kill them up	
	In their assigned and native[19] dwelling-place.	
DUKE SENIOR	And did you leave him in this contemplation?	
SECOND LORD	We did, my lord, weeping and commenting	65
	Upon the sobbing deer.	
DUKE SENIOR	Show me the place;	
	I love to cope[20] him in these sullen fits[21],	
	For then he's full of matter[22].	
FIRST LORD	I'll bring you to him straight[23].	
	Exeunt	

Duke Frederick thinks some of his servants have assisted Rosalind and Celia to flee. Touchstone is reported missing. Frederick orders Orlando or Oliver be brought to him, and the refugees to be hunted down.

剧情简介：弗莱德瑞公爵认为他的一些仆人帮助若泽兰和希丽叶逃跑了，试金石据报也失踪了，于是下令把奥岚铎或奥利沃带到他面前，并抓捕逃亡者。

Stagecraft 导演技巧

Contrasts (in pairs)

Shakespeare ensures that each scene either contrasts with the one that precedes it, or follows on from it in order to offer comment. Imagine that you are co-directing the play with your partner, and carry out the following activities:

a Work out how to emphasise the dramatic contrasts between Scenes 1 and 2 with regard to each of the following:
- setting (the court versus the Forest of Arden)
- character (Duke Frederick versus Duke Senior)
- theme (both scenes have hunting as a theme).

b Consider how you would stage this short scene as dramatically as possible. You should think about giving the audience insight into character as well as information to advance the plot. Discuss the following questions and decide how you would show your ideas:
- Are the lords afraid of Duke Frederick?
- What does he do as the lords speak?
- How does he deliver his instructions in the final five lines?

c In your Director's Journal, compose detailed notes for the stage designer and the actors. Explain your ideas and give instructions for how they should be shown on stage. Remember to refer to costumes, scenery, props and blocking (戏台调度) (the movements of actors in relation to one another on stage) in your notes.

1 Are ... this 认可并默许了这件事
2 untreasured of 空缺
3 roinish 粗俗
4 oft = often
5 wont 惯于
6 gentlewoman 女官
7 parts and graces 外貌和举止
8 sinewy 肌肉发达
9 suddenly = immediately
10 inquisition 调查
11 quail 失败
12 again = back
13 foolish runaways 愚蠢的逃亡者（指希丽叶和试金石，还可能包括若泽兰）

Act 2 Scene 2
Duke Frederick's palace

Enter DUKE FREDERICK *with Lords*

DUKE FREDERICK Can it be possible that no man saw them?
It cannot be: some villeins of my court
Are of consent and sufferance in this[1].

FIRST LORD I cannot hear of any that did see her;
The ladies, her attendants of her chamber,   5
Saw her abed and, in the morning early,
They found the bed untreasured of[2] their mistress.

SECOND LORD My lord, the roinish[3] clown, at whom so oft[4]
Your grace was wont[5] to laugh, is also missing.
Hisperia, the princess' gentlewoman[6],   10
Confesses that she secretly o'erheard
Your daughter and her cousin much commend
The parts and graces[7] of the wrestler
That did but lately foil the sinewy[8] Charles;
And she believes, wherever they are gone,   15
That youth is surely in their company.

DUKE FREDERICK Send to his brother: 'Fetch that gallant hither.'
If he be absent, bring his brother to me –
I'll make him find him. Do this suddenly[9],
And let not search and inquisition[10] quail[11]   20
To bring again[12] these foolish runaways[13].

Exeunt

Adam bemoans the fact that Orlando's good qualities have made him hated in the unnatural world of the court. He reveals that Oliver plots to kill Orlando, and urges Orlando to leave.

剧情简介：亚当哀叹奥岚铎的优良品格使他在无情无义的宫廷世界里遭人嫉恨。他透露说奥利沃密谋杀害他，并敦促奥岚铎离开。

Language in the play 剧中语言

Dramatic language (in pairs)

There is a story that, when he was 30 years old, Shakespeare himself played Adam (who is almost 80 years old) at the Globe Theatre. If the story is true, how do you think he might have played the faithful old servant? Use the following activities to develop your ideas about this.

a Find examples of the following language features in the script opposite (see pp. 180–5 for more detailed descriptions of these and other language features):

- repetition
- rhetorical questions
- **personification** (拟人) (where something that is not human is endowed with personality and human characteristics)
- dramatic pauses
- **apostrophe*** (where an abstract idea or absent person is addressed).

Write out each example you find and describe how it could best be exploited by an actor for dramatic effect on stage.

b These language features might help create a stereotype of a fearful and pitiful old man, or they might produce a comically forgetful and befuddled (迷糊，疑惑) character. Which portrayal do you favour – or have you devised another way of representing Adam?

c Experiment with different ways of speaking Adam's first two speeches in this scene. Write three or four stage directions for the script opposite. Describe in detail the tone of voice, gestures, movements and props that you would want an actor to use.

1 A fallen world? (in small groups)

Orlando does not realise that his good qualities might make him hated in the envious and unnatural world of the court, or that his own house is dangerous because his brother wants him dead.

a Do you think the Forest of Arden would be a safer place for 'virtuous' Orlando? Make a list of what seems immoral or unsavoury (令人不快) about the court, using quotes from the script where you can. Beside this, list your impressions – both positive and negative – of Arden.

b Do you think there is a clear contrast between the court and Arden, or are the two worlds not so different after all? Divide your group in two and debate this question, using evidence from the script.

1 memory 念想
2 fond 热衷
3 bonny 强壮
4 prizer 擂主
5 praise 声誉
6 graces 优点
7 No more do yours 您的也不过如此
8 sanctified 纯洁
9 comely 美好
10 Envenoms him that bears it 毒害具有这种品质的人
11 unhappy = unfortunate
12 lives = lives as (住着)
13 your praises 对您的赞美
14 lodging 住处
15 fail of 未能
16 cut you off 干掉您
17 practices 阴谋
18 butchery 屠宰场
19 so 只要

* apostrophe 转叹，一种修辞手法，指剧中人中断对观众说话，借助一声叹息转而对不在场的某一第三者说话，这第三者多是虚拟或抽象的人或事物（如上帝、爱情等）。

Act 2 Scene 3
Outside Oliver's house

Enter ORLANDO

ORLANDO Who's there?

[*Enter* ADAM]

ADAM What, my young master! O my gentle master,
O my sweet master, O you memory[1]
Of old Sir Roland, why, what make you here?
Why are you virtuous? Why do people love you?
And wherefore are you gentle, strong, and valiant?
Why would you be so fond[2] to overcome
The bonny[3] prizer[4] of the humorous Duke?
Your praise[5] is come too swiftly home before you.
Know you not, master, to some kind of men
Their graces[6] serve them but as enemies?
No more do yours[7]: your virtues, gentle master,
Are sanctified[8] and holy traitors to you.
O what a world is this when what is comely[9]
Envenoms him that bears it[10]!

ORLANDO Why, what's the matter?

ADAM   O unhappy[11] youth,
Come not within these doors: within this roof
The enemy of all your graces lives[12]
Your brother – no, no brother – yet the son –
Yet not the son, I will not call him son
Of him I was about to call his father –
Hath heard your praises[13], and this night he means
To burn the lodging[14] where you use to lie
And you within it. If he fail of[15] that,
He will have other means to cut you off[16]:
I overheard him and his practices[17].
This is no place, this house is but a butchery[18]:
Abhor it, fear it, do not enter it.

ORLANDO Why whither, Adam, wouldst thou have me go?

ADAM No matter whither, so[19] you come not here.

Orlando prefers to face his murderous brother rather than become a beggar or highwayman. Adam offers his life savings and service to Orlando, who accepts and praises Adam's faithfulness.

剧情简介：奥岚铎宁愿直面凶残的哥哥，也不愿沦为乞丐或强盗。亚当把自己毕生积蓄都奉献给了奥岚铎，且愿意一直服侍他，奥岚铎接受并赞扬亚当的忠诚。

Characters 人物分析

Nobility (in small groups)

Both Orlando and Adam reveal signs of their nobility in this scene. Both are loyal, and would rather serve a higher cause than be forced to leave the court.

a Take turns in the hot-seat in role as each character, and question each other about your motivations.

b Discuss each character's reasons for their comments in lines 31–76. Which man is the nobler of the two, and what does this tell us about the world depicted in the play?

Write about it 写作练习

God's providence (保佑) (in pairs)

Adam offers his life savings to Orlando, saying that God will look after him.

a Look up the passage in the Bible that Adam refers to (Matthew 10:29 and Psalms 147:9). What is the significance of the ravens and sparrows? What does this show about Adam's willingness to give all his money to Orlando?

b Adam's actions remind Orlando of past times. Explain how this contrasts with Orlando's view of the modern world in lines 59–62.

c In role as Orlando, write up your ideas about the points above in a diary entry. In his writing, Orlando should reflect on Adam's faith in God, his selfless generosity and his loyalty.

1 How to play Adam? (in pairs)

a Some actors play Adam's lines for laughs in this scene. Discuss what you think of each of these examples from previous performances:

- **Line 45** 'Here is the gold' – he produces a huge bucket of coins.
- **Line 47** 'I am strong and lusty' – he almost faints as he speaks.
- **Lines 48–51** He uses gestures to illustrate his refusals.
- **Line 53** 'Frosty but kindly' – he taps his white-haired head.
- **Lines 54–5** 'I'll do the service of a younger man …' – he totters (蹒跚).

b Try playing the scene straight, and then for laughs. Which do you think works best?

1 base and boisterous 卑贱又暴躁
2 common road 大路上
3 do how I can 无论我怎样干
4 diverted blood 没有骨肉情
5 bloody 嗜血成性
6 The thrifty hire I saved 省吃俭用攒下的工钱
7 foster-nurse 养老的钱
8 unregarded age 被人嫌弃的年纪
9 He … sparrows 依照天意，喂乌鸦者也会喂麻雀（出自《圣经》典故）
10 strong and lusty 强壮有力
11 with unbashful forehead 厚着脸皮
12 woo … debility 讨好那些让人懦弱无力的家伙
13 Frosty but kindly 一头白霜但和蔼可亲
14 the antique world 古道热肠
15 for duty not for meed 只为尽职不为犒赏
16 prun'st 修剪（原形为prune）
17 In lieu of 回报
18 husbandry 栽培
19 youthful wages 年轻时的积蓄
20 light … content 找到可以凑合安身的地方

As You Like It Act 2 Scene 3
各如所愿

ORLANDO What, wouldst thou have me go and beg my food,
Or with a base and boisterous[1] sword enforce
A thievish living on the common road[2]?
This I must do or know not what to do;
Yet this I will not do, do how I can[3].   35
I rather will subject me to the malice
Of a diverted blood[4] and bloody[5] brother.

ADAM But do not so: I have five hundred crowns,
The thrifty hire I saved[6] under your father,
Which I did store to be my foster-nurse[7]   40
When service should in my old limbs lie lame
And unregarded age[8] in corners thrown;
Take that, and He that doth the ravens feed,
Yea providently caters for the sparrow[9],
Be comfort to my age. Here is the gold: 45
All this I give you; let me be your servant –
Though I look old, yet I am strong and lusty[10];
For in my youth I never did apply
Hot and rebellious liquors in my blood,
Nor did not with unbashful forehead[11] woo   50
The means of weakness and debility[12];
Therefore my age is as a lusty winter,
Frosty but kindly[13]. Let me go with you:
I'll do the service of a younger man
In all your business and necessities.   55

ORLANDO O good old man, how well in thee appears
The constant service of the antique world[14],
When service sweat for duty not for meed[15].
Thou art not for the fashion of these times
Where none will sweat but for promotion   60
And, having that, do choke their service up
Even with the having. It is not so with thee;
But, poor old man, thou prun'st[16] a rotten tree
That cannot so much as a blossom yield,
In lieu of[17] all thy pains and husbandry[18].   65
But come thy ways: we'll go along together
And, ere we have thy youthful wages[19] spent,
We'll light upon some settled low content[20].

Adam resolves to be Orlando's faithful servant and bids goodbye to his old home, where he has lived for over sixty years. In Scene 4, Rosalind, Celia and Touchstone seem exhausted as they arrive in Arden.

剧情简介：亚当决心做奥岚铎忠实的仆人，向自己住了六十多年的家告别。在第四场中，若泽兰、希丽叶和试金石筋疲力尽地来到阿登森林。

Language in the play 剧中语言

Rhyming couplets (in pairs)

Shakespeare's scenes often end with a rhyming couplet, in order to give a sense of closure. However, at the end of Act 2 Scene 3, Adam has four rhyming couplets.

a Experiment with reading out lines 69–76 to emphasise the end rhymes and internal rhythm. Notice how the iambic pentameter is interrupted in line 76 by the emphasis on the two words 'die well'.

b Discuss what effect you think Shakespeare wanted to create here and what you predict will happen to Adam.

Stagecraft 导演技巧

Arriving in Arden (in threes)

The beginning of Scene 4 suggests that all three travellers are weary and that Touchstone is particularly disillusioned.

a Take parts and read aloud lines 1–13, then discuss where in this section the following actions might take place. Remember to look out for implicit (含蓄) stage directions in the script.
- Rosalind does something to help Celia.
- Celia collapses and refuses to carry on.
- Touchstone picks up Celia and carries her.

b Experiment with different ways of speaking Rosalind's line 11, 'Well, this is the Forest of Arden.' Choose your favourite of these, and describe the delivery in your Director's Journal. You should include stage directions as well as notes for the actor.

1 *recompense* 犒劳
2 *motley* 彩格衣（丑角的服装，一般带有花格或花斑，类似中国的百衲衣）
3 *Jupiter* 朱庇特（罗马神话中的主神，以性格开朗闻名）
4 *if … weary* 即使我的腿不疲惫（注意weary与merry押韵）
5 *weaker vessel* 弱女子
6 *doublet and hose* 小夹衣和裤袜（伊丽莎白时代男性的典型装束）
7 *bear with me* 担待我一下
8 *bear you* 担着您（这里bear的意思是"背负"）
9 *cross* 十字架（耶稣是背负着十字架被押解到行刑场的；当时金币上也印有十字架；试金石用cross一语双关）
10 *this … Arden* 这儿就是阿登森林了（伊丽莎白时代的剧院没有精致的戏台布景，所以若泽兰的这句台词也是剧中的一个笑点）

ADAM	Master, go on, and I will follow thee	
	To the last gasp with truth and loyalty.	70
	From seventeen years till now almost fourscore	
	Here lived I, but now live here no more.	
	At seventeen years many their fortunes seek,	
	But at fourscore it is too late a week;	
	Yet Fortune cannot recompense[1] me better	75
	Than to die well and not my master's debtor.	

Exeunt

Act 2 Scene 4
The Forest of Arden

Enter ROSALIND *disguised as the boy* GANYMEDE,
CELIA *disguised as a shepherdess* ALIENA,
and the clown TOUCHSTONE *dressed in motley*[2]

ROSALIND O Jupiter[3], how merry are my spirits!

TOUCHSTONE I care not for my spirits, if my legs were not weary[4].

ROSALIND [*Aside*] I could find in my heart to disgrace my man's apparel and to cry like a woman; but I must comfort the weaker vessel[5], as doublet and hose[6] ought to show itself courageous to petticoat; therefore – courage, good Aliena! 5

CELIA I pray you bear with me[7], I cannot go no further.

TOUCHSTONE For my part, I had rather bear with you than bear you[8]; yet I should bear no cross[9] if I did bear you, for I think you have no money in your purse. 10

ROSALIND Well, this is the Forest of Arden[10].

TOUCHSTONE Aye, now am I in Arden, the more fool I! When I was at home I was in a better place; but travellers must be content.

Enter CORIN *and* SILVIUS

ROSALIND Aye, be so, good Touchstone. Look you who comes here:
A young man and an old in solemn talk. 15

CORIN That is the way to make her scorn you still.

SILVIUS O Corin, that thou knew'st how I do love her.

CORIN I partly guess, for I have loved ere now.

Silvius claims that no man's love can equal his, and that the behaviour of lovers is always extreme. Rosalind agrees with his words, but Touchstone's memories show the absurdities of lovers' behaviour.

 剧情简介：悉尔维耶声称没有哪个男人能比他爱得深，还说恋人做事情总是走极端。若泽兰赞同他的话，但试金石的回忆说明恋人会做荒诞之事。

1 A first encounter with pastoral (in pairs)

The travellers' meeting with Corin and Silvius is the court's first encounter with the pastoral (田园生活) tradition in the play (see pp. 165–6). Within this tradition, shepherds living out in the fields with their flocks are seen to inhabit an ideal world, away from the complexity and corruption of the city and the court. What do you think of the Forest of Arden so far in the play? Is it an ideal world, full of limitless possibilities – a place where dreams come true?

- Discuss whether the Forest of Arden is an idealised example of the pastoral tradition or whether it is a more complex place with its own dangers and disappointments. Find an example or a quotation from the play so far to support your views.

Themes 主题分析
Unrequited love (单相思) (in fives)

Silvius's expression of love reminds Rosalind of her own passionate feelings for Orlando.

- How would you want to stage this part of the scene? Should lines 16–37 be played straight or for laughs? Try them both ways. The three actors playing Rosalind, Celia and Touchstone should engage with each other as they react to the conversation with movements, gestures and facial expressions.

Write about it 写作练习
Romantic advice

What advice might Rosalind, Celia or Touchstone have given to Silvius if he had not abruptly left? Write up one character's advice on solving his romantic problem as a letter, a scripted conversation or an agony aunt column (知心大妈栏目). Try to capture the personality and speaking style of the character in your writing.

2 The foolishness of love

Touchstone makes fun of Silvius's words and tells how his love for a milkmaid, Jane Smile, made him behave foolishly. His comic conclusion is that it is inevitable that all lovers behave foolishly.

- Do you agree with Touchstone's conclusion? Write a paragraph about whether you think people behave strangely when they are in love.

---

1 fantasy 痴情
2 slightest folly 最小的傻事
3 Wearing = Wearying (令……厌烦)
4 broke from company 撇下同伴
5 passion 热恋
6 Phoebe 菲妣（与希腊神话中月亮和狩猎女神阿尔媂弥 [Artemis] 的别称同名；这一名字在本剧的其他版本中也作 Phebe）
7 hard adventure 不幸
8 a-night 夜里
9 batler 捣衣棒
10 dugs （母牛、母羊等的）乳房
11 chapped 皲裂
12 peasecod 豌豆荚
13 run into strange capers 做出一些非同寻常的举动（暗指通奸）
14 mortal in folly 傻得要死
15 ware of 意识到，认识到
16 upon my fashion 像我这样
17 grows something stale 变得有些老掉牙了
18 yond man 那边那个人（指考林）
19 Holla, you, clown! 喂，您这土老帽！
20 kinsman 一家人

SILVIUS	No, Corin, being old, thou canst not guess,	
	Though in thy youth thou wast as true a lover	20
	As ever sighed upon a midnight pillow.	
	But if thy love were ever like to mine –	
	As sure I think did never man love so –	
	How many actions most ridiculous	
	Hast thou been drawn to by thy fantasy[1]?	25
CORIN	Into a thousand that I have forgotten.	
SILVIUS	O thou didst then never love so heartily.	
	If thou remembrest not the slightest folly[2]	
	That ever love did make thee run into,	
	Thou hast not loved.	30
	Or if thou hast not sat as I do now,	
	Wearing[3] thy hearer in thy mistress' praise,	
	Thou hast not loved.	
	Or if thou hast not broke from company[4]	
	Abruptly as my passion[5] now makes me,	35
	Thou hast not loved.	
	O Phoebe[6], Phoebe, Phoebe! *Exit*	
ROSALIND	Alas, poor shepherd, searching of thy wound,	
	I have by hard adventure[7] found mine own.	
TOUCHSTONE	And I mine: I remember when I was in love, I broke my sword upon a stone and bid him take that for coming a-night[8] to Jane Smile; and I remember the kissing of her batler[9] and the cow's dugs[10] that her pretty chapped[11] hands had milked; and I remember the wooing of a peasecod[12] instead of her, from whom I took two cods and, giving her them again, said with weeping tears, 'Wear these for my sake.' We that are true lovers run into strange capers[13]; but as all is mortal in Nature, so is all nature in love mortal in folly[14].	40 45
ROSALIND	Thou speak'st wiser than thou art ware of[15].	
TOUCHSTONE	Nay, I shall ne'er be ware of my own wit till I break my shins against it.	50
ROSALIND	Jove, Jove, this shepherd's passion	
	Is much upon my fashion[16].	
TOUCHSTONE	And mine, but it grows something stale[17] with me.	
CELIA	I pray you, one of you question yond man[18]	
	If he for gold will give us any food:	55
	I faint almost to death.	
TOUCHSTONE	Holla, you, clown![19]	
ROSALIND	Peace, fool; he's not thy kinsman[20].	

Rosalind asks where she may buy food and shelter. Corin says that his miserly employer's property is for sale, and offers help. He agrees to buy the sheep farm with Rosalind's and Celia's money.

剧情简介：若泽兰问考林哪里可以买到食物和住处。考林说他那吝啬的雇主正在出售其不动产，他愿意帮忙，用若泽兰和希丽叶的钱把雇主的羊场买下来。

1 'Your betters, sir'

Touchstone's instant response to Corin is sarcastic, but reveals the class differences between the court and the country folk.

a Add to the character web that you began on page 6. (Look at the list of characters on page 1, where the people of Arden are listed as a group).

b Do you think that there are significant differences between people who live in the cities and the countryside today? Is there any snobbery on one side – or perhaps both?

Stagecraft 导演技巧

Meeting Corin (in threes)

This meeting with Corin is the first time that Rosalind and Celia, disguised as Ganymede and Aliena, speak to a stranger. The travellers begin to learn more about what life is like in the Forest of Arden.

a Experiment with different ways of speaking Corin's line 63. Corin might have suspicions about this young person he calls 'gentle sir'. Or he might hesitate after his first three words, wondering just how to address this young boy who is so feminine in appearance. Would you want to show Rosalind being convincing as a boy, or perhaps as a ludicrous (荒唐可笑) figure clumping (踢踢踏踏地走) around the stage? How else could she be perceived?

b In one production, to emphasise there was nothing suitable for the upper-class Rosalind and Celia to eat at the cottage, Corin fished in his pockets and pulled out the remains of an extremely stale loaf, which he broke in disgust as he emphasised 'you' in line 79. How would you advise the actor playing Corin to highlight the unpleasant aspects of the forest?

c Take parts and read aloud lines 68–93. Show through expressions and gestures what Corin thinks of Celia's plight, of his master, of Silvius and of the prospect of working for Rosalind and Celia. Then read through the scene twice more so that everyone has a chance to play Corin. Make notes in your Director's Journal, explaining how you came to your decisions about Corin's **stage business** (戏台动作).

1 **Else** = If not
2 **Good even** 下午好（可在午后的任何时间段使用）
3 **entertainment** 款待（食物和住处）
4 **faints for succour** 急需帮助
5 **shear the fleeces** 剪羊毛
6 **graze** 放牧
7 **of churlish disposition** 生性吝啬
8 **little recks** 很少在意
9 **doing deeds of hospitality** 热情待客
10 **cot** = cottage（村舍）
11 **bounds of feed** 整个牧场
12 **sheepcote** 羊倌房
13 **That you will feed on** 适合你们吃的东西
14 **in my voice** 就我自己而言
15 **young swain** 年轻后生
16 **but erewhile** 刚才
17 **stand with honesty** 公平合理
18 **mend** 改善
19 **waste my time** 打发我的时间
20 **feeder** 羊倌；仆人

CORIN	Who calls?	
TOUCHSTONE	Your betters, sir.	60
CORIN	Else[1] are they very wretched.	
ROSALIND	[*To Touchstone*] Peace, I say –. Good even[2] to you, friend.	
CORIN	And to you, gentle sir, and to you all.	
ROSALIND	I prithee, shepherd, if that love or gold	
	Can in this desert place buy entertainment[3],	65
	Bring us where we may rest ourselves and feed.	
	Here's a young maid with travel much oppressed	
	And faints for succour[4].	
CORIN	Fair sir, I pity her	
	And wish, for her sake more than for mine own,	
	My fortunes were more able to relieve her;	70
	But I am shepherd to another man,	
	And do not shear the fleeces[5] that I graze[6].	
	My master is of churlish disposition[7]	
	And little recks[8] to find the way to heaven	
	By doing deeds of hospitality[9].	75
	Besides, his cot[10], his flocks, and bounds of feed[11]	
	Are now on sale, and at our sheepcote[12] now	
	By reason of his absence there is nothing	
	That you will feed on[13]. But what is, come see,	
	And in my voice[14] most welcome shall you be.	80
ROSALIND	What is he that shall buy his flock and pasture?	
CORIN	That young swain[15] that you saw here but erewhile[16],	
	That little cares for buying anything.	
ROSALIND	I pray thee, if it stand with honesty[17],	
	Buy thou the cottage, pasture, and the flock,	85
	And thou shalt have to pay for it of us.	
CELIA	And we will mend[18] thy wages. I like this place	
	And willingly could waste my time[19] in it.	
CORIN	Assuredly the thing is to be sold.	
	Go with me. If you like upon report	90
	The soil, the profit, and this kind of life,	
	I will your very faithful feeder[20] be,	
	And buy it with your gold right suddenly.	

Exeunt

Amiens sings of the pleasure of forest life. Jaques asks for more singing, hoping it will add to his melancholy. He criticises the singing, politeness in general and Duke Senior.

 剧情简介：阿缅歌唱森林生活的快乐，杰奎要求他多唱一些，希望歌声能增加自己的忧郁。杰奎还评价了歌的好坏、一般的客套和老公爵。

Characters 人物分析

Presenting Jaques (in small groups)

a Read this short scene, and think about what has been said about Jaques so far in the play. What is your opinion of him? Talk together about what each of the following quotations suggests about his personality.

- **Lines 11–12** He compares himself to a weasel (a small, quarrelsome, sharp-toothed animal).
- **Line 14** He criticises Amiens's singing (and often gets a laugh from the audience).
- **Line 17** He seems interested only in the names of people who owe him money.
- **Lines 27–9** He thinks Duke Senior too argumentative, and considers himself as intelligent as him but more humble.

b Count how many times Jaques asks Amiens to sing for him. Discuss together how you think he asks each time – for example, increasingly annoyed or perhaps continuing to entreat him politely. What other evidence of his character is there in this scene?

c Write notes for the actor playing Jaques, describing your interpretation of the character and his behaviour in this scene.

1 greenwood 郁郁葱葱
2 Who = Whoever
3 turn = tune
4 note 歌声
5 throat 歌喉（这里指鸟鸣）
6 Come hither 来吧
7 Monsieur 先生（这里表示杰奎的上等人身份，或带有嘲讽义）
8 weasel 黄鼠狼（在莎士比亚时代以凶猛著称）
9 stanzo = stanza（一段歌词，也指诗的一节）
10 compliment 客套
11 dog-apes 狒狒
12 cover the while 抓紧时间铺餐布（cover指spread the picnic cloth/blanket；the while = in the meantime）
13 disputable 能争善辩
14 warble 高歌吧

Act 2 Scene 5
The camp of Duke Senior

Enter AMIENS, JAQUES, *and other Lords dressed as foresters*

Song

AMIENS   Under the greenwood[1] tree,
             Who[2] loves to lie with me
             And turn[3] his merry note[4]
             Unto the sweet bird's throat[5]:

             Come hither[6], come hither, come hither:
                 Here shall he see
                 No enemy
             But winter and rough weather.

JAQUES   More, more, I prithee more.

AMIENS   It will make you melancholy, Monsieur[7] Jaques.

JAQUES   I thank it. More, I prithee more: I can suck melancholy out of a song as a weasel[8] sucks eggs. More, I prithee more.

AMIENS   My voice is ragged: I know I cannot please you.

JAQUES   I do not desire you to please me, I do desire you to sing. Come, more, another stanzo[9] – call you 'em 'stanzos'?

AMIENS   What you will, Monsieur Jaques.

JAQUES   Nay, I care not for their names; they owe me nothing. Will you sing?

AMIENS   More at your request than to please myself.

JAQUES   Well then, if ever I thank any man, I'll thank you; but that they call 'compliment'[10] is like th'encounter of two dog-apes[11]. And when a man thanks me heartily, methinks I have given him a penny and he renders me the beggarly thanks. Come, sing; and you that will not, hold your tongues.

AMIENS   Well, I'll end the song. – Sirs, cover the while[12]; the Duke will drink under this tree. – He hath been all this day to look you.

JAQUES   And I have been all this day to avoid him: he is too disputable[13] for my company: I think of as many matters as he, but I give heaven thanks and make no boast of them. Come, warble[14], come.

The exiled courtiers sing of the pleasures of leaving court and living simply in the country. Jaques's song mocks such pleasures and implies that Duke Senior's followers are fools.

 剧情简介：流亡的朝臣歌唱离开宫廷的快乐和乡村生活的纯朴。但杰奎唱的歌却嘲讽这种快乐，暗示老公爵的追随者都是傻子。

1 Echoes of Duke Senior (in small groups)

Amiens's song echoes the theme of Duke Senior's first speech at the start of Act 2 ('Sweet are the uses of adversity').

- Re-read Duke Senior's speech and then read through the verses of Amiens's song in lines 1–8 and lines 30–8. Write another verse for Amiens's song, either in the style of Jaques's parody in lines 42–9 or following on from Amiens's original verses. Remember to incorporate ideas from Duke Senior's speech in the same way that the existing song does.

2 Jaques's singing

Jaques's parody of Amiens's song is typically flat and unsentimental. What do you think is the main point of this scene?

- to depict further the character of Jaques
- to show another side of Arden
- to provide some relief from the rest of the plot, which focuses on Rosalind, the court and the pastoral characters
- a critical commentary on the themes of the play as a whole
- another reason not listed above.

Write a paragraph to justify keeping this scene in the play, as opposed to just using the song as background music in your production.

Write about it 写作练习

Two versions of Arden (in small groups)

In *As You Like It*, there is a big difference between life at the court and life in the forest. But even within the forest, there are different ideas about the life it offers.

- How is the Forest of Arden seen differently by Amiens, Jaques, Rosalind and Duke Senior? Write a diary entry for each character that describes what they have done that day and why they like (or hate) living in the forest, away from the world of the court.

1 Who doth ambition shun　放弃飞黄腾达者
2 live i'th'sun　在阳光下生活
3 in despite of my invention　不用我的想象力
4 A stubborn will to please = To please a stubborn will（满足一个固执的意愿）
5 Ducdame　打我呀（读作Du da me，凯尔特人玩一种类似打擂台游戏时擂主口里反复念的词）
6 Gross fools　大傻瓜
7 And if　只要
8 Greek invocation　希腊咒语（来源于谚语"It's all Greek to me."，即"这对我来说完全是希腊文 / 我对此一窍不通。"）
9 rail against　咒骂
10 the first-born of Egypt　埃及的头胎儿（《圣经》中记载，一场瘟疫杀死了埃及所有的头胎孩子，导致哀号遍地，无人能入睡）
11 banquet　野餐

52

Song. All together here

>Who doth ambition shun[1]
>And loves to live i'th'sun[2];
>Seeking the food he eats
>And pleased with what he gets:
>
>Come hither, come hither, come hither:
>   Here shall he see
>   No enemy
>But winter and rough weather.

JAQUES   I'll give you a verse to this note that I made yesterday in despite of my invention[3].

AMIENS   And I'll sing it.

JAQUES   Thus it goes:

>   If it do come to pass
>   That any man turn ass,
>
>Leaving his wealth and ease,
>A stubborn will to please[4],
>
>Ducdame[5], ducdame, ducdame.
>   Here shall he see
>   Gross fools[6] as he,
>And if[7] he will come to me.

AMIENS   What's that 'ducdame'?

JAQUES   'Tis a Greek invocation[8] to call fools into a circle. I'll go sleep if I can: if I cannot, I'll rail against[9] all the first-born of Egypt[10].

AMIENS   And I'll go seek the Duke: his banquet[11] is prepared.

Exeunt

Wandering with Orlando in the forest, Adam fears he is near to death. Orlando comforts him and promises to find food and shelter. In Scene 7, Duke Senior is surprised at Jaques's cheerfulness.

 剧情简介：亚当跟随奥岚铎在森林里游荡，担心自己快死了。奥岚铎安慰他，并保证会找到食物和住处。在第七场中，老公爵对杰奎的乐观感到惊讶。

Stagecraft 导演技巧

The end of the road (in pairs)

How would you bring Scene 6 to life on stage, despite its brief length? Study the two characters' lines, and work out what stage business you would have each actor perform to make the most of his part here. Consider the following:

- **Internal stage directions** Are there any hints in the script as to how the characters could enter or exit and what they could be doing as they speak their lines?
- **Dramatic language** Where can you find repetitions, rhetorical questions and **injunctions** (指令) (commands) in the script? How might you use them for dramatic effect?

1	heart	胆量
2	uncouth	古怪
3	anything savage	任何野兽
4	conceit	想象
5	powers	体力
6	hold … end	暂且将死亡拒于一臂之外
7	presently	马上
8	labour	辛苦
9	Well said	= Well done
10	bleak air	寒风
11	dinner	午餐
12	he	（指杰奎）
13	but even now	= only just now
14	compact of jars	瓶瓶罐罐的组合体（只能发出不和谐音）
15	What, you look merily?	咦，您好像挺开心的？（老公爵看到杰奎快乐的样子很是惊讶）

1 How important is Scene 6? (in fours)

Some critics argue that Scene 6 adds little or nothing to the play, and could be cut in performance.

- Divide the group into two pairs. One pair will argue the case for dropping Scene 6 and the other will defend its inclusion in performances of the play. Prepare your case with your partner, then come together as a group to stage the debate. After the debate, tell the group whether you would include or delete the scene if you were directing the play, and give the main reason for your decision.

2 'discord in the spheres' (天体运行不和谐)

When Duke Senior hears that the melancholy Jaques was 'merry, hearing of a song', he expresses surprise (lines 5–6). His words 'discord in the spheres' echo the common belief of Shakespeare's times that Earth was at the centre of the universe, surrounded by crystal spheres on which the sun, moon and planets orbited. As the spheres moved, they created harmonious music. If Jaques has become happy, it will create chaos in that heavenly order.

- How would you advise Jaques to enter at line 8 to heighten Duke Senior's amazement?
- Consider possible scenarios for his entrance and try them out on one another.

Act 2 Scene 6
The Forest of Arden

Enter ORLANDO *and* ADAM

ADAM Dear master, I can go no further. O, I die for food. Here lie I down and measure out my grave. Farewell, kind master.

ORLANDO Why, how now, Adam, no greater heart[1] in thee? Live a little, comfort a little, cheer thyself a little. If this uncouth[2] forest yield anything savage[3], I will either be food for it or bring it for food to thee. Thy conceit[4] is nearer death than thy powers[5]. For my sake be comfortable; hold death a while at the arm's end[6]. I will here be with thee presently[7], and if I bring thee not something to eat, I will give thee leave to die; but if thou diest before I come, thou art a mocker of my labour[8]. Well said[9], thou look'st cheerly, and I'll be with thee quickly. Yet thou liest in the bleak air[10]. Come, I will bear thee to some shelter, and thou shalt not die for lack of a dinner[11] if there live anything in this desert. Cheerly, good Adam.

Exeunt

Act 2 Scene 7
The camp of Duke Senior

Enter DUKE SENIOR, AMIENS, *and Lords dressed like outlaws*

DUKE SENIOR I think he[12] be transformed into a beast,
For I can nowhere find him like a man.

AMIENS My lord, he is but even now[13] gone hence;
Here was he merry, hearing of a song.

DUKE SENIOR If he, compact of jars[14], grow musical,
We shall have shortly discord in the spheres.
Go seek him; tell him I would speak with him.

Enter JAQUES

AMIENS He saves my labour by his own approach.

DUKE SENIOR Why, how now, monsieur, what a life is this
That your poor friends must woo your company?
What, you look merrily?[15]

Jaques recounts how he enjoyed meeting Touchstone and listening to his moralising. He praises Touchstone, and wishes he were a fool so that he could criticise whoever he wishes.

 剧情简介：杰奎讲述自己与试金石会面并且听他进行道德说教让他如何高兴。他称赞试金石并希望自己是个傻子，这样就能想批评谁就批评谁。

Language in the play 剧中语言
Meeting a fellow pessimist (悲观主义者) (in pairs)

Jaques is happy to have met another cynic (愤世嫉俗者) like himself. Touchstone also takes a negative view of the 'miserable world' (line 13) in which growing old and becoming corrupt is inevitable ('And so, from hour to hour, we ripe and ripe, / And then, from hour to hour, we rot and rot'). Jaques may also be amused at the sexual innuendo (影射，暗示) in Touchstone's words – for example, in Elizabethan times 'hour to hour' was pronounced the same as 'whore to whore'.

a Touchstone's 'moral on the time' and his other observations in lines 19, 24–8 and 37–8 have a few different meanings. Use the glossary on this page to help you work out what these are. Write them out in modern English so that they could be understood by people today.

b Invent your own observation about time, or search the Internet to compile a list of pithy (言简意赅) sayings and proverbs on this theme.

1 Jaques and Touchstone

If Touchstone is the fool of the court of Duke Frederick, then Jaques is the potential fool of Duke Senior's Arden court. Make comparisons between their roles in each realm by copying the table below and adding quotations where you can.

	Jaques	Touchstone
Entertainment		
Wit		
Social commentary		

1 railed on 怒骂
2 In good set terms 用绝妙套话
3 dial = sundial (一种盒装袖珍日晷)
4 poke = pocket
5 lack-lustre eye 无精打采的眼神
6 how the world wags 世界怎么运转
7 thereby hangs a tale 于是就有故事了（tale与tail双关，后者可以委婉地表示"阴茎"）
8 moral = moralise (讲大道理)
9 Chanticleer 打鸣的公鸡
10 deep-contemplative 深思熟虑
11 sans intermission 不停
12 dry 干燥（当时认为，拥有干燥大脑的人记忆能力强，但理解能力弱）
13 remainder biscuit 吃剩的饼干（过去航船上常载有硬饼干供船员食用，到航行结束时这些饼干会异常干燥）
14 observation 所见所闻
15 In mangled forms 以七零八碎的形式
16 suit 要求
17 grows rank 疯长
18 Withal 同时，也
19 as … wind 像风一样大的特权
20 gallèd 伤害，冒犯

JAQUES	A fool, a fool: I met a fool i'th'forest,	
	A motley fool – a miserable world –	
	As I do live by food, I met a fool	
	Who laid him down and basked him in the sun	15
	And railed on[1] Lady Fortune in good terms,	
	In good set terms[2], and yet a motley fool.	
	'Good morrow, fool', quoth I. 'No, sir', quoth he,	
	'Call me not fool till heaven hath sent me fortune.'	
	And then he drew a dial[3] from his poke[4]	20
	And looking on it, with lack-lustre eye[5],	
	Says, very wisely, 'It is ten o'clock.	
	Thus we may see', quoth he, 'how the world wags[6]:	
	'Tis but an hour ago since it was nine,	
	And after one hour more 'twill be eleven;	25
	And so, from hour to hour, we ripe and ripe,	
	And then, from hour to hour, we rot and rot,	
	And thereby hangs a tale[7].' When I did hear	
	The motley fool thus moral[8] on the time,	
	My lungs began to crow like Chanticleer[9]	30
	That fools should be so deep-contemplative[10];	
	And I did laugh, sans intermission[11],	
	An hour by his dial. O noble fool,	
	O worthy fool: motley's the only wear.	
DUKE SENIOR	What fool is this?	35
JAQUES	A worthy fool: one that hath been a courtier	
	And says, 'If ladies be but young and fair,	
	They have the gift to know it'; and in his brain,	
	Which is as dry[12] as the remainder biscuit[13]	
	After a voyage, he hath strange places crammed	40
	With observation[14], the which he vents	
	In mangled forms[15]. O that I were a fool!	
	I am ambitious for a motley coat.	
DUKE SENIOR	Thou shalt have one.	
JAQUES	It is my only suit[16],	
	Provided that you weed your better judgements	45
	Of all opinion that grows rank[17] in them	
	That I am wise. I must have liberty	
	Withal[18], as large a charter as the wind[19],	
	To blow on whom I please: for so fools have.	
	And they that are most gallèd[20] with my folly,	50
	They most must laugh. And why, sir, must they so?	

Jaques claims that people hurt by clever criticism should acknowledge the humour. He wants to cleanse the world with his satire, but the Duke accuses him of hypocrisy. Jaques defends himself against the charge.

剧情简介：杰奎声称那些受到俏皮话伤害的人应该承认其中的幽默。他想用讽刺来净化世界，但公爵指责他虚伪。杰奎为自己辩护，反驳对他的指控。

1 Would you laugh it off? (in small groups)

In lines 50–7, Jaques claims that the people he mocks would be wise to laugh rather than to ignore the criticism or feel hurt because of it.

a Talk about whether you think it is best to shrug off clever but hurtful remarks by joining in with the laughter, or to show that you are offended by confronting the person making the remarks.

b Improvise two different scenes: one in which catty jibes (刻薄的嘲讽) are diffused or ignored, and another in which the criticism is confronted and the target makes their feelings known.

2 Jaques: satirist or hypocrite (伪君子)? (in pairs)

Jaques wants to use his criticism like medicine, cleansing and curing the world's wrongs. He sees the 'motley' costume of a fool as the way he can speak his mind and confront his listeners with their own folly. Yet Duke Senior reveals Jaques's hypocrisy: he has been a lustful womaniser ('libertine') in the past, so it would be a sin for him to try to cure his own diseases in others.

a How does Jaques respond to Duke Senior's criticism? Use the glossary on this page to help you work out what his argument is. Then write out what he means in your own words and decide whether or not you agree with him.

b Discuss whether you agree with Duke Senior. Is Jaques simply a hypocrite who should be ignored?

▼ Decide who you think is Duke Senior and who is Jaques in this image. What are the reasons for your decision? If you imagined the characters differently to how they are shown here, what are the differences?

1 a fool … hit 被傻子聪明地讽刺了一下
2 smart 感到（火辣辣的）疼
3 senseless of the bob 领会不了那俏皮话
4 anatomised 揭露
5 squand'ring glances 漫无目的的暗讽
6 Invest 穿上
7 Fie on thee! 我呸！
8 counter 算筹；小钱
9 libertine 放荡不羁的人
10 brutish sting 兽欲
11 embossèd sores and headed evils 鼓起的脓包和冒头的坏水
12 licence of free foot 我行我素的权利
13 disgorge 呕吐
14 cries out on pride 对高傲大喊大叫
15 tax any private party 批评任何特定个人
16 the weary … ebb 令人厌恶的力量会自行消退
17 cost of princes 贵族的雍容富贵
18 basest function 最卑贱行业
19 bravery 华丽衣服
20 suits … speech 让他的愚蠢印证了我说的话
21 Forbear 不要动

The why is plain as way to parish church:
He that a fool doth very wisely hit[1],
Doth very foolishly, although he smart[2],
If he seem senseless of the bob[3]. If not,
The wise man's folly is anatomised[4]
Even by the squand'ring glances[5] of the fool.
Invest[6] me in my motley; give me leave
To speak my mind, and I will through and through
Cleanse the foul body of th'infected world,
If they will patiently receive my medicine.

DUKE SENIOR Fie on thee![7] I can tell what thou wouldst do.
JAQUES What, for a counter[8], would I do but good?
DUKE SENIOR Most mischievous foul sin in chiding sin:
For thou thyself hast been a libertine[9],
As sensual as the brutish sting[10] itself,
And all th'embossèd sores and headed evils[11]
That thou with licence of free foot[12] hast caught
Wouldst thou disgorge[13] into the general world.
JAQUES Why, who cries out on pride[14]
That can therein tax any private party[15]?
Doth it not flow as hugely as the sea
Till that the weary very means do ebb[16]?
What woman in the city do I name
When that I say the city-woman bears
The cost of princes[17] on unworthy shoulders?
Who can come in and say that I mean her,
When such a one as she, such is her neighbour?
Or what is he of basest function[18]
That says his bravery[19] is not on my cost,
Thinking that I mean him, but therein suits
His folly to the mettle of my speech[20]?
There then! How then? What then? Let me see wherein
My tongue hath wronged him. If it do him right,
Then he hath wronged himself; if he be free,
Why then my taxing like a wild goose flies
Unclaimed of any man. But who come here?

Enter ORLANDO [*with sword drawn*]

ORLANDO Forbear[21], and eat no more!
JAQUES Why, I have eat none yet.

Orlando's threats are met with kindly words from the Duke and scepticism by Jaques. Surprised by the Duke's invitation to eat, Orlando explains his menacing behaviour, asks for pity and is granted hospitality.

剧情简介：奥岚铎的威胁遇上了公爵的好言好语和杰奎的满腹狐疑。奥岚铎对公爵请他吃饭感到诧异，解释自己之前为何咄咄逼人，请求宽恕，获得盛情款待。

Stagecraft 导演技巧

Reaction to Orlando (in small groups)

Duke Senior and Jaques react very differently to Orlando's intrusion. Jaques seems to be mocking Orlando but Duke Senior is trying to understand why he is so desperate. Lines 102–3 change the atmosphere of the scene, as Duke Senior says 'Your gentleness shall force / More than your force move us to gentleness'.

a How would Duke Senior say this line? And how would Orlando respond? Think about the change in character and atmosphere. How would you stage this moment to emphasise the shift in tone?

b How might the rest of the camp, as a group, react to how Jaques and Duke Senior treat Orlando? Rehearse two versions of lines 87–104: one in which the others reflect Duke Senior's tone and appear disapproving of Jaques; the other in which they go along with Jaques's satirical humour by laughing at Orlando. Which version do you think works best?

Language in the play 剧中语言

Civility and gentleness (in pairs)

After bursting in on the peaceful scene with his sword drawn, Orlando asks that the others pardon his threatening appearance. He makes a gentle plea for help, appealing to Duke Senior to remember an earlier, better time. His appeal is made in formal, repetitive verse and Duke Senior replies in the same style.

- Discuss the mood that you would wish to create in lines 105–26. Take parts and perform the lines in ways that you think would evoke that atmosphere.

1 necessity be served 喂饱肚子
2 kind 品种
3 distress 困境
4 civility 礼貌
5 You … first 您一下子就说对了我的秉性
6 the thorny … distress 纯粹困境带来的痛苦
7 inland bred 城里长大
8 nurture 教养
9 answerèd 答复；交代
10 And = If
11 reason 理性（奥兰铎此时眼中只有水果，杰奎想劝奥兰铎不要莽撞行事，看见自己跟前的葡萄，便拿起一串递给奥兰铎，同时说了这句一语双关的俏皮话。raisin在英文中是"葡萄干"，在法文中却是"葡萄"，而raisin与reason读音相同）
12 put I on the countenance 装出样子
13 melancholy boughs 忧郁树枝
14 Lose 忘却
15 knolled 召唤
16 goodman 户主
17 engendered 产生
18 in gentleness 和和气气
19 upon command 根据吩咐
20 wanting 需求
21 doe 母鹿
22 fawn 小鹿

ORLANDO	Nor shalt not, till necessity be served[1].	90
JAQUES	Of what kind[2] should this cock come of?	
DUKE SENIOR	Art thou thus boldened, man, by thy distress[3],	
	Or else a rude despiser of good manners	
	That in civility[4] thou seem'st so empty?	
ORLANDO	You touched my vein at first[5]: the thorny point	95
	Of bare distress[6] hath ta'en from me the show	
	Of smooth civility; yet am I inland bred[7]	
	And know some nurture[8]. But forbear, I say;	
	He dies that touches any of this fruit	
	Till I and my affairs are answerèd[9].	100
JAQUES	And[10] you will not be answerèd with reason[11], I must die.	
DUKE SENIOR	What would you have? Your gentleness shall force	
	More than your force move us to gentleness.	
ORLANDO	I almost die for food, and let me have it.	
DUKE SENIOR	Sit down and feed, and welcome to our table.	105
ORLANDO	Speak you so gently? Pardon me, I pray you:	
	I thought that all things had been savage here	
	And therefore put I on the countenance[12]	
	Of stern commandment. But whate'er you are	
	That in this desert inaccessible,	110
	Under the shade of melancholy boughs[13],	
	Lose[14] and neglect the creeping hours of time –	
	If ever you have looked on better days,	
	If ever been where bells have knolled[15] to church,	
	If ever sat at any goodman's[16] feast,	115
	If ever from your eyelids wiped a tear,	
	And know what 'tis to pity and be pitied,	
	Let gentleness my strong enforcement be,	
	In the which hope, I blush, and hide my sword.	
DUKE SENIOR	True is it that we have seen better days,	120
	And have with holy bell been knolled to church,	
	And sat at goodmen's feasts, and wiped our eyes	
	Of drops that sacred pity hath engendered[17]:	
	And therefore sit you down in gentleness[18]	
	And take upon command[19] what help we have	125
	That to your wanting[20] may be ministered.	
ORLANDO	Then but forbear your food a little while	
	Whiles, like a doe[21], I go to find my fawn[22]	

Orlando leaves to fetch Adam. The Duke's comment that the world presents many sad scenes inspires Jaques to describe the seven ages of man.

剧情简介：奥岚铎起身去找亚当。公爵感慨地说，这个世界的戏台让人看到很多悲惨场景，此话激发了杰奎对人生七个阶段的描述。

Themes 主题分析

The seven ages of man (in sevens)

Prepare and act out your own version of lines 139–66, using some or all of the following suggestions.

- One person speaks the lines while the others perform a mime (哑剧) or a simple collective gesture for each 'age'.
- Divide the speech into seven parts, with each person in the group taking responsibility for an 'age' and speaking it in role as a person in that stage in life. You should use posture, gesture and tone of voice to make each 'age' recognisably different.
- Work out a series of tableaux to illustrate the seven ages; the rest of the 'statues' stay perfectly still as each person in turn speaks the lines. They then change into the next 'age' tableau.
- Replace 'man' with 'woman' and 'he' with 'she' throughout, and think about how a man's life and a woman's life might differ in Shakespeare's time and today. Try one of the above activities again, with this new focus, and discuss any changes.

1 Jaques's tone (in pairs)

a Take turns reading Jaques's 'seven ages of man' speech (lines 139–66) in two different ways. Firstly, use a serious tone to provide a moment of reflection and stillness in the play. Secondly, try it in a more satirical and humorous style, make fun of humankind in its passage from cradle to grave. Which approach do you think works better? Why?

b Think about whom Jaques might be addressing as he speaks these lines. Does he fix on one person in particular or does he make eye contact with different characters as he goes on? Should Jaques mime the ages as he speaks? Consider how these elements might contribute to either the serious or the comic readings described above.

c In your Director's Journal, write up your ideas and opinions on how this speech should be performed.

2 All the world's a … what?

Compose a modern version of Jaques's speech, with a different central metaphor. Use the following prompts to help you:

All the world's a…   circus
                                  festival
                                  city street
                                  garden.

1 sufficed   吃饱
2 bit   一口
3 waste   吃掉
4 ye = 你们；您；你
5 woeful pageants   悲惨的景象
6 Mewling and puking   啼哭又呕吐
7 satchel   书包
8 to his mistress' eyebrow   描写其情人的眉毛（这是在模仿莎士比亚时代矫揉造作的爱情诗）
9 strange   古怪
10 pard   豹子
11 Jealous in honour   珍惜荣誉
12 justice   法官（伊丽莎白时代常由中年人担任）
13 with good capon lined   用肥阉鸡（专供食用的公鸡）喂出来
14 wise saws   智慧格言
15 modern instances   现代案例
16 slippered pantaloon   脚蹬室内鞋的财迷老头儿（意大利即兴喜剧的一个形象滑稽的角色，除了剧中形容的"脚蹬室内鞋""鼻梁架眼镜""腰间挂钱袋""身穿青春紧腿裤"外，还通常蓄着山羊胡，披着大袍子）
17 pouch   钱袋
18 well saved   保存如新
19 a world too wide   肥得不像样
20 shrunk shank   干瘪腿
21 treble   高音号
22 mere oblivion   忘记一切
23 Sans = Without

As You Like It Act 2 Scene 7
各如所愿

          And give it food: there is an old poor man
          Who after me hath many a weary step   130
          Limped in pure love. Till he be first sufficed[1],
          Oppressed with two weak evils, age and hunger,
          I will not touch a bit[2].
DUKE SENIOR   Go find him out,
          And we will nothing waste[3] till you return.
ORLANDO   I thank ye[4], and be blest for your good comfort.   [*Exit*]   135
DUKE SENIOR   Thou see'st we are not all alone unhappy:
          This wide and universal theatre
          Presents more woeful pageants[5] than the scene
          Wherein we play in.
JAQUES   All the world's a stage
          And all the men and women merely players: 140
          They have their exits and their entrances
          And one man in his time plays many parts,
          His acts being seven ages. At first the infant,
          Mewling and puking[6] in the nurse's arms;
          Then the whining schoolboy with his satchel[7]   145
          And shining morning face, creeping like snail
          Unwillingly to school; and then the lover,
          Sighing like furnace, with a woeful ballad
          Made to his mistress' eyebrow[8]; then a soldier,
          Full of strange[9] oaths and bearded like the pard[10],   150
          Jealous in honour[11], sudden, and quick in quarrel,
          Seeking the bubble 'reputation'
          Even in the cannon's mouth; and then the justice[12],
          In fair round belly with good capon lined[13],
          With eyes severe and beard of formal cut,   155
          Full of wise saws[14] and modern instances[15] –
          And so he plays his part; the sixth age shifts
          Into the lean and slippered pantaloon[16],
          With spectacles on nose and pouch[17] on side,
          His youthful hose well saved[18] – a world too wide[19]   160
          For his shrunk shank[20] – and his big manly voice,
          Turning again toward childish treble[21], pipes
          And whistles in his sound; last scene of all
          That ends this strange eventful history
          Is second childishness and mere oblivion[22],   165
          Sans[23] teeth, sans eyes, sans taste, sans everything.

Duke Senior invites Adam to eat. He calls for music. Amiens's song tells that nature, though harsh, is not so cruel as human ungratefulness; that most friendship is merely pretence and that most love is foolishness.

 剧情简介： 老公爵邀请亚当吃饭，并吩咐奏乐。阿缅的歌词是，寒冬凛冽，但不如人世间忘恩负义那般无情；友谊多数是假装，爱情多数是犯痴。

1 venerable burden 背着的尊长
2 So had you need 您可真得这样
3 fall to 请用餐
4 to question 通过探问
5 cousin 爱卿
6 unkind 不近人情
7 keen 尖锐
8 rude 粗暴
9 holly 冬青树（常用于圣诞节装饰，象征快乐和友谊）
10 feigning 假装
11 nigh 靠近（心脏）
12 benefits forgot 忘恩负义
13 warp 结冰

▲ How would you stage Adam's grateful eating of the food Duke Senior gives him? Should Adam be the focus of the onstage action as he eats and Amiens sings?

1 Amiens's song

Consider the following elements of Amiens's song and its staging:

- **Language** Identify repetition, rhyme, personification and apostrophe (see pp. 182–4) in Amiens's song. What effect does each of these poetic devices have on the listener?
- **Content** Amiens's song is about man's ingratitude. How does this fit with the plot of the play so far?
- **Staging** What are the other characters' responses to this song? What are they doing as they listen?
- **Music** What music would you choose to set the lyrics to in a performance? Find a suitable soundtrack, or write your own melody for the song. Devise a performance of the song, adding repetitions, echoes and sound effects (such as rustling leaves, bird noises, rough weather noises and so on).

As You Like It Act 2 Scene 7
各如所愿

Enter ORLANDO *with* ADAM [*on his back*]

DUKE SENIOR Welcome. Set down your venerable burden[1],
And let him feed.
ORLANDO   I thank you most for him.
ADAM So had you need[2]: I scarce can speak
To thank you for myself.   170
DUKE SENIOR Welcome; fall to[3]: I will not trouble you
As yet to question[4] you about your fortunes. —
Give us some music, and, good cousin[5], sing.

Song

AMIENS Blow, blow, thou winter wind,
Thou art not so unkind[6]   175
As man's ingratitude;
Thy tooth is not so keen[7],
Because thou art not seen,
Although thy breath be rude[8].
   Hey-ho, sing hey-ho   180
   Unto the green holly[9],
   Most friendship is feigning[10],
   Most loving mere folly.
   The hey-ho, the holly,
   This life is most jolly.   185

Freeze, freeze, thou bitter sky,
That dost not bite so nigh[11]
As benefits forgot[12];
Though thou the waters warp[13],
Thy sting is not so sharp   190
As friend remembered not.
   Hey-ho, sing hey-ho
   Unto the green holly,
   Most friendship is feigning,
   Most loving mere folly.   195
   The hey-ho, the holly,
   This life is most jolly.

Duke Senior sees in Orlando's face the likeness of his old friend Sir Roland de Boys. He proposes that Orlando tells him the rest of his story later.

 剧情简介：老公爵从奥岚铎的脸上看到了他的老朋友柔岚·德勃伊爵士的模样。他提议让奥岚铎一会儿告诉他那些未讲完的故事。

Stagecraft 导演技巧

An unexpected ending (in pairs)

The end of Act 2 is full of dramatic possibilities for a director, and different productions have interpreted it in different ways. Most productions show Orlando and Adam eating and gaining new strength after their ordeal in the forest. However, in the 1996 Royal Shakespeare Company (RSC) production, the scene ended unexpectedly. As Duke Senior spoke his final line, all the characters moved towards Adam only to find that he had quietly passed away. Everyone stared, frozen in dismay at the sight of Adam's body, and the lights faded as the scene ended.

- Discuss these two options for staging the end of this scene, then suggest how you would direct it yourself. Think about the different ways the characters could exit at the final stage direction, *'Exeunt'*, which means that everybody leaves the stage.

1 whispered 无声地告诉
2 faithfully 令人信服
3 effigies 模拟像
4 limned 画
5 residue of your fortune 您其他的遭遇

Characters 人物分析

Orlando: past and future (in pairs)

a Duke Senior proposes to hear the rest of Orlando's story later. Take turns to step into role as Orlando and recount what has happened to you up to this moment in the play. One person can begin, then give a signal to the other when they are ready for them to take over.

b Write a paragraph predicting what you think will happen to Orlando from this point on. In role as Orlando, write another paragraph describing your plans for the future – these can differ from what you think will actually happen to him.

DUKE SENIOR   If that you were the good Sir Roland's son,
              As you have whispered[1] faithfully[2] you were,
              And as mine eye doth his effigies[3] witness   200
              Most truly limned[4] and living in your face,
              Be truly welcome hither. I am the Duke
              That loved your father. The residue of your fortune[5]
              Go to my cave and tell me. – Good old man,
              Thou art right welcome as thy master is. –   205
              [*To Orlando*] Support him by the arm. [*To Adam*] Give me
                  your hand,
              And let me all your fortunes understand.
                                                                    Exeunt

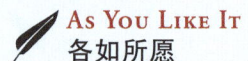

As You Like It
各如所愿

Looking back at Act 2 第2幕回顾
Activities for groups or individuals

1 Contrasts and juxtapositions (并列；并置)

Act 2 continues Shakespeare's dramatic practice of inviting audience members to consider how the scene they are watching contrasts with and comments on the preceding scene. Some themes that run through this act – and are therefore a clear focus for such internal criticism and analysis – include court versus country, virtue versus evil and love versus enmity (敌对；仇恨).

- Look back through the seven scenes of Act 2 and examine how each one is juxtaposed with the one before. For example, Scene 1 is set in the forest with the banished Duke Senior, whereas the last scene of Act 1 was set in Duke Frederick's corrupt court.
- Draw a diagram to show how the scenes in Act 2 are linked together. Annotate it with comments, images and quotations from the script.

2 Opportunities for design

The exiled lords appear dressed as 'foresters' or 'outlaws', and Amiens sings of 'the greenwood tree'.

- Sketch your designs for costumes for the 'outlaws' and the set for the forest. Would you want a modern setting or a historical one? This could be something other than Elizabethan England, such as ancient Rome or the old American West. Would you want the action to take place in winter, spring, summer or autumn? Maybe you want to create a more symbolic set rather than a naturalistic one? Your decisions will affect the mood you create through your designs, and therefore the interpretation of the play that the audience takes away.

3 Learning from nature

At the start of Act 2, Duke Senior claims that nature has a lot to teach humans about moral conduct.

- Do you agree that experiences in the Forest of Arden can teach more about good, evil, courage, honour and love than life in the 'civilised' city? Remember that Arden, as well as being an ideal world away from the corruptions of the court, is also a place of danger, hardship and personal struggles. Write at least one paragraph for each side of the argument. Remember to use examples and quotations from the script.

4 Different perspectives on Act 2

In Scene 2, Hisperia, Celia's lady-in-waiting (女官), appears to answer Duke Frederick's questions about Rosalind and Celia. She is not mentioned again.

- Stage an interview with a partner. Take turns to step into role as Hisperia and tell all you know about events at the court up to the moment that Rosalind and Celia ran away. You might like to present the interview as if it is taking place under duress (胁迫，强迫), as Hisperia 'confesses' to Duke Frederick's lords.

5 Wearing motley

In Scene 7, Jaques longs to play the clown and therefore be able to mock people's shortcomings and pretensions (虚夸；虚饰). He says 'motley's the only wear' and envies the freedom Touchstone has to hide his critical comments in his foolish remarks.

a Research the status and role of a court jester (俳优) or an Elizabethan clown in your library or on the Internet. Write notes on how what have you learnt helps you to better understand the character of Touchstone.

b Look at the photographs of Touchstone opposite, then discuss how you would want to present him in a modern production of the play. Would you keep his 'motley' costume? Or would you think of some other way to represent his unique status in the play?

In Scene 1, Duke Frederick threatens Oliver and orders him to capture Orlando dead or alive. In Scene 2, Orlando praises Rosalind and hangs his love poems to her on trees.

 剧情简介：第三幕第一场中，弗雷德瑞公爵威胁奥利沃，要他无论死活都找到奥岚铎。第二场中，奥岚铎赞美若泽兰，并把为她写的情诗挂在树上。

1 What has just happened? (in small groups)

Scene 1 opens in the middle of a conversation, with Duke Frederick echoing what Oliver has just said: '"Not see him since"?'

a What do you think is happening in this scene? Read the two possible interpretations below and discuss the context to the characters' lines.

- In some productions, a bleeding and battered Oliver is thrown in by the lords. He has obviously been tortured.
- In other productions, Oliver and Duke Frederick are having a secret conversation out of hearing of the lords. There is no physical violence, but their interaction is full of tension.

b Improvise a short scene that might have taken place just before the beginning of Act 3, in which Duke Frederick and Oliver talk about Orlando. Make sure you include the declaration 'Not see him since' in Oliver's last speech.

Write about it 写作练习

Poems in the trees

Orlando has written poems about Rosalind and hung them on trees around the forest so that everyone will read of her beauty and virtue.

a Write your own short poem(s) as if from Orlando to Rosalind, and/or from Rosalind to Orlando. Try to include some striking visual images, or use an extended metaphor to describe the object of the author's affection. Read the suggestions below to get you started:

- You could research the conventions of Elizabethan love sonnets, and use some of the ideas and phrases of love poetry from Shakespeare's day.
- You might choose to look at modern love poetry – for example, by reading through the lyrics of some of your favourite songs.

b When you have finished your poem(s), explain to the rest of the class which love poem or genre influenced your poem and why.

1 **the better part made mercy** 生性仁慈
2 **absent argument / Of my revenge** 我的一个不在场的复仇对象（指奥岚铎）
3 **seizure** 没收
4 **quit thee** 洗刷你
5 **thy brother's mouth** 你兄弟的证词
6 **officers of such a nature** 负责此事的官员
7 **Make an extent upon** 立刻查抄
8 **expediently** 迅速
9 **turn him going** 把他赶走
10 **thrice-crownèd queen of night** 头戴三重王冠的黑夜女王（在罗马神话中，这一女神统治三个世界：作为贞洁和狩猎女神获阿娜 [Diana]，即希腊神话中的阿尔特弥 [Artemis]，统治地上；作为冥界女神普若塞丕娜 [Proserpina]，即希腊神话中的珀尔塞福妮 [Persephone] 或赫卡媂 [Hecate]，统治地下；作为月神卢娜 [Luna]，即希腊神话中的塞丽妮 [Selene]，统治天上）
11 **survey** 俯视
12 **huntress' name** 女猎手的名字（指若泽兰，也暗指罗马神话中的狩猎女神获阿娜）
13 **sway** 支配
14 **character** 雕刻
15 **virtue witnessed** 美德得到见证
16 **unexpressive she** 无法形容的她

Act 3 Scene 1
Duke Frederick's palace

Enter DUKE FREDERICK, *Lords, and* OLIVER

DUKE FREDERICK 'Not see him since'? Sir, sir, that cannot be!
But were I not the better part made mercy[1],
I should not seek an absent argument
Of my revenge[2], thou present. But look to it:
Find out thy brother, wheresoe'er he is; 5
Seek him with candle; bring him dead or living
Within this twelvemonth, or turn thou no more
To seek a living in our territory.
Thy lands and all things that thou dost call thine
Worth seizure[3], do we seize into our hands 10
Till thou canst quit thee[4] by thy brother's mouth[5]
Of what we think against thee.

OLIVER O that your highness knew my heart in this:
I never loved my brother in my life.

DUKE FREDERICK More villain thou. [*To Lords*] Well, push him out of doors 15
And let my officers of such a nature[6]
Make an extent upon[7] his house and lands.
Do this expediently[8] and turn him going[9].

Exeunt

Act 3 Scene 2
The Forest of Arden

Enter ORLANDO *with a sheet of paper in his hand*

ORLANDO Hang there, my verse, in witness of my love;
And thou, thrice-crownèd queen of night[10], survey[11]
With thy chaste eye, from thy pale sphere above,
Thy huntress' name[12] that my full life doth sway[13].
O Rosalind, these trees shall be my books, 5
And in their barks my thoughts I'll character[14]
That every eye which in this forest looks
Shall see thy virtue witnessed[15] everywhere.
Run, run, Orlando, carve on every tree
The fair, the chaste, and unexpressive she[16]. *Exit* 10

Touchstone, using clever-sounding language, says that he likes and dislikes country life. Corin replies in the same empty manner. Touchstone claims that Corin is damned for not having been at court.

剧情简介：试金石用听上去很机智的语言说他既喜欢又不喜欢乡村生活。考林以同样空洞的方式回应。试金石声称考林没救了，因为他没有去过宫廷。

1 Touchstone's wit

Touchstone's lines 2–9 are a series of statements saying that he both likes and dislikes country life.

a Draw up a table with two columns to list your own likes and dislikes of your school or college.

b Write a similar description of your school or college using the same style: 'in respect that it is … but in respect that …' Try to capture Touchstone's style and his ability to hide witty observations in seemingly foolish talk.

2 Empty talk – court versus country (in pairs)

Scene 3 begins with a conversation about one of the major themes of the play: the comparison of country life with court life. To gain a first impression of how Shakespeare mocks the pretentious conversations that often took place among his own contemporaries, take parts as Touchstone and Corin and speak lines 1–64. Then use some of the activities below to help you work out how you would stage the dialogue.

a Does Touchstone treat Corin as an equal or as an inferior? How would this be shown on stage?

b Touchstone dresses up his empty language by calling it 'philosophy'. Corin answers him in the same high-sounding but superficial style, saying banal (平庸) things ('the property of rain is to wet', and so on). Is Corin mocking Touchstone or is he serious about what he says?

c Touchstone makes a number of digs (嘲讽) at Corin. For example, 'a natural philosopher' could mean a foolish thinker, and 'an ill-roasted egg, all on one side' could be Touchstone's way of calling Corin half-baked (愚蠢；肤浅). Decide whether Touchstone should share his sly humour with the audience. How could he show what he really means through his non-verbal actions?

d Write a few detailed stage directions to accompany this scene, so that the actors playing Touchstone and Corin understand how you want them to interact with each other. Remember to advise them on voice (volume, pace, tone), body movements (gesture, posture) and space (where they position themselves on stage or how they move around it).

1 in respect of itself 就其本身而言
2 in respect that 就……这一点而言
3 private 寂寞
4 spare 节俭
5 humour 性情
6 stomach 胃口
7 wants 缺少
8 means, and content 才能和满足
9 wit 心智
10 nature or art 先天或后天
11 complain of good breeding 抱怨缺乏良好教养
12 dull kindred 愚钝的祖先
13 natural philosopher 自然哲学家（意思可以是"科学家"也可以是"白痴"）
14 Wast （be的单数第二人称过去时形式）
15 Nay, I hope = I hope not
16 good manners 礼貌举止
17 parlous （perilous 的一种常见误读）危险

Act 3 Scene 3
The Forest of Arden

Enter CORIN *and* TOUCHSTONE

CORIN   And how like you this shepherd's life, Master Touchstone?

TOUCHSTONE   Truly, shepherd, in respect of itself[1], it is a good life; but in respect that[2] it is a shepherd's life, it is naught. In respect that it is solitary, I like it very well; but in respect that it is private[3], it is a very vile life. Now in respect it is in the fields, it pleaseth me well; but in respect it is not in the court, it is tedious. As it is a spare[4] life, look you, it fits my humour[5] well; but as there is no more plenty in it, it goes much against my stomach[6]. Hast any philosophy in thee, shepherd?

CORIN   No more but that I know the more one sickens, the worse at ease he is; and that he that wants[7] money, means, and content[8] is without three good friends; that the property of rain is to wet and fire to burn; that good pasture makes fat sheep; and that a great cause of the night is lack of the sun; that he that hath learned no wit[9] by nature nor art[10] may complain of good breeding[11], or comes of a very dull kindred[12].

TOUCHSTONE   Such a one is a natural philosopher[13]. — Wast[14] ever in court, shepherd?

CORIN   No, truly.

TOUCHSTONE   Then thou art damned.

CORIN   Nay, I hope[15].

TOUCHSTONE   Truly thou art damned: like an ill-roasted egg, all on one side.

CORIN   For not being at court? Your reason.

TOUCHSTONE   Why, if thou never wast at court, thou never saw'st good manners[16]; if thou never saw'st good manners, then thy manners must be wicked, and wickedness is sin, and sin is damnation. Thou art in a parlous[17] state, shepherd.

Corin argues that to adopt court behaviour in the country would be foolish. Touchstone mocks the examples Corin gives. Corin expresses his contentment with country life, but Touchstone remains cynical.

剧情简介：考林认为，把宫廷举止搬到乡下会显得很滑稽，并举了很多例子。试金石对这些例子加以嘲讽。考林表示他很满足于乡村生活，但试金石仍是愤世嫉俗的样子。

1 Court and country matters: a debate (in pairs)

Verbal jousting (打嘴仗) is much loved by fools in Shakespeare; they enjoy argument for its own sake, and often follow an absurd (荒唐) logic. Corin denies that he is damned for not being at court and he claims that it would be foolish to adopt court manners in the country. Touchstone rejects Corin's example, but his rejection is also a criticism of court manners.

a As you first read through this exchange, discuss whether Touchstone or Corin seems to 'win' the argument. Or is it a draw?

b As you read it the second time, stand opposite your partner. Take a step forward every time you think your character has an advantage over the other character in the debate (the other person takes a step back).

2 Elizabethan jokes, modern audiences (in small groups)

Elizabethans loved jokes about adultery, particularly where the unsuspecting husband did not realise what his wife was up to. Men with unfaithful wives were ridiculed as 'cuckolds' (戴了绿帽子的人) and were said to have horns growing out of their head that were visible to everyone but them. Touchstone criticises breeding sheep as a sin, and calls Corin a pimp (皮条客) who brings together a young female sheep and a lustful, horned old ram.

a Compile a list of questions to ask Touchstone about his attitude and behaviour towards Corin. Is he winding him up (找碴儿)? What response does Touchstone hope to get? What does he mean in lines 61–2 when he says, 'If thou be'st not damned for this, the devil himself will have no shepherds'?

b Take turns to sit in the hot-seat in role as Touchstone and answer the questions asked by the rest of the group.

1 salute 打招呼
2 courtesy 礼貌
3 Instance 证据
4 fells 羊毛
5 grease 油脂
6 tar 焦油（用以治疗羊的伤口）
7 civet 麝香
8 worms' meat 生了蛆的肉
9 in respect of 跟……相比
10 perpend 仔细想想
11 baser birth than tar 出身比焦油还低贱
12 uncleanly flux 不干净的分泌物
13 Mend the instance 举例要得当
14 make incision in 开刀（让知识进入）
15 raw 嫩
16 true 老实
17 that = that which
18 content with my harm 自己倒霉也认命
19 copulation 交配
20 be bawd 拉皮条
21 bell-wether 戴铃的阉公羊（即头羊）
22 crooked-pated 长着弯角
23 'scape = escape

CORIN   Not a whit, Touchstone: those that are good manners at the court are as ridiculous in the country as the behaviour of the country is most mockable at the court. You told me you salute[1] not at the court but you kiss your hands: that courtesy[2] would be uncleanly if courtiers were shepherds.

TOUCHSTONE   Instance[3], briefly; come, instance.

CORIN   Why, we are still handling our ewes, and their fells[4], you know, are greasy.

TOUCHSTONE   Why, do not your courtier's hands sweat, and is not the grease[5] of a mutton as wholesome as the sweat of a man? Shallow, shallow! A better instance, I say — come.

CORIN   Besides, our hands are hard.

TOUCHSTONE   Your lips will feel them the sooner. Shallow again: a more sounder instance, come.

CORIN   And they are often tarred over with the surgery of our sheep, and would you have us kiss tar[6]? The courtiers' hands are perfumed with civet[7].

TOUCHSTONE   Most shallow man! Thou worms' meat[8] in respect of[9] a good piece of flesh, indeed! Learn of the wise and perpend[10]: civet is of a baser birth than tar[11], the very uncleanly flux[12] of a cat. Mend the instance[13], shepherd.

CORIN   You have too courtly a wit for me; I'll rest.

TOUCHSTONE   Wilt thou rest damned? God help thee, shallow man. God make incision in[14] thee, thou art raw[15].

CORIN   Sir, I am a true[16] labourer: I earn that[17] I eat, get that I wear, owe no man hate, envy no man's happiness, glad of other men's good, content with my harm[18]; and the greatest of my pride is to see my ewes graze and my lambs suck.

TOUCHSTONE   That is another simple sin in you: to bring the ewes and the rams together and to offer to get your living by the copulation[19] of cattle; to be bawd[20] to a bell-wether[21] and to betray a she-lamb of a twelvemonth to a crooked-pated[22] old cuckoldly ram out of all reasonable match. If thou be'st not damned for this, the devil himself will have no shepherds. I cannot see else how thou shouldst 'scape[23].

CORIN   Here comes young Monsieur Ganymede, my new mistress's brother.

Enter ROSALIND [*as* GANYMEDE]

Rosalind reads Orlando's poem in praise of her beauty. Touchstone composes a parody of the poem, full of sexual innuendo. Rosalind's reply puns jokingly at Touchstone's expense.

剧情简介：若泽兰朗读奥岚铎赞美其美貌的诗。试金石对这首诗进行戏仿，话里话外都充满下流暗示。若泽兰的回答一语双关，嘲弄了试金石一番。

1 True love or trite (平庸) verses? (in pairs)

Orlando's attempts at poetry demonstrate how difficult it is to say anything 'new' about love. Strong feelings of love can come across as ridiculous when set to rhymes that, according to Touchstone, sound like women trotting to the market! Touchstone is quick to mock Orlando's poetry, but what is Rosalind thinking?

a Write a few asides to insert into this scene, showing Rosalind's private responses to the poems she has just read or heard. Include her reaction to Touchstone's parody.

b Take turns to step into role as Rosalind and practise how you would say these asides. Then use them as the basis for Rosalind's diary entry at the end of the day, in which she reveals her deepest thoughts about Orlando and her hopes and fears for the future.

2 Touchstone's parody (in small groups)

How do your versions of Orlando's and Rosalind's love poems (see p. 70) compare with the example that Rosalind reads out here? You might notice the simple rhythm and the number of words that rhyme with 'Rosalind'. Touchstone picks up on this and criticises the jogging, jerky (不平稳) rhythm of Orlando's verses.

- Write another love poem (from Rosalind to Orlando or from Orlando to Rosalind) in the style of Touchstone's parody. Note that Touchstone makes up a **burlesque** (滑稽模仿) (a comically exaggeration imitation) in the same simple rhythm ('false gallop') as Orlando's poem, and focusing on the physical aspects of love.

Write about it 写作练习

'let the forest judge'

A well-known proverb states that 'many a wise word is said in jest'. What truth might be hidden in Touchstone's jests? What might he be trying to say about Orlando's romantic exaggerations?

- Write a letter from Touchstone to Rosalind describing the problems Rosalind might encounter in a marriage to Orlando if he expects her to be as perfect as his poem describes.

---

1 Western Inde = West Indies （西印度群岛）
2 fairest lined 画得最美丽
3 black to 比起……都黯然失色
4 fair 美貌
5 eight years together 连续八年
6 the right … market 就像卖奶油的大妈一个接一个抢着去市集（讽刺奥岚铎的诗在尾韵和节奏上毫无章法）
7 hart do lack a hind 公赤鹿想要母赤鹿
8 after kind 追母猫
9 Wintered 破旧
10 lined 加内衬
11 They … bind 收割者必须拢起麦子捆成捆
12 to cart 用车载（收割庄稼要用车运输；惩罚妓女也要把她们押上车游街）
13 nut 果子
14 rind 外皮
15 prick 芒刺；锋芒
16 false gallop 不合格的节奏
17 graft 嫁接（若泽兰用一个园艺术语来暗指"性交"）
18 medlar 欧楂果；多管闲事的家伙（与meddler同音双关）
19 right virtue 真正本性

ROSALIND [*Reading from a paper*]
    'From the East to Western Inde[1]
      No jewel is like Rosalind;
    Her worth, being mounted on the wind,
      Through all the world bears Rosalind;
    All the pictures fairest lined[2]
      Are but black to[3] Rosalind;
    Let no face be kept in mind
      But the fair[4] of Rosalind.'

TOUCHSTONE I'll rhyme you so eight years together[5], dinners and suppers and sleeping-hours excepted. It is the right butter-women's rank to market[6].

ROSALIND Out, fool!

TOUCHSTONE For a taste:
    If a hart do lack a hind[7],
      Let him seek out Rosalind;
    If the cat will after kind[8],
      So be sure will Rosalind;
    Wintered[9] garments must be lined[10],
      So must slender Rosalind;
    They that reap must sheaf and bind[11],
      Then to cart[12] with Rosalind;
    Sweetest nut[13] hath sourest rind[14],
      Such a nut is Rosalind;
    He that sweetest rose will find,
      Must find love's prick[15] – and Rosalind.
This is the very false gallop[16] of verses: why do you infect yourself with them?

ROSALIND Peace, you dull fool. I found them on a tree.

TOUCHSTONE Truly, the tree yields bad fruit.

ROSALIND I'll graft[17] it with you, and then I shall graft it with a medlar[18]; then it will be the earliest fruit i'th' country, for you'll be rotten ere you be half ripe, and that's the right virtue[19] of the medlar.

TOUCHSTONE You have said – but whether wisely or no, let the forest judge.

Enter CELIA [*as* ALIENA] *with a writing*

ROSALIND Peace, here comes my sister, reading. Stand aside.

Celia reads Orlando's poem, which tells of the brevity of human life and of broken promises, but is mainly about how Rosalind embodies all beauty and grace. Rosalind calls it a boring sermon.

剧情简介：希丽叶读奥岚铎的诗，诗中感叹人生的短暂和人的失信，但主要称赞若泽兰的美丽和优雅。若泽兰称之为无聊的布道。

1 Echoes of Acts 1 and 2 (in pairs)

Orlando's poem says he will people (让……有人气) the forest with proclamations ('Tongues') on every tree, containing wise sayings about society. Some will tell how human life is as short as the distance enclosed by a handspan (一拃), others will tell of broken promises between friends.

a Compile a list of any events, situations or lines in Acts 1 and 2 that might be echoed in Orlando's poem.

b Would you expect to find social commentary in love poems? Discuss what you expect from love poetry.

2 Heavenly Rosalind (in threes)

Orlando's praise of Rosalind compares her with famous women in ancient Greek and Roman mythology and history:

- She has Helen of Troy's beauty, but not her unfaithfulness.
- She has the majesty of Cleopatra, queen of Egypt.
- She has Atalanta's swiftness of movement – in Greek mythology, this beautiful huntress was given the gift of speed and vowed that any suitor who could not outrun her would be executed.
- She has Lucretia's faithfulness – in Roman mythology, this woman killed herself to prove her honesty and devotion to her husband.

a Identify the references to these women in Orlando's poem. Then discuss whether you think these comparisons really suit Rosalind or if you think they are just poetic, and fairly impersonal, exaggerations.

b What do you think Celia, Rosalind and Touchstone are each thinking as they hear this poem? Take parts and, as Celia experiments with different styles of reading (for example, mocking, passionate, thoughtful), the two listeners should react to the words with gestures and facial expressions.

c Rewrite lines 120–3 of the poem as a modern parody, using four examples of well-known female figures from today.

1 erring pilgrimage 漂泊流浪
2 That = So that
3 Buckles in his sum of age 束缚人的寿命
4 violated vows 背弃的誓言
5 sentence 格言
6 quintessence 精华
7 sprite 精灵
8 in little 在缩影身上（指在若泽兰身上）
9 Nature charged 吩咐大自然
10 heavenly synod 天神聚集
11 touches 特点
12 tedious homily 乏味的说教
13 Backfriends 窃听者
14 sirrah 小子（主人或贵族称呼下人，表示生气或不耐烦）
15 scrip （牧羊人的）钱包
16 scrippage 钱包袋（这是试金石把script和baggage合在一起，拼凑出的一个毫无意义的词）

Stagecraft 导演技巧

Touchstone's exit

How would you direct Touchstone to speak the two lines before his exit (lines 135–6)? In your Director's Journal, make notes on all the possible elements of stage business that the actor could use, including how Touchstone could physically interact with Corin.

As You Like It Act 3 Scene 3
各如所愿

CELIA   'Why should this a desert be?
                  For it is unpeopled? No:
              Tongues I'll hang on every tree,
                  That shall civil sayings show:
              Some how brief the life of man
                  Runs his erring pilgrimage[1]
              That[2] the stretching of a span
                  Buckles in his sum of age[3];
              Some of violated vows[4]
                  'Twixt the souls of friend and friend;
              But upon the fairest boughs
                  Or at every sentence[5] end
              Will I "Rosalinda" write,
                  Teaching all that read to know
              The quintessence[6] of every sprite[7]
                  Heaven would in little[8] show.
              Therefore Heaven Nature charged[9]
                  That one body should be filled
              With all graces wide-enlarged;
                  Nature presently distilled
              Helen's cheek but not her heart,
                  Cleopatra's majesty,
              Atalanta's better part,
                  Sad Lucretia's modesty.
              Thus Rosalind of many parts
                  By heavenly synod[10] was devised,
              Of many faces, eyes, and hearts,
                  To have the touches[11] dearest prized.
              Heaven would that she these gifts should have,
                  And I to live and die her slave.'

ROSALIND   [*Coming forward*] O most gentle Jupiter, what tedious homily[12] of love have you wearied your parishioners withal, and never cried, 'Have patience, good people!'

CELIA   How now? Backfriends[13]! – Shepherd, go off a little. – Go with him, sirrah[14].

TOUCHSTONE Come, shepherd, let us make an honourable retreat, though not with bag and baggage, yet with scrip[15] and scrippage[16].
                              Exeunt Touchstone and Corin

CELIA   Didst thou hear these verses?

Rosalind and Celia joke about the lack of skill in the poems. Celia expresses amazement that Rosalind cannot guess who has written the verses. Rosalind begs to be told the poet's name.

 剧情简介：若泽兰和希丽叶开玩笑说这些诗缺乏技巧。若泽兰猜不出诗是谁写的，希丽叶对此表示惊讶。若泽兰恳求希丽叶说出诗人的名字。

1 But who is it? (in pairs)

The exchange between Rosalind and Celia is full of high spirits, teasing and excitement.

a Read the passage to yourself, then take parts and speak lines 137–212.

b Find the following examples in the script opposite, then discuss in detail how you would want to stage this witty exchange:

- In lines 137–42, Rosalind and Celia joke about Orlando's bad poetry, using puns (双关) on 'feet' and 'bear'.
- There is a series of quick-fire (连发) questions with no real answers in lines 149–57.
- Celia uses repetition in lines 160–1.
- Rosalind uses the metaphor of a corked bottle to show her eagerness to find out who Celia is talking about in lines 165–9.
- The metaphor backfires (事与愿违) on Rosalind (line 170). Why might Rosalind be shocked? What is Celia implying here?

1 feet 音步（这里是说听到的音步比诗的韵律所允许的多）
2 without 在外面
3 should be = was
4 seven … wonder 九天惊奇已有七天不惊奇了（见怪不怪了）
5 palm-tree （这里指柳树）
6 Pythagoras 毕达哥拉斯（古希腊哲学家、数学家，他认为人类的灵魂可以迁移到野兽身上）
7 berhymed … rat （古代爱尔兰人迷信念诗体咒语能灭鼠）
8 Trow you 您是否知道
9 encounter 拥抱（有性暗示）
10 petitionary vehemence 急切恳求
11 out of all hooping 惊奇到无法形容
12 Good my complexion 我的天哪，我脸都红了
13 caparisoned 打扮
14 disposition 秉性
15 South Sea of discovery 南海（南太平洋）探险
16 apace 快
17 of God's making 上帝创造的人

ROSALIND	O yes, I heard them all, and more too, for some of them had in them more feet[1] than the verses would bear.	
CELIA	That's no matter: the feet might bear the verses.	140
ROSALIND	Aye, but the feet were lame and could not bear themselves without the verse, and therefore stood lamely in the verse.	
CELIA	But didst thou hear without[2] wondering how thy name should be[3] hanged and carved upon these trees?	
ROSALIND	I was seven of the nine days out of the wonder[4] before you came, for look here what I found on a palm-tree[5]. I was never so berhymed since Pythagoras'[6] time that I was an Irish rat[7] – which I can hardly remember.	145
CELIA	Trow you[8] who hath done this?	
ROSALIND	Is it a man?	150
CELIA	And a chain that you once wore about his neck? Change you colour?	
ROSALIND	I prithee, who?	
CELIA	O Lord, Lord, it is a hard matter for friends to meet, but mountains may be removed with earthquakes and so encounter[9].	155
ROSALIND	Nay, but who is it?	
CELIA	Is it possible?	
ROSALIND	Nay, I prithee now, with most petitionary vehemence[10], tell me who it is.	
CELIA	O wonderful, wonderful, and most wonderful wonderful, and yet again wonderful, and after that out of all hooping[11].	160
ROSALIND	Good my complexion[12], dost thou think, though I am caparisoned[13] like a man, I have a doublet and hose in my disposition[14]? One inch of delay more is a South Sea of discovery[15]. I prithee tell me who is it – quickly, and speak apace[16]. I would thou couldst stammer that thou might'st pour this concealed man out of thy mouth as wine comes out of a narrow-mouthed bottle: either too much at once or none at all. I prithee take the cork out of thy mouth that I may drink thy tidings.	165
CELIA	So you may put a man in your belly.	170
ROSALIND	Is he of God's making[17]? What manner of man? Is his head worth a hat or his chin worth a beard?	
CELIA	Nay, he hath but a little beard.	
ROSALIND	Why, God will send more if the man will be thankful. Let me stay the growth of his beard, if thou delay me not the knowledge of his chin.	175

Celia reveals that Orlando wrote the poems. Rosalind's first thought is of her disguise as a man. She asks many eager questions and keeps interrupting Celia's story. They hide from Orlando and Jaques.

剧情简介：希丽叶透露这些诗是奥岚铎创作的。若泽兰首先想到的是自己女扮男装的身份，于是急切地问了很多问题，一再打断希丽叶的讲述。最后二人躲起来，偷听奥岚铎和杰奎的对话。

1 Quickfire questions (in pairs)

When Rosalind hears that Orlando is in the forest, she wonders what she will do about her disguise as a man, then launches into a flurry of questions.

a Take turns to speak lines 184–8. How quickly can you deliver the lines while still speaking every word perfectly clearly?

b How does it feel to be on the receiving end of this flurry of questions? Think of a different gesture or action for each question to show Celia's response. Is she confused, frustrated, amused or something else?

2 Rosalind's aside (in threes)

a How is it best to speak Rosalind's aside at line 197? Does she speak to herself, or to the audience? Think of three different ways Rosalind might say this aside, then discuss what each variation suggests.

b Take turns to step into role as Rosalind and speak these different variations. Try out different gestures or facial expressions to help communicate the intended meaning. The others in your group should give you feedback and direction.

c In your Director's Journal, write notes for the actor playing Rosalind to advise her on how best to interpret and perform the aside.

Characters 人物分析

Conversations with the director (in pairs)

Imagine you are working on a new production of this play, and step into role as either the director or the actor playing Rosalind.

- The director thinks that in lines 179–210 Rosalind's tone should be pleading, breathless and self-tormenting.
- The actor thinks that Rosalind should comically exaggerate her speech, teasing Celia in order to hide her strong feelings about Orlando.

Prepare your case by finding words from the script that support your interpretation. Then improvise an argument between the director and the actor, in which each person tries to convince the other that their interpretation is correct and will create the greatest dramatic effect.

1 sad brow and true maid　严肃认真，老老实实
2 Wherein went he?　他穿什么去的？
3 Gargantua　嘎干图阿（一个食量惊人的巨人，16世纪法国作家拉伯雷创作的《巨人传》的主人公）
4 catechism　教义问答
5 freshly　精神抖擞
6 atomies　尘埃
7 resolve　解答
8 propositions　问题
9 relish it with good observance　细心地体会
10 Jove's tree　乔武的树（即橡树；乔武即罗马神话中的主神朱庇特；橡树乃神树，对朱庇特而言是圣物）
11 wounded knight　受伤的骑士（可能是被丘比特的爱之箭射中）
12 holla　吁（让马停下的口令）
13 curvets unseasonably　跃起得不合时宜
14 furnished　打扮
15 ominous　不吉利
16 heart　心肝（与hart [公赤鹿] 谐音）
17 burden　伴奏
18 bring'st me out of tune　让我跑调（提醒对方不要插嘴）
19 bring me out　害我忘了要说什么
20 Soft　嘘（别出声）

CELIA	It is young Orlando, that tripped up the wrestler's heels and your heart both in an instant.	
ROSALIND	Nay, but the devil take mocking! Speak sad brow and true maid[1].	180
CELIA	I'faith, coz, 'tis he.	
ROSALIND	Orlando?	
CELIA	Orlando.	
ROSALIND	Alas the day, what shall I do with my doublet and hose? What did he when thou saw'st him? What said he? How looked he? Wherein went he?[2] What makes he here? Did he ask for me? Where remains he? How parted he with thee? And when shalt thou see him again? Answer me in one word.	185
CELIA	You must borrow me Gargantua's[3] mouth first: 'tis a word too great for any mouth of this age's size. To say 'aye' and 'no' to these particulars is more than to answer in a catechism[4].	190
ROSALIND	But doth he know that I am in this forest and in man's apparel? Looks he as freshly[5] as he did the day he wrestled?	
CELIA	It is as easy to count atomies[6] as to resolve[7] the propositions[8] of a lover; but take a taste of my finding him and relish it with good observance[9]. I found him under a tree like a dropped acorn.	195
ROSALIND	[Aside] It may well be called Jove's tree[10] when it drops such fruit.	
CELIA	Give me audience, good madam.	
ROSALIND	Proceed.	200
CELIA	There lay he stretched along like a wounded knight[11].	
ROSALIND	Though it be pity to see such a sight, it well becomes the ground.	
CELIA	Cry 'holla'[12] to thy tongue, I prithee: it curvets unseasonably[13]. He was furnished[14] like a hunter.	205
ROSALIND	O ominous[15]: he comes to kill my heart[16].	
CELIA	I would sing my song without a burden[17]; thou bring'st me out of tune[18].	
ROSALIND	Do you not know I am a woman? When I think, I must speak. Sweet, say on.	210

Enter ORLANDO *and* JAQUES

CELIA	You bring me out[19]. – Soft[20], comes he not here?
ROSALIND	'Tis he. Slink by, and note him.

[*Rosalind and Celia stand aside*]

Jaques and Orlando engage in a verbal fencing match, with Jaques criticising love. Orlando refuses to join Jaques in rebuking the world. They part, each mocking the other's folly: love and melancholy.

剧情简介：杰奎和奥岚铎展开了一场舌战，杰奎对恋爱大加批判。奥岚铎拒绝跟杰奎一道谴责社会。双方分道扬镳，彼此嘲笑对方愚痴：一方多情，另一方多愁。

Language in the play 剧中语言

'you are full of pretty answers' (in pairs)

In the conversation between Orlando and Jaques, each man tries to score points off (驳倒) the other in politely phrased but insulting language. The exchange is a subversion of normal polite conversation, and Jaques finds Orlando's answers trite and sentimental. He implies that Orlando has made love to goldsmiths' wives and learned ('conned') his answers from the sentimental inscriptions that goldsmiths engraved inside rings. In reply, Orlando implies that Jaques spends his time in tavern bedrooms. These were hung with cheap imitation tapestries ('right painted cloth') with similar commonplace sayings painted on them.

- Take parts and speak the dialogue in the script opposite. Be superficially polite, but try to show up the other character with your wit and sharp delivery. Perform in front of another pair and ask them to judge when either character scores points in this way. The judges should pronounce a winner at the end of the exchange.

Stagecraft 导演技巧

Eavesdropping (偷听) (in small groups)

Characters in Shakespeare's plays often eavesdrop on others, and at this point Rosalind and Celia have stood aside to observe Jaques and Orlando. This means that the audience can see the two women listening as well as the two men talking.

- Stage part of the script opposite, focusing on where you would place the characters in relation to each other and how they would interact with one another and with the audience. Think about the following points:

  Positioning Where should the characters stand on the stage to show that they are (a) eavesdropping and (b) unaware of being overheard? 'Upstage' (戏台上部) means the characters are further away from the audience; 'downstage' (戏台下部) means that they are closer.
  Movement Who should move around the stage? Who is most likely to talk to the audience with an aside or with gestures?
  Stage design What props and scenery will you use to hide Rosalind and Celia from the other characters' view?

1 as lief 宁愿
2 for fashion sake 出于礼貌
3 society 陪伴
4 God buy you = God be with you（goodbye的前身）
5 mar no mo 别再糟蹋（mo = more）
6 ill-favouredly 胡乱
7 just 正是
8 stature 个子
9 pretty 俏皮
10 conned 背诵
11 Atalanta's heels 阿塔兰塔的脚后跟（这位希腊神话中的女猎手以脚步快而著称；见第78页）
12 Will ... will = If you will sit down with me, we two will
13 our mistress the world 我们的女主人，即社会（这里的world指世人或社会）
14 chide 责骂
15 breather 活人，喘气者
16 a fool 傻子（指试金石，但杰奎也可能暗示奥岚铎是傻子）
17 figure 倒影
18 cipher 零符号（本义是"空"或"无"）
19 tarry 耽搁
20 Signor = Sir（这里带讽刺意味）

JAQUES	I thank you for your company, but, good faith, I had as lief[1] have been myself alone.	
ORLANDO	And so had I. But yet, for fashion sake[2], I thank you too for your society[3].	215
JAQUES	God buy you[4]. Let's meet as little as we can.	
ORLANDO	I do desire we may be better strangers.	
JAQUES	I pray you mar no more trees with writing love-songs in their barks.	220
ORLANDO	I pray you mar no mo[5] of my verses with reading them ill-favouredly[6].	
JAQUES	'Rosalind' is your love's name?	
ORLANDO	Yes, just[7].	
JAQUES	I do not like her name.	225
ORLANDO	There was no thought of pleasing you when she was christened.	
JAQUES	What stature[8] is she of?	
ORLANDO	Just as high as my heart.	
JAQUES	You are full of pretty[9] answers: have you not been acquainted with goldsmiths' wives and conned[10] them out of rings?	230
ORLANDO	Not so; but I answer you right painted cloth, from whence you have studied your questions.	
JAQUES	You have a nimble wit; I think 'twas made of Atalanta's heels[11]. Will you sit down with me, and we two will[12] rail against our mistress the world[13] and all our misery.	235
ORLANDO	I will chide[14] no breather[15] in the world but myself, against whom I know most faults.	
JAQUES	The worst fault you have is to be in love.	
ORLANDO	'Tis a fault I will not change for your best virtue: I am weary of you.	240
JAQUES	By my troth, I was seeking for a fool[16], when I found you.	
ORLANDO	He is drowned in the brook: look but in, and you shall see him.	
JAQUES	There I shall see mine own figure[17].	245
ORLANDO	Which I take to be either a fool or a cipher[18].	
JAQUES	I'll tarry[19] no longer with you. Farewell, good Signor[20] Love.	
ORLANDO	I am glad of your departure. Adieu, good Monsieur Melancholy.	

[*Exit Jaques*]

Rosalind, using her disguise as a young man, playfully tells Orlando how time moves at different speeds for different people. He expresses surprise at her refined accent.

 剧情简介：若泽兰以女扮男装的身份戏谑地告诉奥岚铎时间的脚步如何因人而异。奥岚铎对若泽兰的文雅谈吐表示惊讶。

1 First meeting (in pairs)

a To gain an initial impression of Rosalind's meeting with Orlando, take parts and speak from line 250 to the end of the scene. Keep in mind the following comment by an actor:

Rosalind now really tests her disguise. Will she be recognised by the man she loves? She has to speak and act like a man, but all the time she is teasing Orlando. Rosalind conceals her true feelings for Orlando. She hides them behind witty language and play-acting. But the audience knows how she feels, as does Celia.

b What advice would you give the actor playing Rosalind at this point in the play? Talk together with your partner about what Rosalind might be feeling, and how this could be most effectively conveyed by the actor. In your Director's Journal, write up your ideas in the form of actors' notes.

Themes 主题分析

The passing of time (in small groups)

a Use quotes from Rosalind's speeches in lines 261–80 to fill in the first column of the table below, which shows how Rosalind understands the passing of time. In the second column, describe the way you experience time moving at different speeds in your own life – perhaps when you are excited, bored and so on.

Speed at which time passes	When? (according to Rosalind)	When? (according to you)
'ambles' (慢行)		
'trots' (慢跑)		
'gallops' (疾驰)		
'stays it still'		

b Improvise a scenario that depicts one of Rosalind's portrayals of time passing.

c Discuss what insight you gain about Rosalind's feelings at this point in the play by considering her understanding of time.

1 saucy lackey　不知天高地厚的跟班
2 under that habit　以这身行头
3 play the knave　戏耍
4 swift foot of Time　时间的快步（时间的形象在雕塑和谚语中常常显示为脚上长翅膀）
5 ambles withal　与……缓缓而行
6 trots hard　小步急行
7 between … solemnised　在订婚之后和大婚之前
8 sennight　一星期（七夜）
9 lacks　不懂
10 gout　痛风
11 lean and wasteful learning　令人形销骨立的学习
12 heavy tedious penury　贫困乏味生活的重压
13 gallows　绞刑架
14 softly　轻
15 between term and term　两次庭审之间
16 skirts　边沿
17 cony　兔子
18 kindled　出生
19 purchase　学到
20 removed　偏僻

ROSALIND   I will speak to him like a saucy lackey[1], and under that habit[2] play the knave[3] with him. [*To Orlando*] Do you hear, forester?

ORLANDO   Very well. What would you?

ROSALIND   I pray you, what is't o'clock?

ORLANDO   You should ask me what time o'day: there's no clock in the forest.

ROSALIND   Then there is no true lover in the forest, else sighing every minute and groaning every hour would detect the lazy foot of Time as well as a clock.

ORLANDO   And why not the swift foot of Time[4]? Had not that been as proper?

ROSALIND   By no means, sir. Time travels in diverse paces with diverse persons. I'll tell you who Time ambles withal[5], who Time trots withal, who Time gallops withal, and who he stands still withal.

ORLANDO   I prithee, who doth he trot withal?

ROSALIND   Marry, he trots hard[6] with a young maid between the contract of her marriage and the day it is solemnised[7]. If the interim be but a sennight[8], Time's pace is so hard that it seems the length of seven year.

ORLANDO   Who ambles Time withal?

ROSALIND   With a priest that lacks[9] Latin, and a rich man that hath not the gout[10]; for the one sleeps easily because he cannot study, and the other lives merrily because he feels no pain; the one lacking the burden of lean and wasteful learning[11], the other knowing no burden of heavy tedious penury[12]. These Time ambles withal.

ORLANDO   Who doth he gallop withal?

ROSALIND   With a thief to the gallows[13]; for though he go as softly[14] as foot can fall, he thinks himself too soon there.

ORLANDO   Who stays it still withal?

ROSALIND   With lawyers in the vacation; for they sleep between term and term[15], and then they perceive not how Time moves.

ORLANDO   Where dwell you, pretty youth?

ROSALIND   With this shepherdess, my sister, here in the skirts[16] of the forest, like fringe upon a petticoat.

ORLANDO   Are you native of this place?

ROSALIND   As the cony[17] that you see dwell where she is kindled[18].

ORLANDO   Your accent is something finer than you could purchase[19] in so removed[20] a dwelling.

Rosalind says she was taught to speak by a well-educated uncle who also taught her the folly of love. She accuses Orlando of not looking like a man in love.

剧情简介：若泽兰说，是她的一位受过良好教育的叔父教她说话的，叔父还教会了她什么是痴爱。她指责奥岚铎看起来不像个恋爱中的男子。

1 The signs of love

Rosalind lists eight signs by which a man in love can be recognised. All are the marks of someone who does not give a thought to their appearance ('careless desolation').

a Write out, in your own words, the eight signs given in lines 312–18.

b Shakespeare gave another eight-item list of the marks of a lover in *The Two Gentlemen of Verona* (Act 2 Scene 1, lines 17–22):

to wreathe (盘绕) your arms like a malcontent (满腹牢骚者) ; to relish (享受) a love-song like a robin-redbreast; to walk alone like one that had the pestilence (瘟疫) ; to sigh like a schoolboy that had lost his ABC; to weep like a young wench (姑娘) that had buried her grandam; to fast like one that takes diet; to watch like one that fears robbing; to speak puling (哀泣) like a beggar at Hallowmas.

Compare Shakespeare's list in lines 312–18 with the eight items from *The Two Gentlemen of Verona*.

c Make up your own list of eight items by which someone in love can be recognised. Try to use **similes** (comparisons using 'like' or 'as' – see p. 182).

2 Dramatic irony (戏剧反讽)  (in threes)

We, the audience, know what Rosalind knows, and a special relationship develops between us. This is an example of **dramatic irony**, where the audience knows more about what is happening on stage than other characters do, because we have access to all of the characters' experiences and perspectives.

a How is it best to play Rosalind's part in this situation? Cast yourselves as Rosalind, Orlando and an observer (representing the audience). Read through lines 251–357, with the person representing the audience speaking their thoughts out loud at suitable points.

b Discuss how to most effectively convey the dramatic irony of this episode, and work out how to find and exploit the potential humour of Orlando's ignorance and Rosalind's more knowing attitude. Take it in turns to act a few lines from the scene, putting some of your ideas into practice.

1 inland 城市
2 courtship 宫廷举止；谈情说爱
3 touched 沾染
4 giddy offences 轻浮的罪行
5 taxed 指责
6 monstrous 罪大恶极
7 physic 药方
8 elegies 挽歌
9 brambles 荆棘
10 forsooth 确实
11 defying 糟蹋
12 fancy-monger 痴情商
13 counsel 劝导
14 quotidian of love 相思病
15 marks 症状
16 cage of rushes 灯芯草笼子
17 blue 黑眼圈
18 an unquestionable spirit 不愿搭理人的神情
19 your ... revenue 您的胡子就像小兄弟的收入一样少得可怜
20 demonstrating a careless desolation 表明了您失魂落魄，什么都不在乎
21 point-device in your accoutrements 穿戴极为整洁
22 warrant 保证
23 still ... consciences 总是心口不一 (still = always)
24 in good sooth 说真的
25 admired 赞美

ROSALIND I have been told so of many; but indeed an old religious uncle of mine taught me to speak, who was in his youth an inland[1] man, one that knew courtship[2] too well, for there he fell in love. I have heard him read many lectures against it, and I thank God I am not a woman to be touched[3] with so many giddy offences[4] as he hath generally taxed[5] their whole sex withal.

ORLANDO Can you remember any of the principal evils that he laid to the charge of women?

ROSALIND There were none principal; they were all like one another as halfpence are, every one fault seeming monstrous[6] till his fellow-fault came to match it.

ORLANDO I prithee recount some of them.

ROSALIND No. I will not cast away my physic[7] but on those that are sick. There is a man haunts the forest that abuses our young plants with carving 'Rosalind' on their barks; hangs odes upon hawthorns and elegies[8] on brambles[9]; all, forsooth[10], defying[11] the name of Rosalind. If I could meet that fancy-monger[12], I would give him some good counsel[13], for he seems to have the quotidian of love[14] upon him.

ORLANDO I am he that is so love-shaked. I pray you tell me your remedy.

ROSALIND There is none of my uncle's marks[15] upon you. He taught me how to know a man in love, in which cage of rushes[16] I am sure you are not prisoner.

ORLANDO What were his marks?

ROSALIND A lean cheek, which you have not; a blue[17] eye and sunken, which you have not; an unquestionable spirit[18], which you have not; a beard neglected, which you have not – but I pardon you for that, for, simply, your having in beard is a younger brother's revenue[19]. Then your hose should be ungartered, your bonnet unbanded, your sleeve unbuttoned, your shoe untied, and everything about you demonstrating a careless desolation[20]. But you are no such man; you are rather point-device in your accoutrements[21], as loving yourself than seeming the lover of any other.

ORLANDO Fair youth, I would I could make thee believe I love.

ROSALIND Me believe it? You may as soon make her that you love believe it, which I warrant[22] she is apter to do than to confess she does. That is one of the points in the which women still give the lie to their consciences[23]. But, in good sooth[24], are you he that hangs the verses on the trees wherein Rosalind is so admired[25]?

Rosalind tells how, as Ganymede, she once cured a lover by pretending to be his love and behaving capriciously. This drove the lover insane, and he became a monk. Orlando agrees to follow her cure.

 剧情简介：若泽兰讲述她曾如何以甘尼密的身份，假扮一位恋爱中人的恋人，以反复无常的行为治这位恋爱中人的痴情病，逼得他发疯，最后做了修士。奥岚铎同意接受她的治疗。

1 The cure for madness (in pairs)

In Elizabethan times, mentally ill people were sometimes thought to be possessed by devils. They were cruelly locked in a dark room and whipped to drive out the evil spirits. Rosalind says 'Love is merely a madness', although she points out that even the people who whip the supposedly mad are themselves susceptible to the common insanity of falling in love. Shakespeare often made comparisons between lunatics and lovers, as in *A Midsummer Night's Dream*:

> *The lunatic, the lover, and the poet*
> *Are of imagination all compact [composed].*
> *One sees more devils than vast hell can hold,*
> *That is the madman. The lover, all as frantic,*
> *Sees Helen's beauty in a brow of Egypt.*
>
> (Act 5 Scene 1, lines 7–17)

- Do you agree that love is a kind of madness? Discuss this proposition with your partner, then each prepare an argument either for or against it. To support your case, you should collect examples of people's behaviour when they are in love – think about historical figures as well as modern ones, and also consider how people you know have acted when they have been in love. Stage a debate with your partner and try to decide which argument is the most convincing.

2 Three staging decisions (in threes)

a At line 349 Orlando refuses to undergo a cure for love, but in line 352 he agrees. How does Rosalind get him to change his mind by how she speaks and behaves at lines 350–1? Practise different ways of saying these lines.

b In one production, Orlando gave Rosalind a hearty slap on the back at line 355, making her line 356 a kind of rebuke. Discuss how you would stage the final few lines of this scene.

c The 'Come, sister' in line 356 is addressed to Celia, who has not spoken a word throughout Rosalind's conversation with Orlando. What has she been doing? Does she approve of Rosalind's approach? Discuss how Celia reacts as she watches Rosalind's play-acting, and how she finally leaves the stage. Take parts as Celia, Rosalind and Orlando and try acting out some of your ideas to see what works best.

1 a dark-house and a whip 需要关进黑屋子，用鞭子抽（莎士比亚时代治疗精神病的方法，人们相信鞭打可以驱病魔）
2 lunacy 疯病
3 profess 主张
4 moonish 多变
5 effeminate 温柔
6 fantastical 思想怪诞
7 apish 猿猴似的（比其他动物鬼，比人傻）
8 for every … anything 各种情都有一点儿，没有一种情是真情
9 cattle of this colour 这种面目
10 forswear him 不跟他好
11 drave = drove （逼迫）
12 a nook, merely monastic 一个角落，修道而已
13 take upon me 使用
14 liver 肝脏（被视为爱和激情的源泉）
15 sound sheep's heart 健全的羊心
16 faith 真诚

ORLANDO I swear to thee, youth, by the white hand of Rosalind, I am that he, that unfortunate he.

ROSALIND But are you so much in love as your rhymes speak?

ORLANDO Neither rhyme nor reason can express how much. 330

ROSALIND Love is merely a madness and, I tell you, deserves as well a dark-house and a whip[1] as madmen do; and the reason why they are not so punished and cured is that the lunacy[2] is so ordinary that the the whippers are in love too. Yet I profess[3] curing it by counsel.

ORLANDO Did you ever cure any so? 335

ROSALIND Yes, one, and in this manner. He was to imagine me his love, his mistress, and I set him every day to woo me. At which time would I, being but a moonish[4] youth, grieve, be effeminate[5], changeable, longing and liking, proud, fantastical[6], apish[7], shallow, inconstant, full of tears, full of smiles; for every passion something, and for no passion truly anything[8], as boys and women are, for the most part, cattle of this colour[9]; would now like him, now loathe him; then entertain him, then forswear him[10]; now weep for him, then spit at him; that I drave[11] my suitor from his mad humour of love to a living humour of madness, which was to forswear the full stream of the world and to live in a nook, merely monastic[12]. And thus I cured him, and this way will I take upon me[13] to wash your liver[14] as clean as a sound sheep's heart[15], that there shall not be one spot of love in't. 340 345

ORLANDO I would not be cured, youth.

ROSALIND I would cure you if you would but call me Rosalind and come every day to my cot and woo me. 350

ORLANDO Now, by the faith[16] of my love, I will. Tell me where it is.

ROSALIND Go with me to it and I'll show it you; and by the way you shall tell me where in the forest you live. Will you go?

ORLANDO With all my heart, good youth. 355

ROSALIND Nay, you must call me 'Rosalind'. – Come, sister, will you go?

Exeunt

Touchstone's literary jokes are lost on Audrey, although they amuse Jaques. Touchstone reflects that lovers and poets are both given to deception. He says he intends to marry Audrey.

剧情简介：试金石的文字游戏让奥卓依摸不着头脑，不过却逗乐了杰奎。试金石认为恋人和诗人都容易骗人。他说他打算娶奥卓依为妻。

Characters 人物分析

Audrey and Touchstone (in small groups)

After the meeting of Rosalind and Orlando in Scene 3, Shakespeare now presents a lampoon (parody) of love.

a What is Audrey like? Many productions present her as simple-minded, dressed in old tattered clothes, speaking in a rustic accent and with her face covered in dirt. What evidence can you gather from the script about her appearance?

b In Shakespeare's time, 'goats' and 'Goths' (哥特人) (lines 5–6) had the same pronunciation. Ovid was a Roman poet (43 BC–AD 17) who was sent into exile among the Goths (an East Germanic people), perhaps because of his erotic poetry and sexual misbehaviour (for Elizabethans, 'capricious' meant goat-like or lustful). What do you think Touchstone is trying to say here? Look for clues in the script that show whether or not Audrey understands his jokes and allusions.

c How would you want Touchstone and Audrey to interact with each other? Is there some tenderness to the comedy here, or does Touchstone ruthlessly exploit Audrey's inferior wit and apparently placid nature?

1 Come apace 快来
2 simple feature 朴素长相
3 warrant 保佑
4 capricious … Goths 羊气的罗马诗人奥维德老哥在一群哥特羊中间（capricious的词源义是"山羊"）
5 ill-inhabited 放错了地方
6 seconded with 支持，赏识
7 forward child, understanding 有前途／早慧的孩子，能解人意
8 a great … room 大账单遇上小客栈（表示非常失望）
9 poetical 听懂诗
10 honest 懂事
11 feigning 虚假，会装
12 honest 贞洁
13 hard-favoured 老天让你长得不争气
14 material 实实在在
15 foul slut 丑破鞋
16 in … forest 在林中这个地方
17 couple 结为两口子
18 meeting 会面

Stagecraft 导演技巧

Jaques's unheard lines (in threes)

Presumably, Touchstone and Audrey do not hear Jaques's lines – they certainly do not seem to react or respond to them.

- How would you advise the actor playing Jaques to speak these lines? Think about how he relates to the audience at each line.

1 Relationships (in pairs)

a Discuss the couples that have come together in the play so far. How are the romantic relationships similar and different? Who is notably without a partner, and why?

b Draw up a list of the relationships in the play, then discuss the types of love represented in each one.

c Write a few notes on each relationship and predict how it will end.

Act 3 Scene 4
The Forest of Arden

Enter TOUCHSTONE, AUDREY, *with* JAQUES *behind, watching them*

TOUCHSTONE Come apace[1], good Audrey; I will fetch up your goats, Audrey. And how, Audrey, am I the man yet? Doth my simple feature[2] content you?

AUDREY Your features, Lord warrant[3] us – what features?

TOUCHSTONE I am here with thee and thy goats as the most capricious poet honest Ovid was among the Goths[4].

JAQUES O knowledge ill-inhabited[5], worse than Jove in a thatched house!

TOUCHSTONE When a man's verses cannot be understood, nor a man's good wit seconded with[6] the forward child, understanding[7], it strikes a man more dead than a great reckoning in a little room[8]. Truly, I would the gods had made thee poetical[9].

AUDREY I do not know what 'poetical' is. Is it honest[10] in deed and word? Is it a true thing?

TOUCHSTONE No, truly; for the truest poetry is the most feigning[11], and lovers are given to poetry; and what they swear in poetry may it be said, as lovers, they do feign.

AUDREY Do you wish then that the gods had made me poetical?

TOUCHSTONE I do, truly; for thou swear'st to me thou art honest[12]. Now if thou wert a poet, I might have some hope thou didst feign.

AUDREY Would you not have me honest?

TOUCHSTONE No, truly, unless thou wert hard-favoured[13]: for honesty coupled to beauty is to have honey a sauce to sugar.

JAQUES A material[14] fool.

AUDREY Well, I am not fair, and therefore I pray the gods make me honest.

TOUCHSTONE Truly, and to cast away honesty upon a foul slut[15] were to put good meat into an unclean dish.

AUDREY I am not a slut, though I thank the gods I am foul.

TOUCHSTONE Well, praised be the gods for thy foulness: sluttishness may come hereafter. But be it as it may be, I will marry thee, and to that end I have been with Sir Oliver Martext, the vicar of the next village, who hath promised to meet me in this place of the forest[16] and to couple[17] us.

JAQUES I would fain see this meeting[18].

剧情简介：试金石暗示所有妻子都不忠，但又说做已婚男还是比打光棍好。杰奎警告不要找奥利沃牧师，可试金石在糟糕牧师的身上看到了好处。

1 Unfaithful wives and shamed husbands (in pairs)

Although it was a great insult for a man to be called a cuckold, Touchstone here jokes about it in an outrageous, comic way.

a What exactly is Touchstone saying? Find the points in lines 36–47 opposite where Touchstone makes the following statements:

- Many husbands are cuckolded but do not know it.
- All women are inevitably unfaithful.
- Rich men and poor men alike are cuckolded.
- Even a cuckold is better than a bachelor, just as a fortified (设防) city is better than a village.

b What is Audrey thinking and doing on stage during this speech? Does she understand what Touchstone is saying? Work out some suitable stage business for Touchstone's monologue and Audrey's reaction, and take parts to rehearse it.

▼ Do you think Audrey is listening to Touchstone as he talks on and on? Or is she distracted by something else entirely, as she appears to be in this image?

1 fearful 胆小
2 stagger 踌躇
3 temple 教堂
4 assembly 教众
5 horn-beasts 头上长角的野兽（伊丽莎白时代说丈夫头上长角就等于说丈夫被妻子戴了绿帽子）
6 necessary 无法避免
7 the dowry of his wife 他妻子的嫁妆
8 rascal 公鹿崽子
9 by how … want 有防御比无本领强多少，头上长角就比头上无角强多少
10 dispatch us 把我们打发了（即"为我们主婚"）
11 on = as（暗指别的男人不要的）
12 Monsieur What-Ye-Call't 这位什么大爷来着（试金石故意不说 Jaques，因为 Jaques 与 Jakes 谐音，后者在伊丽莎白时代是"厕所"的一种委婉说法）
13 God'ild you = God yield you（上帝感谢您）
14 toy in hand 小意思
15 be covered 戴上帽子
16 bow 轭
17 curb 辔头，笼头
18 bells 铃铛（猎鹰腿上挂着铃铛，可以被发现和重新捕获）
19 bill 碰喙
20 wedlock 结婚仪式
21 nibbling 亲嘴（指新婚夫妇的亲昵动作）
22 wainscot 木墙板
23 shrunk panel 缩小的木板
24 warp 弯

AUDREY	Well, the gods give us joy.	35
TOUCHSTONE	Amen. A man may, if he were of a fearful[1] heart, stagger[2] in this attempt; for here we have no temple[3] but the wood, no assembly[4] but horn-beasts[5]. But what though? Courage! As horns are odious, they are necessary[6]. It is said, 'Many a man knows no end of his goods.' Right: many a man has good horns and knows no end of them. Well, that is the dowry of his wife[7], 'tis none of his own getting. Horns? Even so. Poor men alone? No, no: the noblest deer hath them as huge as the rascal[8]. Is the single man therefore blessed? No: as a walled town is more worthier than a village, so is the forehead of a married man more honourable than the bare brow of a bachelor. And, by how much defence is better than no skill, by so much is a horn more precious than to want[9].	40 45

Enter SIR OLIVER MARTEXT

	Here comes Sir Oliver. – Sir Oliver Martext, you are well met. Will you dispatch us[10] here under this tree, or shall we go with you to your chapel?	50
MARTEXT	Is there none here to give the woman?	
TOUCHSTONE	I will not take her on[11] gift of any man.	
MARTEXT	Truly, she must be given, or the marriage is not lawful.	
JAQUES	[*Coming forward*] Proceed, proceed: I'll give her.	
TOUCHSTONE	Good-even, good Monsieur What-Ye-Call't[12]. How do you, sir? You are very well met. God'ild you[13] for your last company; I am very glad to see you. Even a toy in hand[14] here, sir.	55
	[*Jaques removes his hat*]	
	Nay, pray be covered[15].	
JAQUES	Will you be married, Motley?	
TOUCHSTONE	As the ox hath his bow[16], sir, the horse his curb[17], and the falcon her bells[18], so man hath his desires, and as pigeons bill[19], so wedlock[20] would be nibbling[21].	60
JAQUES	And will you, being a man of your breeding, be married under a bush like a beggar? Get you to church, and have a good priest that can tell you what marriage is. This fellow will but join you together as they join wainscot[22], then one of you will prove a shrunk panel[23] and, like green timber, warp[24], warp.	65
TOUCHSTONE	I am not in the mind; but I were better to be married of him than of another, for he is not like to marry me well and, not being well married, it will be a good excuse for me hereafter to leave my wife.	70

Touchstone's song mocks Sir Oliver, who claims he is not put off by such foolery. In Scene 5, Celia makes fun of Rosalind's distress over Orlando's non-appearance.

 剧情简介：试金石唱歌嘲弄奥利沃牧师，可奥利沃牧师声称并没有受到这种嘲弄的影响。第五场中，希丽叶取笑若泽兰，因为若泽兰因奥岚铎久不露面而郁郁寡欢。

1 Reverse psychology (in pairs)

Celia mocks Rosalind's lovesick moodiness by exaggerating agreeing with whatever she says, even comparing Orlando with Judas – the disciple who, in the Bible, betrayed Jesus with a kiss.

a Take parts as Celia and Rosalind and speak lines 1–37. As you read through the lines a second time, stand a metre apart: whenever Rosalind and Celia seem to agree, take a step towards each other; when they disagree, take a step backwards. Which character seems to take the most steps forwards? Which character seems to take the most steps away from the other?

b What are Celia's strategies for dealing with Rosalind's mood swings? Do you think Rosalind is aware that she is being teased or indulged, or is she too absorbed in her own concerns to notice? Write notes in your Director's Journal advising the actors on how the two characters should interact with each other here.

2 Rosalind drops her disguise (in pairs)

In earlier scenes, Rosalind mocked the foolishness of love. However, here she seems to drop her disguise as Ganymede and give way to her feelings. What is the significance of Rosalind throwing off her disguise at this point in the play?

a In role as Celia, both you and your partner write a diary entry for that day. The writing should describe your response to seeing Rosalind behave as she has. Is she really revealing her true feelings or is she just performing another role?

b Exchange diary entries with your partner. In role as Rosalind, read through the entry and make notes on any parts that you feel are understanding, unfair, hurtful and so on. What do you remember thinking and feeling at the time? Do you have any criticisms of how Celia treated you? Take turns to act the part of Rosalind and confront Celia about the diary entry.

1	in bawdry 淫奔
2	brave 漂亮
3	Wind away 一边去
4	fantastical knave 荒唐的无赖
5	flout … calling 忽悠我放弃这个职业
6	have the grace to consider 有勇气想一想
7	become 与……相称
8	dissembling 迷惑人
9	Something = Somewhat (有些)
10	Judas 犹大（背叛耶稣的人，常被人描述成红头发）
11	sanctity 圣洁
12	holy bread 圣餐饼
13	cast lips 如雕像一样冰冷的嘴唇

Stagecraft 导演技巧

Rosalind and Celia's cottage (in small groups)

Imagine you are set designers. Make a list of any items you could use to give the impression of a cottage in the forest, including props for the actors to use. Note down your ideas on how to use lighting, music, sounds – even smells! – to enhance your creation.

JAQUES	Go thou with me and let me counsel thee.
TOUCHSTONE	Come, sweet Audrey, we must be married or we must live in bawdry[1]. – Farewell, good Master Oliver. Not

[*Sings*] O sweet Oliver, 75
O brave[2] Oliver,
Leave me not behind thee;

but [*Sings*]

Wind away[3],
Begone, I say, 80
I will not to wedding with thee.

MARTEXT [*Aside*] 'Tis no matter; ne'er a fantastical knave[4] of them all shall flout me out of my calling[5].

Exeunt

Act 3 Scene 5
Outside the cottage of Rosalind and Celia

Enter ROSALIND (*disguised as* GANYMEDE) *and* CELIA (*disguised as* ALIENA)

ROSALIND	Never talk to me; I will weep.
CELIA	Do, I prithee; but yet have the grace to consider[6] that tears do not become[7] a man.
ROSALIND	But have I not cause to weep?
CELIA	As good cause as one would desire: therefore weep. 5
ROSALIND	His very hair is of the dissembling[8] colour.
CELIA	Something[9] browner than Judas's[10]: marry, his kisses are Judas's own children.
ROSALIND	I'faith, his hair is of a good colour.
CELIA	An excellent colour: your chestnut was ever the only colour. 10
ROSALIND	And his kissing is as full of sanctity[11] as the touch of holy bread[12].
CELIA	He hath bought a pair of cast lips[13] of Diana. A nun of winter's sisterhood kisses not more religiously: the very ice of chastity is in them. 15
ROSALIND	But why did he swear he would come this morning and comes not?

Celia doubts whether Orlando is truly in love. Rosalind recounts how she met her father, Duke Senior, who failed to recognise her. Corin invites them to watch Silvius attempting to woo Phoebe.

 剧情简介：希丽叶怀疑奥岚铎是否真的处在恋爱之中。若泽兰讲述她与父亲老公爵相遇，但老公爵没有认出她来。考林邀请她们一同观看悉尔维耶如何向菲妣求爱。

Language in the play 剧中语言
Jousting (马上长矛竞技)

Renaissance tournaments (骑士比武) included the aristocratic sport of jousting, where knights on horseback tried to hit one another with long lances (wooden poles). Tournaments were popular, and a knight would often compete for fame, and a lady's honour and attention.

a Celia uses imagery that relates to jousting in lines 33–7, but what does she suggest when using this metaphor? What does the metaphor itself imply? And is she being serious or ironic? Celia's teasing of Rosalind contains many opportunities for humour, so devise actions that would suit her lines here.

b What other imagery would you use to describe someone head over heels (完全地) in love and eager to impress their beloved? Write a comic example like Celia's, as well as a more serious example. Use imagery drawn from the modern world and your own experiences.

1 **pickpurse** 扒手，小偷
2 **verity** 真诚
3 **concave** 中空，空心
4 **covered goblet** 加盖的酒杯
5 **tapster** 酒保
6 **the confirmers of false reckonings** 能把假的说得像真的一样的家伙
7 **traverse** 直截了当
8 **athwart** 刺穿
9 **puny tilter** 嘴上无毛的骑士
10 **noble goose** 大名鼎鼎的呆鹅
11 **youth mounts** 年轻人干的事
12 **pageant** 好戏
13 **pale complexion of true love** 真爱显出的白脸（当时人们相信恋人叹息会抽出心脏里的血）
14 **remove** 出发

1 From prose to poetry (in threes)

There is a shift from prose to poetry at line 38. When Corin enters speaking in verse, Rosalind and Celia switch from prose to verse. The characters use **blank verse** (无韵诗；素体诗), which consists of unrhymed lines that have alternate stressed and unstressed syllables (see p. 183). Each line has five iambs (抑扬音步) (feet), each with an unstressed (×) and stressed (/) syllable that sounds like a heartbeat (da DUM, da DUM, da DUM, da DUM, da DUM):

×　　/　×　　/　×　/　×　　/　×　　/
Who you saw sitting by me on the turf (line 40)

a Take parts and read aloud lines 38–50. Try to hear the rhythmic beat of the blank verse by tapping a beat on the table.

b Why do you think the play changes from prose to verse at line 38? Remember that Celia gives a very unflattering description of Orlando: as hollow as an empty wine glass or nutshell (lines 21–2), and a cheating bartender who adds up the bill wrongly (lines 26–8). In contrast, Corin invites them to 'see a pageant truly played' of rural lovers who could have featured in the common pastoral poetry of the day (see pp. 165–6).

CELIA	Nay, certainly, there is no truth in him.	
ROSALIND	Do you think so?	
CELIA	Yes, I think he is not a pickpurse[1] nor a horse-stealer but, for his verity[2] in love, I do think him as concave[3] as a covered goblet[4] or a worm-eaten nut.	20
ROSALIND	Not true in love?	
CELIA	Yes, when he is in; but I think he is not in.	
ROSALIND	You have heard him swear downright he was.	25
CELIA	'Was' is not 'is'; besides, the oath of a lover is no stronger than the word of a tapster[5]: they are both the confirmers of false reckonings[6]. He attends here in the forest on the Duke your father.	
ROSALIND	I met the Duke yesterday and had much question with him; he asked me of what parentage I was. I told him of as good as he: so he laughed and let me go. But what talk we of fathers when there is such a man as Orlando?	30
CELIA	O that's a brave man: he writes brave verses, speaks brave words, swears brave oaths, and breaks them bravely, quite traverse[7], athwart[8] the heart of his lover as a puny tilter[9] that spurs his horse but on one side, breaks his staff like a noble goose[10]. But all's brave that youth mounts[11] and folly guides. – Who comes here?	35

Enter CORIN

CORIN	Mistress and master, you have oft enquired After the shepherd that complained of love Who you saw sitting by me on the turf, Praising the proud disdainful shepherdess That was his mistress.	40
CELIA	Well, and what of him?	
CORIN	If you will see a pageant[12] truly played Between the pale complexion of true love[13] And the red glow of scorn and proud disdain, Go hence a little, and I shall conduct you If you will mark it.	45
ROSALIND	O come, let us remove[14], The sight of lovers feedeth those in love. – Bring us to this sight and you shall say I'll prove a busy actor in their play.	50

Exeunt

Silvius begs Phoebe to show him some kindness. She mocks the notion that her look might kill him. He warns that she might one day feel the pangs of love.

 剧情简介：悉尔维耶央求菲妣对自己仁慈一些。菲妣嘲笑那种认为她的眼神有杀伤力的想法。悉尔维耶警告说总有一天菲妣会尝到爱情的痛苦。

1 'I'll prove a busy actor' (in small groups)

Rosalind says she will 'prove a busy actor' as she eavesdrops on Silvius and Phoebe.

a Discuss to what extent Rosalind is 'a busy actor' throughout the play. Then compile a list of the different roles Rosalind plays (for example, daughter, traveller, relationship advisor). Discuss how convincingly you think she plays each of these roles.

b Remember that on Shakespeare's stage, Rosalind would have been played by a boy actor. Discuss the particular challenges faced by the actor. Do you think Rosalind is more or less comfortable in role as Ganymede than she is as herself? Why might this be?

2 If looks could kill (in pairs)

Elizabethans thought that the eyes were the 'windows to the soul', and that rejected lovers were wounded by the disdainful glances of the one they loved. Phoebe points out how ridiculous this idea is in lines 10–27.

- Take turns to read through these lines. Identify two moments of comedy that you would want to draw attention to in your own production of the play, and invent some stage business that would effectively emphasise it.

1 Falls 落下
2 But first begs pardon 先说一声对不起
3 dies ... drops 以杀人滴血为生
4 fly thee for 逃避你是因为
5 'Tis pretty 说得漂亮
6 sure 没错
7 coward gates 懦夫的眼帘
8 counterfeit 假装
9 swoon 昏倒
10 rush 灯芯草
11 cicatrice 伤痕
12 capable impressure 压痕
13 fresh cheek 清新面孔
14 power of fancy 仰慕的力量
15 love's keen arrows 爱情的利箭

Themes 主题分析

Love and passion

a Search in the library or on the Internet for the following two poems: Christopher Marlowe's 'The Passionate Shepherd to his Love' (1599) and Sir Walter Raleigh's reply, 'The Nymph's Reply to the Shepherd' (1600). One is an example of the pastoral tradition in literature, and the other is a parody of this tradition. (See pp. 165–6 for more information about these traditions).

b Consider how closely these poems evoke the behaviour of Silvius and Phoebe. Choose one of the poems and rewrite parts of it according to the perspective of either Silvius or Phoebe.

Act 3 Scene 6
The Forest of Arden

Enter SILVIUS *and* PHOEBE

SILVIUS Sweet Phoebe, do not scorn me, do not, Phoebe.
Say that you love me not, but say not so
In bitterness. The common executioner,
Whose heart th'accustomed sight of death makes hard,
Falls[1] not the axe upon the humbled neck
But first begs pardon[2]. Will you sterner be
Than he that dies and lives by bloody drops[3]?

Enter ROSALIND [*as* GANYMEDE], CELIA [*as* ALIENA],
and CORIN[; *they stand aside*]

PHOEBE I would not be thy executioner;
I fly thee for[4] I would not injure thee.
Thou tell'st me there is murder in mine eye,
'Tis pretty[5], sure[6], and very probable
That eyes, that are the frail'st and softest things,
Who shut their coward gates[7] on atomies,
Should be called tyrants, butchers, murderers!
Now I do frown on thee with all my heart;
And if mine eyes can wound, now let them kill thee.
Now counterfeit[8] to swoon[9], why, now fall down;
Or, if thou canst not, O for shame, for shame,
Lie not to say mine eyes are murderers.
Now show the wound mine eye hath made in thee.
Scratch thee but with a pin, and there remains
Some scar of it; lean upon a rush[10],
The cicatrice[11] and capable impressure[12]
Thy palm some moment keeps. But now mine eyes,
Which I have darted at thee, hurt thee not,
Nor I am sure there is no force in eyes
That can do hurt.

SILVIUS   O dear Phoebe,
If ever – as that 'ever' may be near –
You meet in some fresh cheek[13] the power of fancy[14],
Then shall you know the wounds invisible
That love's keen arrows[15] make.

Rosalind rebukes Phoebe for having no pity for Silvius, and criticises her looks and marriage prospects. Rosalind also censures Silvius for loving Phoebe. But Phoebe falls in love with the disguised Rosalind.

 剧情简介：若泽兰斥责菲妡对悉尔维耶毫无怜悯，并批评她相貌丑陋，嫁人无望。若泽兰也申斥悉尔维耶，说他不该爱上菲妡。菲妡反倒爱上了乔装的若泽兰。

1 'Sell when you can' (in pairs)

Rosalind gives Phoebe a dose of her own medicine, pouring scorn on her upbringing and her beauty, and urging her to marry while she has the chance.

a Take turns to speak Rosalind's lines 35–63, trying to bring out the humour of her words and to make the insults strike home. The following explanations should help you to better understand what Rosalind says.

- **Line 39** 'Than without candle … bed' = 'your looks wouldn't exactly light up a room'.
- **Lines 42–3** 'I see no more … sale-work' = 'you look like common, cheap goods'.
- **Lines 46–7** 'inky (漆黑) brows … eyeballs' – in Shakespeare's time, dark hair and features were not considered beautiful.
- **Line 54** "Tis not her glass … her' = 'she thinks she's beautiful, not because of what she sees in the mirror but because you tell her she is'.
- **Line 60** 'Sell when you can … markets' – this is Rosalind's most cutting insult, so think about how to deliver it as a climactic (最重要) line (it is followed by three less harsh lines of advice).

b Discuss why you think Rosalind launches into this long tirade (长篇激烈讲话) against a complete stranger. Make predictions about how this episode might affect the future plot of the play.

1 Who might be your mother 您母亲有可能是谁啊
2 exult 践踏
3 all at once 同时
4 the wretched 可怜人（指悉尔维耶）
5 What = Even
6 sale-work 大路货
7 Od's my little life 上帝保佑我的小命（Od's = God save）
8 tangle my eyes 迷住我的双眼
9 hope not after it 别妄想
10 bugle 黑玻璃球似的
11 follow 追
12 foggy South 湿漉漉的南风
13 puffing with wind and rain 呼呼地又是风又是雨
14 properer 更加仪表堂堂
15 out of you 从您那里
16 lineaments 容貌
17 fasting 斋戒
18 Cry 求
19 Foul … scoffer 最丑的丑八怪是嘲讽人的丑八怪
20 take her to thee 你收下她吧
21 chide a year together 一起吵一年

PHOEBE	But till that time
	Come not thou near me; and, when that time comes,
	Afflict me with thy mocks, pity me not,
	As till that time I shall not pity thee.
ROSALIND	[*Coming forward*] And why, I pray you? Who might be your mother[1]
	That you insult, exult[2], and all at once[3]
	Over the wretched[4]? What[5] though you have no beauty,
	As, by my faith, I see no more in you
	Than without candle may go dark to bed,
	Must you be therefore proud and pitiless?
	Why, what means this? Why do you look on me?
	I see no more in you than in the ordinary
	Of Nature's sale-work[6] – Od's my little life[7],
	I think she means to tangle my eyes[8] too. –
	No, faith, proud mistress, hope not after it[9];
	'Tis not your inky brows, your black silk hair,
	Your bugle[10] eyeballs, nor your cheek of cream
	That can entame my spirits to your worship. –
	You, foolish shepherd, wherefore do you follow[11] her
	Like foggy South[12], puffing with wind and rain[13]?
	You are a thousand times a properer[14] man
	Than she a woman. 'Tis such fools as you
	That makes the world full of ill-favoured children.
	'Tis not her glass but you that flatters her,
	And out of you[15] she sees herself more proper
	Than any of her lineaments[16] can show her. –
	But, mistress, know yourself. Down on your knees,
	[*Phoebe kneels to Rosalind*]
	And thank heaven, fasting[17], for a good man's love;
	For I must tell you friendly in your ear,
	Sell when you can: you are not for all markets.
	Cry[18] the man mercy, love him, take his offer,
	Foul is most foul, being foul to be a scoffer[19]. –
	So take her to thee[20], shepherd; fare you well.
PHOEBE	Sweet youth, I pray you chide a year together[21];
	I had rather hear you chide than this man woo.

Rosalind rejects Phoebe and tells her to be kinder to Silvius. Phoebe acknowledges that she loves Ganymede and proposes to use Silvius as a go-between. Silvius is grateful for anything from Phoebe.

剧情简介：若泽兰拒绝了菲妣，并告诉她要对悉尔维耶好一些。菲妣承认自己爱上了甘尼密，提出让悉尔维耶做媒。悉尔维耶愿意任何事情都为菲妣效劳。

1 To whom? (in pairs)

Rosalind has indeed proved 'a busy actor' in this episode with Silvius and Phoebe. Her final two speeches are especially 'busy', as they address both Phoebe and Silvius in turn. Her comments might also be addressed to the audience or muttered under her breath.

- As one person speaks Rosalind's part in lines 66–79, the other says to whom they think each line is addressed. Afterwards, discuss what might be achieved by addressing the audience directly.

Themes 主题分析

Love at first sight (in small groups)

Lines 80–1 are probably a reference to the playwright Christopher Marlowe, who was killed in a tavern quarrel in 1593. One of his poems contained the line: 'Who ever loved that loved not at first sight?' Phoebe calls Marlowe 'Dead shepherd', and declares that she now finds his saying to be very true indeed.

Discuss the idea of love at first sight:

- Is there such a thing as love at first sight? Do you not have to know someone in order to really fall in love with them?
- Do you think you can love someone even when it is not love at first sight? Is it perhaps better to get to know someone as a friend before you begin a romantic relationship with them?
- Where does love come into a marriage that is (a) arranged by your family or (b) where the romance seems to have gone? How is new love different from seasoned love, and is one more valuable than the other?

1	sauce	逗一逗
2	vows made in wine	醉酒时的誓言
3	tuft of olives	橄榄树丛
4	hard by	附近
5	ply her hard	使劲去追她
6	abused in sight	被眼见所蒙蔽
7	saw	名言
8	might	力量
9	sorrow	难过
10	sorrow	哭泣
11	extermined	消除
12	neighbourly	友善
13	covetousness	贪婪
14	erst was irksome to me	过去很令我讨厌
15	glean the broken ears	拾一些碎麦穗
16	Loose	露出
17	scattered	不经意的

Write about it 写作练习

Phoebe/Silvius (in pairs)

Rosalind's intervention in the lovers' quarrel has an unexpected outcome: Phoebe falls in love with her, thinking her to be Ganymede – an attractive and forthright boy.

- In role as Phoebe, write out a diary entry. Describe your feelings about meeting this exciting new 'man'. What exactly has attracted you to him, and how do you compare him to Silvius?

ROSALIND	He's fallen in love with your foulness – [*To Silvius*] and she'll fall in love with my anger. If it be so, as fast as she answers thee with frowning looks, I'll sauce[1] her with bitter words. – Why look you so upon me?	
PHOEBE	For no ill will I bear you.	70
ROSALIND	I pray you do not fall in love with me	
	For I am falser than vows made in wine[2];	
	Besides, I like you not. – [*To Silvius*] If you will know my house,	
	'Tis at the tuft of olives[3], here hard by[4]. –	
	Will you go, sister? – Shepherd, ply her hard[5]. –	75
	Come, sister. – Shepherdess, look on him better	
	And be not proud, though all the world could see,	
	None could be so abused in sight[6] as he. –	
	Come, to our flock. *Exeunt Rosalind, Celia, Corin*	
PHOEBE	Dead shepherd, now I find thy saw[7] of might[8]:	80
	'Who ever loved that loved not at first sight?'	
SILVIUS	Sweet Phoebe, –	
PHOEBE	Ha, what say'st thou, Silvius?	
SILVIUS	Sweet Phoebe, pity me.	
PHOEBE	Why I am sorry for thee, gentle Silvius.	
SILVIUS	Wherever sorrow[9] is, relief would be.	85
	If you do sorrow[10] at my grief in love,	
	By giving love your sorrow and my grief	
	Were both extermined[11].	
PHOEBE	Thou hast my love: is not that neighbourly[12]?	
SILVIUS	I would have you.	
PHOEBE	Why, that were covetousness[13].	90
	Silvius, the time was that I hated thee,	
	And yet it is not that I bear thee love;	
	But since that thou canst talk of love so well,	
	Thy company, which erst was irksome to me[14],	
	I will endure – and I'll employ thee too.	95
	But do not look for further recompense	
	Than thine own gladness that thou art employed.	
SILVIUS	So holy and so perfect is my love,	
	And I in such a poverty of grace	
	That I shall think it a most plenteous crop	100
	To glean the broken ears[15] after the man	
	That the main harvest reaps. Loose[16] now and then	
	A scattered[17] smile, and that I'll live upon.	

Phoebe's detailed description of Ganymede shows how much she loves him. But she denies that she does, and says she will write a taunting letter that Silvius will deliver.

剧情简介：菲妞对甘尼密的详细描述显出她有多爱他，可她偏偏不承认自己的爱慕之情，她说她要给甘尼密写一封嘲讽信，让悉尔维耶送给他。

Language in the play 剧中语言

Dramatic grammar (whole class)

Read through Phoebe's long speech by yourself as you walk around the room. Remember to use the following rules, as you did in the activity on page 2:

- At each full stop make a full 'about-turn' (180 degrees).
- At each comma, colon, semi-colon or dash make a half turn (90 degrees to your right or left).
- Devise a gesture to make at every question mark (such as stamping your foot or clicking your fingers).

Which words or lines stood out for you during this activity? How might the grammatical structure of the script reflect Phoebe's feelings at this point in the play?

2 Enjoy the language! (in pairs)

Phoebe's speech, which expresses the emotional turmoil that Ganymede has provoked in her, displays many of Shakespeare's characteristic language techniques.

a   Use the following tips to help you speak lines 108–34 in a way that brings out the humour of the situation. Take turns to perform the speech to each other, and note down what works well in both readings.

- **Antithesis** (对比) A string of oppositions is created through the use of antithesis, where something is said and then contradicted.
- **Monosyllables** (单音节词) A long succession of monosyllables (single-sound words) helps the actor to speak each word sharply and emphatically. Shakespeare gives Phoebe long stretches of language full of monosyllables.
- **Lists** Shakespeare loved to pile up item on item to intensify meaning and dramatic effect. This speech is a long catalogue of how Phoebe has 'marked him / In parcels' (appraised him feature by feature).
- **Repetition** Shakespeare adds subtle repetition of words and phrases – such as 'yet' and 'he'/'his' – to capture Phoebe's confusion and gradual understanding of the situation and her own feelings.

b   For each example of the language techniques listed above, write stage directions in your Director's Journal for an actor to follow. Make sure they are detailed enough to give the actor playing Phoebe inspiration about tone of voice, gesture and movement on stage.

1 erewhile 刚刚
2 bounds 牧场
3 old carlot 老农民
4 peevish 傻乎乎
5 complexion 肤色
6 not very … tall （在成年男子中）个儿不太高，但在他这个岁数，个儿就算高的了
7 lusty 艳
8 mingled damask 白里透红
9 In parcels 仔细
10 gone … him 马上就要爱上他
11 had he to do 凭什么他要
12 black 黑（莎士比亚时代black是fair [美] 的反义词）
13 answered not again 没有回敬他几句
14 Omittance is no quittance 不反驳不代表原谅
15 taunting 嘲弄
16 straight 立即
17 matter 内容
18 passing short 特别简短

PHOEBE	Know'st thou the youth that spoke to me erewhile[1]?	
SILVIUS	Not very well; but I have met him oft	105
	And he hath bought the cottage and the bounds[2]	
	That the old carlot[3] once was master of.	
PHOEBE	Think not I love him, though I ask for him;	
	'Tis but a peevish[4] boy – yet he talks well.	
	But what care I for words? Yet words do well	110
	When he that speaks them pleases those that hear.	
	It is a pretty youth – not very pretty;	
	But sure he's proud – and yet his pride becomes him;	
	He'll make a proper man. The best thing in him	
	Is his complexion[5]; and faster than his tongue	115
	Did make offence, his eye did heal it up;	
	He is not very tall, yet for his years he's tall[6];	
	His leg is but so-so, and yet 'tis well;	
	There was a pretty redness in his lip,	
	A little riper and more lusty[7] red	120
	Than that mixed in his cheek: 'twas just the difference	
	Betwixt the constant red and mingled damask[8].	
	There be some women, Silvius, had they marked him	
	In parcels[9] as I did, would have gone near	
	To fall in love with him[10]: but, for my part,	125
	I love him not nor hate him not – and yet	
	Have more cause to hate him than to love him.	
	For what had he to do[11] to chide at me?	
	He said mine eyes were black[12], and my hair black,	
	And, now I am remembered, scorned at me.	130
	I marvel why I answered not again[13];	
	But that's all one. Omittance is no quittance[14].	
	I'll write to him a very taunting[15] letter	
	And thou shalt bear it – wilt thou, Silvius?	
SILVIUS	Phoebe, with all my heart.	
PHOEBE	I'll write it straight[16]:	135
	The matter's[17] in my head and in my heart;	
	I will be bitter with him and passing short[18].	
	Go with me, Silvius.	

Exeunt

As You Like It 各如所愿

Looking back at Act 3 第3幕回顾
Activities for groups or individuals

1 Staging Arden

At the beginning of Act 3, the play leaves the court for the last time and establishes itself in Arden. What characteristics of this new setting would you want to represent on stage? Look at the examples of sets from other productions on the page opposite and elsewhere in this edition as you think about your own ideas.

- ◆ Imagine that you are part of the set design team for a new production of the play. Make initial sketches and/or detailed drawings of how you would like to stage Arden. Then present your plans to the class, and explain why you would want to represent the Forest of Arden in this way.

2 Life in Arden

Critics have had many different opinions about what Arden represents. Here are a few of them:

- Arden is the complete antithesis (对照) of the court.
- Arden is a kind of Eden (伊甸园), just as the court is akin (相似) to a fallen world.
- The characters undergo a positive transformation when they live in or travel to Arden.
- Arden represents an upside-down world where the usual conventions and hierarchies of social and political life are overturned.
- The people of Arden are all of a kind: rustic, simple and lacking in refined feelings.

- ◆ Arrange the statements above in order of preference, and be prepared to justify your arrangement to a partner.

- ◆ Write a short article about Arden for the programme of a new production of *As You Like It*, using one of the above observations as the title. Develop the central idea in the title and refer to characters, events and quotations from the play.

3 Parallel relationships

- ◆ How do the romantic relationships that emerge in the play – Rosalind/Orlando, Phoebe/Silvius and Audrey/Touchstone – show different forms of 'love' and different kinds of relationships between men and women?

- ◆ If you were directing the play and had to shorten Act 3 because of time constraints, which couple you would drop from the play? Discuss in groups whether you think any of the couples are an unnecessary distraction from the main plot, and which of them are absolutely crucial to the play's themes. Give reasons for your choices.

4 Time and time again

Time is a recurring (反复出现) theme in Shakespeare's work, both in his plays and his sonnets. The word 'time' is mentioned on eighty occasions in Shakespeare's 154 sonnets (小歌).

- ◆ Find a sonnet by Shakespeare that explores the theme of time. (You might like to choose sonnets 18, 19, 60, 64 or 73). What ideas about time are developed here?

- ◆ Write two paragraphs about how time is a theme that is developed in *As You Like It*. Remember to refer to the following passages as you do so:
  - Adam's reflection on the passing of time in his life from hard-working youth to strong old age (Act 2 Scene 3, lines 38–55)
  - Jaques's description of the seven ages of man (Act 2 Scene 7, lines 139–66)
  - Rosalind's example of the way times moves at different speeds for different people (Act 3 Scene 3, lines 265–80).

109

Rosalind says that extremes of both melancholy or merriness are detestable. Jaques claims that his melancholy is more complex than anyone else's. Rosalind mocks his pretentiousness. She ignores Orlando.

 剧情简介：若泽兰说极度忧郁和极度快乐都可憎。杰奎声称他的忧郁比任何人的都复杂。若泽兰嘲笑他自命不凡。她无视奥岚铎的存在。

1 Melancholic manifestations (in pairs)

Today, the word 'melancholy' is usually used to describe someone who is sad, but in Shakespeare's time it included other meanings: serious, cynical, world-weary, neurotic (神经质). Elizabethans used the theory of the four humours to explain people's behaviour, personalities or moods (see p. 132), and 'melancholy' was one of these humours.

a Discuss the difference between Jaques's melancholy and Orlando's melancholy. Would you describe Rosalind as melancholy? If so, how does her mood differ from Jaques's and Orlando's. Look again at Act 3 Scene 3, as well as the script opposite, and select particular words or phrases that illustrate your interpretation.

b Imagine how a costume designer for a modern production might use costume to portray these different kinds of melancholy. Describe or sketch the costumes and props for each of the characters above.

Language in the play 剧中语言

Blank verse of a melancholic lover (in pairs)

Jaques thinks that Orlando is going to speak to Rosalind (Ganymede) 'in blank verse' (see p. 183), but in fact he speaks to her in prose.

a What is different about Orlando's greeting that makes Jaques think he is speaking verse? What else about Orlando's diction might make Jaques think he will speak in blank verse?

b Imagine that Orlando was going to speak in verse to Rosalind, but Jaques made him self-conscious and he changed his mind. Write out what he might have said to Rosalind if Jaques had not interrupted him. Use rhythms, rhymes, diction and imagery that would be suitable to a lover addressing his mistress.

2 Playing the melancholic

Jaques is perhaps the most famous stage depiction of 'the melancholy man'. Many Elizabethan gentlemen affected his pose: the world-weary cynic who feels that he has seen it all.

- Read lines 26–30 as Rosalind teases Jaques about his melancholic disposition. Then write a paragraph of your own advice to Jaques. Decide whether you will write in the same light-hearted manner as Rosalind or in a more serious style to try to help him deal with his emotions.

---

1 in extremity of either 两方面走极端（要么极端忧伤，要么极端快乐）
2 abominable 令人讨厌
3 modern censure 通常的指责
4 sad 发愁
5 emulation 争锋
6 politic 手腕
7 nice 挑剔
8 simples 成分
9 sundry contemplation 各种思索
10 often rumination 经常沉思
11 humorous sadness 忧郁的哀伤
12 travel 跋涉（与travail [劳作] 谐音）
13 Look you 您务必
14 lisp 洋腔洋调
15 disable 贬低
16 nativity 故乡
17 swam in a gondola 坐贡多拉船游过威尼斯（指出国访问过）

Act 4 Scene 1
The Forest of Arden

Enter ROSALIND [*as* GANYMEDE], *and* CELIA [*as* ALIENA] *and* JAQUES

JAQUES I prithee, pretty youth, let me be better acquainted with thee.
ROSALIND They say you are a melancholy fellow.
JAQUES I am so: I do love it better than laughing.
ROSALIND Those that are in extremity of either[1] are abominable[2] fellows, and betray themselves to every modern censure[3] worse than drunkards.
JAQUES Why, 'tis good to be sad[4] and say nothing.
ROSALIND Why then, 'tis good to be a post.
JAQUES I have neither the scholar's melancholy, which is emulation[5]; nor the musician's, which is fantastical; nor the courtier's, which is proud; nor the soldier's, which is ambitious; nor the lawyer's, which is politic[6]; nor the lady's, which is nice[7]; nor the lover's, which is all these; but it is a melancholy of mine own, compounded of many simples[8], extracted from many objects, and indeed the sundry contemplation[9] of my travels, in which my often rumination[10] wraps me in a most humorous sadness[11].
ROSALIND A traveller! By my faith, you have great reason to be sad. I fear you have sold your own lands to see other men's. Then to have seen much and to have nothing is to have rich eyes and poor hands.
JAQUES Yes, I have gained my experience.

Enter ORLANDO

ROSALIND And your experience makes you sad. I had rather have a fool to make me merry than experience to make me sad – and to travel[12] for it too!
ORLANDO Good day, and happiness, dear Rosalind.
JAQUES Nay then, God buy you, and you talk in blank verse!
ROSALIND Farewell, Monsieur Traveller. Look you[13] lisp[14] and wear strange suits; disable[15] all the benefits of your own country; be out of love with your nativity[16], and almost chide God for making you that countenance you are, or I will scarce think you have swam in a gondola[17].

[*Exit Jaques*]

Rosalind berates Orlando for his lateness, and doubts whether he is truly in love. She jokes about deceived husbands, then demands that Orlando woo her and teases him about tongue-tied lovers.

剧情简介：若泽兰痛斥奥岚铎迟到，怀疑他并非真的在恋爱。她拿被戴了绿帽子的丈夫们开玩笑，然后要求奥岚铎向她求婚，并取笑奥岚铎是个笨嘴拙舌的恋人。

1 The wooing scene (in small groups)

Lines 31–176 are often called 'the wooing scene', in which Rosalind tricks Orlando into wooing her. He thinks he is talking to a young man, Ganymede, who has promised to act as Rosalind to cure him of his love. But it really is Rosalind – and she loves the deception!

a Discuss whether you think Orlando really believes that this exercise will cure him of his love for Rosalind. Does he actually think that 'Ganymede' is a man?

b Compile a list of questions to ask Orlando in order to find out what he is thinking. Then take turns to sit in the hot-seat in role as Orlando, and answer the questions that the rest of the group asks.

Language in the play 剧中语言

Many-layered meaning (in pairs)

The script opposite has many opportunities for comic moments because of the different meanings of the words Rosalind uses as she talks with Orlando. Her language is both playful and funny.

a Find the two following examples in the script opposite and note down the different meanings that Rosalind uses. What effect do Rosalind's witty speeches have on Orlando?

- Rosalind says that she would rather be wooed by a snail, but she does not just mean to reprimand (斥责) Orlando for being late. She refers to ideas of cuckoldry to make a comment on relationships and trust between men and women.

- Rosalind says that a lover should kiss his mistress when he runs out of things to say; and Orlando asks who could be lost for words in front of his mistress. Rosalind's reply in lines 66–7 could mean different things, because for Elizabethans the word 'ranker' had two different meanings (see the glossary).

b Which interpretation of 'ranker' seems most appropriate for this section of the play? Discuss how easy you think it would be for an audience to understand these different meanings. How would you advise the actors to help make the meanings clearer?

1 Cupit ... o'th'shoulder 丘比特拍过他的肩膀
2 heart-whole 心脏完好（没有陷入爱情）
3 tardy 慢腾腾
4 jointure 房产
5 are ... for 应该感谢你们妻子替你们戴的
6 leer 相貌
7 holiday humour 假日的愉悦
8 and I ... very 假如我真的是您千真万确的
9 gravelled 卡壳了
10 lack of matter 缺少话题
11 out （台词）忘光了
12 cleanliest shift 最卫生的补救办法
13 puts you to entreaty 要您求她
14 ranker 比……多 / 臭
15 What, of my suit? 我的请求呢？
16 Not ... suit 不是您的衣服走光了，而是您的请求忘光了（双关）

As You Like It Act 4 Scene 1
各如所愿

Why, how now, Orlando, where have you been all this while? You a lover? And you serve me such another trick, never come in my sight more.

ORLANDO My fair Rosalind, I come within an hour of my promise.

ROSALIND Break an hour's promise in love? He will divide a minute into a thousand parts and break but a part of the thousand part of a minute in the affairs of love, it may be said of him that Cupid hath clapped him o'th'shoulder[1], but I'll warrant him heart-whole[2].

ORLANDO Pardon me, dear Rosalind.

ROSALIND Nay, and you be so tardy[3], come no more in my sight — I had as lief be wooed of a snail.

ORLANDO Of a snail?

ROSALIND Aye, of a snail; for though he comes slowly, he carries his house on his head; a better jointure[4], I think, than you make a woman. Besides, he brings his destiny with him.

ORLANDO What's that?

ROSALIND Why, horns; which such as you are fain to be beholden to your wives for[5]. But he comes armed in his fortune and prevents the slander of his wife.

ORLANDO Virtue is no horn-maker, and my Rosalind is virtuous.

ROSALIND And I am your Rosalind.

CELIA It pleases him to call you so, but he hath a Rosalind of a better leer[6] than you.

ROSALIND Come, woo me, woo me; for now I am in a holiday humour[7] and like enough to consent. What would you say to me now and I were your very, very[8] Rosalind?

ORLANDO I would kiss before I spoke.

ROSALIND Nay, you were better speak first, and when you were gravelled[9] for lack of matter[10] you might take occasion to kiss. Very good orators when they are out[11], they will spit, and for lovers, lacking — God warrant us — matter, the cleanliest shift[12] is to kiss.

ORLANDO How if the kiss be denied?

ROSALIND Then she puts you to entreaty[13], and there begins new matter.

ORLANDO Who could be out, being before his beloved mistress?

ROSALIND Marry, that should you if I were your mistress, or I should think my honesty ranker[14] than my wit.

ORLANDO What, of my suit?[15]

ROSALIND Not out of your apparel, and yet out of your suit[16]. Am not I your Rosalind?

Orlando claims that he will die for love. Rosalind lampoons his claim, telling of famous lovers who died – but not for love. She asks Celia to act as priest and marry her to Orlando.

剧情简介：奥岚铎声称他愿意为爱而死。若泽兰嘲讽了他的说法，讲了一些著名恋人并非殉情而死的例子，又要希丽叶扮作牧师，把她嫁给奥岚铎。

Characters 人物分析

Teasing Orlando

Rosalind teases Orlando in lines 92–8 by being deliberately tricky in her replies to his questions and requests.

- How would you stage this exchange and what advice would you give to the actors? Would you want them to bring out Orlando's genuine confusion and Rosalind's slippery contrariness or, alternatively, would you highlight both characters' fun and flirtatious bantering (逗乐)? Write notes in your Director's Journal.

Themes 主题分析

Marriage: 'Give me your hand' (in pairs)

A 'hand-fast' marriage was a serious betrothal contract (婚约) between a man and a woman. Although the church made it a legal requirement for marriages to be publicly announced in a church by a priest, 'hand-fast' marriages were thought to be legally binding. The couple held hands, vows were exchanged and this 'hand-fast' marriage was solemnised (隆重庆祝) in a church soon afterwards.

- In line 102, Celia says 'I cannot say the words'. Why? Is she laughing too much because she knows that Ganymede is really Rosalind? Is she shocked because Rosalind has basically proposed to Orlando? Or is she horrified that Orlando has just 'married' Ganymede (a man)?

1 **by attorney** 还是让替死鬼
2 **The poor ... old** 这可怜的世界已将近六千岁了（伊丽莎白时代人们根据《圣经》推算世界是将近六千年前创造的）
3 **videlicet** 即（拉丁文）
4 **in a love-cause** 因为恋情
5 **Troilus ... club** 特洛伊勒（希腊神话中的特洛伊王子。按照中世纪和文艺复兴时期的传说，特洛伊勒与本城预言家凯尔柯 [Calchas] 的女儿克莱希达 [Cressida] 相爱。凯尔柯预见到特洛伊的毁灭，投奔了希腊联军，后通过人质交换让克莱希达来到自己身边。特洛伊勒夜晚潜入敌营，窥见联军大将狄俄墨德 [Diomed] 勾引克莱希达，发誓与之对决。第二天二人战场上交手，狄俄墨德受伤后逃脱。特洛伊勒的最后结局是被联军第一勇士阿喀琉斯 [Achilles] 斩首。若泽兰的说法明显与当时的传说不符）
6 **patterns** 模式
7 **Leander** 勒安卓（古希腊文的拉丁文转写是 Léandros。希腊神话里的一个小伙子，住在希腊海峡 [Hellespont，今达达尼尔海峡] 亚洲一侧阿比多城 [Abydos]，爱上了海峡对岸塞斯托城 [Sestos] 的姑娘赫婼 [Hero，又译作"赫洛"]，每晚游过海峡与之幽会。一个暴风雨的冬夜，勒安卓照样下了海，可是赫婼为他点着的灯被风吹灭，导致勒安卓因迷失方向而淹死。天亮后赫婼看到崖下被潮水冲到岸上的恋人尸体，跳崖殉情而亡。若泽兰关于勒安卓死因的说法明显与神话不符）
8 **though** 即使
9 **cramp** 抽筋
10 **found it was** 认定是因为
11 **my ... mind** 我真正的若泽兰是这种观念
12 **coming-on** 顺从；宽容
13 **Fridays and Saturdays** 周五和周六（斋戒的日子）
14 **Go to** 来吧

ORLANDO   I take some joy to say you are, because I would be talking of her.
ROSALIND   Well, in her person, I say I will not have you.
ORLANDO   Then, in mine own person, I die.
ROSALIND   No, faith, die by attorney[1]. The poor world is almost six thousand years old[2] and in all this time there was not any man died in his own person, videlicet[3], in a love-cause[4]. Troilus had his brains dashed out with a Grecian club[5], yet he did what he could to die before, and he is one of the patterns[6] of love; Leander[7], he would have lived many a fair year though[8] Hero had turned nun, if it had not been for a hot midsummer night, for, good youth, he went but forth to wash him in the Hellespont and, being taken with the cramp[9], was drowned, and the foolish chroniclers of that age found it was[10] Hero of Sestos. But these are all lies: men have died from time to time – and worms have eaten them – but not for love.
ORLANDO   I would not have my right Rosalind of this mind[11], for I protest her frown might kill me.
ROSALIND   By this hand, it will not kill a fly. But come, now I will be your Rosalind in a more coming-on[12] disposition and, ask me what you will, I will grant it.
ORLANDO   Then love me, Rosalind.
ROSALIND   Yes, faith, will I, Fridays and Saturdays[13] and all.
ORLANDO   And wilt thou have me?
ROSALIND   Aye, and twenty such.
ORLANDO   What sayest thou?
ROSALIND   Are you not good?
ORLANDO   I hope so.
ROSALIND   Why then, can one desire too much of a good thing? – Come, sister, you shall be the priest and marry us. – Give me your hand, Orlando. – What do you say, sister?
ORLANDO   Pray thee, marry us.
CELIA   I cannot say the words.
ROSALIND   You must begin: 'Will you, Orlando –'
CELIA   Go to[14]. – Will you, Orlando, have to wife this Rosalind?
ORLANDO   I will.
ROSALIND   Aye, but when?
ORLANDO   Why, now, as fast as she can marry us.
ROSALIND   Then you must say, 'I take thee, Rosalind, for wife.'
ORLANDO   I take thee, Rosalind, for wife.

Rosalind jokes at her own forwardness, then comments on how time sours marriages. She warns of her future giddy behaviour and hints that wives and husbands are unfaithful. She criticises Orlando's proposed absence.

 剧情简介：若泽兰拿自己的主动上门开玩笑，接着又评论时间如何让婚姻变酸。她警示说，自己将来会举止轻佻，并暗示夫妇会有二心。奥岚铎提出要走，若泽兰批评了他。

Themes 主题分析

Love through the year (in pairs)

In lines 114–25, what do the different seasons suggest about the behaviour, motivations and desires of men and women? Discuss what Rosalind means here, then create a tableau that represents your interpretation of these lines.

1 Who's in charge? (in pairs)

The wooing scene is comic because of the role reversals that take place on stage. The added irony on Shakespeare's stage was that Rosalind would have been a boy actor playing a woman dressed as a man. Within the play, Rosalind is also a woman taking the lead in wooing the man she wants to marry.

- Try reading through the script opposite (lines 110–49) in two different ways: in one version, Orlando takes the upper hand and drives the conversation; in the other, Rosalind is the dominant force. Which version seems more plausible? When you have tried both interpretations, stage a third one in which you find a balance between the two characters.

Stagecraft 导演技巧

What is Celia doing?

Celia is present throughout the wooing scene, but says very little until Orlando leaves (line 161). What might she be thinking as she watches the encounter between Orlando and Rosalind?

a Compose stage directions for two points in the script opposite, to advise the actor playing Celia on how she can reveal her thoughts. What actions might Celia use, and where might she stand on the stage so that her feelings can be clearly expressed to the audience?

b Sketch an outline of the stage, and mark on it where you would want the characters to stand, sit and move in relation to one another. You might like to draw arrows and annotate your diagram to show what movement occurs at various points. Keep this plan in your Director's Journal.

1 commission 保证
2 a girl … priest 姑娘比祭司先行了一步
3 possessed 娶
4 April 四月天（阵雨多，隐喻泪水）
5 May 五月天（快乐多，隐喻嬉戏）
6 Barbary cock-pigeon 巴巴里雄鸽（对雌鸽盯得很紧）
7 against = before
8 new-fangled 追新求异
9 giddy 无脑
10 Diana in the fountain 喷泉里的荻阿娜（可能指建造于16世纪晚期的伦敦齐普赛街 [Cheapside] 上一个喷泉里的荻阿娜雕像，也可能指建造于16世纪中期的意大利蒂沃利市 [Tivoli] 埃斯特别墅 [Villa d'Este] 里一尊多乳房荻阿娜雕像，其每个乳房的乳头都喷水。该别墅实际是一座景观优美的大庄园，以喷泉众多而闻名于世）
11 waywarder 越一意孤行
12 Make the doors upon 给……闩上门
13 casement 窗棂
14 whither wilt? 哪里走？（伊丽莎白时代的流行语，表达一种斥责；前面的Wit是拟人化，wilt是will的单数第二人称现在时形式）
15 check 斥责
16 And … that? 机智有什么机智为这种行为（指通奸）开脱呢？
17 'Tis but one cast away 不过是个被人甩了的玩意儿

ROSALIND	I might ask you for your commission[1], but I do take thee, Orlando, for my husband. There's a girl goes before the priest[2], and certainly a woman's thought runs before her actions.
ORLANDO	So do all thoughts: they are winged.
ROSALIND	Now, tell me how long you would have her after you have possessed[3] her?
ORLANDO	For ever and a day.
ROSALIND	Say a day without the 'ever'. No, no, Orlando: men are April[4] when they woo, December when they wed; maids are May[5] when they are maids, but the sky changes when they are wives. I will be more jealous of thee than a Barbary cock-pigeon[6] over his hen; more clamorous than a parrot against[7] rain, more new-fangled[8] than an ape; more giddy[9] in my desires than a monkey. I will weep for nothing, like Diana in the fountain[10], and I will do that when you are disposed to be merry. I will laugh like a hyena, and that when thou art inclined to sleep.
ORLANDO	But will my Rosalind do so?
ROSALIND	By my life, she will do as I do.
ORLANDO	O, but she is wise.
ROSALIND	Or else she could not have the wit to do this: the wiser, the waywarder[11]. Make the doors upon[12] a woman's wit, and it will out at the casement[13]; shut that, and 'twill out at the keyhole; stop that, 'twill fly with the smoke out at the chimney.
ORLANDO	A man that had a wife with such a wit, he might say, 'Wit, whither wilt?[14]'
ROSALIND	Nay, you might keep that check[15] for it till you met your wife's wit going to your neighbour's bed.
ORLANDO	And what wit could wit have to excuse that?[16]
ROSALIND	Marry, to say she came to seek you there: you shall never take her without her answer unless you take her without her tongue. O, that woman that cannot make her fault her husband's occasion, let her never nurse her child herself for she will breed it like a fool.
ORLANDO	For these two hours, Rosalind, I will leave thee.
ROSALIND	Alas, dear love, I cannot lack thee two hours.
ORLANDO	I must attend the Duke at dinner, by two o'clock I will be with thee again.
ROSALIND	Aye, go your ways, go your ways. I knew what you would prove – my friends told me as much, and I thought no less. That flattering tongue of yours won me. 'Tis but one cast away[17], and so come, Death! Two o'clock is your hour?

Rosalind warns Orlando not to be late. Celia rebukes Rosalind for her criticism of women, but Rosalind declares she is immeasurably deeply in love. Celia remains sceptical.

 剧情简介：若泽兰警告奥岚铎不要迟到。希丽叶责备若泽兰诋毁女性，若泽兰却宣称她已经深深陷入爱河。希丽叶将信将疑。

1 Rosalind's mood changes

How many mood changes can you identify in Rosalind during this scene? Record exactly where the shifts in mood occur, and think of an action or gesture that the actor playing Rosalind could make at these points to illustrate each emotion. In your Director's Journal, write out these stage directions with their relevant line references.

Characters 人物分析

Is Celia genuinely upset? (in pairs)

In the early scenes of the play, Celia had quite a large speaking role. Now, as Rosalind plays her love scenes with Orlando, Celia has less and less to say. She was silent in Act 3 Scene 6, and here she only gets the chance to act as 'priest' to 'marry' the lovers. At the scene's end, she has only six lines to express her feelings.

a At the end of this episode, is Celia exasperated or does she speak good-humouredly, using a mocking style that conceals genuine affection? What do Celia's comments below tell us about her at this point in the play?

- Celia criticises Rosalind for what she has said about women by referencing the proverb 'It is the foul bird that defiles its own nest' (only bad women criticise women) in line 164.
- When Rosalind tells of her deep love, Celia remarks that her love runs out as fast as it runs in (lines 168–9).
- To Rosalind's desire to find a shady spot to sigh for Orlando, Celia merely says 'And I'll sleep.' (line 176)

b Take parts as Celia and Rosalind, and read through lines 162–76 several times to explore different versions of Celia's feelings (exasperated, joking, genuinely annoyed, and so on). Does Rosalind listen to Celia at all, or is she completely caught up in her own emotions? Use the script to support your interpretation.

c Imagine Celia is sharing her observations of Rosalind's behaviour with a friend, or pouring her heart out to a counsellor. What would she say about the way things are going in the Forest of Arden? Improvise this imaginary conversation in modern English to further explore Celia's thoughts and feelings.

1 **in good earnest** 说真的
2 **by … dangerous** 凭着一切不危险（指亵渎神灵）的美丽（指恋人之间）誓言来发誓
3 **jot** 一点点
4 **pathetical** 可怜
5 **the gross band** 那一大帮人
6 **censure** 责备，批评
7 **religion** 信仰；真诚
8 **try** 裁判
9 **simply misused** 完全是在诋毁
10 **love-prate** 关于爱情的喋喋不休
11 **how many fathom deep** 多少寻深（fathom是英语国家测量水深的单位，合6英尺或1.8米；"寻"是中国古代长度单位，1寻等于8尺）
12 **sounded** 探测
13 **bastard of Venus** 维纳斯生的野种（指丘比特）
14 **begot of thought** 发端自相思
15 **conceived of spleen** 受孕于激情
16 **that blind rascally boy** 那个瞎眼的捣蛋鬼
17 **abuses** 捉弄

ORLANDO	Aye, sweet Rosalind.	150
ROSALIND	By my troth, and in good earnest[1], and so God mend me, and by all pretty oaths that are not dangerous[2], if you break one jot[3] of your promise or come one minute behind your hour, I will think you the most pathetical[4] break-promise, and the most hollow lover, and the most unworthy of her you call Rosalind that may be chosen out of the gross band[5] of the unfaithful. Therefore beware my censure[6], and keep your promise.	155
ORLANDO	With no less religion[7] than if thou wert indeed my Rosalind. So adieu.	
ROSALIND	Well, Time is the old justice that examines all such offenders, and let Time try[8]. Adieu.	160

Exit [Orlando]

CELIA	You have simply misused[9] our sex in your love-prate[10]. We must have your doublet and hose plucked over your head, and show the world what the bird hath done to her own nest.	
ROSALIND	O coz, coz, coz, my pretty little coz, that thou didst know how many fathom deep[11] I am in love! But it cannot be sounded[12]: my affection hath an unknown bottom like the Bay of Portugal.	165
CELIA	Or rather bottomless, that as fast as you pour affection in, it runs out.	
ROSALIND	No, that same wicked bastard of Venus[13] that was begot of thought[14], conceived of spleen[15], and born of madness, that blind rascally boy[16] that abuses[17] everyone's eyes because his own are out, let him be judge how deep I am in love. I'll tell thee, Aliena, I cannot be out of the sight of Orlando. I'll go find a shadow and sigh till he come.	170

175 |
| CELIA | And I'll sleep. | |

Exeunt

剧情简介： 杰奎提议把杀死鹿的大臣像凯旋的功臣一样引荐给老公爵。朝臣们唱的歌声称戴绿帽子是男人的宿命。

1 How would you present the scene?

Act 4 Scene 2 has been played in many different ways:

- as a celebration of hunting, of masculine strength and unity
- as a nightmare, where Celia dreams of Rosalind being hunted out of the forest
- as a reminder of the role reversals that take place in the Forest of Arden (the 'hunters' are in fact poachers [偷猎者] who are not authorised to kill the deer)
- as a continuation of the jokes about cuckoldry and marriage that have been linked to references to 'horns' in the play so far.

How would you stage the scene, and what would you want the audience to take away from it? Write programme notes in your Director's Journal to explain your choice, and to give your audience more information about what they are seeing on stage.

▼ Do you think that the production pictured here is presenting the scene in any of the ways described above? If not, what central interpretation do the costumes, postures and expressions of the actors suggest?

1	Roman conqueror	罗马征服者（凯旋的罗马军人会被授予橄榄枝头环）
2	branch of victory	胜利花环
3	burden	重担（这里指鹿皮和鹿角）
4	Take ... horn	戴这鹿角别脸红
5	a crest ... born	你出生之前它曾是英雄冠
6	lusty	雄姿勃发
7	laugh to scorn	取笑

Act 4 Scene 2
A glade in the Forest of Arden

Enter JAQUES *and* LORDS, FORESTERS
bearing the antlers and skin of a deer

JAQUES Which is he that killed the deer?

FIRST LORD Sir, it was I.

JAQUES Let's present him to the Duke like a Roman conqueror[1] – and it would do well to set the deer's horns upon his head for a branch of victory[2]. – Have you no song, forester, for this purpose?

FIRST FORESTER Yes, sir.

JAQUES Sing it. 'Tis no matter how it be in tune, so it make noise enough.

Music
Song

LORDS
What shall he have that killed the deer?
His leather skin and horns to wear.
Then sing him home,
The rest shall bear this burden[3]:

Take thou no scorn to wear the horn[4],
It was a crest ere thou wast born[5];
   Thy father's father wore it,
   And thy father bore it;
The horn, the horn, the lusty[6] horn,
Is not a thing to laugh to scorn[7].

Exeunt

Celia mocks Rosalind's impatience that Orlando is late. Silvius says that Phoebe's letter contains an angry message. Rosalind seems annoyed and criticises Phoebe.

 剧情简介：希丽叶嘲笑若泽兰对奥岚铎约会迟到缺乏耐心。悉尔维耶说菲妯的信中有一股恼怒之意。若泽兰似乎生气了，责骂菲妯。

1 Celia's prose and Silvius's verse (in pairs)

At the beginning of this scene, Celia seems tired of Rosalind and bored with her friend's game of love with Orlando. She speaks of going to sleep.

a Think about Celia's tone and mood here. What words convey her attitude, and how would you speak her lines of prose?

b The script changes from prose to verse with Silvius's entrance. Rewrite at least five lines of Silvius's poetry in prose, then read both versions out loud. Discuss what difference it makes to have Silvius speak in either verse or prose.

c In Shakespeare's plays, it is usually the aristocratic characters that speak in verse and the low-status or comic characters who speak in prose. Here, the pattern seems reversed. Discuss why you think this is, and what effect it might have on the audience.

2 Why is Rosalind so critical?

Silvius's 'Pardon me, / I am but as a guiltless messenger', spoken with an air of wide-eyed innocence, often gets a big laugh from the audience. Yet, after reading the letter, Rosalind calls Silvius a fool and launches an attack on Phoebe.

a Write out some of the insults that Rosalind uses in the script opposite. Then, in role as Rosalind, describe in writing what exactly you mean by these insults. Use the glossary on this page to help you.

b As Rosalind, write a confession to explain why you insulted Silvius and Phoebe so harshly, and why you are so critical of the messenger as well as the writer.

1 **And here much Orlando!** 这里来了不少奥岚铎！（这里是反话，正着说就是"哪里有奥岚铎的影子！"）
2 **I warrant you** 我向您保证
3 **waspish** 马蜂一般
4 **angry tenor** 恼怒之意
5 **play the swaggerer** 暴跳如雷
6 **bear this, bear all** 忍了这口气，一切都得忍；是可忍孰不可忍
7 **Her ... hunt** 她的爱并不是我要猎取的野兔（hare：野兔，指追猎的对象）
8 **protest** 发誓
9 **turned ... love** 被爱情冲昏了头
10 **leathern** 牛皮般
11 **freestone-coloured** 砂岩色
12 **hussif** = housewife
13 **she ... letter** 这封信绝非出自她的手
14 **man's invention and his hand** 男人的语言、男人的笔迹

Write about it 写作练习

An insulting letter

Read through lines 12–28, where Rosalind reacts to the contents of the letter. Write the insulting letter that you imagine Phoebe has sent to 'Ganymede'. Think about the following:

- In line 12, Rosalind says that even the personified figure of patience itself would lose its temper with the letter's author.
- In line 13, she says the letter is written to provoke her to violence.
- In line 19, she accuses Silvius of writing the letter because it is so masculine in its insulting content.

Act 4 Scene 3
The Forest of Arden

Enter ROSALIND (*as* GANYMEDE) *and* CELIA [*as* ALIENA]

ROSALIND How say you now, is it not past two o'clock? And here much Orlando![1]

CELIA I warrant you[2], with pure love and troubled brain he hath ta'en his bow and arrows and is gone forth – to sleep. Look who comes here.

Enter SILVIUS [*with a letter*]

SILVIUS My errand is to you, fair youth. 5
My gentle Phoebe did bid me give you this:
I know not the contents but, as I guess
By the stern brow and waspish[3] action
Which she did use as she was writing of it,
It bears an angry tenor[4]. Pardon me, 10
I am but as a guiltless messenger.

ROSALIND [*After reading the letter*] Patience herself would startle at this letter
And play the swaggerer[5]: bear this, bear all[6].
She says I am not fair, that I lack manners;
She calls me proud, and that she could not love me 15
Were man as rare as phoenix. Od's my will,
Her love is not the hare that I do hunt[7] –
Why writes she so to me? Well, shepherd, well?
This is a letter of your own device.

SILVIUS No, I protest[8], I know not the contents; 20
Phoebe did write it.

ROSALIND Come, come, you are a fool
And turned into the extremity of love[9].
I saw her hand, she has a leathern[10] hand,
A freestone-coloured[11] hand. (I verily did think
That her old gloves were on, but 'twas her hands.) 25
She has a hussif's[12] hand – but that's no matter.
I say she never did invent this letter[13]:
This is a man's invention and his hand.[14]

SILVIUS Sure, it is hers.

Rosalind claims that Phoebe's letter is full of insults. But when she reads the letter, it reveals that Phoebe is passionately in love with Ganymede and wants him to send a secret reply by Silvius.

 剧情简介：若泽兰声称菲妶的信充满羞辱之词，但读完此信却发现菲妶已疯狂爱上了甘尼密，而且想让甘尼密给自己秘密回个话，由悉尔维耶转达。

1 Silvius's reaction (in threes)

Rosalind so passionately denounces the insulting content of Phoebe's letter that Silvius wants to read what she has written. However, when Rosalind reads out the letter, it turns out to be quite different from what the listeners expected. Instead of attacking Ganymede, it describes him as a god who has become a man and conquered Phoebe's heart.

a Discuss why you think Rosalind is offended by the letter.

b Take turns to give a dramatic reading of the letter as if you are:
- the lovesick Phoebe
- the irritated and insulted Rosalind
- the confused Silvius.

c What effect does the revelation of the letter's actual content have on Silvius? Take parts and act out lines 30–62 to show Silvius's reactions to Rosalind's irritation and to the letter itself. Look especially at lines 36–7, 41 and 62.

2 Elizabethan language (in pairs)

Imagine that the actor playing Rosalind wants to cut lines 31–5 because they contain an offensive reference, using 'Ethiop' as a negative adjective to describe Phoebe's words. The director wants to keep these lines, and argues that Shakespeare's words are a reflection of his culture and not an indication that he is racist. In role as the actor or director, argue your case with your partner. Would you cut these lines, or change them, if you were directing the play?

Language in the play 剧中语言

New words

Shakespeare loved making up new words by putting two words together with a hyphen (连字符) or by using a noun as a verb (and vice versa).

a Find examples of both types of linguistic inventions in the script opposite. Then invent some new hyphenated words of your own – for example, alligator-hungry, dragon-scary, and so on.

b In line 38, Rosalind uses Phoebe's name as a verb: 'She Phoebes me' (meaning 'she insults me in her own typical style'). Invent similar phrases using your own name as a verb. What would your name mean and how would it be used?

1 boisterous 气势汹汹
2 A style for challengers 挑战的口气
3 defies 蔑视；挑战
4 Turk to Christian 土耳其人蔑视基督徒（二者是宿敌）
5 drop forth 生出
6 Ethiop 埃塞俄比亚人一般（喻指黑透了；这个词如今有种族主义色彩）
7 blacker … countenance 内容之黑甚于外表
8 Phoebes me 以她菲妶的一贯方式对我
9 rail thus 这样骂人
10 thy godhead laid apart 把你那圣洁的相放一边
11 Warr'st thou = Do you make war
12 do no vengeance to 奈何不了
13 eyne = eyes
14 mild aspect 和颜悦色
15 chid (chide的过去时形式)
16 seal up thy mind = make up your mind and seal it in a letter
17 kind 情爱
18 make 获得，赢得

ROSALIND	Why, a boisterous[1] and a cruel style,	30
	A style for challengers[2]. Why, she defies[3] me	
	Like Turk to Christian[4]. Woman's gentle brain	
	Could not drop forth[5] such giant-rude invention,	
	Such Ethiop[6] words, blacker in their effect	
	Than in their countenance[7]. Will you hear the letter?	35
SILVIUS	So please you, for I never heard it yet,	
	Yet heard too much of Phoebe's cruelty.	
ROSALIND	She Phoebes me[8]. Mark how the tyrant writes:	
	Reads 'Art thou god to shepherd turned,	
	That a maiden's heart hath burned?'	40
	Can a woman rail thus[9]?	
SILVIUS	Call you this railing?	
ROSALIND	*Reads* 'Why, thy godhead laid apart[10],	
	Warr'st thou[11] with a woman's heart?' –	
	Did you ever hear such railing? –	
	'Whiles the eye of man did woo me,	45
	That could do no vengeance to[12] me.' –	
	Meaning me a beast!	
	'If the scorn of your bright eyne[13]	
	Have power to raise such love in mine,	
	Alack, in me what strange effect	50
	Would they work in mild aspect[14]?	
	Whiles you chid[15] me, I did love;	
	How then might your prayers move?	
	He that brings this love to thee	
	Little knows this love in me;	55
	And by him seal up thy mind[16],	
	Whether that thy youth and kind[17]	
	Will the faithful offer take	
	Of me and all that I can make[18],	
	Or else by him my love deny,	60
	And then I'll study how to die.'	
SILVIUS	Call you this chiding?	
CELIA	Alas, poor shepherd.	

Rosalind rebukes Silvius for being made so feeble by love. Oliver recognises Aliena (Celia) and Ganymede (Rosalind) by their descriptions, and brings a bloody handkerchief from Orlando. He begins his story.

剧情简介：若泽兰责备悉尔维耶被爱情弄得憔悴不堪。奥利沃根据听到的描述，认出爱丽艾娜（希丽叶）和甘尼密（若泽兰），拿出来自奥岚铎的一条带血的手帕，开始讲述他的故事。

1 Dramatic grammar (by yourself)

Read the script opposite to yourself as you walk around the room. Repeat the grammar activity you did on pages 2 and 106, changing direction and making gestures as you walk to mark the punctuation.

- How might the grammatical structure of the script reflect Rosalind's feelings and experiences? What actions or gestures and what tone of voice might an actress use on stage to capture this?
- In your Director's Journal, write detailed stage directions describing how Rosalind might behave on stage and how Silvius might behave in response.

2 'Enter OLIVER' (in pairs)

Oliver, Orlando's wicked brother, was last seen in Act 3 Scene 1. He was being manhandled (推搡) by Duke Frederick's officers and was then sent off to capture Orlando, dead or alive. Now he appears again, seemingly a changed man. He brings news of Orlando, along with a bloodstained handkerchief.

- Before you read on in the script, discuss your predictions about how the handkerchief became stained. Make a guess about the part the handkerchief will play in the rest of the story.

Language in the play 剧中语言

The language of love at first sight (in small groups)

Although it is more obvious when you watch the play than when you read the script, Oliver and Celia fall in love at first sight.

a Suggest how you would stage lines 70–85 to give the audience the first hint of their mutual attraction. Does Oliver's and Celia's language hold any suggestion that they are immediately smitten (打击), or will you have to rely on stage business to show this?

b When Oliver enters at line 70, there is an abrupt movement from prose to verse. List any other poetic language features (for example, vocabulary, imagery, and so on) that you can find in the script opposite. Discuss what this shift in language might suggest about Oliver and the effect his sudden appearance might have on the women.

1 make thee an instrument 把你当作工具
2 false strains 虚情假意
3 tame snake 可怜虫
4 purlieus 边沿
5 down in the neighbour bottom 附近山谷里
6 rank of osiers 一排杨柳
7 the house doth keep itself 房子空守着屋子
8 an eye … tongue 眼睛受益于舌头
9 bestows himself 言谈举止
10 ripe sister 成熟的大姐
11 low 矮
12 napkin 手帕
13 Within an hour 一个钟头内；用不了多久
14 Chewing … fancy 咀嚼爱情结出的既甜蜜又苦涩的果子
15 Lo what befell 瞧，出什么事了
16 threw （目光）投向

ROSALIND	Do you pity him? No, he deserves no pity. – Wilt thou love such a woman? What, to make thee an instrument[1] and play false strains[2] upon thee? Not to be endured! Well, go your way to her – for I see love hath made thee a tame snake[3] – and say this to her: that if she love me, I charge her to love thee; if she will not, I will never have her, unless thou entreat for her. If you be a true lover, hence, and not a word; for here comes more company.	65

Exit Silvius

Enter OLIVER

OLIVER	Good morrow, fair ones. Pray you, if you know	70
	Where in the purlieus[4] of this forest stands	
	A sheepcote fenced about with olive-trees.	
CELIA	West of this place, down in the neighbour bottom[5];	
	The rank of osiers[6] by the murmuring stream,	
	Left on your right hand, brings you to the place.	75
	But at this hour the house doth keep itself[7]:	
	There's none within.	
OLIVER	If that an eye may profit by a tongue[8],	
	Then should I know you by description:	
	Such garments, and such years. 'The boy is fair,	80
	Of female favour, and bestows himself[9]	
	Like a ripe sister[10]; the woman low[11]	
	And browner than her brother.' Are not you	
	The owners of the house I did enquire for?	
CELIA	It is no boast, being asked, to say we are.	85
OLIVER	Orlando doth commend him to you both,	
	And to that youth he calls his Rosalind	
	He sends this bloody napkin[12]. Are you he?	
ROSALIND	I am. What must we understand by this?	
OLIVER	Some of my shame, if you will know of me	90
	What man I am, and how, and why, and where	
	This handkerchief was stained.	
CELIA	I pray you tell it.	
OLIVER	When last the young Orlando parted from you,	
	He left a promise to return again	
	Within an hour[13] and, pacing through the forest,	95
	Chewing the food of sweet and bitter fancy[14],	
	Lo what befell[15]. He threw[16] his eye aside	
	And mark what object did present itself.	

Oliver relates how Orlando saw an unkempt sleeping man threatened by a snake and lion. Orlando recognised the man as his brother, and killed the lion. Oliver reveals he was the sleeping man.

剧情简介：奥利沃讲述奥岚铎看到一个衣衫褴褛的昏睡男子受到蛇和狮子的威胁，认出这男子是自己的兄长，于是杀死了狮子。奥利沃透露自己就是那个昏睡男子。

Stagecraft 导演技巧

Staging the story (in small groups)

The story Oliver tells is improbable and melodramatic (耸人听闻). It is an example of the conventions of literary pastoral, in which forests can contain all kinds of exotic animals and give rise to fantastical events.

Work out how you would present Oliver's story on stage, and how you would direct the two women to react. Use the following points to help your preparation:

- To whom does Oliver tell his story: Celia, Rosalind, or both?
- Identify the personal pronoun in line 127 – is it a slip of the tongue or the way by which Oliver tactfully identifies himself?
- How does Celia behave when Oliver reveals his identity?
- Does Oliver listen to Rosalind, or is he completely caught up with (迷上) Celia?
- How could you use different visual effects to show Oliver's story as he recounts it? For instance, the different events could be acted out by people in costume, shown in silhouette (剪影) behind a curtain or illustrated by artworks and video clips.

1 bald 光秃
2 dry antiquity 干瘪老旧
3 green and gilded 金绿交错
4 wreathed 缠绕
5 indented glides 蜿蜒滑行
6 with udders all drawn dry 乳房完全干瘪了 (udder: 乳房)
7 couching 蹲伏
8 render 描述
9 unnatural 没有天良
10 kindness 善心
11 just occasion 正当（即复仇）的时机
12 hurtling 打斗
13 miserable slumber 悲催的昏睡（奥利沃改头换面之前的精神状态）
14 contrive 设计
15 do not shame 不以为耻
16 conversion 改过自新
17 for = what about

	Under an old oak whose boughs were mossed with age,	
	And high top bald[1] with dry antiquity[2],	100
	A wretched ragged man, o'ergrown with hair,	
	Lay sleeping on his back; about his neck	
	A green and gilded[3] snake had wreathed[4] itself,	
	Who, with her head, nimble in threats, approached	
	The opening of his mouth. But suddenly	105
	Seeing Orlando, it unlinked itself	
	And with indented glides[5] did slip away	
	Into a bush; under which bush's shade	
	A lioness, with udders all drawn dry[6],	
	Lay couching[7] head on ground, with cat-like watch	110
	When that the sleeping man should stir – for 'tis	
	The royal disposition of that beast	
	To prey on nothing that doth seem as dead.	
	This seen, Orlando did approach the man	
	And found it was his brother, his elder brother.	115
CELIA	O, I have heard him speak of that same brother,	
	And he did render[8] him the most unnatural[9]	
	That lived amongst men.	
OLIVER	And well he might so do,	
	For well I know he was unnatural.	
ROSALIND	But to Orlando – did he leave him there,	120
	Food to the sucked and hungry lioness?	
OLIVER	Twice did he turn his back and purposed so.	
	But kindness[10], nobler ever than revenge,	
	And nature, stronger than his just occasion[11],	
	Made him give battle to the lioness,	125
	Who quickly fell before him; in which hurtling[12]	
	From miserable slumber[13] I awaked.	
CELIA	Are you his brother?	
ROSALIND	Was't you he rescued?	
CELIA	Was't you that did so oft contrive[14] to kill him?	
OLIVER	'Twas I, but 'tis not I. I do not shame[15]	130
	To tell you what I was, since my conversion[16]	
	So sweetly tastes, being the thing I am.	
ROSALIND	But for[17] the bloody napkin?	

Oliver relates how Orlando fainted, then recovered and sent Oliver with the bloodstained handkerchief to Rosalind. She faints, recovers and pretends her swooning is a pretence.

 剧情简介：奥利沃说奥岚铎先是昏迷，然后苏醒，并派奥利沃把那条带血的手帕带给若泽兰。若泽兰听后昏倒，醒来后谎称自己的昏倒是假装的。

Stagecraft 导演技巧

Ganymede or Rosalind? (in small groups)

The final moments of Act 4 are rich in comic and dramatic possibilities. While some critics think that Oliver is totally caught up with Celia, with whom he has fallen in love, others think that he sees through Rosalind's disguise and realises she is a woman.

a Talk together about the different comic and dramatic effects that could be achieved if Oliver knows or suspects that Ganymede is really Rosalind in disguise. Use the following questions to guide your discussion:

- At what moments does Rosalind seem close to blowing her cover (卸下伪装)?
- Does Celia give the game away at line 154?
- Does Oliver begin to suspect that Ganymede is not a boy when he carries out the stage direction '*Raising Rosalind*' at line 155?
- Is Oliver's use of Rosalind's name at line 170 a good-humoured signal that he has seen through her disguise?

b Decide what interpretation you think would work best on stage, and make detailed notes in your Director's Journal.

Characters 人物分析

Oliver's conversion (in pairs)

What conversion did Oliver have? Oliver uses religious language to describe the difference between his shameful past and his converted present (lines 130–2). He also employs religious language when, a few lines earlier, he recounts Orlando's forgiveness and his willingness to suffer harm so Oliver could escape injury.

a What do you think it was that caused such a dramatic change of heart, and character, in Oliver? Was Oliver converted by Orlando's acts of forgiveness and mercy towards him? Or do you believe something else happened before this? Discuss these questions with your partner. Try to support your ideas with evidence from the script.

b Take parts and improvise a conversation between Oliver and Orlando just after the rescue from the lion. How does Oliver describe his conversion to Orlando? How does Orlando respond?

1 By and by   很快
2 recountments   讲述
3 kindly   自然，亲切
4 As   比如
5 desert place   荒野
6 array   衣物
7 Brief = In brief
8 recovered   使苏醒
9 after some small space   过了一小会儿
10 in sport   戏谑
11 lack a man's heart   缺少男人的心肠
12 a body   任何人
13 well counterfeited   装得很像
14 testimony   证据
15 passion of earnest   真情实意
16 draw = let's turn (回转)
17 excuse   原谅

OLIVER	By and by[1].	
	When from the first to last betwixt us two,	
	Tears our recountments[2] had most kindly[3] bathed –	135
	As[4] how I came into that desert place[5] –	
	In brief, he led me to the gentle Duke	
	Who gave me fresh array[6] and entertainment,	
	Committing me unto my brother's love,	
	Who led me instantly unto his cave;	140
	There stripped himself and here, upon his arm,	
	The lioness had torn some flesh away,	
	Which all this while had bled; and now he fainted,	
	And cried in fainting upon Rosalind.	
	Brief[7], I recovered[8] him, bound up his wound,	145
	And, after some small space[9], being strong at heart,	
	He sent me hither, stranger as I am,	
	To tell this story that you might excuse	
	His broken promise, and to give this napkin,	
	Dyed in this blood, unto the shepherd youth	150
	That he in sport[10] doth call his Rosalind.	
	[*Rosalind faints*]	
CELIA	Why, how now? Ganymede, sweet Ganymede!	
OLIVER	Many will swoon when they do look on blood.	
CELIA	There is more in it. – Cousin! Ganymede!	
OLIVER	[*Raising Rosalind*] Look, he recovers.	155
ROSALIND	I would I were at home.	
CELIA	We'll lead you thither. – I pray you, will you take him by the arm.	
OLIVER	Be of good cheer, youth. You a man? You lack a man's heart[11].	
ROSALIND	I do so, I confess it. Ah, sirrah, a body[12] would think this was well counterfeited[13]. I pray you tell your brother how well I counterfeited. Heigh-ho!	160
OLIVER	This was not counterfeit: there is too great testimony[14] in your complexion that it was a passion of earnest[15].	
ROSALIND	Counterfeit, I assure you.	
OLIVER	Well then, take a good heart, and counterfeit to be a man.	165
ROSALIND	So I do. But, i'faith, I should have been a woman by right.	
CELIA	Come, you look paler and paler: pray you, draw[16] homewards. – Good sir, go with us.	
OLIVER	That will I. For I must bear answer back how you excuse[17] my brother, Rosalind.	170
ROSALIND	I shall devise something. But I pray you commend my counterfeiting to him. Will you go?	

Exeunt

As You Like It
各如所愿

Looking back at Act 4 第4幕回顾
Activities for groups or individuals

1 Jaques's melancholy – the four humours

In Scene 1, Jaques declares that he has his own, very special melancholy. A popular belief in Shakespeare's time was that personality was determined by four 'humours' (fluids in the human body). These were blood (producing bravery), phlegm (痰) (producing calmness), 'yellowe' (黄胆汁) (producing anger) and black bile (黑胆汁) (pro-ducing melancholy). The belief was that if the four humours were in balance, a person would be healthy and temperate, but if one humour dominated, the result was an unbalanced personality.

◆ Imagine what Jaques would be like if he had an excess of 'blood' or 'phlegm', rather than 'black bile'. What would he say or do at key points in the play if his personality and behaviour were influenced by a different imbalance of humours? How might his language and ideas change?

2 A transitional act?

Act 4, with its three scenes, is the shortest in the play, but it seems to include several key turning points.

◆ What important transitions have taken place in this act? What do you think is the significance of Scene 2 within the action of the play so far?

◆ Imagine that you are writing notes on Act 4 to help a younger student who has also just finished reading the act. They have not had a chance to see a performance of the play, so how would you encourage them to visualise this act's key moments and characters?

3 Oliver's conversion

Oliver's conversion from a vengeful (心存报复), hateful brother into a kind and thoughtful one is extreme; the actor playing Oliver faces a challenging task in making this change appear credible.

◆ In role as an actor playing Oliver, write out the challenges of making such a change in the way you portray the character. How do you understand the conversion that Oliver has had? How can you make his reformed character believable, and how do you change the way he looks, speaks and moves to show this change of heart?

4 Rosalind's mood changes

Rosalind experiences violent swings of emotion during Scenes 1 and 3.

◆ Find three different ways of visually presenting her shifts of mood – perhaps as a graph, a mime and a trio of drawings. Write notes on each, explaining what it shows and why you chose to use this method of representation.

5 Love is in the air

There are four pairs of lovers in the play so far: Rosalind/Orlando; Touchstone/Audrey; Phoebe/Silvius; Celia/Oliver.

◆ In pairs, create a tableau for each couple. Try to capture their relationship so that another pair can guess who you are representing each time. When the other pair guesses correctly, stay in role for a minute longer and speak your thoughts and feelings about the other person.

Write an extended piece in which you compare and contrast the different kinds of love that have been explored in the play so far. Include a discussion of other kinds of love in addition to romantic love, such as the sisterly love between Rosalind and Celia or the strong loyalty that Adam has for Orlando.

Audrey regrets that Sir Oliver Martext did not marry her to Touchstone. She denies that William has any claim on her. William enters, and Touchstone begins to mock him.

 剧情简介：奥卓依对奥利沃•马泰克斯牧师没有把她嫁给试金石感到遗憾，否认威廉向自己求婚。威廉上场，试金石开始嘲笑他。

1 Touchstone's wisecracks (in threes)

Touchstone takes great delight in taunting (嘲笑) William, who he thinks is also interested in Audrey. Take parts and read through the script opposite. Discuss the following questions and make notes to help you refine a second reading of this section.

- Does Touchstone speak lines 8–10 to Audrey, to himself or to the audience? What option would you advise the actor to take, and why? How does each variation indicate a different intent?
- What comic business might you make out of the internal stage direction 'cover thy head', which is repeated in lines 14–15?
- William thanks God that he was born in the forest. Touchstone echoes (附和) him and agrees, but what else might he mean here? How might he share this joke with the audience or with Audrey?
- The 'saying' Touchstone suddenly remembers in lines 27–8 provides another comic moment. Write out in modern English what Touchstone is really saying. Bear this clearer meaning in mind when delivering – or reacting to – these lines.
- Do you think William would understand what Touchstone is saying on stage?

1	gentle	好
2	the old gentleman	那位老绅士（指杰奎）
3	lays claim to	向……求婚
4	He … world	他跟我毫无关系
5	clown	乡巴佬
6	have good wits	脑子健全
7	shall be flouting	要取笑他人
8	cannot hold	按捺不住
9	God ye good ev'n	= God give you a good evening
10	ripe age	大好年纪
11	so-so	马马虎虎

Write about it 写作练习

William's role in the play (in pairs)

Why did Shakespeare include William in the play? In the pairings that appear to be shaping up, Touchstone and Audrey already seem committed. To introduce a new character so late in the play, when everyone is apparently coupled up already, seems odd.

a Discuss whether William is there:
- to show who Audrey's 'natural' partner should be, and thus to challenge Touchstone
- to provide yet another perspective on love
- and/or as further fun, to keep the audience amused throughout the final act.

b Improvise a conversation between a director and the actor playing William, to show how each of them understands William's role in the play.

Act 5 Scene 1
The Forest of Arden

Enter TOUCHSTONE *and* AUDREY

TOUCHSTONE We shall find a time, Audrey; patience, gentle[1] Audrey.

AUDREY Faith, the priest was good enough, for all the old gentleman's[2] saying.

TOUCHSTONE A most wicked Sir Oliver, Audrey, a most vile Martext. But, Audrey, there is a youth here in the forest lays claim to[3] you.

AUDREY Aye, I know who 'tis. He hath no interest in me in the world[4].

Enter WILLIAM

Here comes the man you mean.

TOUCHSTONE It is meat and drink to me to see a clown[5]. By my troth, we that have good wits[6] have much to answer for. We shall be flouting[7]; we cannot hold[8].

WILLIAM Good ev'n, Audrey.

AUDREY God ye good ev'n[9], William.

WILLIAM [*Taking off his hat*] And good ev'n to you, sir.

TOUCHSTONE Good ev'n, gentle friend. Cover thy head, cover thy head. Nay prithee, be covered. How old are you, friend?

WILLIAM Five and twenty, sir.

TOUCHSTONE A ripe age[10]. Is thy name William?

WILLIAM William, sir.

TOUCHSTONE A fair name. Wast born i'th'forest here?

WILLIAM Aye, sir, I thank God.

TOUCHSTONE 'Thank God': a good answer. Art rich?

WILLIAM Faith, sir, so-so[11].

TOUCHSTONE 'So-so' is good, very good, very excellent good – and yet it is not: it is but so-so. Art thou wise?

WILLIAM Aye, sir, I have a pretty wit.

TOUCHSTONE Why, thou say'st well. I do now remember a saying: 'The fool doth think he is wise, but the wise man knows himself to be a fool.'

Touchstone bamboozles William with impressive-sounding but empty language. He says that he, not William, must marry Audrey, and threatens William with all kinds of punishments.

剧情简介：试金石用一些听着高深实则空洞的语言来忽悠威廉，说他，而非威廉，一定要娶奥卓依，还用各种惩罚吓唬威廉。

1 'Country bumpkin'? (in pairs)

The encounter between Touchstone and William is another example of the conflict between court and country. Touchstone is determined to show the superiority of the court, and he talks a good deal of high-flown (浮夸) nonsense in order to get the better of William. He contemptuously (轻蔑) refers to ordinary language as 'the vulgar (粗俗)' and 'the boorish (粗野)' and translates everything into 'common' language so that William can understand.

a Is William cleverer than Touchstone gives him credit for? Would you want Touchstone to be obviously condescending (居高临下) and patronising (高傲) in this scene, or to hide his sharp wit behind friendly gestures and mannerisms (言谈举止)?

b Take parts for a dramatic reading of lines 31–50. Before you begin, prepare by carefully selecting specific words for emphasis and thinking of gestures that will complement your interpretation of each character.

2 Act out the scene

a How would you cast William and how you would advise him to act towards Touchstone? Think especially about how you want the audience to feel towards William. In one production, William stood wide-eyed and open-mouthed – this provoked Touchstone's remark about the heathen (异教徒) philosopher in lines 29–31. In another, as Touchstone finished his threats, William seized him and almost strangled (勒死) him until Audrey pleaded 'Do, good William.'

b Look at the image on this page, and list the directorial choices that have gone into the production. Beside this list, write what features you would either keep or change if you were directing a production of the play.

1 learned 念过书
2 figure in rhetoric 修辞格
3 consent 承认
4 *ip*se 他（拉丁文）
5 to wit 或者说
6 translate 把……变成
7 deal in 用……打交道
8 bastinado 棒子
9 steel 钢刀
10 bandy with thee in faction 用行动跟你过招
11 o'errun 打倒
12 policy 阴谋诡计
13 Trip 快走
14 I attend 我就来

[William gapes]

The heathen philosopher, when he had a desire to eat a grape, would open his lips when he put it into his mouth, meaning thereby that grapes were made to eat and lips to open. You do love this maid?

WILLIAM   I do, sir.

TOUCHSTONE   Give me your hand. Art thou learned[1]?

WILLIAM   No, sir.

TOUCHSTONE   Then learn this of me: to have is to have. For it is a figure in rhetoric[2] that drink, being poured out of a cup into a glass, by filling the one doth empty the other. For all your writers do consent[3] that '*ipse*'[4] is he. Now you are not *ipse*, for I am he.

WILLIAM   Which he, sir?

TOUCHSTONE   He, sir, that must marry this woman. Therefore, you clown, abandon, which is in the vulgar 'leave', the society, which in the boorish is 'company', of this female, which in the common is 'woman': which together is 'abandon the society of this female'; or, clown, thou perishest or, to thy better understanding, 'diest', or, to wit[5], 'I kill thee', 'make thee away', 'translate'[6] thy life into death, thy liberty into bondage'! I will deal in[7] poison with thee, or in bastinado[8], or in steel[9]! I will bandy with thee in faction[10], I will o'errun[11] thee with policy[12] – I will kill thee a hundred and fifty ways! Therefore, tremble and depart.

AUDREY   Do, good William.

WILLIAM   God rest you merry, sir.

Exit

Enter CORIN

CORIN   Our master and mistress seeks you. Come away, away.

TOUCHSTONE   Trip[13], Audrey, trip, Audrey. – I attend[14], I attend.

Exeunt

Oliver confirms that he instantly fell in love with Celia. He promises to give Orlando all his inheritance. Rosalind describes how Oliver and Celia fell in love at first sight and now long for marriage.

 剧情简介：奥利沃确认他一眼就爱上了希丽叶，答应把所有继承的财产都留给奥岚铎。若泽兰描述奥利沃和希丽叶如何一见钟情，现在渴望结婚。

Language in the play 剧中语言

The speed of love, the speed of speech? (in threes)

The prevailing theme in the script opposite is the speed of love. Shakespeare provides Orlando, Oliver and Rosalind with a language style that matches the rapidity of falling in love at first sight. All three have speeches that pile item on item, event on event, in rapid succession.

a Take parts and experiment with ways of speaking the three characters' speeches on time (lines 1–3, 4–9 and 24–33). Do you think they should be spoken as quickly as possible, or with distinct pauses between each section? Or perhaps in some other way?

b Identify the following language features in the script opposite, and devise a suitable form of delivery or dramatic gesture for each one:

- **polyptoton** (一词多形法) – the repetition of words that are derived from the same root, but have different endings or forms
- **anaphora** (首语叠用) – the repetition of the same word at the beginning of successive sentences or clauses
- **alliteration** (头韵) – the repetition of consonants at the beginning of successive words.

c In role as voice and language coaches for a modern production, write out advice for the actors playing Orlando, Oliver and Rosalind. Help them to understand the meanings and nuances (细微差别) of the words in their speeches at this point then advise on their pronunciation and dramatic delivery.

1 grant 答应
2 persevere 坚持
3 Neither … question 一定别考虑考虑不周的问题
4 the poverty of her 她家太穷（她结婚带不来任何金钱、土地或嫁妆）
5 sudden 仓促
6 revenue 收入
7 estate upon 赠予
8 all's contented followers 所有他那些自得的追随者
9 scarf 绷带
10 I know where you are 我明白您的意思
11 thrasonical brag 自吹自擂
12 in these degrees 这样一步一步
13 climb incontinent 迫不及待地爬上去
14 be incontinent before marriage 婚前就耐不住了
15 wrath of love 热恋
16 clubs 棍棒

1 Does Orlando know Ganymede is Rosalind?
(in threes)

Oliver greets Rosalind as 'fair "sister"' (line 13) and Orlando says that his brother told him of 'greater wonders' than how Ganymede pretended to faint. Rosalind replies that Oliver is referring to his and Celia's love at first sight. But are these 'greater wonders' the fact that Orlando now sees through her disguise as Ganymede?

a Take parts and act out lines 1–58 in two ways:

- first, as if Orlando is still innocent of the disguises and counterfeits of Rosalind
- second, as if he is fully aware that she has been playing an elaborate game with him.

b Discuss which interpretation feels most appropriate to you at this point in the play, and the implications of each.

Act 5 Scene 2
The Forest of Arden

Enter ORLANDO *and* OLIVER

ORLANDO Is't possible that on so little acquaintance you should like her, that, but seeing, you should love her, and, loving, woo, and, wooing, she should grant[1]? And will you persevere[2] to enjoy her?

OLIVER Neither call the giddiness of it in question[3]; the poverty of her[4], the small acquaintance, my sudden[5] wooing, nor her sudden consenting. But say with me I love Aliena; say with her that she loves me; consent with both, that we may enjoy each other. It shall be to your good, for my father's house and all the revenue[6] that was old Sir Roland's will I estate upon[7] you, and here live and die a shepherd.

Enter ROSALIND [*as* GANYMEDE]

ORLANDO You have my consent. Let your wedding be tomorrow; thither will I invite the Duke and all's contented followers[8]. Go you, and prepare Aliena, for look you, here comes my 'Rosalind'.

ROSALIND God save you, brother.

OLIVER And you, fair 'sister'.   [*Exit*]

ROSALIND O, my dear Orlando, how it grieves me to see thee wear thy heart in a scarf[9].

ORLANDO It is my arm.

ROSALIND I thought thy heart had been wounded with the claws of a lion.

ORLANDO Wounded it is, but with the eyes of a lady.

ROSALIND Did your brother tell you how I counterfeited to swoon when he showed me your handkerchief?

ORLANDO Aye, and greater wonders than that.

ROSALIND O, I know where you are[10]. Nay, 'tis true, there was never anything so sudden but the fight of two rams, and Caesar's thrasonical brag[11] of 'I came, saw, and overcame.' For your brother and my sister no sooner met but they looked; no sooner looked, but they loved; no sooner loved, but they sighed; no sooner sighed, but they asked one another the reason; no sooner knew the reason, but they sought the remedy; and in these degrees[12] have they made a pair of stairs to marriage, which they will climb incontinent[13] – or else be incontinent before marriage[14]. They are in the very wrath of love[15], and they will together – clubs[16] cannot part them.

Orlando says that Oliver's joy at marriage will match his own sadness in not having Rosalind. She claims special powers, and promises he will marry her tomorrow. Phoebe complains about Rosalind's unkind action.

 剧情简介：奥岚铎说，奥利沃对婚姻的喜悦与自己没有娶到若泽兰的悲伤相互映衬。若泽兰声称自己有特异功能，并许诺奥岚铎第二天娶到若泽兰。菲妪抱怨若泽兰不与人为善。

Characters 人物分析

Orlando's heavy heart

Whether he is aware or not of Rosalind's real identity, Orlando seems to be tiring of the game. Oliver's happiness appears to plunge Orlando into sadness and bitterness.

- How realistic do you think Shakespeare's depiction of Orlando's state of mind is at this point? When others close to you are happy, do you feel yourself reflecting on your own unhappiness? Consider this as you write advice to Orlando to try to lift his spirits.

1 A change of language? (in pairs)

Rosalind wants Orlando to believe she has benign magical powers and will ensure he marries her the next day when Celia and Oliver marry.

a Read lines 41–54 and discuss how you think Rosalind should deliver this speech. Do not worry if you find the third sentence difficult to understand: most people do. It means something like: 'I say that you are intelligent, not to get you to think well of me; the only esteem I want is from helping you, not to improve my own reputation.'

b Take turns to experiment with different styles (mysterious, business-like, serious, provocative, formal, humorous, and so on) of reading out Rosalind's speech. Then write a detailed stage direction at line 46, giving advice to the actor playing Rosalind.

2 A change of pace? (in small groups)

The entrance of Silvius and Phoebe is again marked by a change from prose to verse. The first instance of this, in Act 4 Scene 3, was explored in Activity 1 on page 122.

a Discuss the following questions in groups:
- What do you think the shift from prose to verse, along with the entrance of Silvius and Phoebe, might indicate at this point in the play?
- What do you predict will happen from now until the end of the play?

b Write a paragraph each, describing and explaining what you think will happen from this point on. Think about ideas that other people raised in the discussion and whether or not you agree with them. You should also refer to what Rosalind has just said in lines 56–9.

1 nuptial 婚礼
2 serve your turn for 为您效力 充当
3 speak to some purpose 说正经的
4 good conceit 明晓事理
5 insomuch = in that（因为）
6 grace me 给我脸上贴金
7 do strange things 做出奇妙的事情
8 art 法术
9 not damnable 不作恶
10 gesture 外表
11 straits of fortune 艰难处境
12 Speak'st thou in sober meanings? 你说话当真？
13 tender dearly 珍贵，珍视
14 bid 邀请
15 study 故意为之
16 despiteful 鄙夷一切，不可一世
17 followed 追求

ORLANDO They shall be married tomorrow and I will bid the Duke to the nuptial[1]. But O, how bitter a thing it is to look into happiness through another man's eyes. By so much the more shall I tomorrow be at the height of heart-heaviness, by how much I shall think my brother happy in having what he wishes for.

ROSALIND Why then, tomorrow, I cannot serve your turn for[2] Rosalind?

ORLANDO I can live no longer by thinking.

ROSALIND I will weary you then no longer with idle talking. Know of me, then – for now I speak to some purpose[3] – that I know you are a gentleman of good conceit[4]. I speak not this that you should bear a good opinion of my knowledge, insomuch[5], I say, I know you are; neither do I labour for a greater esteem than may in some little measure draw a belief from you to do yourself good, and not to grace me[6]. Believe then, if you please, that I can do strange things[7]. I have, since I was three year old, conversed with a magician, most profound in his art[8], and yet not damnable[9]. If you do love Rosalind so near the heart as your gesture[10] cries it out, when your brother marries Aliena shall you marry her. I know into what straits of fortune[11] she is driven, and it is not impossible to me, if it appear not inconvenient to you, to set her before your eyes tomorrow, human as she is, and without any danger.

ORLANDO Speak'st thou in sober meanings?[12]

ROSALIND By my life, I do, which I tender dearly[13], though I say I am a magician. Therefore put you in your best array, bid[14] your friends. For if you will be married tomorrow, you shall, and to Rosalind, if you will.

Enter SILVIUS *and* PHOEBE

Look, here comes a lover of mine and a lover of hers.

PHOEBE Youth, you have done me much ungentleness
To show the letter that I writ to you.

ROSALIND I care not if I have. It is my study[15]
To seem despiteful[16] and ungentle to you.
You are there followed[17] by a faithful shepherd;
Look upon him, love him: he worships you.

As Silvius speaks his litany of what it is to love, Phoebe, Orlando and Rosalind echo and endorse his feelings. Rosalind gives orders for them all to meet tomorrow, when their desires will be fulfilled.

剧情简介：悉尔维耶喋喋不休地阐述爱情时，菲妣、奥岚铎和若泽兰纷纷给予回应并赞同他的观点。若泽兰命令他们明天碰头，届时他们会各如所愿。

At the end of the scene, Rosalind promises to fulfil everyone's desires as long as they keep to their word. Should she deliver these lines in a comic or a serious style?

1 fantasy 幻想
2 observance 服从
3 trial 验证；磨炼
4 Irish wolves 爱尔兰的狼群（或许是因为狼的嚎叫十分单调，或出自爱尔兰人可以变化成狼的典故）
5 fail 缺席，失约

Write about it 写作练习

'what 'tis to love' (in pairs)

Phoebe's request in line 66 is interrupted until line 78, when Silvius gives his description of what it is to love. Read lines 78–82. Do you agree with his definition of true love? Write your own response to Phoebe's request. Use the same style as Silvius but include your own ideas.

1 Howling of Irish wolves (in fives)

In line 92, Rosalind tells everyone to stop speaking, saying ''tis like the howling of Irish wolves against the moon'. What might be happening on stage to make her say this?

Take parts and read through lines 67–91. Experiment with ways of bringing to life the repetition and language patterns in this part of the script. You should also consider:

- giving each character a different gesture or movement at each echo of the other characters' lines
- having the characters talk over each other or at the same time, like an operatic chorus (歌剧合唱)
- depicting the increasing frustration of Rosalind until her outburst in line 92.

PHOEBE	Good shepherd, tell this youth what 'tis to love.	
SILVIUS	It is to be all made of sighs and tears,	
	And so am I for Phoebe.	
PHOEBE	And I for Ganymede.	70
ORLANDO	And I for Rosalind.	
ROSALIND	And I for no woman.	
SILVIUS	It is to be all made of faith and service,	
	And so am I for Phoebe.	
PHOEBE	And I for Ganymede.	75
ORLANDO	And I for Rosalind.	
ROSALIND	And I for no woman.	
SILVIUS	It is to be all made of fantasy[1],	
	All made of passion, and all made of wishes,	
	All adoration, duty, and observance[2],	80
	All humbleness, all patience, and impatience,	
	All purity, all trial[3], all obedience;	
	And so am I for Phoebe.	
PHOEBE	And so am I for Ganymede.	
ORLANDO	And so am I for Rosalind.	85
ROSALIND	And so am I for no woman.	
PHOEBE	[*To Rosalind*] If this be so, why blame you me to love you?	
SILVIUS	[*To Phoebe*] If this be so, why blame you me to love you?	
ORLANDO	If this be so, why blame you me to love you?	
ROSALIND	Who do you speak to 'Why blame you me to love you'?	90
ORLANDO	To her that is not here, nor doth not hear.	

ROSALIND Pray you no more of this: 'tis like the howling of Irish wolves[4] against the moon. [*To Silvius*] I will help you, if I can. [*To Phoebe*] I would love you, if I could. – Tomorrow meet me all together. – [*To Phoebe*] I will marry you, if ever I marry woman, and I'll be married tomorrow. [*To Orlando*] I will satisfy you, if ever I satisfy man, and you shall be married tomorrow. [*To Silvius*] I will content you, if what pleases you contents you, and you shall be married tomorrow. [*To Orlando*] As you love Rosalind, meet; [*To Silvius*] As you love Phoebe, meet – and as I love no woman, I'll meet. So fare you well: I have left you commands.

SILVIUS I'll not fail[5], if I live.
PHOEBE Nor I.
ORLANDO Nor I.

Exeunt

Touchstone and Audrey look forward to their marriage. The two Pages sing of springtime as the time for young lovers, even though life is brief.

 剧情简介：试金石和奥卓依期待着他们的婚礼。老公爵的两位侍童把春天歌颂为年轻人恋爱的季节，哪怕生命短暂。

1 Sing it! (in large groups)

The Pages' song seems to have two dramatic purposes:

- first, to mark the passage of time between Scenes 2 and 4 (between Rosalind's instructions to prepare for marriage and the ceremony in the final scene)
- second, to echo the theme of love now that all the lovers are preparing for marriage.

a Choose a new soundtrack (配乐) for this scene. Which modern songs can you think of that would be appropriate?

b Try singing the original song from the script. Theatre productions of the play often set the song's lyrics to the music below, which was composed in 1600 by Thomas Morley. Play this tune on a piano or keyboard, and perform it to another group. Try to use gestures and actions that relate to the lyrics.

1	dishonest 不正当
2	woman of the world 出嫁的女人（本义指进入社会之后的女人）
3	honest gentleman 尊贵的大人
4	clap into't roundly 拍手就唱
5	hawking 清嗓子
6	only 主要
7	prologues 开场白
8	like … horse 像两个吉卜赛人同骑一匹马
9	ring-time 戴婚戒的时间（ring 有多重意思：交换戒指、奏响快乐的婚礼钟声、跳圆圈舞）
10	carol 欢快的歌曲

Act 5 Scene 3
The Forest of Arden

Enter TOUCHSTONE *and* AUDREY

TOUCHSTONE Tomorrow is the joyful day, Audrey; tomorrow will we be married.

AUDREY I do desire it with all my heart, and I hope it is no dishonest[1] desire to desire to be a woman of the world[2]?

Enter two PAGES

Here come two of the banished Duke's pages.

FIRST PAGE Well met, honest gentleman[3].

TOUCHSTONE By my troth, well met. Come, sit, sit, and a song.

SECOND PAGE We are for you; sit i'th'middle.

FIRST PAGE Shall we clap into't roundly[4], without hawking[5], or spitting, or saying we are hoarse, which are the only[6] prologues[7] to a bad voice?

SECOND PAGE Aye, faith, i'faith, and both in a tune like two gipsies on a horse[8].

FIRST AND SECOND PAGE It was a lover and his lass,
　　　With a hey, and a ho, and a hey nonny-no,
　　　That o'er the green cornfield did pass,
　　　　In spring-time,
　　　　The only pretty ring-time[9],
　　　　　When birds do sing;
　　　　Hey ding a-ding, ding,
　　　　　Sweet lovers love the spring.

　　　Between the acres of the rye,
　　　With a hey, and a ho, and a hey nonny-no,
　　　These pretty country folks would lie,
　　　　In spring-time,
　　　　The only pretty ring-time,
　　　　　When birds do sing;
　　　　Hey ding a-ding, ding,
　　　　　Sweet lovers love the spring.

　　　This carol[10] they began that hour,
　　　With a hey, and a ho, and a hey nonny-no,
　　　How that a life was but a flower;
　　　　In spring-time,
　　　　The only pretty ring-time,

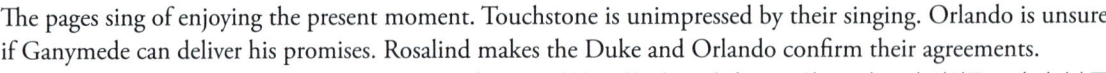

The pages sing of enjoying the present moment. Touchstone is unimpressed by their singing. Orlando is unsure if Ganymede can deliver his promises. Rosalind makes the Duke and Orlando confirm their agreements.

剧情简介：两位侍童哼唱着纵情享乐的歌谣。面对他们的歌唱试金石不为所动。奥岚铎不确定甘尼密能否兑现其承诺。若泽兰让公爵和奥岚铎重申其约定。

Themes 主题分析

Carpe diem (把握现在) – seize the day

The Pages' song highlights the brevity of human life, and advises that present happiness should be seized and enjoyed. The theme of the song is *carpe diem*, a Latin quotation meaning 'seize the day', taken from the Roman poet Horace.

- One of the themes of the play is time and timelessness. Revisit your responses to the activities on page 56, then compare your ideas about this theme with some of the aspects of time that have been evoked in the Pages' song.

Stagecraft 导演技巧

'the note was very untunable' (in pairs)

Why is Touchstone so unimpressed by the song and its sentiments? The Page's response to Touchstone that 'we kept time; we lost not our time' could be simply about their timing in the singing; but it could also refer to their immersion in the moment and their enjoyment of the present time.

- Write either stage directions or asides at various points throughout the song to give more information about what might be happening on stage. Do the Pages really sing in tune, and did Touchstone actually get lost in the song? Or were the singers totally out of tune, and did they interrupt Touchstone's romantic moment with Audrey?

1 Orlando's state of mind (in pairs)

At the beginning of the play's final scene, Orlando still seems unsure about his fate: 'I sometimes do believe and sometimes do not'.

- Imagine Orlando has been discussing his position with Duke Senior and others in Arden since we last saw him. Improvise these conversations, taking turns to play Orlando. Consider what Orlando might say about his thoughts and feelings since last talking to Rosalind. Think about the dreams or visions that have haunted him or inspired him, and the advice that other people have given him.

1 prime 风华之年
2 ditty 歌词
3 note 调子
4 untunable 不和谐
5 deceived 错了
6 time 节拍
7 yes （即you did lose your time；试金石将time理解为"时间"）
8 mend 改善
9 the boy （指甘尼密）
10 those that fear they hope 担心希望落空的人
11 whiles our compact is urged 我们的约定被拿出来讨论
12 bestow her on 把她许配给

> When birds do sing;
> Hey ding a-ding, ding,
> Sweet lovers love the spring. 35
>
> And therefore take the present time;
> With a hey, and a ho, and a hey nonny-no,
> For love is crownèd with the prime[1],
> In spring-time,
> The only pretty ring-time, 40
> When birds do sing;
> Hey ding a-ding, ding,
> Sweet lovers love the spring.

TOUCHSTONE Truly, young gentlemen, though there was no great matter in the ditty[2], yet the note[3] was very untunable[4]. 45

FIRST PAGE You are deceived[5], sir: we kept time[6]; we lost not our time.

TOUCHSTONE By my troth, yes[7]. I count it but time lost to hear such a foolish song. God buy you, and God mend[8] your voices. – Come, Audrey.

Exeunt

Act 5 Scene 4
Duke Senior's camp in the forest

Enter DUKE SENIOR, AMIENS, JAQUES, ORLANDO, OLIVER, CELIA [*as* ALIENA]

DUKE SENIOR Dost thou believe, Orlando, that the boy[9]
Can do all this that he hath promisèd?

ORLANDO I sometimes do believe and sometimes do not,
As those that fear they hope[10] and know they fear.

Enter ROSALIND [*as* GANYMEDE], SILVIUS, *and* PHOEBE

ROSALIND Patience once more whiles our compact is urged[11]. – 5
You say, if I bring in your Rosalind,
You will bestow her on[12] Orlando here?

DUKE SENIOR That would I, had I kingdoms to give with her.

ROSALIND And you say you will have her, when I bring her?

ORLANDO That would I, were I of all kingdoms king. 10

Rosalind promises to fulfil every character's wishes. Duke Senior and Orlando remark on Ganymede's resemblance to Rosalind. Touchstone boasts of his skills as a courtier.

 剧情简介：若泽兰许诺实现每个人的愿望。老公爵和奥岚铎点评了甘尼密和若泽兰的相似之处。试金石夸耀自己作为朝臣的技能。

1 Promise-keeping (in small groups)

In lines 5–25, Rosalind asks for patience while she gets each character to confirm his or her own promise: that Duke Senior will give his daughter in marriage to Orlando, that Orlando will marry her, and so on.

- List the promises that Rosalind asks each of the characters to confirm. In your Director's Journal, write stage directions for each time that she makes one of these requests. How might her attitude, and therefore her actions and postures, differ in each case? Explain why.
- Use these stage directions as you act out lines 5–25. Think about what additional notes you might write to advise the other actors on stage how to react to Rosalind's speech and actions.

Characters 人物分析

Reminders of Rosalind

The exchange between Orlando and Duke Senior seems to confirm that Rosalind's disguise as Ganymede is still intact (未被识破). But is it possible that Orlando has guessed the truth, yet wishes to keep the secret from her father?

- In role as the director of a modern production, write notes in your Director's Journal to advise the actor playing Orlando how to speak lines 28–34. Refer to what he says in lines 3–4 in this scene as you consider what Orlando might be thinking.

2 Touchstone as courtier (in pairs)

In lines 42–5, Touchstone lists the skills that prove he has been a courtier:

- dancing (a 'measure' is a stately dance)
- flattery, diplomacy and deceit ('politic')
- false friendship ('smooth with mine enemy')
- non-payment of bills (he has ruined – 'undone' – three tailors).

a Discuss how Touchstone mocks the life and fashions of the court. Do you think he really was once a courtier?

b Devise gestures to accompany each of Touchstone's criticisms or jokes about the court. Take turns to read lines 42–5 aloud, using these gestures to try to make your partner laugh.

c Prepare and stage an interview with a courtier who would have known a younger Touchstone at court. What was Touchstone like then? Did he criticise the court or did he try to be a popular, fashionable courtier?

1 make all this matter even 把这件事全部搞定
2 give your daughter 把令爱嫁出去
3 lively touches 相像之处
4 favour 容貌
5 rudiments 入门知识
6 desperate studies 危险法术
7 Obscurèd 隐居
8 flood 洪水（杰奎的话使人想起了《圣经》中的大洪水）
9 toward 要来了
10 motley-minded 傻头傻脑
11 purgation 清洗，净化（试金石在这里明显误用了这个词）
12 measure 宫廷舞
13 like 很可能
14 ta'en up 造成
15 the seventh cause 第七个原因

ROSALIND	You say you'll marry me, if I be willing.	
PHOEBE	That will I, should I die the hour after.	
ROSALIND	But if you do refuse to marry me,	
	You'll give yourself to this most faithful shepherd.	
PHOEBE	So is the bargain.	15
ROSALIND	You say that you'll have Phoebe if she will.	
SILVIUS	Though to have her and death were both one thing.	
ROSALIND	I have promised to make all this matter even[1]. –	
	Keep you your word, O Duke, to give your daughter[2]. –	
	You yours, Orlando, to receive his daughter. –	20
	Keep you your word, Phoebe, that you'll marry me	
	Or else, refusing me, to wed this shepherd. –	
	Keep your word, Silvius, that you'll marry her	
	If she refuse me – and from hence I go	
	To make these doubts all even.	25

Exeunt Rosalind and Celia

DUKE SENIOR	I do remember in this shepherd boy	
	Some lively touches[3] of my daughter's favour[4].	
ORLANDO	My lord, the first time that I ever saw him,	
	Methought he was a brother to your daughter;	
	But, my good lord, this boy is forest-born	30
	And hath been tutored in the rudiments[5]	
	Of many desperate studies[6] by his uncle	
	Whom he reports to be a great magician,	
	Obscurèd[7] in the circle of this forest.	

Enter TOUCHSTONE *and* AUDREY

JAQUES	There is sure another flood[8] toward[9], and these couples are com-	35
	ing to the ark. Here comes a pair of very strange beasts which, in all	
	tongues, are called fools.	
TOUCHSTONE	Salutation and greeting to you all.	
JAQUES	Good my lord, bid him welcome. This is the motley-minded[10]	
	gentleman that I have so often met in the forest: he hath been a	40
	courtier, he swears.	
TOUCHSTONE	If any man doubt that, let him put me to my purgation[11].	
	I have trod a measure[12]; I have flattered a lady; I have been politic	
	with my friend, smooth with mine enemy; I have undone three	
	tailors; I have had four quarrels, and like[13] to have fought one.	45
JAQUES	And how was that ta'en up[14]?	
TOUCHSTONE	Faith, we met and found the quarrel was upon the	
	seventh cause[15].	

Touchstone declares that he too wishes to be married, because Audrey's roughness conceals inner virtues. He lists the sequence of insults that lead up to a duel, explaining how to avoid it.

 剧情简介：试金石宣称，他也希望与奥卓依结婚，因为她表面粗俗，内心却良善。他列举出了导致对决的一系列冒犯，解释如何避免对决。

1 'amongst … the country copulatives'

Touchstone continues to mock the country ways as well as the court. But he is keen not to be left out of the impending marriages. Unlike Jaques, he wants to be inside, not outside, the action.

a How does Touchstone treat Audrey? Make notes on how you would want to present their relationship to an audience.

b Suggest what Audrey might be doing when Touchstone orders her 'Bear your body more seeming, Audrey.' Write notes in your Director's Journal.

c What is Touchstone's view of marriage (see line 53)? Rewrite it in your own words. Predict how a modern audience might feel about Touchstone's statement.

Write about it 写作练习

The seventh cause: the etiquette of quarrelling

Touchstone lists how a quarrel develops and how a fight can be avoided by an 'if'. Shakespeare is satirising manuals on correct behaviour for courtiers. Many of these handbooks were about how to behave in a duel when one's honour had been insulted. The table below shows the stages of a quarrel when an insult is repeated.

Name of response	Meaning of reply	Result
1 Retort courteous (客气反驳)	Oh, yes it is	Avoid duel (决斗)
2 Quip modest (适度嘲讽)	It's my affair	Ditto (同上)
3 Reply churlish (粗暴回复)	You are a poor judge	Ditto
4 Reproof valiant (大胆责备)	That isn't true	Ditto
5 Countercheck quarrelsome (争吵反击)	You lie	Ditto
6 Lie circumstantial (间接说谎)	You lie, because…	Ditto
7 Lie direct (直接说谎)	You definitely lie	Duel – although it could be also still be avoided!

- Touchstone says 'we quarrel in print, by the book' (line 78). What would a modern rulebook for quarrellers look like? Use the table above to help you create a contemporary version of seven rules for how to avoid a quarrel. Then write a modernised speech for Touchstone that is based upon these new rules.

1 desire you of the like 祝愿您也一样
2 copulatives 对象们
3 blood breaks 淫欲爆发（将婚姻破碎）
4 humour 怪脾气
5 swift and sententious 伶牙俐齿
6 bolt 箭
7 dulcet diseases 甜蜜的病患
8 seeming 端庄
9 in the mind 以为
10 countercheck 反申斥
11 circumstantial 间接
12 durst 敢（dare的过去时形式）
13 measured swords 量了一下剑长（决斗之前量一量双方剑的长短是否一致，免得一方占便宜）
14 nominate 说出来
15 circumstance 委婉说法
16 take up 受理
17 as 换句话说
18 swore brothers 结拜为兄弟

JAQUES	How, 'seventh cause'? – Good my lord, like this fellow.	
DUKE SENIOR	I like him very well.	50
TOUCHSTONE	God'ild you, sir; I desire you of the like[1]. I press in here, sir, amongst the rest of the country copulatives[2], to swear and to forswear according as marriage binds and blood breaks[3]. A poor virgin, sir, an ill-favoured thing, sir, but mine own. A poor humour[4] of mine, sir, to take that that no man else will. Rich honesty dwells like a miser, sir, in a poor house, as your pearl in your foul oyster.	55
DUKE SENIOR	By my faith, he is very swift and sententious[5].	
TOUCHSTONE	According to 'the fool's bolt[6]', sir, and such dulcet diseases[7].	
JAQUES	But, for 'the seventh cause': how did you find the quarrel on 'the seventh cause'?	60
TOUCHSTONE	Upon a lie seven times removed. – Bear your body more seeming[8], Audrey. – As thus, sir: I did dislike the cut of a certain courtier's beard. He sent me word, if I said his beard was not cut well, he was in the mind[9] it was: this is called 'the retort courteous'. If I sent him word again it was not well cut, he would send me word he cut it to please himself: this is called 'the quip modest'. If again it was not well cut, he disabled my judgement: this is called 'the reply churlish'. If again it was not well cut, he would answer I spake not true: this is called 'the reproof valiant'. If again it was not well cut, he would say I lied: this is called 'the countercheck[10] quarrelsome'. And so to 'the lie circumstantial[11]' and 'the lie direct'.	65

70 |
JAQUES	And how oft did you say his beard was not well cut?	
TOUCHSTONE	I durst[12] go no further than the lie circumstantial, nor he durst not give me the lie direct; and so we measured swords[13], and parted.	75
JAQUES	Can you nominate[14], in order now, the degrees of the lie?	
TOUCHSTONE	O sir, we quarrel in print, by the book – as you have books for good manners. I will name you the degrees: the first, the retort courteous; the second, the quip modest; the third, the reply churlish; the fourth, the reproof valiant; the fifth, the countercheck quarrelsome; the sixth, the lie with circumstance[15]; the seventh, the lie direct. All these you may avoid but the lie direct, and you may avoid that too with an 'if'. I knew when seven justices could not take up[16] a quarrel but when the parties were met themselves, one of them thought but of an 'if': as[17], 'If you said so, then I said so.' And they shook hands and swore brothers[18]. Your 'if' is the only peacemaker: much virtue in 'if'.	80

85 |

Duke Senior praises Touchstone. Hymen enters with Rosalind and Celia (undisguised) and asks the Duke to receive his daughter. Rosalind promises to be Orlando's wife. Hymen ordains four marriages.

剧情简介：老公爵赞扬试金石。亥门带着若泽兰和希丽叶（不再伪装）上场，并要求公爵认领其女儿。若泽兰答应做奥岚铎的妻子。亥门主持了四对新人的婚礼。

Stagecraft 导演技巧

'Enter HYMEN' (in small groups)

The entry of Hymen, the Greek and Roman god of marriage, is a great moment of theatre. The episode may have been staged as a masque. Masques were spectacular entertainments that drew imaginatively on Classical mythology to present gods and goddesses. They used elaborate scenery and costumes, and were filled with music, poetry and dance. Masques revelled in visual effects, often using stage machinery and lighting to create striking illusions.

a Discuss your ideas for a masque, and draw up a list to describe the atmosphere you would like to create at the end of a stage production of *As You Like It*.

b Work out a staging of lines 93–134 for a modern production, with all the possibilities of modern set design, machinery, costume, special effects and lighting. Use the following considerations to help you with this plan:
- Will you present Hymen as a god or as a human character?
- Hymen's language is formal and ritualistic and uses rhyming verse. Will you emphasise the rhymes? If so, how?

1 stalking-horse 掩护马（当猎人们向猎物靠近时，掩护马能够让猎人们隐身其后）
2 *Still music* 舒缓柔和的音乐
3 mirth 欢乐
4 made even 公平处理
5 Atone together 诸事如意
6 Peace, ho 安静啦
7 bar confusion 禁止喧闹
8 Hymen's bands 婚礼誓言
9 cross 磨难
10 accord 和谐一致
11 sure together 形影相随
12 Whiles 直到
13 That reason, wonder may diminish 道理可以减少惊奇

1 Hymen (in pairs)

a Some directors cut Hymen from the play altogether. Discuss whether the play needs a ritualistic moment at this point, or whether the marriages could be carried out more simply and informally.

b Improvise a conversation between a set designer who wants to include Hymen (because of the opportunities for elaborate special effects) and a director who thinks this character can be cut.

Themes 主题分析

'If truth holds true contents'

One critic has suggested that line 114 in this scene has at least 168 possible interpretations! One is 'If revealing who Ganymede and Aliena really are brings genuine happiness'. The characters' disguises, shifting moods, changing personalities and uncertain positions make 'the truth' a complex and ambiguous concept.

- Make one or two suggestions for what line 114 might mean. Then write a paragraph on how 'truth' is represented in the play.

JAQUES	Is not this a rare fellow, my lord? He's as good at anything, and yet a fool.	90
DUKE SENIOR	He uses his folly like a stalking-horse¹, and under the presentation of that he shoots his wit.	

Still music². Enter HYMEN, [*with*] ROSALIND *and* CELIA
[*as themselves*]

HYMEN	Then is there mirth³ in heaven,	
	When earthly things made even⁴	
	Atone together⁵.	95
	Good Duke, receive thy daughter;	
	Hymen from heaven brought her,	
	Yea, brought her hither	
	That thou mightst join her hand with his,	
	Whose heart within his bosom is.	100
ROSALIND	[*To the Duke*] To you I give myself, for I am yours.	
	[*To Orlando*] To you I give myself, for I am yours.	
DUKE SENIOR	If there be truth in sight, you are my daughter.	
ORLANDO	If there be truth in sight, you are my Rosalind.	
PHOEBE	If sight and shape be true, why then, my love, adieu.	105
ROSALIND	[*To the Duke*] I'll have no father, if you be not he.	
	[*To Orlando*] I'll have no husband, if you be not he.	
	[*To Phoebe*] Nor ne'er wed woman, if you be not she.	
HYMEN	Peace, ho⁶: I bar confusion⁷,	
	'Tis I must make conclusion	110
	Of these most strange events.	
	Here's eight that must take hands	
	To join in Hymen's bands⁸,	
	If truth holds true contents.	
	[*To Orlando and Rosalind*] You and you no cross⁹ shall part.	115
	[*To Oliver and Celia*] You and you are heart in heart.	
	[*To Phoebe*] You to his love must accord¹⁰,	
	Or have a woman to your lord.	
	[*To Touchstone and Audrey*] You and you are sure together¹¹	
	As the winter to foul weather. –	120
	Whiles¹² a wedlock hymn we sing,	
	Feed yourselves with questioning,	
	That reason, wonder may diminish¹³	
	How thus we met and these things finish.	

After the song celebrating marriage and fertility, Phoebe accepts Silvius. Jacques de Boys brings news of Duke Frederick's conversion and penitence. Duke Senior orders revelry.

 剧情简介：庆祝婚姻和生育的歌唱完后，菲妣接受了悉尔维耶。雅克·德勃伊带来了弗莱德瑞公爵觉悟和忏悔的消息。老公爵下令狂欢。

1 Snapshots of the action (in large groups)

a Discuss the questions below, and then write stage directions based on what you decide will work best.

- How does Duke Senior acknowledge Celia? (lines 131–2)
- Does Phoebe accept Silvius grudgingly, willingly or with a different emotion? (lines 133–4)
- How do Oliver and Orlando respond to the sight of their brother?

b Create tableaux that illustrate your stage directions. One member of the group is the photographer, who can call out 'Ready … Snap!' to signal that the moment has been captured.

Stagecraft 导演技巧

A believable happy ending? (in small groups)

The news of Duke Frederick's conversion is sudden and improbable. But this unlikely surprise is part of the pastoral romance tradition, which Shakespeare was satirising in the play. The tradition delighted in happy endings in which order was restored, with reconciliations (和解), conversions to goodness, forgiveness, marriages, and the prospect of harmony for individuals and society.

a Consider how you would want Jacques de Boys deliver his news (for example, using pauses to add dramatic effect, or moving and gesturing when he recognises his brothers).

b How would you want your audience to respond to the news of Frederick's conversion? How could you convey the satirical edge of Shakespeare's writing, both in the actors' delivery and through other staging decisions? Write notes in your Director's Journal.

Themes 主题分析

Return to court

In one production, the members of the banished court threw off their country clothes at lines 158–9 to reveal their true court apparel. In a filmed version of the play, the 'rustic revelry' started out as a dance in the forest, then the characters ran through the forest and finished the dance in the very places in the court where the play started.

- In role as director, write notes about how you would stage this final movement from country to court? Would you want to suggest liberation or a return to corruption at the end of the play?

---

1 Juno 茱娜（婚姻女神）
2 board and bed 同食同寝
3 peoples 让人居住于
4 High wedlock 崇高的婚姻
5 Even 如同
6 tidings 消息
7 resorted to 躲避到
8 Addressed a mighty power 调集大军
9 conduct 率领
10 crown 君权
11 bequeathing to 归还
12 offer'st fairly 送来漂亮的贺礼
13 the other （有两种解释：一种指若泽兰；另一种指老公爵）
14 at large 大片
15 potent 强大
16 do those ends 做好扫尾工作
17 shrewd 艰难
18 the measure of their states 他们的身份地位
19 new-fall'n dignity 新近得来的尊荣（他的公国）
20 rustic revelry 乡村狂欢

Song

    Wedding is great Juno's[1] crown,
        O blessed bond of board and bed[2].
    'Tis Hymen peoples[3] every town,
        High wedlock[4] then be honourèd.
    Honour, high honour, and renown
    To Hymen, god of every town.

DUKE SENIOR O my dear niece: welcome thou art to me,
Even[5] daughter; welcome in no less degree.

PHOEBE I will not eat my word now thou art mine:
Thy faith my fancy to thee doth combine.

Enter [JACQUES DE BOYS, the] second brother

JACQUES DE BOYS Let me have audience for a word or two.
I am the second son of old Sir Roland,
That bring these tidings[6] to this fair assembly.
Duke Frederick, hearing how that every day
Men of great worth resorted to[7] this forest,
Addressed a mighty power[8] which were on foot
In his own conduct[9], purposely to take
His brother here and put him to the sword;
And to the skirts of this wild wood he came,
Where, meeting with an old religious man,
After some question with him, was converted
Both from his enterprise and from the world,
His crown[10] bequeathing to[11] his banished brother,
And all their lands restored to them again
That were with him exiled. This to be true,
I do engage my life.

DUKE SENIOR   Welcome, young man.
Thou offer'st fairly[12] to thy brothers' wedding:
To one his lands withheld, and to the other[13]
A land itself at large[14], a potent[15] dukedom. –
First, in this forest, let us do those ends[16]
That here were well begun and well begot;
And after every of this happy number
That have endured shrewd[17] days and nights with us
Shall share the good of our returnèd fortune
According to the measure of their states[18].
Meantime forget this new-fall'n dignity[19]
And fall into our rustic revelry[20]. –

Jaques resolves to join Duke Frederick. He predicts honour and success to all except Touchstone, and declines to join the celebrations. Rosalind asks the audience to approve the play with their applause.

 剧情简介：杰奎决定和弗莱德瑞公爵一同归隐。他预言，除了试金石，所有新人都将获得荣耀和幸福，不过他拒绝参加婚庆。若泽兰邀请观众为演出鼓掌以示肯定。

1 Jaques's farewell

Jaques refuses to join in the celebrations, preferring to join Duke Frederick in abandoning court life.

- Why do you think Shakespeare adds this 'serious' episode to the closing festivities? Why might Jaques still be melancholy? Write a stage direction to advise the actor playing Jaques on how to make his farewell.

Stagecraft 导演技巧

Staging the Epilogue (in pairs)

Discuss the following points about the play's **epilogue** (the section at the end of a play or book that concludes or comments on the preceding action), then make notes in your Director's Journal in response.

- **'Exeunt all but Rosalind'** In Shakespeare's day, it was customary for the actor giving the epilogue to remain on stage after everyone else had left it. This is not necessarily the case in modern productions. Decide whether you would have the rest of the cast on view behind Rosalind or whether she should speak to the audience by herself. What effect would each of these two versions have on the audience?
- **Lines 7–8** These lines play on the theme of appearance and reality, which has been complicated by the play's many disguises and role changes. Consider whether Rosalind should stay in role as she speaks the Epilogue, or address the audience as an actor.
- **Line 13** In Shakespeare's time, Rosalind was played by a (usually very young) man. But today, nearly all Rosalinds are female. Consider the effect you would want to achieve with this line, and how you would advise a female actor to deliver it.
- **Lines 13–17** Rosalind teases the audiences by implying that if they don't applaud, they have beards that don't please her, ugly faces and bad breath. How would you expect the audience to respond? How could the actor maximise the audience reaction?

2 Final image (in large groups)

Discuss the final 'stage picture' that you would want the audience to see at the end of your production, and think about what final impression of the play it would give. Stage a tableau of this moment. Script a voiceover (画外音) that describes the different elements of the tableau and the reasons behind including them.

---

1 by your patience 且慢
2 thrown into neglect 扔下不管
3 convertites 悟道者
4 matter 教训
5 great allies 贵戚
6 wrangling 争吵
7 Is … victualled 只有两个月的食粮
8 pastime 寻欢作乐
9 bush 招牌（酒铺常在店门外挂一簇常春藤）
10 case 情形
11 insinuate with 讨好
12 furnished 穿着打扮
13 become 合适
14 conjure 召唤
15 simpering 傻笑的样子
16 liked me 讨我喜欢
17 defied 让人厌恶
18 offer （指亲吻观众）
19 curtsey 屈膝礼
20 bid me farewell 以掌声与我告别

	Play, music – and you, brides and bridegrooms all,
	With measure heaped in joy to th'measures fall.
JAQUES	Sir, by your patience[1]. [*To Jacques de Boys*] If I heard you rightly,
	The Duke hath put on a religious life
	And thrown into neglect[2] the pompous court.
JACQUES DE BOYS	He hath.
JAQUES	To him will I: out of these convertites[3]
	There is much matter[4] to be heard and learned.
	[*To the Duke*] You to your former honour I bequeath:
	Your patience and your virtue well deserves it.
	[*To Orlando*] You to a love that your true faith doth merit.
	[*To Oliver*] You to your land and love and great allies[5].
	[*To Silvius*] You to a long and well-deservèd bed.
	[*To Touchstone*] And you to wrangling[6], for thy loving voyage
	Is but for two months victualled[7]. – So to your pleasures;
	I am for other than for dancing measures.
DUKE SENIOR	Stay, Jaques, stay.
JAQUES	To see no pastime[8], I. What you would have
	I'll stay to know at your abandoned cave. *Exit*
DUKE SENIOR	Proceed, proceed. – We will begin these rites
	As we do trust they'll end, in true delights.
	[*They dance.*] *Exeunt all but Rosalind who speaks the Epilogue:*

ROSALIND It is not the fashion to see the lady the Epilogue, but it is no more unhandsome than to see the lord the Prologue. If it be true that good wine needs no bush[9], 'tis true that a good play needs no Epilogue. Yet to good wine they do use good bushes, and good plays prove the better by the help of good Epilogues. What a case[10] am I in, then, that am neither a good Epilogue nor cannot insinuate with[11] you in the behalf of a good play? I am not furnished[12] like a beggar, therefore to beg will not become[13] me. My way is to conjure[14] you, and I'll begin with the women. I charge you, O women, for the love you bear to men, to like as much of this play as please you. – And I charge you, O men, for the love you bear to women – as I perceive by your simpering[15] none of you hates them – that between you and the women the play may please. If I were a woman, I would kiss as many of you as had beards that pleased me, complexions that liked me[16], and breaths that I defied[17] not. And I am sure as many as have good beards, or good faces, or sweet breaths will, for my kind offer[18], when I make curtsey[19], bid me farewell[20]. *Exit*

 As You Like It
各如所愿

Looking back at the play 本剧回顾
Activities for groups or individuals

1 Ending the play

◆ In groups, develop your ideas on the final 'stage picture' you created on page 156 by considering the context (time and place) in which you would want to set the play. This should affect your choice of stage set, music, costume and choreography (编舞) (dance steps). You could use the images on the page opposite for inspiration.

Imagine you are a team of theatrical experts, preparing a presentation on your vision for the final scene. You will need to answer certain questions:

- **Lighting designer:** what mood would you want to create at the end of the play, and how would you use lighting to enhance this?
- **Sound designer:** some productions of *As You Like It* end with the whole company on stage singing a song from the play. Which song would you choose?
- **Costume designer:** what colours and styles of costume would you choose for each character at the end of the play?
- **Set designer:** where and when would you want the play to be set? What stage scenery and props could you use to portray this setting?
- **Choreographer:** at which points in the play might a choreographer work with the actors? Write notes for where and how you might want to choreograph a fight scene or a dance sequence in the play.

◆ Develop and prepare your presentation.

2 Did Shakespeare believe it?

Do you think Shakespeare believed in the possibility of a rural utopia where happiness and community spirit reigned? Or was his intention to subvert the notion of that ideal world, showing its impossibility?

◆ In role as Shakespeare, take turns to sit in the hot-seat and answer questions about your ideas of an ideal world in *As You Like It*.

3 Happily ever after?

Several predictions are made about the couples at the end of the play:

- Jaques says that Touchstone's and Audrey's happiness will not last – they will soon quarrel.
- Hymen says that no troubles will come between Rosalind and Orlando.
- When Phoebe realises that Ganymede is actually a woman, she tells Silvius that his faith (constancy) has finally won her love.
- Rosalind says that Celia and Oliver are so much in love that violence will not part them.

◆ Imagine that the main characters from the play come together for an anniversary party five years after this last scene. What do you think has happened to each of them? Step into role as one of these characters and write your diary entry after the party has taken place. Describe how life is for you and for everyone else, and record some of the things the other characters said and did during the party.

5 A missing scene?

Dr Samuel Johnson, a famous editor and critic of Shakespeare's work, thought that Shakespeare should have taken the opportunity to teach a moral lesson by writing a scene showing Duke Frederick's meeting with the 'old religious man'.

◆ Remind yourself of the report of the meeting (Act 5 Scene 4, lines 138–49). Then write this 'missing scene' in modern English to show what happened to Duke Frederick. Explain his conversion and his decision to withdraw from the world and to renounce all his ill-gotten land and titles.

As You Like It 各如所愿

Perspectives and themes 视角与主题

What is the play about?

One way of answering the question 'What is *As You Like It* about?' is to identify the themes of the play. Themes are ideas or concepts of fundamental importance that recur throughout the play, linking together plot, characters and language. Themes echo, reinforce and comment upon one another and upon the whole play in interesting ways. It would be difficult to write about appearance and reality in the play without referring to the manifestation (显现) of evil. It would be equally problematic to write about kingship and masculinity without talking about the themes of loyalty and ambition.

As you can see, themes are not individual categories but a 'tangle' (乱糟糟一团) of ideas and concerns that are interrelated in complex ways. In your writing, you should aim to explore the way these themes cross over and illuminate each other, rather than simply listing each of the themes. You might also like to think about the way the themes work at different levels: the individual level (psychological or personal); the social level (linked to society and nation); and the natural level (the natural or supernatural world). For example, in *As You Like It*, you can clearly see how the theme of appearance and reality works across all three of these levels. The following themes can be traced through the play; there are, of course, others – some of which you may have already identified.

Themes

Court versus country

The tradition of pastoral romance (see pp. 165–6) portrayed rural life as an ideal world of innocence and freedom. It was a world into which kings, queens and courtiers could escape, disguised as shepherds and shepherdesses, to enjoy the tranquillity and harmony of country life. On the surface, Shakespeare seems to follow that tradition: *As You Like It* is full of contrasts between court and country. In the court, brother is set against brother, and ambition, envy and intrigue (阴谋) are commonplace. Duke Frederick has usurped his brother, and he exiles his niece Rosalind on pain of death. In contrast, the exiles in the Forest of Arden seem to live contentedly as a friendly community. The court appears to be an unnatural and unhappy place, corrupt and artificial; in contrast, the country has a more benign, joyful air of freedom. However, all might not be as clear-cut as it seems.

◆ Devise a dramatic presentation that contrasts life at 'court' with life in the 'country'. Create a series of contrasting tableaux, and set them to a brief narrative voiceover or a suitable musical accompaniment. Try to portray the complexity and contradictory nature of each world beyond its superficial appearance (read through the next section for more ideas).

The Forest of Arden as a utopia

Arden appears to be a refuge from the hypocrisy, deceit and ambition of the court. It seems a place of harmony, free from the anger of fathers and brothers, from envy and malice, and from the false friendship of flattering courtiers. It is an enchanted, innocent world where happiness is truly possible and where community, brotherhood and welcoming hospitality can be found. It apparently fosters (促进) regeneration and reconciliation, as characters are changed by their experience, discovering truths about themselves and others. As Charles the wrestler says, Arden is like the 'golden world' of Classical writing (see p. 165) or the simple, egalitarian (人人平等) world of Robin Hood and his merry men.

But the Forest of Arden is not an idealised utopia. It has its own perils: harsh winds, cold weather, low wages, hard masters, dangerous creatures, weariness, hunting and death, hunger and exhaustion. The critic Jan Kott called it 'Bitter Arcadia (阿卡迪亚 [世外桃源])', and characters in the play refer to it as a 'desert'. The man who employs Corin is a hard taskmaster (工头), and Jaques cynically comments on the foolishness of the man who leaves 'his wealth and ease' for the rough pleasures of the forest.

PERSPECTIVES AND THEMES

Phoebe cruelly scorns the besotted (痴迷) Silvius, and is quite unlike the idealised shepherdess of the romantic tradition. The native deer are hunted to death by the exiled lords, and snakes and lions threaten people's lives.

◆ Look up some accounts of either the Garden of Eden or the 'golden world' of Classical writings, and compare their features with those of Arden as it is described in the play (particularly at the beginning of Act 2 Scene 1). Write an essay entitled 'What kind of Eden is Arden?' Consider Arden's function in *As You Like It* and look carefully at what happens when the characters bring their issues and problems into this supposedly utopian world.

Love

Love is the driving force of the play. Within a few minutes of her first appearance, Rosalind asks the question 'what think you of falling in love?' and the rest of the play explores love in many of its forms and expressions:

- brotherly love
- love as friendship and service
- self-love
- love as lust
- idealised love
- cruel love
- sincere love
- love at first sight.

As You Like It considers a variety of viewpoints as characters express and criticise the absurdities and contradictions of love. But in spite of (or perhaps because of) all the trials and tribulations (艰难困苦) of love, the play ends happily in the marriages of the four pairs of lovers.

◆ Find as many examples as you can in the script of the different forms and expressions of love listed opposite. Describe how your example fits each heading. For example:

- **Brotherly love:** Orlando saves Oliver from a lion.
- **Love as friendship and service:** Adam's devotion to Orlando and his late father (and Orlando's compassion towards Adam).

Gender

As You Like It may be a play partly about love, but it is also about gender and sexuality. Rosalind is a young woman who dresses as a young man as she flees from the court. Although she is a woman, it is as Ganymede that she woos Orlando and inadvertently (不经意) attracts Phoebe. She uses her disguise as Ganymede to encourage Orlando to woo Rosalind, and tricks Orlando into promising to marry her. Through these complicated arrangements, the play shows how Rosalind seems able to subvert traditional gender roles and question the boundaries her society places on sexuality and gender.

Cross-dressing characters are a common feature of Shakespeare's plays, and manifest some of the gender transformations mentioned above. In Shakespeare's time, the sexual ambiguity was heightened in performance: the audience saw a boy actor playing a girl (Phoebe), falling in love with a boy (Ganymede), who is a girl (Rosalind) played by a boy actor! The comedy here might also come from the fact that Rosalind overacts (夸张地表演) to draw attention to the role reversal. These kind of jokes are **meta-theatrical** (元戏剧) in that they draw attention to the play as an illusion and to the conventions of acting that sustain this illusion, even while they break it.

◆ As you can see by looking at the photos of Rosalind in this edition, the appearance of Ganymede can vary dramatically from play to play. Some productions have a more traditionally masculine Ganymede, some aim to blur the distinction between the genders and present a thinly disguised, very feminine Ganymede. Choose which type of disguise you would have in a modern production of the play, and explain why you think it would work best.

Appearance and reality – 'Most friendship is feigning'

Things are not as they seem in *As You Like It*. Oliver deceives Charles about Orlando; Amiens sings of false friendship; the seemingly benign Forest of Arden conceals hardships and dangers. The play sets an ongoing puzzle about the nature of the different types of love it portrays: which are real and which are merely pretence?

The most obvious way in which the play explores the theme of appearance and reality is through disguise. Celia, a princess, disguises herself as a shepherdess called Aliena. Rosalind disguises herself as a youth, the boy Ganymede, and fools the inhabitants of the forest. Most notably, she uses her disguise to conceal and to reveal her true feelings for Orlando. Under cover of her disguise, Rosalind can speak as she really feels and enjoy Orlando's wooing. The dramatic irony of the deception lies in the fact that Orlando does not recognise the truth of what Rosalind says, but the audience does.

◆ Some characters are aware that things are not as they seem, but most are duped (欺骗) by outward appearance. Select four key moments from the play and describe what evidence of false impressions you can find there. How are these moments perceived differently by each of the characters involved? For example, one key moment is where Celia knows that Ganymede is Rosalind in disguise, but Orlando does not.

Order and disorder – 'there begins my sadness'

The play begins with a portrait of disorder. Orlando is rebelling against his cruel treatment by his brother, and Duke Frederick has already disrupted the moral and social fabric (结构) of the kingdom by overthrowing his brother and seizing his dukedom. The long middle section of the play then takes place in the apparently peaceful world of Arden. The disorder here is created by the trials of love, as well as the conflict between appearance and reality. The play ends with order restored: Orlando and Oliver are reconciled, four marriages are proclaimed and Duke Senior is returned to his rightful position of Duke.

◆ Some stage productions portray the theme of order and disorder by showing the Forest of Arden as a harsh winter setting that changes to one of high summer for the celebrations of marriage and happiness at the end of the play. How would you use costume, lighting, music and set design to illustrate the theme of order and disorder in a modern production?

Time and change – 'there's no clock in the forest'

Time is discussed in various ways in the play: Rosalind claims that time travels at different speeds, and gives examples of its 'diverse paces'; Jaques remarks bitingly (犀利) that 'from hour to hour, we rot and rot'. After the hectic (忙碌) speed of the first act, time seems to stand still in the Forest of Arden. The forest itself marks a sort of holiday, a time away from the hurried drama of the court. But holidays don't last forever, and at the end the Duke and his court leave Arden. Jaques's 'seven ages of man' is the play's best-known expression of the passage of time, and the unavoidable changes that accompany it.

As in every Shakespeare play, change is a major theme of *As You Like It*. Celia and Rosalind disguise themselves as Aliena and Ganymede, changing from princesses to a shepherdess and her brother. At the end of the play, both return to their status as princesses. Orlando begins penniless, a victim of his brother's hatred. He ends the play married to Duke Senior's daughter with the prospect of becoming heir to the dukedom. The 'villains' of Act 1, Oliver and Duke Frederick, are converted to goodness in the final scenes. Only Jaques seems unchanged at the play's end.

◆ In groups, discuss each character in turn. Describe how they change, if at all, over the course of the play (in social status, moral awareness or understanding, knowledge of others/love/themselves). Then take turns in the hot-seat to answer questions from the rest of the group while in role as different characters.

▼ Why do you think Jaques is the only character that remains apparently unchanged at the end of the play?

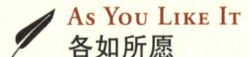

As You Like It
各如所愿

Perspectives

Another way of thinking about the play is to explore the range of interpretations that can be applied to it. Early critics of As You Like It were overwhelmingly concerned with Rosalind and with the play as entertainment. Recent criticism has dealt with issues of gender, patriarchy (父权制), social hierarchy and personal identity, as you will see below. Of course, there are many other perspectives to the play, and it is up to you to engage with the variety of meanings and to decide what you think the play is about. The following strands of criticism concentrate on particular aspects of the play, and evaluate its meaning based on these primary concerns.

Cultural materialist criticism
A cultural materialist critique of As You Like It argues that the play offers a subversive (颠覆性) critique of the social and political beliefs of Shakespeare's time. It looks at the way politics, wealth and power strongly influence every human relationship, and considers how these ideas are thrown into relief by the play's movement from court to country.

Feminist criticism
In feminist readings of the play, gender issues are politicised and critiqued from women's perspectives. This includes looking at the way women and their experiences are represented in literature. In As You Like It, the social and symbolic construction of gender, as shown in Rosalind's cross-dressing (异装), allows for exploration of the roles and experiences of women in Shakespeare's time and today.

New-historicist criticism
This strand of criticism places the play firmly in its historical context, to explore ideas about society and power that were current at the time. With regard to As You Like It, important factors include the acts of subversion and the way these moments of disorder are contained within the action of the play.

Performance criticism
This approach explores As You Like it as a performance text, analysing past and present theatrical productions to consider the changing ways in which the play has been interpreted. In more recent years, this also encompasses film and other moving-image interpretations.

Psychoanalytical (精神分析) criticism
A psychoanalytical critique focuses on currents of desire and repressed sexuality that run beneath the surface of the play and drive its action. It pays particular attention to aspects of cross-dressing and construction of gender that are explored in the play.

None of these readings could be claimed to be the 'correct' one, and at the heart of modern forms of criticism is the belief that all interpretation carries certain assumptions (for example, about society, about what literature is and about political issues referenced in the play).

◆ Working in small groups, devise a short series of tableaux that illustrate some of the themes or possible perspectives of the play. Present your tableaux to other groups, freezing each one for one minute so your audience can guess which theme or perspective you are portraying.

◆ Afterwards, discuss as a class why your group chose to portray those particular themes or perspectives, and try to find links between them. Talk together about whether some of the critical perspectives described above might focus on certain themes, and why that might be. You might like to undertake further research on some of these interpretive approaches to the play in order to understand them more fully.

Contexts and sources 背景与来源

The educated members of Shakespeare's audience would have enjoyed *As You Like It*'s many literary, biblical (《圣经》的) and Classical allusions. They would have recognised in the play the influence of the books they read for pleasure, picking up its references to the Roman poet Ovid and to the various elements of Classical mythology. They would have also been aware of the elements of pastoral romance in the play, the parody of this type of romance, and the allusions to a story by Thomas Lodge with a similar heroine named Rosalynde.

The pastoral romance tradition

As Shakespeare wrote *As You Like It*, he was greatly influenced by what is now called the pastoral romance tradition. This was made up of two major strands: 'pastoral' and 'romance'.

Pastoral

Pastoral literature and drama idealised nature and rural life. It presented the country as a place of escape, far superior to the city. The country taught moral lessons ('books in the running brooks, / Sermons in stones, and good in everything', Act 2 Scene 1, lines 16–17). In the country, far away from the town, human nature could be changed for the better.

The Greek poet Theocritus (310–250 BC), and other writers of Classical antiquity, imagined a golden world of peaceful and harmonious country life. This rural idyll (田园；田园生活) was peopled by beautiful shepherdesses and shepherds (often aristocrats in disguise as humble country folk) who were poets, philosophers and lovers. Before the French Revolution, Queen Marie Antoinette created her own rural idyll, without dirt or labour, where she and her attendants dressed up as shepherdesses and shepherds.

See pages 46, 98, 100, 128 and 154 for discussion and activities relating to the pastoral tradition.

Romance

The romance tradition largely derives from stories of love and chivalry (骑士风范), which were very popular in the Middle Ages. Famous examples of these are the tales of King Arthur, the 'Chanson de Roland', 'Roman de la Rose' and Chaucer's 'Knight's Tale' in *The Canterbury Tales*. The stories dealt with the trials of young knights, and presented two views of love: courtly and romantic.

Courtly love was sexless. It was the idealised love between a love-struck, languishing man and an unattainable woman whom he worshipped as a goddess. Only by long devotion, many trials and much suffering could a man attract the attention of this woman, the 'fair, cruel maid' of literature.

Romantic love was also idealised, but it included the spontaneous and emotional feature of 'love at first sight', and a happy marriage was seen as its natural result.

See pages 70, 76, 88, 90 and 98 for discussion and activities relating to romantic love.

Pastoral romance

The two earlier traditions described above increasingly merged into pastoral romance as time went on. Pastoral romance literature often included certain major features:

- **Shepherds** Lovesick shepherds yearn for scornful shepherdesses.
- **Forest** In this setting, magical transformations occur and true love flourishes after rigorous testing; it is a place of deposed (废黜) rulers, 'merry men', kindly outlaws and magicians.
- **Journeys** A young knight leaves court to travel and seek his fortune.
- **Adventures** The knight has many adventures in remote places.
- **Adversity** Misfortune besets (困扰) the knight and he undergoes many trials, from which he learns.
- **Love** The knight loves a beautiful woman, and she occupies all his thoughts.

As You Like It
各如所愿

- **Faithfulness** Constancy (fidelity) is highly valued.
- **Coincidence** All kinds of improbabilities and coincidences occur.
- **Female beauty** A beautiful woman has a harsh father, and is much prized.
- **Disguise** Mistaken identity and disguise feature in many stories.
- **Happy endings** The knight marries his beloved, and the stories end with forgiveness, reconciliation and the triumph of virtue.

Many members of Shakespeare's audience came to the Globe Theatre with a deep knowledge of pastoral romance literature. They expected to see its themes, characters and conventions portrayed on stage. Shakespeare fulfilled their expectations, but he also gave his audience something radically different. As You Like It shows that women can more than hold their own in the battle of the sexes. Rosalind takes the lead, directing and controlling the process of wooing – and falling head over heels in love herself. As You Like It also shows that the forest is a place of hardship and suffering as well as one of magical transformations and kindly outlaws.

◆ In pairs, identify how each element of pastoral romance in the list above is represented in *As You Like It*. You should note where any of these elements are contrasted, questioned or parodied in the play. Use the photographs of different interpretations of Arden opposite to prompt your ideas and discussion.

The name 'Arden' would have resonated (使人联想起) with Shakespeare on different levels. To begin with it is, as Juliet Dunisberre suggests, a combination of 'Arcadia' and 'Eden' – two imagined sites of earthly paradise and harmony. In addition, 'Arden' is the name of an actual forest in Warwickshire. This ancient woodland lay to the north-west of the Avon River, near the village of Wilmcote where Shakespeare's mother was born. There was also another woodland called Arden, near to where Shakespeare lived as a child. Interestingly, Shakespeare's mother's maiden name was also 'Arden'. You can see why this name would have been significant to Shakespeare!

Shakespeare would certainly have been aware of the pastoral tradition in English folk tales – such as that of Robin Hood and his merry men in Sherwood Forest, fugitives (逃亡者) who lived out in the woodland and stole from the rich to feed the poor. It is possible that these stories originated in Warwickshire, where a man called Robin of Loxley became an outlaw and lived in the local woodlands until Richard the Lionheart came back from the Crusades and restored his lands to him. Whether the Robin Hood stories originated near Stratford-on-Avon or further up north, it is clear they made an impact on Shakespeare. In *As You Like It*, Charles likens (把……比作) Duke Senior to Robin Hood:

> They say he is already in the Forest of Arden, and a many merry men with him; and there they live like the old Robin Hood of England. They say many young gentlemen flock to him every day, and fleet the time carelessly, as they did in the golden world.

These side-by-side references to Robin Hood and to the 'golden world' were significant because in Shakespeare's day poets liked to draw comparisons between Queen Elizabeth and the goddess Astraea – a goddess of justice who lived on Earth during the mythical Golden Age, but fled from it due to the increasing wickedness of humans. Many of Elizabeth's supporters believed she had established a new 'Golden Age' in England.

A statue of Robin Hood stands today beside the walls of Nottingham Castle.

As You Like It
各如所愿

Shakespeare finds his story

As pages 165–6 show, the stories and plays of the pastoral romance tradition were very popular in Shakespeare's time. Shakespeare used one of these stories, *Rosalynde, Euphues Golden Legacie* (1590) by Thomas Lodge, as the inspiration for the plot of *As You Like It*. He added the characters of Jaques, Touchstone, Audrey and William, but retained most of the original story.

The following summary of *Rosalynde* shows how closely Shakespeare followed Lodge's tale (the names of Shakespeare's characters are included in brackets the first time they appear):

> *A nobleman dies, leaving three sons. The youngest son, Rosader (Orlando) is kept in poverty by the oldest son, Saladyne (Oliver).*
>
> *Saladyne plots that a wrestler kill Rosader. But Rosader defeats the wrestler. Rosalynde (Rosalind) watches the fight and falls in love with Rosader. She is the daughter of the rightful king, who has been overthrown and now lives in exile.*
>
> *Saladyne again plots to kill Rosader, who flees to the Forest of Arden together with his loyal servant Adam Spencer (Adam). He and Adam receive hospitality from the exiled king.*
>
> *Rosalynde is banished from court. She flees with Alinda (Celia), daughter of the wrongful king, to the Forest of Arden. They disguise themselves as Ganymede and Aliena.*
>
> *They overhear a young shepherd (Silvius) telling an old shepherd (Corin) of his unrequited love for Phoebe (Phoebe), a shepherdess. They give money to the shepherds.*
>
> *Rosader writes love poems to Rosalynde, who, as Ganymede, encourages Rosader to woo her as if she were Rosalynde. Aliena conducts a mock wedding of Rosalynde and Rosader. Phoebe falls in love with Ganymede.*
>
> *Rosader rescues his brother from a lion. Saladyne and Aliena fall in love. Rosalynde drops her disguise as Ganymede.*
>
> *Three marriages are celebrated.*

◆ In Shakespeare's day, plots were borrowed and adapted from many different sources as a normal part of creating a new play. Discuss the difference between using sources in this way and copying other people's work (plagiarising [剽窃]). You might like to research Shakespeare's use of sources as you consider this question.

◆ Step into role as Shakespeare. How would you defend yourself against an accusation of plagiarism? Prepare your argument while your partner thinks of questions to ask you as part of a tough interview.

Characters 人物分析

A good deal of recent literary theory assumes that the most important aspect of a 'character' is the dramatic function they fulfil within the social and political context of the play and the fact that they exist only whilst on stage within the play's dramatically created world.

In every performance of As You Like It, a different interpretation of each character is forged (缔造). There is no one definitive portrayal of the characters: they are complex, at times ambiguous or riddled with contradictions, and yet always reinvented afresh in each new performance or reading of the play. Keep all these considerations in mind as you explore Shakespeare's characters in the following pages.

Rosalind

Rosalind is one of the longest parts in all Shakespeare: she has more lines than Macbeth or Prospero. Rosalind appears first as a typical court lady, enjoying witty wordplay with her cousin Celia. In her early scenes, she seems to accept a subordinate role to Celia (it is Celia's suggestion that they leave the court and go to Arden). But as the play moves to the forest and she takes up her male disguise as Ganymede, Rosalind takes the initiative (占据主动) more and more. She controls the action, manipulating other characters and exercising her strong sense of humour as she alternately mocks and celebrates love.

In the forest, as Ganymede, Rosalind befriends and tests Orlando, with whom she is head over heels in love. Rosalind displays the range of emotions that one might expect someone in love to feel: she is downcast (心情低落) at Orlando's lateness; she fires a breathless list of questions at Celia, demanding to know who has written poems to her; she delights in hearing Celia talk about Orlando, and relishes the flirting and wordplay in the 'wooing scene' (Act 4 Scene 1, lines 31–161); she expresses sheer exuberance (兴高采烈) in 'O coz, coz, coz'; and she faints at the sight of a handkerchief stained with her lover's blood.

However, Rosalind's love is also clear-sighted and sceptical (怀疑). She is not fooled by the bad verses that Orlando writes about her, and she mocks his claim that he will love for ever and a day. There is stark (明显；完全) realism in her recognition that 'men have died … but not for love'. Rosalind finally becomes a kind of 'mistress of ceremonies', and arranges the happy ending of multiple marriages.

Below are three comments about Rosalind.

> Dorothy Tutin plays Rosalind in the disguise scenes with an air of bewildered (困惑) self-mockery; her comic timing is superb, especially in her deliciously funny attempts to play the man …
>
> Critic Doreen Tanner

> [She] never allowed her clothes to distract us from her basic femininity. Her gauche (拘谨) walk, the awkward movement of her hands into her trouser pockets, the timorous (羞怯) way in which she bunched a fist, were there to remind us that she was first and foremost a woman in love.
>
> Critic Milton Schulman

> The popularity of Rosalind is due to three main causes. First, she only speaks blank verse for a few minutes. Second, she only wears a skirt for a few minutes … Third, she makes love to the man instead of waiting for the man to make love to her – a piece of natural history which has kept Shakespeare's heroines alive, whilst generations of properly governessed young ladies, taught to say 'No' three times at least, have miserably perished.
>
> Playwright and critic George Bernard Shaw

◆ How do you see Rosalind? Choose one of the critics' quotes above, then gather evidence from the play to show why you agree or disagree with these comments. Display your evidence in a mind map, and then perhaps write it up as a few paragraphs of continuous prose.

As You Like It
各如所愿

So we discover immediately that Rosalind is a divided spirit, part of her in exile with her father, and displaced; and that, for Celia, the wounds of the past lie between them, ever present, and can be healed only through the generosity of her affection. There is a sense of urgency about their respective declarations which suggests that the situation for them both is gathering momentum (势头) with time, not easing with it.

Actors Fiona Shaw and Juliet Stevenson

◆ Script an imaginary conversation with the actors quoted above, in which you discuss their interpretation of the characters. Express your own views and consider what they might say in response.

Characters

Celia

Celia is the daughter of the wicked Duke Frederick, and the cousin and best friend of Rosalind. She stands up to her angry father and proposes the plan of escape to Arden, where she disguises herself as a shepherdess. She seems to become more reserved (矜持) as the play progresses, taking a subordinate role to Rosalind and having less and less to say (she is silent in Act 5).

- ◆ Discuss Celia in pairs, and ask yourselves: is she genuinely critical of Rosalind in the wooing episode? Does she become increasingly separated from Rosalind, aware that she is losing her best friend?

The friendship and familial (家族的) bond between Rosalind and Celia is another central 'love' in the play. Fiona Shaw and Juliet Stevenson talk about the strength and humanity of this attachment:

> *If the struggle for women is a struggle to be human in a world which declares them only to be female, then this was the territory of* As You Like It *which most engaged and challenged us. If we even in part gave resonance to the story of Rosalind and Celia, then the struggle was richly rewarded.*

Celia and Rosalind's relationship can be interpreted in many ways, and the deep, shifting, complex nature of their connection invites a multi-faceted (多面) approach within each different production.

> *Deirdre Mullins and Beth Park have charming chemistry as the slapstick duo (搭档) of Rosalind (Mullins) and Celia. Their on-stage relationship begins with flirtatious play-fighting and solidarity against men (they spit audibly whenever the opposite sex is mentioned) and good-hearted rivalry for Orlando's affections, to a deep appreciation of each other's character.*
>
> Review of a performance at Shakespeare's Globe, Emily Jupp, *The Independent*, 2012

Samantha Spiro as a fiery, bespectacled (戴眼镜的) Celia was forever eyeing (审视，注视) anxiously Rosalind's meetings with Orlando, because from the moment he first appeared it was comically obvious that she also rather fancied him.

Editors Mike Clamp and Perry Mills, Cambridge School Shakespeare Picture Collection

- ◆ How would you want to portray Celia on stage to show her character and her relationship with the other characters? In role as a director of a new production, write separate emails to the costume designer and the actor playing Celia. Tell them your ideas about the costume, props and behaviour that you think should be used in bringing Celia's character to life on stage.

As You Like It
各如所愿

Orlando

Just as Rosalind is despised and threatened by her uncle despite her innocence, Orlando is wrongly treated by a close relative who hates him only for his goodness. His eldest brother, Oliver, has denied him education and money, and now plans to murder him. After defeating Charles the wrestler, Orlando flees to the Forest of Arden with Adam, his old servant. In the forest, he plays out the role of a foolish courtly lover, writing bad verses to his beloved Rosalind and hanging them on trees. But Rosalind, in disguise as Ganymede, persuades him to woo her and he discovers true love. Towards the end of the play, he is wounded as he saves his wicked brother Oliver from a hungry lion. At the end of the play, he is set to marry Rosalind and become heir to Duke Senior.

Although he defeats Charles in the wrestling match early in the play, Orlando is portrayed as 'gentle' and 'sweet' – a downtrodden (被欺负), hard-done-by (受到不公正待遇) romantic character, tending to foolishness in his verses – until at the end of the play he rescues his brother from the lion and re-establishes his 'manly', heroic qualities. Orlando's 'gentleness' is more than our present-day associations of 'gentle' with 'kindness' and 'softness'. Rather, he is a gentleman of aristocratic birth (he, like Oliver, is the son of Roland de Boys), with associations of nobility and selflessness.

Several actors who have not themselves played Orlando have yet been struck by the dynamism and complexity of Orlando's character and role in the play:

> *The wrestling match is crucially important to the first part of the play because of what it releases in all those attending it ... the lid springs off Duke Frederick's latest tyranny, Rosalind's passion, and Celia's grief at her father's wrongs. Orlando finds his heart in love and his life at stake.*
>
> Actors Fiona Shaw and Juliet Stevenson

> *... a very tricky part, at once full of bullish machismo (男子气概), then suddenly prancing through the trees in the depths of romantic gooey-ness.*
>
> Actor David Tennant

◆ Consider each of the comments above about Orlando. Talk with a partner about which of them you think is most helpful in defining the essence of Orlando's character, and why that is. When you have identified the one that you think gets closest to the truth, present your thoughts to the rest of the class. Be prepared to explain and defend your views with examples from the text.

CHARACTERS

Oliver

Oliver de Boys ignores his father's dying wishes. He refuses to give Orlando the wealth, status and schooling that is properly due to him. Early in the play, Oliver appears violent and ruthless. He remains relentless (无情，苛刻) , hard and uncompromising (强硬) in his attitude to his brother and even to Adam, the old servant who served his father for most of his life. Oliver appears to be a usurper similar to Duke Frederick, and in the scenes where the two villains are together we see their greed and violence as they plot to get rid of any contender (竞争者) to their unlawful authority.

However, Oliver undergoes a dramatic change of heart. His journey into the forest starts off with murderous intentions, but away from the corrupt court he experiences a new vulnerability (弱点) and a new understanding of life and death. When his wronged brother, Orlando, finds him asleep and in danger of being killed by wild forest beasts, he does not choose revenge but selflessly rescues him, incurring (招致) injuries of his own. Oliver is swayed (动摇) by his brother's generosity in saving him from death, and his conversion is complete: he renounces his former way of life and his unjust treatment of Orlando. When Oliver brings news of Orlando's injury to Rosalind, he meets Celia and falls instantly in love with her. He marries Celia, and gives all his lands and possessions to Orlando.

◆ Oliver's perspective is interesting because he undergoes such a dramatic change of heart towards Orlando and the other exiles. What questions would you want to ask him? In groups, put Oliver in the hot-seat: prepare some questions, and then take turns to step into role as Oliver and answer them.

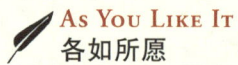

As You Like It
各如所愿

Duke Senior and Duke Frederick

Duke Senior has been deposed by his brother, Frederick, and has escaped into the forest with his loyal courtiers. In the Forest of Arden, they live as outlaws – hiding away from the court, eating the food of the forest and practising hospitality to those they meet there (such as the hungry Orlando and Adam). Their simple lives are contrasted with the corrupt and greedy court, and Duke Senior relishes the lessons that country life can teach. At the end of the play, he is happy to return to court life – perhaps because he has become bored of the simple life of the forest, or maybe because he knows that the lessons he has learnt there will make him a better ruler.

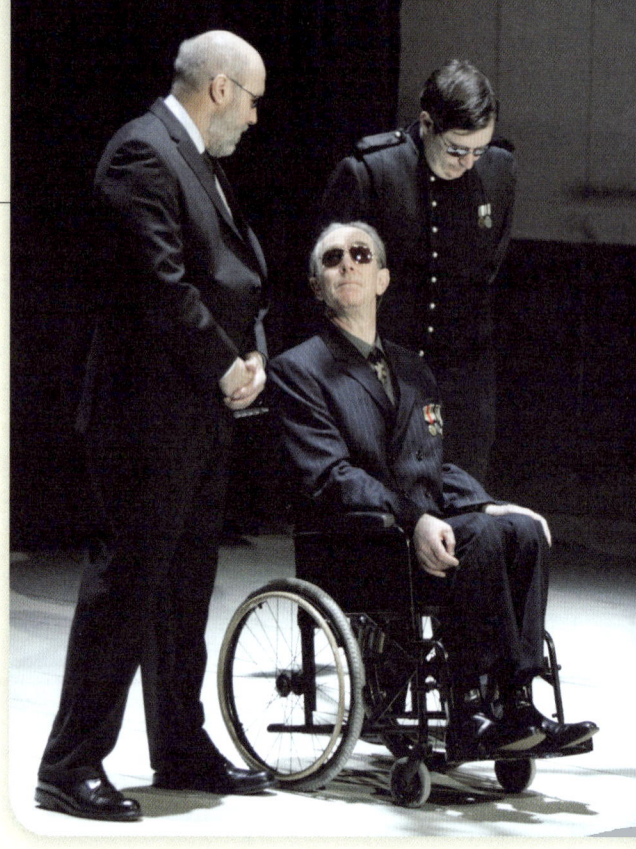

Duke Frederick is the usurper who has seized his brother's dukedom. Injustice and vindictiveness (恶心) reign in his court, and he is a violent ruler who is always seeking to protect his authority. He threatens Rosalind with death, and in so doing alienates (疏远) his own daughter, Celia, who sees her cousin Rosalind as her sister and closest friend. Duke Frederick's cruelty and selfishness then leads him to take an army into the Forest of Arden to kill his brother. Surprisingly, he meets an old religious man while in the forest and is condemned for his evil intentions. He undergoes a striking change of mind, gives up all his former wickedness, and resolves to live the simple life of a hermit (隐士) in the forest rather than the luxurious life of an unlawful ruler. At the end of the play, he is happy to give the dukedom back to his brother.

◆ In pairs, step into roles as Duke Senior and Duke Frederick. Improvise a scene in which each of you tells the story of the play from the point of view of your character. Include any developments that are mentioned in the play but are not seen by the audience. You could also imagine what happens to Duke Senior when he returns to court to rule again, and how Duke Senior fares (成功) in the humble life of a country hermit.

Characters

Touchstone

Touchstone is the court jester or fool, who joins Rosalind and Celia in their escape to the Forest of Arden. His loyalty to the two exiles and his witty remarks make him a valuable companion in this dangerous journey. When not in disguise, Touchstone would traditionally wear the distinctive costume of a fool, which might include a patchwork (拼布) coat, colourful breeches (马裤), and a hood (风帽) or cape (披肩) decorated with donkey's ears or the crest (羽冠) of a rooster. As a fool, he would often carry a short stick – his 'sceptre' (权杖) – and be accompanied by the jangling sound of the small bells sewn into his costume. This costume was referred to as 'motley' – a word that describes the incongruous colours and diverse fabrics of his outfit. Jaques admires not only the wit of Touchstone, but also his costume: 'O noble fool! A worthy fool! Motley's the only wear.'

Touchstone's role in court was that of licensed fool: to comment on what he saw around him, exposing folly and dishonesty. His name signifies his dramatic function: a touchstone was used to reveal if a metal was true gold. Touchstone similarly tests the genuineness of characters with his sceptical comments. In Act 5 Scene 4, Duke Senior says of Touchstone, 'He uses his folly like a stalking-horse, and under the presentation of that he shoots his wit'. However, as Celia reminds Touchstone, he could also be whipped for speaking the truth.

The clown role in Shakespeare's plays was influenced by two very different actors in his theatre company. William Kempe, who was part of the company from 1594 to 1599 was famous as a clown who performed comic jigs (吉格舞), bawdy (下流) tales or satirical songs. Robert Armin, who took over from 1599 (until 1610), was known as a more intellectual fool, contributing to the development of the plot and able to sing and provide music on stage. There is a marked difference in the kind of fools presented by these two actors, and this is reflected in Shakespeare's plays. Kempe's clowning and jigging was not to everyone's taste, and some people preferred Armin's more philosophical and intellectual fool. His witty repartee and critical comment on social superiors was licensed by his status, and he often improvised satirical lines directed at members of the audience as well.

◆ Find out more about William Kempe and Robert Armin, and about the first performance of *As You Like It*. Which actor do you think would have played Touchstone originally? Who would you prefer to see in the role? Can you think of any modern actors or comedians that you think could play the part well?

The flights of ideas, the energy of thought and the inability to shut up are all traits of manic episodes in a bipolar (躁狂抑郁性) mental illness. It is perhaps an actor's affectation to think of Shakespearean characterisation in this way, but it helped me to make sense of some of Touchstone's less easily motivated moments.

Actor David Tennant, on playing Touchstone

Touchstone, authentically witty, is rancidly (令人反感) vicious, while Jaques is merely rancid … Both of them are in As You Like It to serve as touchstones for Rosalind's more congenial wit, and she triumphantly (大获全胜) puts them in their places.

Critic and editor Harold Bloom

◆ Can you find examples of where Touchstone tests the genuineness of characters with his sceptical comments and witty remarks, as his name suggests he should?

As You Like It
各如所愿

Audrey

Audrey is a goatherd, and her personality is simple and down to earth. Unlike Phoebe or Celia, she is a 'real' rural character, and on stage she is often played as a dirty, rough country wench.

- Draw a prop that you feel would give important information to the audience about Audrey. Make notes on how the actor playing Audrey could use it for maximum effect – perhaps in multiple ways. Find instances in the script where other characters – for example, Touchstone or Rosalind – could pick up the prop and interact with it themselves. Describe how you would use these moments to show how their personalities differ from Audrey's rustic and unpretentious (朴实) image.

Jaques – 'They say you are a melancholy fellow'

Today, the melancholy Jaques would probably be called neurotic or unbalanced. He is the malcontent – a familiar role in Elizabethan times: a sardonic (爱嘲讽的) observer who comments cynically on everything and everybody around him, seeing only foolishness, absurdities and ingratitude. He has a jaundiced (狭隘；有偏见), pessimistic view of the world, and would almost certainly agree with Hamlet's description of it as 'weary, stale, flat and unprofitable'. Duke Senior accuses him of having been 'a libertine' who now wishes to make the world as corrupt as himself.

◆ As you think about Jaques's character, explore possible answers to some of the following questions:
- Is he playing a role to hide his true feelings, and what might these be?
- Why does Duke Senior enjoy his company? Does he have a genuine sense of humour?
- What do you make of his final decision not to take part in the celebrations, but to join Duke Frederick in rejecting court life?
- Audrey calls him 'the old gentleman'. How old do you think he is, and why?
- What is your own attitude towards Jaques?

◆ If Jaques were a real person living today, what do you think he would list as his:
- favourite movie?
- favourite book and/or magazine?
- favourite television programme?
- favourite type of music?
- favourite sport?
- occupation?
- leisure activities?
- views of key current affairs?

◆ Construct a social media profile for the character of Jaques. Include five examples of his 'recent activity' – this could be status updates, comments made on other characters' photos or statuses, or 'liked' pages.

As You Like It
各如所愿

The shepherds: Silvius and Phoebe

Elizabethans would recognise Silvius and Phoebe as stock characters (常备角色) from pastoral literature. Speaking in elegant, polished verse, they are traditional figures of the court in the country. Silvius is the lovelorn faithful shepherd, who suffers the pains of unrequited love. Phoebe is the disdainful shepherdess, the cruel mistress of pastoral literature, whose beautiful face conceals a hard heart. She rejects and humiliates Silvius, but falls for Rosalind disguised as Ganymede. When Rosalind throws off her disguise, Phoebe agrees to marry Silvius.

- Think of two actors that you think would work well together as Silvius and Phoebe. Draft a letter asking them to take on the roles in your next production. In the letter, outline your vision for their characters, and for the wider context of the play's setting, and explain why you think they are perfect for this role.

The two old men: Adam and Corin

Adam represents an older world of loyal and faithful service. He gives his life savings to Orlando and goes with him into exile in Arden. He disappears from the play after Act 2: what do you think happens to him? Remember also that actors often played more than one character in Shakespeare's day. What role might the actor playing Adam have taken after Act 2?

Corin is content in his modest life as a shepherd in the forest and calls himself 'a true labourer'. He has served a hard master, but finds better employment with Celia and Rosalind. He counsels Silvius on love, and endures Touchstone's condescension (傲慢) with good humour.

- With a partner, discuss whether you think the roles of Adam and Corin should be played seriously, with quiet wisdom and dignity, or as comic characters with exaggerated infirmities (弱点) and eccentricities (古怪，怪癖). Design costumes and props, and write actors' notes on movement and gestures, for either serious or comic interpretations of both characters.

Characters

Visions of the characters

- In small groups, make a list of all the 'main' characters in the play. You will have to discuss this, and agree on who you would include or exclude in this category. Take each selected character in turn and look through all the images of them in this edition (including the photo gallery at the beginning). Make notes on what characteristics are emphasised in the various images, making sure you consider age, ethnicity, physical features, facial expressions, clothes and props as appropriate. Then individually decide which photo best fits your idea of how the role should be portrayed, and give reasons for your choice. Which aspects are most important, and which are least important, for each character? Present your choice for each character, along with your reasons, to the rest of the group.

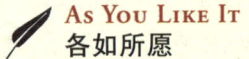

As You Like It
各如所愿

The language of *As You Like It*
《各如所愿》的语言

Dramatic language

Clues in the script

Shakespeare was writing at a time when theatres could only create a very few special effects, so he used language to establish atmosphere, mood and setting. To set the scene for the audience, he included vivid descriptions in the dialogue; to give actors clues about their actions, embedded stage directions were included in the script. Here are some examples:

> Are not these woods
> More free from peril than the envious court?
> (Act 2 Scene 1, lines 3–4)

> I pray you bear with me, I cannot go no further.
> (Act 2 Scene 4, line 7)

> Forbear, and eat no more!
> (Act 2 Scene 7, line 88)

> In the which hope, I blush, and hide my sword.
> (Act 2 Scene 7, line 119)

> Welcome. Set down your venerable burden,
> And let him feed.
> (Act 2 Scene 7, line 167–8)

> Will you dispatch us here under this tree, or shall we go with you to your chapel?
> (Act 3 Scene 4, lines 49–50)

◆ Consider the lines shown and identify the internal clues given to guide the actors and the audience. In pairs, decide on the actions each character might perform at that point in the script. Try to make the actions appropriate for the character delivering the lines.

Soliloquies and asides

A **soliloquy** is a monologue spoken by a character who is alone (or assumes they are alone) on stage. It gives the audience direct access to the character's mind, revealing their inner thoughts and motives. There are no soliloquies in *As You Like It*, although Orlando's reflections at the end of Act 1 Scene 2 and in Act 3 Scene 2 come close. Instead, there are many monologues in which characters develop their thoughts while addressing others on stage, such as when Jaques gives his explanation of the 'seven ages of man' in Act 2 Scene 7, or when Phoebe talks about Ganymede in Act 3 Scene 6.

An **aside** is a brief comment or address to the audience that gives voice to a character's inner thoughts, unheard by other characters on stage. The audience is taken into this character's confidence, or can see deeper into their motivations and experiences. Asides can also be used for characters to comment on the action as it unfolds. Although not marked as such, Jaques's lines at the start of Act 3 Scene 4 are generally performed as asides.

The language of As You Like It

- Identify some of the play's monologues and asides. Choose one and speak it to a partner. Then write notes on how you would perform it on stage to maximise its dramatic effect. Remember to comment on how the other characters on stage might react to the speech.

- Choose one of the photographs in this book and use it as inspiration to write your own aside for one of the characters. This brief comment should reveal the character's thoughts at a particular point in the play, and should be accompanied by appropriate gestures and/or expressions.

- Write a soliloquy for one of the characters at a key point in the play, when the audience would benefit from finding out more about their inner feelings and intentions.

Imagery

As You Like It abounds in **imagery**. Imagery is created by using vivid words and phrases to conjure up mental pictures and associations. It provides insight into character and helps the audience use its imagination to transform a bare stage into Duke Frederick's court or the 'golden world' of the Forest of Arden. It deepens the dramatic impact of particular moments, and helps to create distinctive atmospheres and themes.

As You Like It contains a wide range of imagery, particularly that of animals, country life, hunting and theatre. On every page of the play you will find at least one example of imagery, and there are often many more.

Recurring imagery

Animals

There is a wealth of animal imagery in the play. For example, Duke Senior says: 'Sweet are the uses of adversity / Which like the toad, ugly and venomous, / Wears yet a precious jewel in his head' (Act 2 Scene 1, lines 12–14). In Act 4 Scene 1, Rosalind 'had as lief be wooed of a snail' (line 42) and 'will laugh like a hyena' (line 124). It is not so much that animals appear in the Forest of Arden or elsewhere in the play's imagined settings, but more that animal references are used to comment on human nature and various characters' actions and attributes. For an extended example of this, see Act 4 Scene 3, lines 93–115.

Hunting

Images of hunting, particularly of the deer in the Forest of Arden, are prevalent in the play. Celia compares Orlando to a hunter ('furnished like a hunter', Act 3 Scene 3, line 205), and Rosalind pictures the 'pursuit that will be made / After my flight' (Act 1 Scene 3, lines 126–7). But Rosalind is not just Orlando's quarry (猎物); he describes her as possessing a 'huntress' name' (Act 3 Scene 2, line 4), too. Many of the characters in the forest are both hunted and hunter. Duke Senior and his court have taken refuge there away from the corruptions of the city court, and their own hunting of the deer ('Come, shall we go and kill us venison?', Act 2 Scene 1, line 21) is symbolic of their new-found power and their part in nature.

Nature's bounty and wisdom

In a play that draws strongly on the pastoral tradition (see pp. 165–6), there are inevitably many images of nature – and connections and comparisons between nature and humanity are often made. In Act 3 Scene 3, Celia says of Orlando that she 'found him under a tree like a dropped acorn' (line 196), and Orlando's poems are hung in trees. Touchstone, in criticising Orlando's verse, remarks that 'Truly, the tree yields bad fruit.' Rosalind's response continues the metaphor of trees and fruit, revealing her wit and mastery of language: 'I'll graft it with you, and then I shall graft it with a medlar; then it will be the earliest fruit i'th' country, for you'll be rotten ere you be half ripe, and that's the right virtue of the medlar' (lines 94–6). (Grafting has the technical sense of splicing one type of tree with another to make a hardier version, and also means to work hard.)

That nature should judge the actions of humans is one of the abiding (永恒) themes of later Shakespeare plays, and this idea is often contrasted with the corruptions of the city court. As is often the case, wise words on this subject are placed in the mouth of the fool, Touchstone.

As You Like It
各如所愿

Wrestling

Other images that appear in the play are those of sport ('sport for ladies', Act 1 Scene 2, line 109) – in particular, wrestling. The significance of Orlando defeating Charles early in the play is about more than Orlando proving his manhood and attractiveness to Rosalind. Wrestling is court entertainment (of a fairly brutal nature, in this play), and also suggests the complicated moves that Rosalind makes throughout the play to secure her victory – not just in winning Orlando, but also in teaching him how to truly love. Wrestling is both a sport and a deadly serious activity, in which one can be gravely injured. Love is presented as a similarly multi-faceted endeavour, bringing joy and witty frivolity (愚蠢的行为，可笑的表现) but also pain and anxiety to the play.

The theatre

Shakespeare's preoccupation (专注) with the theatre is evident throughout *As You Like It*. The play is full of acting and playing, particularly for those in disguise – like actors, these characters take on new costumes and identities. The many monologues scattered throughout the play, and the different roles portrayed by the characters (romantic lover, melancholic misanthrope [遁世者], reformed oppressor [压迫者]) remind the audience of other popular dramatic traditions. As Rosalind says of Phoebe and Silvius, 'I'll prove a busy actor in their play'. The theatre is also the central metaphor used by Jaques in his famous reflection on the stages of life:

> *All the world's a stage*
> *And all the men and women merely players:*
> *They have their exists and their entrances*
> *And one man in his time plays many parts,*
> *His acts being seven ages.*
>
> (Act 2 Scene 7, lines 139–43)

- Many of the examples of imagery given above are from Acts 1–4. Look at Act 5 to identify the imagery Shakespeare uses there, and how it contributes to the meaning of the play as a whole.

- In small groups, list what you think are the key images of the play. Create a collage on a large sheet of paper, using images that you have collected from magazines and pictures that you have drawn yourselves. You can combine images and words, and include pictures from any other sources you come across. Present your collage to other groups, explaining its content by referring closely to the script.

- Look at Act 3 Scene 6, lines 8–27, where Shakespeare gently mocks the use of imagery. He gives Phoebe twenty lines, in which she ridicules the imagery based around the idea that a lover's disdainful eyes could inflict cruel wounds. Look closely at these lines, then write your own parody of some of the imagery that Shakespeare uses in this play. Use modern English, and try to identify some of the limitations of the imagery used in the play.

Metaphor, simile and personification

Shakespeare's imagery uses **metaphor**, **simile** or **personification**. All of these language devices are comparisons. A simile compares one thing to another by using 'like' ('creeping like snail / Unwillingly to school') or 'as' ('my age is as a lusty winter'). A metaphor does not use 'like' or 'as', but suggests that two dissimilar things are the same. Examples are Rosalind labelling Silvius 'a tame snake', Orlando calling himself 'a rotten tree' and Touchstone insulting Corin as 'worms' meat'. Personification is a particular type of imagery. It imagines things or ideas as people ('the good housewife Fortune'), giving them human feelings or body parts ('the swift foot of Time'). Jaques and Orlando use personification to bid each other a mocking farewell as 'Signor Love' and 'Monsieur Melancholy'.

- Compile a list of metaphors, similes and personification from the script. What do they add to your understanding of the characters or the events of the play?

The language of As You Like It

Verse and prose – 'Didst thou hear these verses?'

Most of the verse in the play is **blank verse** (unrhymed verse with a five-beat rhythm known as iambic pentameter). Each ten-syllable line has five alternating unstressed (×) and stressed (/) syllables, as shown in the line below:

× / × / × / × / × /
Because that I am more than common tall

This rhythmic pattern is what distinguishes verse from prose, rather than rhyming lines. Prose is different from blank verse: it is everyday language with no specific rhythm, metric scheme or rhyme. Shakespeare uses prose to break up the verse in his plays, to signify characters' madness or low status, to draw attention to changes in plot or character, and for other less consistent and obvious reasons (see below for more discussion of this). It is easy to tell the difference: verse passages begin with a capital letter and the lines do not reach the other side of the page, whereas prose passages have lines that reach both sides of the pages and only use capital letters at the beginning of sentences.

- ◆ To experience the rhythm of iambic pentameter, read a few lines aloud from any of the verse speeches in the play. Pronounce each syllable very clearly, as if it were a separate word. As you speak, beat out the five-beat rhythm by clapping your hands or tapping your desk.

- ◆ The songs, Orlando's poems, Phoebe's letter and Hymen's blessings are all in verse, but not in the five-beat rhythm of iambic pentameter. Speak a few lines of each aloud to discover their distinctive rhythms.

- ◆ Invent a few lines of blank verse to describe your response to the play. Make sure that it has the correct structure and rhythm of iambic pentameter.

Over half of *As You Like It* is in prose: almost 1300 lines against just over 1100 lines of verse. How did Shakespeare decide whether to write in verse or prose?

In his time, the play-writing convention was that high-status characters spoke in verse and that prose was used for comedy or by low-status characters. However, Rosalind and Celia are high-status characters (they are both the daughters of dukes), yet much of their language is in prose. Silvius and Phoebe, the shepherd and shepherdess (low status), speak in verse.

It may be that as he wrote *As You Like It*, Shakespeare used prose or verse depending on whether he felt the situation to be 'comic' or 'serious'. But even this is not always the case: Oliver uses prose as he urges Charles the wrestler to harm Orlando (a 'serious' episode).

- ◆ Look through the play to discover which characters speak only in verse or in prose, and which use both forms of speech. Then select one act and work through it, identifying where prose switches to verse, or verse to prose. Explain why you think Shakespeare decided to use prose and verse in this way, referring to specific examples in the script.

Repetition

Shakespeare uses repetition to give dramatic force to his language. Lines that incorporate this language device are rich in the repeated sounds of rhyme and the hypnotic (催眠) effects of rhythm. At various points in the play, repeated words, phrases, rhythms and sounds add to the emotional intensity of a scene. This repetition can occur on many levels: sounds, words, phrases and rhythms, and patterns across sentences or clauses.

Repetition of sounds

Alliteration is the repetition of consonant sounds at the beginning of words:

Time travels in diverse paces with diverse persons

Assonance (半谐音；半韵) is the repetition of vowel sounds (in the middle of words):

Take thou no scorn to wear the horn,
It was a crest ere thou wast born

Rhymes (which are repeated sounds) are most obvious in songs, Orlando's poems, Phoebe's letter and the rhyming couplets that often end long speeches or signal the end of a scene. These repetitions are opportunities for actors to intensify emotional impact and draw attention to changes in character or action.

> *Now go we in content,*
> *To liberty, and not to banishment.*

Repetition of words
Sometimes the same word is repeated several times in rapid succession, in order to increase pace and tension:

> *O Phoebe, Phoebe, Phoebe!*
>
> *More, more, I prithee more*
>
> *O wonderful, wonderful, and most wonderful wonderful, an yet again wonderful…*

Repeated phrases and rhythms
One example of the use of repeated phrases and rhythms to underscore a particular moment is when the three lovers repeat Silvius's litany of love, 'And so am I for Phoebe' (Act 5 Scene 2, lines 67–90); and when Rosalind promises to satisfy the wishes of each lover, 'I will help you, if I can' (Act 5 Scene 2, lines 92–100). At other times, particular phrases and rhythms are repeated throughout a passage so that an idea can be developed or extended. Examples of this are Silvius's refrain 'Thou hast not loved' (Act 2 Scene 4, lines 27–36), and the echoing exchange between Orlando and Duke Senior: 'If ever you have looked on better days'.

Repetition of patterns
Anaphora is the repetition of the same word or phrase at the beginning of successive sentences or clauses:

> *I'll tell you who Time ambles withal, who Time trots withal, who Time gallops withal, and who he stands still withal.*

Epistrophe (尾词重复) is the repetition of the same word or phrase at the end of successive sentences or clauses:

> *Live a little, comfort a little, cheer thyself a little.*
>
> *A lean cheek, which you have not; a blue eye and sunken, which you have not; an unquestionable spirit, which you have not; a beard neglected, which you have not.*

◆ Look at one or two of the seven songs in this play:
- 'Under the greenwood tree' (Act 2 Scene 5)
- 'If it do come to pass' (Act 2 Scene 5)
- 'Blow, blow, thou winter wind' (Act 2 Scene 7) 'O sweet Oliver' (Act 3 Scene 4)
- 'What shall he have that killed the deer?' (Act 4 Scene 2)
- 'It was a lover and his lass' (Act 5 Scene 3)
- 'Wedding is great Juno's crown' (Act 5 Scene 4)

Identify all the ways in which Shakespeare uses repetition in these songs.

◆ Read through the last two lines of each scene. See how many of these closing lines are rhyming couplets, and suggest why Shakespeare chooses to end scenes in this way.

Lists

Shakespeare liked to accumulate many words or phrases at certain moments in the script, rather like a list. He knew that 'piling up' item on item, image on image, view on view, can intensify description, atmosphere, character and dramatic effect.

The most famous example is Jaques's 'seven ages of man' speech, and there are many other points in the play where lists are used to great effect. A few of the longer ones are:

- Corin's list of his contentments (Act 3 Scene 3, lines 53–6)
- Rosalind's breathless list of questions about Orlando (Act 3 Scene 3, lines 185–8)
- Rosalind's ten 'marks' of a man in love (Act 3 Scene 3, lines 312–18)
- Rosalind's many ways of having 'cured' a lover (Act 3 Scene 3, lines 336–46)
- Jaques's description of different kinds of melancholy (Act 4 Scene 1, lines 9–16)
- Silvius's list of what it is to love (Act 5 Scene 2, lines 68–83)
- Touchstone's repeated catalogue of how to avoid a duel (Act 5 Scene 4, lines 62–88).

The language of As You Like It

◆ Choose an example of how this listing technique is used in the script, either from the examples given here or from elsewhere in the play. Take turns with a partner to speak the lines in a way that maximises the impact of the repetition. Think about how you can use gestures and expressions as well as your voice.

Antithesis

Antithesis, the use of contrasting words or phrases within the same sentence or short section of text, is used to bring out oppositions and express conflict. Although *As You Like It* is a comedy, it is full of conflict: brother versus brother, court versus country and lover against lover.

Antithesis is most clearly seen in the verse sections of the play. The first time that verse is spoken, Duke Frederick says to Orlando: 'The world esteemed thy father honourable / But I did find him still mine enemy' (Act 1 Scene 2, lines 177–8). Here 'world' opposes 'I', and 'honourable' contrasts with 'enemy'.

◆ Working through the play, collect ten examples of antithesis. Write an essay in which you show how antithesis helps create a sense of conflict in *As You Like It*. You might like to base your discussion on the following statement: 'Much of the conflict in *As You Like It* is created through language.'

Puns and wordplay – 'How now, wit, whither wander you?'

People in Shakespeare's time loved wordplay of all kinds, and **puns** were especially popular. A pun is a play on words where the same sound or word has different meanings. Rosalind puns on 'hart' (female deer) when, hearing that Orlando is dressed like a hunter, she cries 'he comes to kill my heart'. However, the most intriguing wordplay comes when Rosalind (disguised as Ganymede) persuades Orlando to woo her/him.

◆ Take parts and read aloud the 'wooing scene' (Act 4 Scene 1, lines 31–161). Orlando thinks he is speaking to a boy, but Rosalind revels in the ambiguity that her disguise gives. She can speak as herself without Orlando knowing it. After you have read through the scene, take it in turns to speak only Rosalind's lines: every time she uses a personal pronoun (I, me, myself, and so on), pause and say whom she might have in mind.

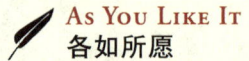

As You Like It
各如所愿

Critics' forum 评论家论坛

Use the following quotations from a range of critics to explore your own responses to the play. As you read through them, think about its usefulness to you in your understanding of *As You Like It*. Remember, you do not have to agree with any of them, but you should be able to justify your own interpretation.

> It is the most ideal of any of [Shakespeare's] plays. It is a pastoral drama in which the interest arises more out of the sentiments and characters than out of the action or situation ... Caprice (反复无常) and fancy reign and revel here, and stern (苛刻) necessity is banished to the court.
>
> William Hazlitt, 1817

> *As You Like It* is a criticism of the pastoral sentiment, an examination of certain familiar ideas concerning the simple life and the golden age ... The result is something very curious. When Rosalind has made her last curtsy and the comedy is done, the pastoral sentiment is without a leg to stand on, and yet it stands; and not only stands but dances. The idea of the simple life has been smiled off the earth, and yet here it is, smiling back at us from every bough of Arden ... The doctrine of the golden age has been as much created as destroyed.
>
> Mark Van Doren, 1939

> The pastoral region is a place of refuge and the dominant symbol of relief from danger, weariness, want, every ill ... And what is Arden but a pastoral region where lost children are found, parted lovers reunited, dispossessed men come to their own again, and repentance (忏悔) and reconciliation grow like leaves on the trees?
>
> Mary Lascelles, 1959

> Shakespeare is not interested in a comforting pastoral dream. From the dark corridors (走廊) of the duke's palace, the forest has all the inviting warmth of the escape world of the Golden Age. But those who make the journey find 'a desert inaccessible', where the wind bites shrewdly, and food is only to be had by hunting. Expecting a womb, they are faced with a challenge. The forest only helps those who help themselves.
>
> David Jones, 1968

> The play shows us not a court made simple, but a simple place made courtly (恭敬有礼).
>
> D. Nuttall, 1972

> Behind Rosalind's disguise ... lies the great Renaissance wish-dream of harmony between the masculine and feminine principles.
>
> Anne Barton, 1973

> [The play's] aristocratic protagonists (主角) formulate and enact an ideology: they express the particular interests of their own class as if these were identical with universal interests, with the interests of the whole society.
>
> Elliot Krieger, 1979

> [Rosalind's] disguise as Ganymede permits her to educate him about himself, about her, and about the nature of love. It is for Orlando, not for Rosalind that the masquerade (乔装) is required; indeed the play could fittingly, I believe, be subtitled 'The Education of Orlando.'
>
> Marjorie Garber, 1986

Critics' Forum

Elizabeth's court by the end of the sixteenth century was increasingly adopting Duke Frederick's style of arbitrary and personalised decision-making. Thus the many angry comments by Rosalind, Orlando, Adam and others about the 'fashion of these times', as well as Jaques' desire to 'cleanse the foul body of the infected world', must have held an extraordinary power over an audience caught up in a whirlwind of change, social disintegration (瓦解) and ultimately Civil War.

Stephen Unwin, 1994

With Orlando what you see is what you get. Rosalind on the other hand needs to be freed from the feminine role that projects so pale a version of the resourceful, noisy, energetic person she really is before she can love Orlando with all her might … He has no wish to be cured; it is she who needs to replace bad poetry and stereotyped reactions by true love and loyalty and these she draws from him in the person of a boy.

Germaine Greer, 1996

The forest people in As You Like It do not, actually, 'fleet (消磨) the time carelessly'. They have hierarchy, property and money, and give little serious thought to living without them … [They] are not outside the state system; they are a government in waiting. The play presents a conflict within the ruling elite (掌权精英): which faction is to control the state and its resources?

Alan Sinfield, 1996

Feminist thought has highlighted the audacity (大胆行为) and originality of Shakespeare's conception of Rosalind, analysing the ways in which the play participates in an Elizabethan questioning of attitudes to women.

Juliet Dusinberre, 2006

As You Like It is poised before the great tragedies; it is a vitalizing work, and Rosalind is a joyous representative of life's possible freedoms.

Harold Bloom, 2009

The place of 'banishment' turns out to be the home of 'liberty' — free from the constraints of court hierarchy and customary deference (遵从), Arden is where you can play at being someone different and find out who you really are. It's where you learn to live alongside people who come from very different backgrounds from your own. And where, in the end, you all come together for a big party in celebration of multiple mixed marriages that cut across the traditional social order.

Jonathan Bate, 2010

◆ **Choose three of the quotations above and make notes on them. Decide whether you agree or disagree with the view expressed in each one, using examples and direct quotations from the script in order to justify your decision.**

◆ **Afterwards, use your notes to write your own extended response to these three perspectives on the play. Structure your response in the form of a formal essay, with an introduction, paragraphs giving your perspective on each view you chose (one view per paragraph), and a conclusion.**

As You Like It
各如所愿

As You Like It in performance
《各如所愿》的演出

Shakespeare probably wrote *As You Like It* around 1600, perhaps in response to the popularity of pastoral plays at that time. It is traditionally believed that this was the very first play acted at the Globe Theatre on London's Bankside, and that Shakespeare played Adam in the production. Another claim is that *As You Like It* was performed before King James I in 1603. However, no one knows for sure if these stories are true. There is no record of a performance during Shakespeare's lifetime.

Performance on Shakespeare's stage

In Shakespeare's time, plays staged in outdoor amphitheatres (圆形剧场) such as the Globe Theatre were performed in broad daylight during the summer months. So, at 2:00 p.m. people would assemble with food and drink to watch a play with no lighting and no rule of silence for the audience. There were high levels of background noise and interaction during performances, and audience members were free to walk in and out of the theatre.

In the Globe Theatre, the audience was positioned on three sides of the stage: the 'groundlings' (站票观众) stood in the pit (无座观众池) around the stage, while those who paid more were seated in three levels around the pit. Actors would see around three thousand faces staring up or down at them. The positioning of the audience made it difficult for everyone to hear all that was going on. Inevitably, the actors would have their backs to sections of the audience at times. The best place for an actor to stand, especially for a soliloquy or an aside, was at the front of the stage – so that he could directly address almost all of the audience. However, it would be tedious if all the action occurred in this area of the stage.

Shakespeare's use of repetition helped to overcome the problem of addressing the different sections of the audience. There are times when the same idea is stated or developed in three ways in order to allow an actor to address each section in turn. These repetitions were never simply word-for-word repeats but were used to create rhythm, accumulate details and build on an idea through different metaphors and imagery (see 'Repetition' on pp. 183–4). If you spot significant repetition, it may be a clue that Shakespeare intended the character to move around the stage and engage with different parts of the audience.

In Shakespeare's time, where a character was placed on stage gave the audience clues about their role or authority in the play. Characters that were absorbed in their own lives, or characters that played out literary or conventional stereotypes, were often placed centre-stage or upstage (furthest away from the audience). Characters that had a comic role, that performed many roles, or that commented on the action on stage, were often placed downstage (closer to the audience) and were sometimes at the edge of the stage. In this way, these comic characters straddled (横跨) the divide between the play and its audience.

- Look at the images opposite, which give an idea of what the Globe Theatre and its surrounding area would have looked like in Shakespeare's time. A faithful modern recreation of the Globe now stands on the same site, and it is called Shakespeare's Globe. Use the library or the Internet (the Shakespeare's Globe website may be helpful) to research what kind of experiences Elizabethan theatregoers – both rich and poor – would have had watching one of Shakespeare's plays at the Globe.

- Actors at Shakespeare's Globe often comment on how effectively its stage layout (布局) can be made to work dramatically. They particularly praise the way in which the theatre's design encourages a close rapport (亲近) with the audience. What parts of *As You Like It* do you think would work well on a stage where the audience is so close to the actors, and why? What parts do you think it would be difficult to stage convincingly, and why?

As You Like It in performance

The exterior and interior of Shakespeare's Globe have been designed to look just like the original Globe Theatre that stood on the same site beside the Thames (泰晤士河) hundreds of years ago.

139

As You Like It
各如所愿

Performances after Shakespeare

The first historical record of a performance since Shakespeare's time is of an adaptation of the play in 1723, which was called *Love in a Forest*. This version cut all of the lower-class characters, such as Touchstone, Audrey, Phoebe, Silvius and Corin. It also replaced the wrestling match with a bout (回合) of fencing (击剑) with rapiers (thin swords), and it included lines, songs and characters from other Shakespeare plays. Jaques married Celia, and the mechanicals from *A Midsummer Night's Dream* performed their 'Pyramus and Thisbe' play.

In 1740, the play was performed largely as Shakespeare had written it, and from then on it became one of the most popular and frequently performed of all his plays. In the eighteenth and nineteenth centuries, many leading actresses played Rosalind, and the success of a production was largely judged on who played the part. The popularity of *As You Like It* was also in part due to the audience's enjoyment at the sight of a woman dressed in breeches and showing off her feminine ankles and legs. Around this time, Shakespeare's comedies rose in popularity compared to the tragedies and histories, and they were seen as opportunities for songs, dances and comic episodes.

In the last half of the nineteenth century, and early in the twentieth century, many productions of *As You Like It* were staged outdoors and attempted to create a realistic Forest of Arden on stage. These forests included running streams, real trees, logs, grass, leaves and ferns (蕨). Some productions brought live animals on stage, and sheep and rabbits were common. One staging, in Manchester, presented a whole herd of deer, while another used leaves that covered the stage up to the actors' ankles!

For many years, annual productions of *As You Like It* at Stratford-upon-Avon included a stuffed deer (标本鹿) from nearby Charlecote Park. Shakespeare was supposed to have poached (偷猎) deer from this park, and consequently fled to London to escape the wrath of the landowner. In 1919, the director of that year's production refused to include the stuffed deer. Many local people were outraged at the break with tradition and the director was insulted in the street.

◆ **Create a list of props for your production of *As You Like It*.** You might want to take ideas from the list below, which includes some different props that have been used by directors in the past. Annotate your prop list, explaining the significance and intended use of each prop you have chosen. You should also think about the practical considerations of including certain props.

- a clock that does not tick (time is not measured and controlled as it is at court)
- mirrors (a reflection of the audience?)
- real grass or leaves on the stage
- animals such as sheep and deer
- sheets of white silk for different, magical effects
- a bare tree with a few apples on it
- a boar spear for Rosalind
- a rabbit, dead or alive (a dead rabbit was skinned and beheaded on stage by Corin in an RSC production in 2009)

As You Like It in performance

More recent productions

By the second half of the twentieth century, the earlier emphasis on the play as a vehicle for the actor playing Rosalind had given way to 'company productions', in which all the actors contributed significantly to the success of each performance. More recent productions have often been bold in identifying a theme or perspective on the play that sheds new, sometimes glaring light on it.

Adrian Noble's production for the Royal Shakespeare Company in the 1980s focused on the idealism of the forest, but with a new emphasis on feminism. It explored the liberal, feminist notions of gender – in particular, Rosalind's switching of gender and her cross-dressing. In this production, the concept was to see Arden as an imaginative landscape rather than as a real place to which the courtiers had escaped. The characters' escape from Duke Frederick's court was like an extended dream, and Jaques's world-weary cynicism appeared to be that of someone disappointed by a dream unfulfilled.

Social issues have also been more prominently stressed in more recent productions, with the emphasis both on the harsh political realities of Duke Frederick's court and on the exploitation of the natural world by the exiled court. A 1992 film version of *As You Like It* set Arden in a modern urban wasteland, to bring home messages about social deprivation (社会剥削) to contemporary audiences. This transposition of a green, pastoral, ecologically vital England to a background of despair and dereliction (荒废) gave the play a darker tone, especially when contrasted with the extravagance and wealth of the court scenes. Banishment from the court meant exile from the good life to a bleaker (不乐观，无望) world in Arden, as if the utopian dreams projected in other productions were transformed into a dystopia (反乌托邦) in this one.

Such social commentary upset many viewers, who thought the movie had lost much of the joyous, comic exuberance of the play. Rosalind became a boyish Ganymede in jeans, parka and hat, and her interplay (互动) with Orlando was cut down. There was also a good deal of doubling in the movie, with the lovers looking much like each other by the end of the play, and the city court being mirrored by the court in Arden. Such doubling, which is easier to achieve on film than on stage – challenges you to think about the structure, the characters and the significance of the play as a whole.

▲ The 1992 film version of *As You Like It* used a contemporary setting and style of dress to address issues in modern society.

As You Like It is a popular play outside the UK, too. Salvador Dalí once designed surrealist (超现实主义) sets and costumes for a lavish (耗资巨大) 1948 production in Rome, choosing to represent the Forest of Arden as a single large apple painted on the backdrop (背景幕布) behind the stage. Before the reunification of Germany, a famous 1977 production in Berlin implied that the Forest of Arden (a 'free' place) was like West Berlin surrounded by the socialist German Democratic Republic.

As You Like It
各如所愿

A 1990s Cheek by Jowl production featured an all-male cast in modern dress. By revisiting this single-gendered approach, which was exclusively used for performances in Shakespeare's time, the director invited a modern reappraisal (重新评估) of how the play represents gender. Rather than a female actor stepping into the female role of Rosalind and then 'acting like a man' when disguised as Ganymede, in this production a male actor had to realistically embody a female character and then interrogate what it meant to be a man in order to self-consciously act like one when required. Adrian Lester played Rosalind and was widely praised for his grace, humour and sensitivity in the role.

Some productions have focused on the festive and romantic elements of the play. Lucy Bailey's 1998 Shakespeare's Globe production flirted with the idea of street theatre by bringing the wrestling match between Charles and Orlando off the stage and into the central pit of the theatre, thus immediately placing the action right in the heart of the audience. Rosalind was played as a woman whose femininity was emphasised so that when she was disguised as Ganymede, the disguise was superficial. Beneath Ganymede's exterior, there was clearly a young woman with a strong passion for Orlando. In this production, there was a renewed focus on the joy and earnestness of the script.

In a 2006 production directed by Louisa Fitzgerald for Castle Theatre Company at Durham University, the emphasis was on colour in a garden setting. The production seemed, indeed, like a garden fête (露天游乐会) – with a bandstand (乐队演奏台) of musicians providing accompaniment, a wrestling match arranged in a hastily erected ring (竞技场), and the pastoral seeming to overpower the forest and the court. The audience sat on chairs on the lawn, and the action surrounded them. There was both a sense of the surreal (超现实), prompted by the garish (花哨) colours of Touchstone and some deckchairs, and a real sense of the outdoors being essential to the Englishness of the play. The production as a whole had the feeling of a glorious romp (风流韵事): a youthful, concentrated exploration of love, society and the breaking of convention.

▼ **Adrian Lester and Simon Coates as Rosalind and Celia in the widely praised Cheek by Jowl production.**

An Australian production in 2011 was described as 'cheeky', 'accessible', 'hilarious' and 'tightly paced' in theatre reviews. The world of the corrupt Duke Frederick was full of social injustices that were easily recognised by the local audience, but all this was quickly swept away as the play moved into the forest. Here, the musically talented cast performed song and pantomime (哑剧) routines in a rollicking, fun-filled performance of the play.

An RSC production in 2011 was considered by some to be similarly gloomy. The anger and discontent at the beginning of the play created a harsh atmosphere that was followed by a focus on the trials and tribulations of love in all its forms. Even Rosalind and Celia embarked on their adventure to the forest with a sense of dismal woe. However, as winter turned to spring in the forest, the focus changed to the transformative power of love and there was 'love, and jokes, and pleasure' for the rest of the play.

Other recent productions have tempered the fun and festive aspects of the play with more serious and melancholic overtones (弦外之音). Sam Mendes's 2010 production of the play, with a mixed cast of American and British actors, presented a cold and unfriendly Arden full of adversity and melancholy. In this production, Orlando seemed to border on deep despair; and Adam, despite his assertions that he was still young and healthy, died as he and Orlando journeyed into the forest. The hardships and difficulties encountered by the characters were reflected in the intensity of some of the dramatic scenes, as well as in the stage set for the forest – which was covered at times by drifts of snow, before gradually blossoming as the play moved through its final scenes.

In 2013, a vibrant and youthful performance of the play by the RSC evoked the atmosphere of an English summer music festival, complete with lots of mud that Rosalind and Orlando smeared (涂抹) all over each other at the end. Arden was a place of escape and joyous freedom, rather than the site of arduous trials and eventual redemption (拯救，救赎) as in the productions described above.

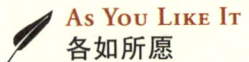

As You Like It
各如所愿

Staging Shakespeare

Any script by Shakespeare should be read as a blueprint (plan) for a live performance, so it is essential that you think about how it can or should be staged. There is no substitute for seeing a live performance of the play at the theatre (or a filmed performance of such a production) in order to gain an appreciation of the play as a script that has been brought to life.

When creating sets for specific theatres, professional set designers often produce three-dimensional models of the stage, and reproduce the key features of the set in miniature to see how all the components will work together and with the space.

- In groups, have a go at creating this kind of model, perhaps by using a shoebox as the basic structure. Compare your set designs with those of other groups in the class. How different do you think the audience's response will be to the different sets? (See images of the sets from other productions in this book.)

Programme notes that are sold at performances of the play sometimes include information on how the stage set links to the director's interpretation and characterisation.

- In role as a director, write your own programme notes on how the key features (themes, setting, tone, and so on) of your interpretation and vision for the production have informed the set design and other staging decisions such as casting choices, costumes, sound design and lighting.

Film versions

In 1936, a film version of *As You Like It* was released, starring Laurence Olivier (in his first Shakespeare film) as Orlando and the Austrian actress, Elisabeth Bergner, as Rosalind. Bergner, who was Jewish, had played Rosalind on the stage in Germany more than 500 times, but she had to leave the country when the Nazis took power there. She had a strong German accent, which confused some of the movie's viewers, while others thought she was too small and slight to play the robust Rosalind. Despite this, she was one of the most sprightly, vivacious (活泼) and flirtatious Rosalinds that most people had seen.

Olivier was not as famous as Bergner when he took on the role of Orlando, but by the time the movie was released his name was in large letters on all the publicity posters. His Orlando was both poetic and impressively athletic, taking on a wrestler who was twice his size. Interestingly, this was the only Shakespeare role for which Olivier did not receive an award, and he did not count his performance as a personal success.

The film was an extravagant production with a forest set over 90 metres long (the largest ever made for a film studio) and a cast of famous actors, many of whom were star performers in their own right. A number of animals were also included in the movie: swans and ostriches were seen in scenes at the court, and in the Forest of Arden, pigs, cows, sheep and even a serpent and lioness, made appearances.

In 1978, a production of *As You Like It* was filmed for the BBC at Glamis Castle in Scotland. It starred Helen Mirren as Rosalind. It was famed for the lush greenery of its Arden Forest. Although the director, Basil Coleman, wanted to film the changing seasons over the course of the year, he was unable to do so and had to complete most of the filming in May. The action therefore takes place in a summer climate, while the characters speak incongruously (不相称) of the winter weather and their harsh life in the forest.

As You Like It in performance

In 1992, Christine Edzard directed a film version of *As You Like It* with young, unknown actors as Rosalind and Orlando. The same actor played Orlando and Oliver, and the two characters were never in the same shot together. The Welsh comedian and TV personality Griff Rhys Jones was cast as Touchstone. Edzard set the play in an urban wasteland where the exiled Duke Senior and his courtiers live like homeless people, in tents and cardboard boxes, hiding from a violent overlord. Rosalind and Celia live in a taxi shelter and Audrey runs a café from her caravan (宿营拖车). The characters are dressed in modern clothes, with Rosalind wearing a jumper and jeans, and Orlando writes his love poems to Rosalind using an aerosol (喷雾) can. Despite this setting, and the urban noise that was part of the movie's soundtrack, all Shakespeare's references to life in the forest – including animals, trees and weather – remained in the script.

Kenneth Branagh's 2006 film version of *As You Like It* sets the play in Japan. The graphics at the start of the film indicate 'a dream of Japan', with associations of exotica (异域事物), formality and the distant 'Orient'. As in some productions in the theatre, as well as on film, Duke Senior and Duke Frederick are played by the same actor – their respective costumes indicate that they are extreme opposites in character. The movie starts in a court, with Duke Senior and his followers, including Celia and Rosalind, enjoying a Kabuki (歌舞伎) theatre performance. The courtiers' costumes are from nineteenth-century Japan, and Duke Senior bases his court on Japanese culture and ceremony.

An attack by the usurping court abruptly disturbs this tranquillity. Duke Frederick and his entourage (随从) appear like samurai warriors (格斗武士) – or like Darth Vader and his stormtroopers (突击队员) from *Star Wars*.

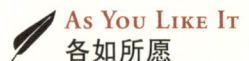

As You Like It
各如所愿

The movie depicts the moments in which Duke Frederick usurps his brother and, with his ninja warriors, takes control. The new rulers' sinister (阴险，邪恶) presence broods (让人不安) over the court, while Duke Senior and his courtiers are chased into the forest, to be followed later by the banished Rosalind and Celia. In the court of Duke Frederick, Orlando and Oliver engage in a full-scale fight rather than just the mutual threats of one. In keeping with the formal Japanese setting, Charles is a sumo (相扑) wrestler.

In this film, Arden appears as a kind of paradise. It is a place where meditation, soft-spoken exchanges and gentleness (in the sense of gentility and nobility, as well as softness) are the order of the day. Jaques is the principal source of humour in the movie, and his changing moods, his melancholy observations and his love of the forest are all emphasised in this production. Interestingly, the minor characters in the pastoral romance – such as Silvius, Corin and Phoebe – are given prominence and status, as if their way of life is seen as equally heroic and important to the play as a whole. Indeed, it is they who seem to be the centre of moral power and goodness in the movie, rather than any character from the court.

◆ Plan a movie pitch (电影推介). Imagine that you are making the pitch to a group of investors. They have the money to finance a new film version of the play – if you can convince them of the merits of your concept. Work through the following points to create your presentation, and remember that your production can be big-budget!

◆ Consider your audience: why would people go to see this movie, and why would it appeal to a modern audience?

◆ How will your movie begin? Where (and when) will it be set? What music or sound effects will you use? What atmosphere are you seeking to create? Will you want to reorder/cut the script? Storyboard the opening of the play. If you have access to cameras, film the opening three or four minutes and share the video with other groups in your class. Which group's video do you like best, and why do you think it is the most successful?

◆ Summarise the storyline in approximately 500 words, and include a list of characters.

◆ Describe the setting and time – this could be any place at any point in the past, present or future. Suggest a series of locations, matched to specific scenes, within your chosen setting. Add further ideas about how lighting, costume and music could contribute to the overall effect.

◆ Cast your production with known actors, comedians or other celebrities, and explain your choices. Then identify several speeches that you think are particularly important, and write instructions on how they should be delivered.

◆ Draw some costume designs, or use pictures taken from magazines or the Internet to create collages of the costumes.

◆ Design a DVD cover with the title, strapline and production photo(s) on the front and a short promotional 'blurb' (宣传性简介) on the back.

◆ Create a publicity poster. What elements of your movie will you emphasise in order to persuade people to see it? Will you include a quotation as a 'slogan'? Which image from the play, and which character, will you give most prominence to? Or will you use an abstract image that ties in with a particular theme? For inspiration, look at the promotional posters opposite.

As You Like It in performance

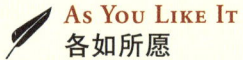

As You Like It
各如所愿

Writing about Shakespeare 笔论莎士比亚

The play as text

Shakespeare's plays have always been studied as literary works – as words on a page that need clarification, appreciation and discussion. When you write about the plays, you will be asked to compose short pieces and also longer, more reflective pieces like controlled assessments, examination scripts and coursework – often in the form of essays on themes and/or imagery, character studies, analyses of the structure of the play and on stagecraft. Imagery, stagecraft and character are dealt with elsewhere in this edition. Here, we concentrate on themes and structure. You might find it helpful to look at the 'Write about it' boxes on the left-hand pages throughout the play.

Themes

It is often tempting to say that the theme of a play is a single idea, like 'death' in *Hamlet*, or 'the supernatural' in *Macbeth*, or 'love' in *Romeo and Juliet*. The problem with such a simple approach is that you will miss the complexity of the plays. In *Romeo and Juliet*, for example, the play is about the relationship between love, family loyalty and constraint; it is also about the relationship of youth to age and experience; and the relationship between Romeo and Juliet is also played out against a background of enmity between two families. Between each of these ideas or concepts there are tensions. The tensions are the main focus of attention for Shakespeare and the audience; this is also how the best drama operates – by the presentation of and resolution of tension.

Look back at the 'Themes' boxes throughout the play to see if any of the activities there have given rise to information that you could use as a starting point for further writing about the themes of the specific play you are studying.

Structure

Most Shakespeare plays are in five acts, divided into scenes. These acts were not in the original scripts, but have been included in later editions to make the action more manageable, clearer and more like 'classical' structures. One way to get a sense of the structure of the whole play is to take a printed version (not this one!) and cut it up into scenes and acts, then display each scene and act, in sequence, on a wall, like this:

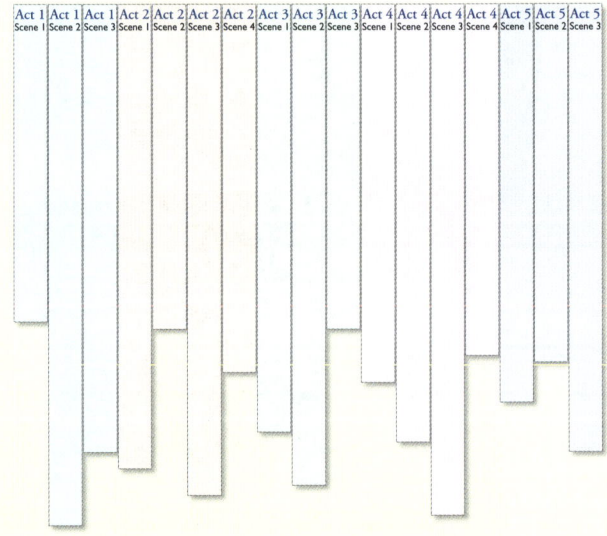

As you set out the whole play, you will be able to see the 'shape' of each act, the relative length of the scenes, and how the acts relate to each other (such as whether one act is shorter, and why that might be). You can annotate the text with comments, observations and questions. You can use a highlighter pen to mark the recurrence of certain words, images or metaphors to see at a glance where and how frequently they appear. You can also follow a particular character's progress through the play.

Such an overview of the play gives you critical perspective: you will be able to see how the parts fit together, to stand back from the play and assess its shape, and to focus on particular parts within the context of the whole. Your writing will reflect a greater awareness of the overall context as a result.

The play as script

There are different, but related, categories when we think of the play as a script for performance. These include stagecraft (discussed elsewhere in this edition and throughout the left-hand pages), lighting, focus (who are we looking at? Where is the attention of the audience?), music and sound, props and costumes, casting, make-up, pace and rhythm, and other spatial relationships (for example, how actors move around the stage in relation to each other). If you are writing about stagecraft or performance, use the notes you have made as a result of the Stagecraft activities throughout this edition of the play, as well as any information you can find about the plays in performance.

What are the key points of dispute?

Shakespeare is brilliant at capturing a number of key points of dispute in each of his plays. These are the dramatic moments where he concentrates the focus of the audience on difficult (sometimes universal) problems that the characters are facing or embodying.

First, identify these key points in the play you are studying. You can do this as a class by discussing what you consider to be the key points in small groups, then debating the long-list as a whole class, and then coming up with a short-list of what the class thinks are the most significant. (This is a good opportunity for speaking and listening work.) They are likely to be places in the play where the action or reflection is at its most intense, and which capture the complexity of themes, character, structure and performance.

Second, drill down at one of the points of contention and tension. In other words, investigate the complexity of the problem that Shakespeare has presented. What is at stake? Why is it important? Is it a problem that can be resolved, or is it an insoluble one?

Key skills in writing about Shakespeare

Here are some suggestions to help you organise your notes and develop advanced writing skills when working on Shakespeare:

- Compose the title of your writing carefully to maximise your opportunities to be creative and critical about the play. Explore the key words in your title carefully. Decide which aspect of the play – or which combination of aspects – you are focusing on.
- Create a mind map of your ideas, making connections between them.
- If appropriate, arrange your ideas into a hierarchy that shows how some themes or features of the play are 'higher' than others and can incorporate other ideas.
- Sequence your ideas so that you have a plan for writing an essay, review, story – whichever genre you are using. You might like to think about whether to put your strongest points first, in the middle, or later.
- Collect key quotations (it might help to compile this list with a partner), which you can use as evidence to support your argument.
- Compose your first draft, embedding quotations in your text as you go along.
- Revise your draft in the light of your own critical reflections and/or those of others.

The following pages focus on writing about *As You Like It* in particular.

As You Like It
各如所愿

Writing about *As You Like It* 笔论《各如所愿》

Any kind of writing about *As You Like It* will be informed by your responses to the play. Your understanding of how characters, plot, themes, language and stagecraft are all interrelated will contribute to your unique perspective. This section will help you locate key points of entry into the play, so that your writing will be engaging and original. The best way to capture your reader's attention is to take them with you on a journey of discovering a new pathway into *As You Like It*.

But first, how do you find your unique perspective? You may want to start with the title *As You Like It*, and think about Shakespeare's hints as to the play's meaning. *As You Like It* may be Shakespeare saying to his Elizabethan audiences: 'whoever you are, whatever your social background and interests, there's something here for you'. All kinds of meanings and interpretations are possible in the play, and there is something in it for everyone – whether you like spectacle, some violent action, songs, clowns and jokes, disguise, lots of talk about love, or the silliness of people in love.

The title may have also promised Elizabethan audiences that they would find many reminders of their own world. In Jaques they would see the malcontent – the world-weary cynic who was such a familiar figure in Shakespeare's London. They would recognise certain figures from society in Jaques's 'seven ages of man' speech: brave soldiers, justices who accepted bribes, and so on. Despite containing reminders of the audience's own world, the Forest of Arden that lies at the heart of this play is a world of its own. It is a place of escape, an illusion of perpetual holiday and freedom where time stands still. This contented 'Never-Never Land' of make-believe exists under many names: Utopia, Xanadu (世外桃源), Arcadia, the Land of Cockaigne (安乐乡), the Golden Age, Shangri-La and Camelot (传说中亚瑟王的王宫所在地). These are festive worlds of romance, full of magical possibilities, where anything can happen: disguises are adopted and all kinds of confusions, errors and mistakes occur. But the end result is marriage and happiness because these are places where dreams come true and harmony can be restored.

At this point, you may think about Rosalind – the character who seems to orchestrate (精心安排) events to make sure her dream (and everyone else's) comes true! Like Rosalind, who is disguised as Ganymede for much of the play, life in the forest is not always what it seems. It is full of people with their own agendas, and it also has its own hardships and injustices. And yet, in this world that is set apart from the everyday formality of the court, there is a special freedom that allows Rosalind (as Ganymede) to take on different roles in order to shape events in general and woo Orlando in particular. Shakespeare's use of theatrical metaphors and imagery reminds the audience of the play's central theme of illusion, and at the same time sets Rosalind apart as a character who can play on the border between illusion and reality. Indeed, Shakespeare gives Rosalind the very last word, as she talks directly to the audience in the epilogue.

While thinking through the range of possible perspectives on the play, you might find that reflecting on the performance possibilities offered in the play script is helpful. Your own perspective on the play will begin to develop as you think about what you are interested in, and allow yourself to make connections between the dramatic, contextual, linguistic and thematic features of the play.

Creative writing

At different times during your study of *As You Like It*, and during assessments and examinations, you will write about the play and your personal responses to it. Creative responses to the play, such as those encouraged in the activities in this book, can allow you to be as imaginative as you want. This is your chance to develop your own voice and to be adventurous as well as sensitive to the words and images in the play. *As You Like It* is a rich, multilayered play that benefits from many different approaches, both in performance and in writing. Don't be afraid of larger questions or implications that cannot be reduced to simple resolutions. It is often the problematic and complex issues, for which you do not have easy answers, that can be the most interesting.

- ◆ Duke Frederick's usurpation of Duke Senior takes place 'off stage', before the play opens. Imagine how this rebellion might have taken place and how Duke Senior could have been overthrown. Write the missing scene.

- ◆ What happens to Silvius and Phoebe or Touchstone and Audrey after the play has finished? Choose one of the characters and write their story, extending it to cover the times before and after they appear in the play. You might like to write this as a monologue or a diary entry. You could also compose a scene showing one of the couples after five years of married life.

Essay writing

Other types of written response to the play, such as essays, have a set structure and specific requirements. Writing an essay gives you a chance to explore your own interpretations, to use evidence that appeals to you, and to write with creativity and flair (才华). You can approach the play from a number of critical perspectives and with a focus on various different themes. Don't forget to consider the social, literary, political and cultural contexts of the play, both in Shakespeare's day and when it is experienced today.

Your essay should present a strong, reasoned argument, using evidence and structural requirements to persuade your readers that you have an important perspective on the play. You will need to integrate evidence from the script into your own writing by using embedded quotations and by explaining the significance of each quotation and reference to the play. Some people like to remember the acronym (首字母缩略词) PEA to help them here. P is the POINT you are making. E is the EVIDENCE you are taking from the script, whether it is a direct quotation, a summary of what is happening, or a reference to character, plot and themes. A is the ANALYSIS you give for using this evidence, which will reflect back on the point you are making and also contain your own personal response and original ideas.

The following are typical examination essays on *As You Like It*:

- Choose two or three central themes and explain how each is developed linguistically and dramatically through the play.
- Write about an aspect of language that interests you in *As You Like It*.
- The pastoral romance tradition is parodied throughout *As You Like It*. Discuss the effect this has on your understanding of characters and events in the play.
- 'Although, in the Forest of Arden, women seem to be temporarily empowered, male dominance is re-established at the end of the play.' Consider the events of the play in the light of this comment.
- How does Rosalind's disguise help her to orchestrate the events leading up to the marriages at the end of *As You Like It*? Write about the significance of her disguise at different points in the play.
- 'The Forest of Arden is a setting where simple, natural love is able to develop.' To what extent do you agree with this view?

- ◆ Pick at least two of the essay titles above, and sketch out an essay plan for each. Swap plans with two other students in your class, giving constructive feedback and making suggestions for improvements.

- ◆ Select the two essay titles that you think are the most difficult to answer. Try to pinpoint what aspects of the questions you find most challenging, then get together with a partner and share ideas about how to address these challenging aspects of each question.

As You Like It
各如所愿

William Shakespeare 莎翁年表
1564–1616

1564	Born Stratford-upon-Avon, eldest son of John and Mary Shakespeare.
1582	Marries Anne Hathaway of Shottery, near Stratford.
1583	Daughter Susanna born.
1585	Twins, son and daughter Hamnet and Judith, born.
1592	First mention of Shakespeare in London. Robert Greene, another playwright, described Shakespeare as 'an upstart crow beautified with our feathers'. Greene seems to have been jealous of Shakespeare. He mocked Shakespeare's name, calling him 'the only Shake-scene in a country' (presumably because Shakespeare was writing successful plays).
1595	Becomes a shareholder in The Lord Chamberlain's Men, an acting company that became extremely popular.
1596	Son, Hamnet, dies aged eleven.
	Father, John, granted arms (acknowledged as a gentleman).
1597	Buys New Place, the grandest house in Stratford.
1598	Acts in Ben Jonson's *Every Man in His Humour*.
1599	Globe Theatre opens on Bankside. Performances in the open air.
1601	Father, John, dies.
1603	James I grants Shakespeare's company a royal patent: The Lord Chamberlain's Men become The King's Men and play about twelve performances each year at court.
1607	Daughter Susanna marries Dr John Hall.
1608	Mother, Mary, dies.
1609	The King's Men begin performing indoors at Blackfriars Theatre.
1610	Probably returns from London to live in Stratford.
1616	Daughter Judith marries Thomas Quiney.
	Dies. Buried in Holy Trinity Church, Stratford-upon-Avon.

The plays and poems

(no one knows exactly when he wrote each play)

1589–95	*The Two Gentlemen of Verona, The Taming of the Shrew, First, Second* and *Third Parts* of *King Henry VI, Titus Andronicus, King Richard III, The Comedy of Errors, Love's Labour's Lost, A Midsummer Night's Dream, Romeo and Juliet, King Richard II* (and the long poems *Venus and Adonis* and *The Rape of Lucrece*).
1596–99	*King John, The Merchant of Venice, First* and *Second Parts* of *King Henry IV, The Merry Wives of Windsor, Much Ado About Nothing, King Henry V, Julius Caesar* (and probably the Sonnets).
1600–05	*As You Like It, Hamlet, Twelfth Night, Troilus and Cressida, Measure for Measure, Othello, All's Well That Ends Well, Timon of Athens, King Lear.*
1606–11	*Macbeth, Antony and Cleopatra, Pericles, Coriolanus, The Winter's Tale, Cymbeline, The Tempest.*
1613	*King Henry VIII, The Two Noble Kinsmen* (both probably with John Fletcher).
1623	Shakespeare's plays published as a collection (now called the First Folio).

Acknowledgements 鸣谢

Cambridge University Press would like to acknowledge the contributions made to this work by Rex Gibson, Richard Andrews and Perry Mills.

p. 171 extract from a review of a performance of *As You Like It* at Shakespeare's Globe by Emily Jupp, 10 September 2012, reproduced courtesy of *The Independent*.

Picture Credits

p. iii & 69 top: Courtyard Theater 2011, © Chicago Shakespeare Theater (photo by Liz Lauren, dir. Gary Griffin, actors pictured are Philip James Brannon, Chaon Cross and Kate Fry); p. v top: Curve Theatre 2009, © Donald Cooper/Photostage; p. v bottom: Bath Theatre Royal 2003, © Donald Cooper/Photostage; p. vi top: Royal Shakespeare Theatre 1992, © Donald Cooper/Photostage; p. vi bottom: Bath Theatre Royal 2003, © Donald Cooper/Photostage; p. vii top: Shakespeare's Globe 1998, © Donald Cooper/Photostage; p. vii bottom: Bath Theatre Royal 2003, © Donald Cooper/Photostage; p. viii Wyndham's Theatre 2005, © Donald Cooper/Photostage; p. ix top: Shakespeare's Globe 1998, © Donald Cooper/Photostage; p. ix bottom: Royal Shakespeare Theatre 1985, © Donald Cooper/Photostage; p. x top: Royal Shakespeare Theatre 1992, © Donald Cooper/Photostage; p. x bottom: Old Vic 2010, © Nigel Norrington/ArenaPAL; p. xi top: Wyndham's Theatre 2005, © Donald Cooper/Photostage; p. xi bottom: Bath Theatre Royal 2003, © Donald Cooper/Photostage; p. xii: Royal Shakespeare Theatre 1992, © Donald Cooper/Photostage; p. 4: Curve Theatre 2009, © Donald Cooper/Photostage; p. 10: Illustration from John Lydgate's *Siege of Troy*, showing the Wheel of Fortune held by the Queen of Fortune; p. 12 Shakespeare's Globe 2009, © Robbie Jack/Corbis; p. 14: Barbican 2001, © Donald Cooper/Photostage; p. 16: Regent's Park Open Air Theatre 2002, © Donald Cooper/Photostage; p. 18: Barbican 2001, © Donald Cooper/Photostage; p. 26: Curve Theatre 2009, © Donald Cooper/Photostage; p. 33: Regent's Park Open Air Theatre 2002, © Donald Cooper/Photostage; p. 38: Still from 2006 As You Like It film directed by Kenneth Branagh, © REX/Moviestore Collection; p. 44: Royal Shakespeare Theatre 2007, © Donald Cooper/Photostage; p. 50: Shakespeare's Globe 1998, © Donald Cooper/Photostage; p. 58: Wyndham's Theatre 2005, © Donald Cooper/Photostage; p. 60: Royal Shakespeare Theatre 2007, © Donald Cooper/Photostage; p. 64: Bath Theatre Royal 2003, © Donald Cooper/Photostage; p. 66: Bath Theatre Royal 2003, © Donald Cooper/Photostage; p. 69 bottom left: Regent's Park Open Air Theatre 2002, © Donald Cooper/Photostage; p. 69 bottom right: Shakespeare's Globe 1998, © Donald Cooper/Photostage; p. 74: Royal Shakespeare Theatre, © Donald Cooper/Photostage; p. 80: Old Vic 2010, © Donald Cooper/Photostage; p. 88: Bath Theatre Royal 2003, © Donald Cooper/Photostage; p. 94: Royal Shakespeare Theatre 1992, © Donald Cooper/Photostage; p. 102: Shakespeare's Globe 2012, © Donald Cooper/Photostage; p. 109 top: Royal Shakespeare Theatre 2007, © Donald Cooper/Photostage; p. 109 bottom: Clywd Theatre 2012, © Clark Nobby/ArenaPAL; p. 114: Lyric 2000, © Donald Cooper/Photostage; p. 120 Royal Shakespeare Theatre 2000, © Donald Cooper/Photostage; p. 128 Regent's Park Open Air Theatre 2002, © Donald Cooper/Photostage; p. 133 top: Swan Theatre 2003, © Donald Cooper/Photostage; p. 133 bottom left: Bath Theatre Royal 2003, © Donald Cooper/Photostage; p. 133 bottom right: Royal Shakespeare Theatre 2000, © Donald Cooper/Photostage; p. 136: Royal Shakespeare Theatre 1992, © Donald Cooper/Photostage; p. 142: Swan Theatre 2003, © Donald Cooper/Photostage; p. 159 top: Old Vic 1989, © Donald Cooper/Photostage; p. 159 bottom: Bath Theatre Royal 2003, © Donald Cooper/Photostage; p. 161: Bath Theatre Royal 2003, © Donald Cooper/Photostage; p. 163: Bath Theatre Royal 2003, © Donald Cooper/Photostage; p. 166: Statue of Robin Hood in Nottingham, © Deniskelly/Dreamstime; p. 167 top:

As You Like It
各如所愿

Rose of Kingston 2011, © Donald Cooper/Photostage; p. 167 bottom: Bath Theatre Royal 2003, © Donald Cooper/Photostage; p. 168: Lyric Theatre 2000, © Donald Cooper/Photostage; p. 170 left: Curve Theatre 2009, © Donald Cooper/Photostage; p. 170 top right: Royal Shakespeare Company 2009, © Donald Cooper/Photostage; p. 170 bottom right: Bath Theatre Royal 2003, © Donald Cooper/Photostage; p. 171: Old Vic Theatre 2010, © Donald Cooper/Photostage; p. 172: Royal Shakespeare Company 1992, © Donald Cooper/Photostage; p. 173: Bath Theatre Royal 2003, © Donald Cooper/Photostage; p. 174 left: Royal Shakespeare Theatre 2000, © Colin Willoughby/ArenaPAL; p. 174 right: Crucible Theatre 2007, © Donald Cooper/Photostage; p. 176: Royal Shakespeare Company 1985, © Donald Cooper/Photostage; p. 177: Shakespeare's Globe 1998, © Donald Cooper/Photostage; p. 178 left: Bath Theatre Royal 2003, © Donald Cooper/Photostage; p. 178 right: Shakespeare's Globe 1998, © Donald Cooper/Photostage; p. 179 top: Royal Shakespeare Company 2000, © Donald Cooper/Photostage; p. 179 bottom: Royal Shakespeare Company 2013, © Donald Cooper/Photostage; p. 180: Lyric Theatre Hammersmith 1991, © Donald Cooper/Photostage; p. 185: Old Vic 1989, © Donald Cooper/Photostage; p. 189 top left: Exterior of Shakespeare's Globe, © Lance Bellers/Shutterstock; p. 189 top right: Interior of Shakespeare's Globe 2011, © Kamira/Shutterstock; p. 189 bottom: Wencelaus Holler's 1675 map of London, Wikimedia; p. 190: Old Vic 1989, © Donald Cooper/Photostage; p. 191: Still from *As You Like It* 1992, Sands Films/The Kobal Collection; p. 192: Albery Theatre 1995, © Donald Cooper/Photostage; p. 193: Royal Shakespeare Company 2013, © Donald Cooper/Photostage; p. 195 Still from *As You Like It* 2006, © PicHouse/Everett/Rex Features; p. 197 top left: Orgeon Shakespeare Festival poster 2012, © Toni Bright; p. 197 top right: The Hazlitt Arts Centre 2012, © Michael Yeowell, Changeling Theatre Company Ltd; p. 197 bottom left: © Mortimer and Ransom, Peterborough Mask Theatre 2010; p. 197 bottom right: Lion & Unicorn Theatre 2012, © Custom/Practice, designer Lee Daniels, photo by Boris Mitkov.

Produced for Cambridge University Press by White-Thomson Publishing
+44 (0)843 208 7460
www.wtpub.co.uk

Project editors: Alice Harman and Sonya Newland
Designer: Clare Nicholas
Concept design: Jackie Hill